PRAISE FOR HIDE AWAY

"Pinter is in fine form with *Hide Away*. You'll burn through the pages."
—David Baldacci, #1 *New York Times* bestselling author of
Long Road to Mercy

"Pinter has crafted a wonderful mix of a domestic family saga, a suburban thriller, and a crime novel. It's a blend of Michael Connelly and Harlan Coben with a dash of Batman, and Rachel is a single-mother version of Bruce Wayne. Grab this and hide away somewhere until the last page is turned."

—*Associated Press*

"Pinter does a masterful job of ramping up suspense about the Marin family's past and the current case, spinning an absolutely riveting plot with a cast of full-bodied, fallible characters, in what seems the start of a promising series. Fans of both domestic thrillers and police procedurals should get in at the start."

—*Booklist* (starred review)

"Pinter's (*The Darkness*) outstanding series launch is a deft combination of domestic suspense and police procedural that recalls the works of Harlan Coben and Linwood Barclay. Both an unstoppable force of nature and painfully human, Rachel is a heroine readers will not soon forget."

—*Library Journal* (starred review)

"Pinter builds a complex plot on the dual mysteries of Constance's murder and Rachel's transformation from suburban mom to crack investigator and lethal street fighter . . . Pinter creates engaging characters . . . and keeps the suspense taut."

—*Kirkus Reviews*

A
STRANGER
AT THE
DOOR

OTHER BOOKS BY JASON PINTER

RACHEL MARIN SERIES

Hide Away

HENRY PARKER SERIES

The Mark
The Guilty
The Stolen
The Fury
The Darkness

STAND-ALONE

The Castle

FOR CHILDREN

Zeke Bartholomew: Superspy!
Miracle

A
STRANGER
AT THE
DOOR

JASON
PINTER

THOMAS & MERCER

Published by Thomas & Mercer, Seattle

www.apub.com

Amazon, the Amazon logo, and Thomas & Mercer are trademarks of Amazon.com, Inc., or its affiliates.

ISBN-13: 9781542005944
ISBN-10: 1542005949

Cover design by Micaela Alcaino

Printed in the United States of America

For Dana
Warrior. Protector. Mother. Wife.
It begins and ends with you.

"You cannot watch him all the time.
I will take him in the end."
She was gone. But I said it anyway, to that great
empty room and my son's dreaming ears:
"You do not know what I can do."
—Madeline Miller, *Circe*

"Knock knock."

"Who's there?"

"A burglar."

"A burglar who?"

"No, Mom, this isn't a knock-knock joke. It's a real burglar. You're supposed to be scared."

"Oh, right. Sorry, sweetie. Oh no, a burglar! Whatever shall we do?"

"I'm a mean old burglar, and I smell, and I'm going to come in and shoot you."

"Megan, burglars don't shoot people. They're cowards. They just want to steal things and run away."

"That's not true, Mom. When a burglar came into our home, he had a gun and wanted to shoot you. Remember, Mommy?"

". . ."

"Mommy?"

"Yes. I remember, darling. I'll never forget it. But he didn't."

"But he could have. He could have shot you. Right?"

"Yes, Megan. But you and your brother are safe. Now and always."

"Are you safe?"

"Right now I am, baby."

"So in my story, the burglar is like the one who came to our house. He didn't only want to steal things. He wanted to hurt people."

"You shouldn't be writing such scary things, Megan."

"But Sadie Scout is the hero of my books, Mom. She doesn't get scared by bad people because she's brave."

"Being brave doesn't mean you're not scared of the bad things. Being brave means you stay strong even though you're scared."

"Don't worry, Mom. Nothing that bad is going to happen to Sadie Scout."

"Oh? How do you know?"

"Because I want to write a lot of Sadie Scout books. Like a hundred. I can't write a hundred Sadie Scout books if something really bad happens to her. It's not like real life, where if something really bad happens, the person doesn't come back. Like Dad."

"Oh, sweetie . . ."

"I think that's what people want, isn't it? A happy ending?"

"They do, baby. They do."

"Even if happy endings don't always happen in real life, they're going to happen to Sadie Scout. Because she's a hero. She'll always stop the bad guy. Even if that doesn't always happen in real life."

"Megan?"

"Yes, Mom?"

"You are truly amazing."

"Mom?"

"Yes?"

"Our last name. Marin. I know it's not our real last name. Right?"

"That's right."

"Did you make that name up, like out of nowhere? Did you read it in a book? Or did it come from somewhere?"

"It came from somewhere. Or something, actually. Something that once made Mommy very happy—the happiest she'd ever been before you and your brother were born. And so I chose Marin because I thought about that time I was so happy, and I wanted our family to be happy in the same way."

"What was that something? The reason you chose the name Marin for our family."

"Oh, hon, let's not get into that right now."

"Will I ever know?"

"One day. One day I'll show you. I promise."

"Mom? Do you think wherever Dad is, he's happy?"

"Oh, Megan, I know he is. He's happy, and he loves you and your brother and is proud of you every second of every day."

"I wish he was here so he could read my Sadie Scout books. I think he'd like them."

"I know he would, baby. Your daddy loved a good mystery."

CHAPTER 1

The day Matthew Linklater was murdered, he taught three social studies classes, caught Becca Matheson and Steve D'Agosta making out in the north stairwell, refused to loan his sister any more money on account of the fact that she'd already borrowed nearly six grand from him and there was as much chance of getting repaid as there was of finding coffee on the moon, and responded to three messages on dating apps during his lunch break.

Though never married, Linklater had steadfastly refused to participate in the fetid swamp that was online dating, despite the sadistic urging of his (married) friends. He found no dignity in crafting a focus-group biography expected to contain a measure of wit, a soupçon of self-deprecation, a hint of worldliness, and a heap of confidence, all in support of curated, flattering photographs of himself doing exotic things like posing alongside tigers while holding a freshly caught three-hundred-pound swordfish. But Edward Li, the school's forty-six-year-old chemistry teacher, had met his wife on one of those infernal swipey things, and as Li recalled it, they knew from the moment they met that they had "an immediate and unbreakable covalent bond." Three cheers for chemistry humor.

Had Linklater known the date and manner of his death, he would have tried to squeeze as much happiness into his relatively short life as possible before it was taken from him with an unimaginable amount of pain and terror.

But once Linklater acquiesced and downloaded the dating apps, he was shocked by the opposite sex's appetite for single, employed, reasonably put-together middle-aged men who still possessed the majority of their hair. It was addictive—that spark of excitement when he swiped right and got a notification that they, too, would at the very least *consider* having sex.

Every so often he'd come across the mother of one of his students, and suddenly he would understand why Suzanne Winger or Jamal Phillips or any number of students had become sullen or angry: their parents had split up, leaving confused, bitter children in their wake. He tried to use this concealed knowledge to be more understanding, more patient, with those kids he learned were suffering, often in the midst of oblivious parents solely focused on their own miseries.

Yet despite all the matches, his overflowing in-box, all the couplings and conversations and carnality, Matthew Linklater was selective. He was not an unhappy man and did not want a prospective partner to think he was looking for something serious when, the truth was, he was largely content. Lonely sometimes, sure. But who wasn't? Linklater's parents were divorced by the time he was eight, and being shuffled joylessly from home to home every other weekend had been as pleasurable as a trip to the dentist.

So he'd drifted through life on the fringes of academia. Earned a master's in history from Loyola, bounced around the Midwest until landing at Ashby High thirteen years ago. He'd bought a house before the market boom and had nearly paid off his thirty-year fixed-rate mortgage in less than half the time. Soon enough he would be debt-free, and every spare penny from his $68,000-a-year salary could be earmarked for retirement. Or better yet, a long-overdue vacation. He had been seeing someone on and off—an Ashby High mother, no less. It went against his rules, but there was something about Gabrielle. She stuck in his mind, and even when he'd tried to call it off, his heart had refused to call it quits. Who knew what the future held? He'd always wanted to visit Machu Picchu. Maybe he would invite Gabrielle. Maybe it could be more.

So on the day he would experience more agony than he ever thought possible, Matthew Linklater arrived home, went for a two-point-two-mile jog around his neighborhood, and mixed himself a Moscow mule (he even had a copper mug chilling in the freezer). Then he planned to settle in, grade some papers, watch an hour of television, and prepare to repeat it all again the following day. But before he did that, he had one order of business to take care of. Something had been bothering him, but he had been unsure of how to deal with it and whom he could trust. The issue was possibly criminal, so it was not fully a school matter. But he'd read about the recent corruption at the Ashby Police Department and felt he couldn't trust them either. He needed to tell someone smart and persistent. And, more importantly, someone who could work outside the law.

Which was why he emailed Rachel Marin.

He typed out an email from his personal, private account:

Dear Ms. Marin—

We have only met briefly at Parent/Teacher nights, but I am your son Eric's social studies teacher at Ashby High. Before you get concerned, this note does not actually pertain to Eric, who is sharp as a tack, if a little withdrawn (as you surely must know).

This is about something else entirely. Information has come into my possession regarding a few of our students, and their dealings with people who, to put it mildly, do not have their best interests at heart. For reasons of safety and security, I cannot go into further detail over email. I do not have proof of my suspicions, which, among other reasons, is why I have not yet gone to the police. As an admirer of your dogged pursuit of justice for the killer of Mayor Constance Wright, I would like to speak with you in order to figure out the appropriate course of action here. I care deeply about my students, and I cannot sit idly by after having learned some may be in peril. I apologize for the vagueness of this note, but hopefully all will be made clear when we speak in person.

My phone number is below. Please call me at your earliest convenience. I abhor dramatics, but it may be a matter of life and death.

Yours,
Matthew Linklater

He reviewed the email, took a deep breath, and pressed "Send." He then poured himself another drink. Linklater had just put the cup to his lips when he heard a knock at the door. For a moment, he was unsettled. Linklater rarely had visitors, and when he did, they were meticulously scheduled in advance. But it was just a knock, he told himself, and he ignored the unease.

Linklater looked through the peephole and immediately sighed with relief. He opened the door and said, "Is everything all right?"

Linklater didn't see the second person, just the flicker of a shadow. Then he heard a strange skittering sound, like tiny claws scraping against metal, and then the wrench connected with his left temple.

He did not feel it when his head hit the floor. It was as though one moment he was standing and the next he was at ground level. He tried to blink, but his eyes refused to focus. He felt a stickiness beneath his temple. He opened his mouth, but nothing came out. He tried to move but could not. Fear flooded his body.

Linklater saw his cell phone lying a few feet away. He had one thought: *police.*

He reached for it, but a hand came down and picked up his phone. Linklater heard voices. They sounded far away, as if he were listening to sounds from ashore while deep, deep underwater. He tried to scream, but his body would not cooperate.

"Phone is locked. It has facial-recognition software," a disembodied voice said. "Good thing he still has a face. For now."

The last thing Matthew Linklater saw, before the wrench came down again and the light behind his eyes flickered out for the second-to-last time, was the reflection of his own bloodied face in the inky-black screen of his cell phone.

CHAPTER 2

She still couldn't get used to it. The man in her bed. The way his body smelled in the morning, the way his cheeks had pillow marks when he woke up, how he always left the bathroom door open a crack while showering, as if egging her on to take a quick glimpse. She took the bait more often than not but couldn't shake the feeling of unrest, as though she'd just eaten a five-course gourmet meal and was waiting for the crippling heartburn to set in.

Rachel Marin had been dating Detective John Serrano of the Ashby Police Department for about six months, and they were the happiest months she'd had in a long, long time. She'd hesitated to get involved romantically. She was concerned with how her children, Eric and Megan, would react to having a boyfriend around the house. The only man they had ever seen Rachel with was their father, and when he'd died, Rachel had wondered if they would ever approve of seeing her with anyone else. But they had warmed to John Serrano and, in doing so, allowed her to feel more comfortable. More like herself again.

Serrano spent time with her kids. Asked them questions. Listened, patiently. Never smothered them or made his presence feel forced. He had befriended Eric, even if only for a few brief months, until her son retreated back into his shell. Serrano now sat on the floor, rapt, as Megan read from her latest Sadie Scout story, remarking on the pint-size heroine's uncanny ability to both fight evil and look super cute while doing so.

He watched movies with the Marin family. Ate dinner with them. And when the children were in bed (and confirmed by Rachel's CCTV monitors in their bedrooms to be asleep), they made love. Quietly but passionately, both knowing that the children were far more aware than they might let on.

She had received Matthew Linklater's disturbing email the previous night as Megan read them a new Sadie Scout tale, and in an effort to be present for her daughter, she'd promised herself to respond the next day.

Rachel lay in bed. She watched John Serrano as he snored lightly, his face mashed against the pillow. She stretched and stepped into the shower. She heard him stir and left the door open a crack in case he felt like joining her. He did not. And when Rachel stepped out, Serrano was sitting up, on his cell phone, a look of grave concern on his face.

"Text me the address," he said, pinching the bridge of his nose. "You said the fire is out. Has anybody been inside the house? Tell Montrose and Beene to wait. Even if it's out, we need to assess any structural damage before sending in forensics. Call Tally. I'm on my way."

"What is it?" she said.

"House fire," John said. He stood up, cracked his back, and headed for the shower. "North Ashby. Possible arson."

"Was anyone home?"

"Yes," Serrano said. "They've found one body so far, but we're waiting on dental records to confirm the victim's identity."

"So the victim died in the fire."

Serrano nodded.

"Once the kids are out the door, I'll meet you there," Rachel said.

Serrano nodded again. "Tell Eric and Megan I'm sorry I couldn't eat breakfast with them."

"I will. You know, when we started seeing each other, Eric seemed to get better. He was opening up. But the last couple of months, it's like he's been . . . gone."

"I've noticed," Serrano said. "That boy has been through things I can't imagine. If you want me to talk to him, let me know. I can't be his father. But I can be his friend."

"Thanks, John. He's not a kid anymore, but he'll always be my baby. Seeing him in pain . . . there's nothing worse. I know you know."

"I do." The detective gave Rachel a quick but firm kiss.

After Serrano showered, he put on a clean white shirt, socks, and underwear; a pair of freshly pressed pants; and a suit jacket. Rachel had cleaned out space in her closet for his clothes, and she couldn't help but smile as he dressed. After dating for several months, they'd both agreed it had become silly for him to carry a gym bag of dirty linens to and from her house. To Serrano, it might have just been an empty drawer, a couple of coat hangers. But to Rachel, it signified that she was moving on. Making room for him not just in her house but in her life.

"Can I tie your tie?" she said.

Serrano laughed. "You still haven't learned how to do it. You're the only woman I've ever met who can clean a shotgun but not tie a tie."

"To be honest, only one of those skills is practical knowledge. If push comes to shove, I'd rather be able to pump a load of bird shot into a criminal than try to strangle him with a necktie."

"Now that sounds like a romantic evening."

Serrano did his tie, then leaned down and kissed Rachel deeply.

"See you in a bit," he said.

"Remember," she replied, "if the floors are hardwood, see if they squeak. If they do, they've suffered severe fire damage and could collapse. If they think it's an electrical fire, check for soot or black streaks near any outlets. If you find any, there could be—"

"Damage inside the walls. I know, Rachel. You forget I've been doing this a lot longer than you have."

"Doesn't make you any better at it," she said with a knife-edge smile.

"Say bye to the kids for me."

He blew her a kiss and disappeared. Rachel stood there, wondering whether it was stranger that Serrano had not yet said *I love you* to her or that part of her didn't want him to.

CHAPTER 3

Serrano could see the thick black smoke pouring into the sky as he approached Glenmore Lane in North Ashby. It was a wooded residential neighborhood, tree lined and quiet. A decent-size three-bedroom ranch style ran about $400,000. A lifetime ago, he and his ex-wife, Deirdre, had looked at homes here. If they'd ever tried for the second kid they'd talked about for so long, they would've needed the extra bedroom.

A lifetime ago.

Fire trucks and cop cars blocked off the roads adjacent to Glenmore. Residents lined the streets, most still in their pajamas, several holding cups of coffee in one hand while taking cell phone photos with the other.

Images and video of the fire had already begun blanketing social media. It wasn't long ago, Serrano thought, that cops could control the flow of information from a crime scene. There were savvy reporters, and sure, occasionally a citizen would trundle by with a camcorder. But local news stations hardly ever needed camera crews anymore; they could just sift through Twitter and Instagram, and suddenly some teenager's shaky cell phone video would lead the morning news.

Serrano pulled up to the curb and got out of the car. The stench of smoke and burnt wood was pungent. He saw his partner, Detective Leslie Tally, standing in the driveway, speaking to Isaac Montrose from forensics. Montrose towered over Detective Tally, an easy six four both vertically and horizontally. His bald head, dotted with sweat, peeked out from his breathable protective coverall. He had on latex gloves and protective eyewear. A NIOSH-approved particle respirator hung from his neck. Tally was about five six, black, her hair tightly braided on the sides and curly on top. Just the other day she'd come into work in a mood that suggested the IRS had notified her about a tax audit but was actually because she'd noticed her first gray hair. She told him she'd named it Serrano, her reasoning being that either her partner or old age would be the death of her.

"Detective," Montrose said as Serrano approached. "Sorry to ruin your morning."

Serrano pointed at the smoking remains of the house at the end of the driveway. "What do we got?"

"One victim," Tally said, "as yet unidentified. Male, likely Caucasian. Hector Moreno already has the body at the medical examiner's office, and he's running dental records as we speak. It's likely that the body belongs to the owner of the home, but we don't want to confirm anything before Moreno gets a positive ID. For that reason we haven't yet contacted next of kin."

"Where was the body found?" Serrano asked.

"Still in bed," Tally replied. Serrano looked at her, confused. "I know. We don't have an answer for that yet. It's possible he was drunk or on drugs and slept through the first kindlings. With the extensive damage to the body and organs, Moreno said they'll be lucky to get any sort of accurate tox screen."

"Time of death?"

"We couldn't make that determination at the scene," Montrose said. "Liver was cooked, so we couldn't get a good internal temp reading."

"Hopefully Hector can work his magic," Tally said.

Montrose said, "We removed the body, but we're still assessing the foundation to make sure the structure won't collapse with us in it."

Serrano said, "I seem to remember another murder not that long ago where we were worried about the ice swallowing us up. Now it's fire."

"Constance Wright," Montrose said. "And speaking of the Constance Wright investigation . . ."

"So, what did I miss?" The trio turned around to see Rachel Marin walking toward the house. Serrano had left the Marin home barely twenty minutes ago. She must have shooed the kids out the door and ignored all posted speed limits.

"Ms. Marin," Montrose said. "Pleasure to see you, despite the circumstances."

"Hey, Rachel," Tally said as they shook hands. "How are Eric and Megan?"

She sighed. "Megan is going to be a famous writer by the time she's in high school. Eric is . . . I don't know. I might know my way around a crime scene. But I'm like the blind leading the limbless when trying to understand the mind of an adolescent boy."

"You should talk to Claire," Tally said. "When she and her ex-husband split, her kids didn't speak to her for a month."

"I appreciate that, and I'll take you up on it," Rachel said. "So what's the story here with Cinderville?"

"I was just filling the detectives in," Montrose said. "What do you think, Rachel?"

Rachel took a few steps closer and surveyed the property. Then she pointed at the charred remnants of the house.

"See the blackening on the eastern and western walls? How they're much darker than the material around them?" she said. Serrano, Tally, and Montrose looked, noted the discoloration. "Now look at the roof. You'll see a similar blackening. Normally a fire starts from one specific flash point: faulty wiring, a space heater, a candle. But from what I can tell, there appear to be at least three separate flash points. Home fires don't begin from three separate spots concurrently. And we haven't even examined the rest of the house. There could be even more."

"That would suggest arson," Montrose said.

"Not only that," Rachel said, "but it would mean that someone took the time to prep the house to go up fast and burn down fast. That would be one way to make sure whoever was inside wouldn't be able to get out."

"We don't know that the victim was alive when the house went up," Tally said.

"Yes, we do," Rachel said. "The arsonist wanted it to burn fast. Any one of those flash points would have eventually done the job. But we have at least three. Meaning they wanted all exits blocked by fire. You don't seal off the exits for a corpse. Check the windows and staircases. If you find other flash points, it was the killer sealing off the tomb."

Serrano thumbed his lip. "If the arsonist was smart enough to get inside the home, subdue the victim, and prep numerous flash points, they'd also have to know we'd determine quickly that the fire was intentional."

Tally said, "That would mean they didn't care if we knew it was arson. In fact, the obviousness of it might have been the entire point. They wanted us to know it was arson and that the victim, presuming he was inside, was murdered."

Rachel said, "And someone either wanted us to know immediately this was not an accidental fire or didn't care one way or the other. Speaking of which, do we have an ID on the victim?"

"Moreno needs to wait until dental records come back to officially make an ID so we can notify next of kin. But the house was owned by a man named Matthew Linklater."

Rachel's head snapped up, eyes wide.

"What?" Serrano said. "What is it?"

Rachel took out her cell phone and showed them her email account.

"Matthew Linklater is my son's social studies teacher," she said. "He emailed me yesterday—right before he was murdered."

CHAPTER 4

Eighteen-year-old high school senior Benjamin Ruddock was eating a bowl of cereal, his third helping, when he felt his cell phone vibrate in his right pocket. An incoming text. He immediately froze. This cell phone rang infrequently, but when it did, it necessitated an immediate answer. He checked the text. One word.

Call.

"Dad, turn the TV down," the younger Ruddock said. His father, Timothy, was sunk so deep into his faded green easy chair that it looked like the piece had tried to swallow him whole but gave up. The elder Ruddock simply stared at the state-of-the-art sixty-inch LCD, which looked out of place in the dilapidated home.

The remote was on the coffee table a whole six inches away from his father's grasp, which meant there was a higher chance of him suddenly deciding to get a degree in thermal engineering than lifting a finger to help his son.

Benjamin grabbed the remote and turned the volume down from twelve to two.

"I can barely hear it now," his father rasped. Benjamin eyed the man with furious contempt, the rage thick in his veins like motor oil in a straw.

"Who bought you the TV?" Benjamin asked pointedly. "Oh. That's right. *I did*. So I'll turn down the volume if I want. I'll throw it out the damn window if I want. That's *my* television. You're lucky I even let you use it."

"Kid gets a little money and suddenly he's a big shot," Timothy Ruddock said to nobody in particular. "You just better hope nobody asks me how you got it."

"What's that?" Benjamin said, looming over his father's lethargic form.

Ruddock senior snorted and spat a glob of tobacco juice into a red Solo cup. Benjamin Ruddock was bigger, stronger, and smarter than his father and spent far too much energy just cleaning up his old man's (literal) messes. But Benjamin would be out of the house soon enough and would leave skid marks on his way out of this miserable town. Not only that, he would leave with a full bank account, thanks to the man who'd sent the text, and a future of endless possibility. Which is more than his old man could ever say.

Benjamin went into his bedroom, closed the door, and dialed the number he knew by heart.

"Good response time," the voice on the other end said.

"What do you need?" Ruddock said.

"There's a boy in your school. A few years younger. A freshman. His name is Eric Marin. Do you know him?"

"Not personally, but I've heard the name a few times. Has a bit of a rep. One of those kids who's just a little too quiet, know what I mean? Like if he ever murders a bunch of people with a ballpoint pen, everyone's gonna say, 'Yeah, I saw it coming.'"

"Your amateur psychiatric evaluations aside," the voice said, "what else do you know about him?"

"Not much. He's a freshman, so we don't have any classes together. Just pass him in the hall sometimes. Don't think I've ever said a word to him."

"Does he have friends?"

"He seems like kind of a loner. There's one girl I've seen hanging around him: Penny Wallace. I know that Wallace's stepmom is a cop."

"What else do you know about him?"

"Wasn't his mom in the news a little while back? Something to do with a murder? I feel like a lot of people at school were talking about her, like she was some kind of vigilante—"

"Never mind what people might have been talking about. I need you to get closer to this Marin boy."

Benjamin Ruddock was silent for a moment. "I thought I just said that his mom—"

"And I thought I just said I need you to get closer to *him*."

"Is this related to what happened yesterday?"

"I think you know the answer to that question, Benjamin."

The high schooler was silent.

"We need to bring Eric Marin into the fold. His mother, Rachel, may try to get involved in our business, and I'd like her attentions diverted. Besides, sometimes boys who are, to use your delicate phrasing, *loners* wind up being our most valuable assets. Troubled children have tremendous potential. They just need guidance. What have I taught you to do?"

"Know the customer. Learn what they need. Make them believe what you have to offer is the key to their happiness."

"So what might a young man like Eric Marin—a loner, as you say—what might he need? What does a lonely child need?"

"Someone who listens to him. Makes him feel like he's being heard. Like he's full of untapped potential that only you can see." Ruddock paused. "I can do that."

"You're a good kid, Ben. Offer him a little signing bonus as well. The usual. I've taken care of the arrangements. Just make sure Eric Marin is at the next meeting. We're about to change his life."

CHAPTER 5

"I'm telling you, there's something wrong," Penny Wallace whispered. "Mr. Linklater has never even been ten seconds late for class. And it's already ten ten."

"Maybe he won the lottery," Ronnie Parness said. "Got a new wardrobe and moved to LA to be an actor. That's what happened to my cousin. He was a school superintendent in Chicago, but just last year he got cast in a five-minute role as a pedophile on some cop show, and now he acts like he's Brad Pitt."

"Mr. Linklater isn't hot enough to be an actor," Lucy Wiles replied.

"I don't know, he's got kind of a cool, schlumpy, middle-aged-librarian vibe," Aaron Middlestein said. "Not like cool as in *hot*, but cool like he'd be comfy to snuggle up against and binge a few episodes of something with."

Eric Marin listened to all this speculation but remained silent. Though he was maintaining an A minus average, he did not speak in Mr. Linklater's freshman social studies class unless explicitly called on and never joined in on the conversations that dominated pre- and postclass. Not that anyone ever tried to bring him in.

Eric had joined Ashby Middle School in the seventh grade following the death of his father and his mother's decision to move their family to the middle of nowhere. By seventh grade, friendships had already been established, cliques hardened into concrete. There was no room for a "random" like Eric Marin. That's what kids like him were called—randoms—since they joined the school at random times, usually due to unstable family lives: divorces, relocation, abuse. Even prison, like Tony Vargas's father. Eric had enrolled at Ashby alone, and for the most part, he'd remained that way.

He was friendly with Penny Wallace, but they weren't quite friends. Penny was the stepdaughter of Leslie Tally, John Serrano's partner on the Ashby police force. Since Eric's mom had begun . . . seeing . . . Detective John Serrano, Penny's and Eric's families had become friendly. Tally's wife, Claire Wallace, had a husband and three kids before she married Tally. Eric's mom had a husband before she met John Serrano. Both families had been blown up: one by divorce, the other by tragedy. Eric couldn't stand their loud, boisterous family dinners. He felt like a shard from a broken glass being glued together with other pieces that didn't fit.

But Penny . . . Penny was always kind to him. Even when he didn't return that kindness. There was a reason he couldn't allow himself to get close to her. He could never tell her the truth.

"I know what you've been through," she'd said to him once. "I can't say I know what it's like to lose a parent like you did, but if you ever want to talk, I'm a pretty good listener."

Eric had thanked her. And he'd meant it. But never took her up on it. He had to keep a distance between them. For her own good.

John Serrano wasn't a bad guy. Eric's mom was happy around him, he liked fantasy and science fiction, and he could keep up with Eric when they talked about books and movies. Since Eric's father had died, his mom had mostly kept to herself. And Eric knew why. She didn't trust anyone. *Couldn't* trust anyone. Sometimes Eric wondered if his mom wanted John Serrano around because she genuinely cared for him or if she just liked having another gun in the house.

The classroom door opened, and the gossip stopped. Eric could feel his pulse thumping in his temples. Principal Tamara Alvi entered, talking softly on a cell phone. Her eyes were red, and mascara ran in rivulets down her cheeks.

Principal Alvi put her phone in the pocket of her gray blazer, took a deep breath, and faced the classroom. She was about five two with short legs and deep-set eyes. She was in her early fifties, usually well put together, but looked like she'd aged ten years that morning.

"Where's Mr. Linklater?" came a voice from the back of the room.

Principal Alvi nodded, as though acknowledging the question but unsure how to answer it.

"At this point," Ms. Alvi said, "you are all young adults, and many of you have dealt with tremendously difficult situations in your lives. These days, information spreads as fast as a text message. It's important you hear this from me and not on social media. Mr. Linklater is both friend and family to our school, its faculty, and its students. Today I have the terrible responsibility to inform you that Mr. Linklater has passed away."

Several students audibly gasped. A few began to cry. Eric felt a lump rise in his throat. *Passed away?* he thought. *Healthy-looking fortysome-things don't just pass away.* He knew Alvi was either lying or withholding the truth.

"We have informed your parents and guardians about this terrible tragedy," Ms. Alvi said, her voice shaking. "We will have grief counselors on hand for any student who would like to speak with them. No doubt you will hear more about Mr. Linklater's passing. All I ask is that you treat him with the same respect he treated all of you."

"How did he die?" Cory Stuber shouted. Cory was an asshole. Everyone knew it, but because he had an enormous summer home right on Lake Springfield and a key to his parents' liquor cabinet, nobody wanted to piss him off. Eric hated Cory's asshole voice, his asshole wavy blond hair, and the way that even though he was an asshole, girls still smiled at him.

Alvi shook her head. "His death was . . . unnatural. That's all I can say right now. You may see members of the Ashby Police Department around school over the next few days. If any of them try to speak with you, please let me or your parents or guardians know before talking to them. We will have a schoolwide assembly tomorrow morning."

"Oh, so he was *definitely* killed," Cory Stuber said.

"You're a soulless shithead," Adaline Wylie chided.

"Don't be so naive," Cory snapped back. "Do you think cops would be here if he choked on a chicken bone? So how did Linklater kick the bucket?"

Eric felt flames rise up through his gut and into his shoulders. He clenched his fists and said, "Shut the hell up, Cory."

"Why?" Cory said with a smug laugh. "Did *you* kill him?"

"Enough, Cory," Penny yelled.

"Why? Are you gonna call one of your two moms on me?"

"That's *enough*, Mr. Stuber," Alvi said. The anger that always bubbled in Eric's gut was now inching up his neck, roiling inside of him. "There is no room right now for hate or anger. We all loved Mr. Linklater, and we will get through this. Together."

Principal Alvi left the classroom. Once she was gone, the students slowly got up and filed out. Eric listened to the whispers, the theories, the gossip. He went to his locker and removed his copy of *Discovering Our Past: A History of the United States* from his backpack. The spine was new, barely cracked. Most students were forced to buy used copies of the curriculum textbooks, but Eric's mother always made sure his were brand new. New books. New clothes. New everything. He felt embarrassed reading from his pristine copy when his classmates read from books with pages falling out. He never asked his mother where the money came from.

Back when his father was alive, his parents had rarely argued. But when they did, it was always about money. And the walls were so thin he could hear every word. How they could ever afford college for two. If they'd be stuck in the same house forever. One morning Eric had asked them about it. "If you love each other," he'd said, "why do you yell at each other?"

They'd both kissed him and hugged him, and his father had said, "Parents fight. Your mom and I fight because we care about you and about our family. But I love her more than I did yesterday." And Eric knew he meant it.

But after their father died, the Marin family had never wanted for anything. New computers. New textbooks. New clothes every season. Things they'd never had before. Eric wondered how they suddenly had money, but he never asked. He had a feeling the answer would make him angry.

As he put his books into his backpack, Eric knew Penny Wallace had come up behind him. He could always smell her before he saw her. Her deodorant had a sweet scent, like too much sugar poured into too little lemon juice. He liked that he could tell when she was close; it made him feel like a detective or an FBI agent. He closed his locker, spun the lock, and turned around to see Penny there.

"Oh, hey, Penny," he said, pretending to be surprised.

"Hey, Eric," she said. He felt something twisting in his stomach, her presence washing away his anger like cool water over burning embers. He tried to force back a smile but failed.

"Well, look at that," Penny said. "I was starting to wonder if you had teeth. You should smile more often."

A witty reply did not come to him, so Eric just said, "Yeah."

"You didn't respond to my text last night."

"I was asleep," Eric lied. *Keep her at arm's length,* he thought. *For her own sake.*

"No, you weren't. I got a read receipt."

He shrugged. "Caught."

"So," she repeated. "How *are* you?"

"OK, I guess."

"OK, I guess," Penny said. "The only time someone says they're 'OK' is when they're really *not* OK. Talk to me."

"About what?"

"Come on, Eric. The last few months you've been . . . I don't know, not there."

"I'm right here."

"You know what I mean. The last few times your family has come over for dinner, I don't think you've said more than two words."

"Were you counting?"

"Maybe," she said, with a faint smile.

The first time his mother had told them they were having dinner with Detective Tally's family, Eric had refused to go. "I don't have to listen to you," he'd shouted. "When has anything good ever come from me listening to you?" Then he'd stormed off to his room, leaving his mother and sister standing in the foyer, shocked.

A few minutes later, Eric had heard his mother quietly weeping in the hallway. When he opened his bedroom door, he saw her sitting on the floor, knees held to her chin, head in her arms. He could not recall ever seeing his mother look defeated before. Guilt sliced through him like a sharpened blade.

Eric knew the hell his mother had been through. And even though his brain had said, *Fight, you idiot; you've got her on the ropes!* his heart had reminded him that his mother would trade her life for his in an instant. And that he was at least partially responsible for her sadness.

And so he'd come out and told her he'd changed his mind, and they'd gone to the Wallace family's home. To his surprise, it hadn't been that bad. Tally's wife, Claire, had cooked enough osso buco to feed an infantry division. And the Wallace kids were pretty cool. Penny especially. They talked about school and music and who had the best Instagram feeds. At the end of the night, they exchanged numbers. Before they went to bed, they followed each other on social media. They filled each other's feeds with chaste "likes." And every time Penny spoke to him unprovoked, Eric wondered—maybe even hoped—it might be something more.

"I know you want to talk," she said. "Talk to me."

"I didn't realize you could read minds," he said, more flirtatiously than he'd hoped.

"Actually, I can. One look at your hand, and I'll be able to tell you what you're going to get on Mr. Meador's English exam next week."

"Is that right?" Eric said, this time striking the right tone. He knew it because he could see the color rising in her cheeks.

She nodded and gently took his hand. Penny looked at it for a moment, then gently placed her right hand underneath his and ran her finger along the creases in his skin.

Eric felt strange. Warm. Like all the words he knew had been removed from his brain and replaced with mush. He wanted to tell her to stop, but his brain had ceased responding to instructions. Penny traced her finger from the tips of his fingers down to his wrist.

"What does my hand tell you?" Eric said.

"Shh," Penny replied. Her eyes were shut tight as she concentrated. Or at least pretended to concentrate. "This line says you're going to get an eighty-eight on your English test."

"That's a B plus," Eric said. "Can my palm bump that to maybe a ninety or ninety-one?"

"I don't make up what your lines say," Penny replied. "This line says you're a *Placidochromis*."

"A what, now?"

"A *Placidochromis*. It's a type of fish that comes from Lake Malawi in Mozambique."

"And why would I be a . . ."

"*Placidochromis*. Actually its full name is *Placidochromis phenochilus Mdoka*."

"Bless you."

"It's a fish with lips that look bizarrely human. That's what you are. You have all these traits that *appear* human . . . but you don't really use them."

"That was quite a leap," Eric said.

26

"Tell me I'm wrong. Because you want to say more than you actually do. Maybe you don't think anyone wants to listen. But they will."

"Like who?"

Penny took her hand from Eric's. She toed the ground. "People."

To Eric, the following moment of silence seemed to last forever. Then he said, "So did you learn anything else from my palm, Ichthyologist Wallace?"

She took his hand and said, "This line says . . ."

"That Eric Marin killed Mr. Linklater."

Eric turned to see Cory Stuber standing there, a smirk on his face that practically begged to be punched away. Two girls stood on either side of him: Vanessa Jackson and Odette Meyers. They looked at Eric like he was a tetherball that would be fun to bat around.

"Go away, Cory," Eric said.

"I'm sorry, what did you say?" Cory said, mock-cupping his ear and leaning in. "Was that a confession? Did you just confess to cutting off Mr. Linklater's head and making it into a fishbowl?"

"Stop it, Cory," Penny said.

"Know what I just remembered? Penny's mom is a cop. Wouldn't that be embarrassing if you got arrested by your girlfriend's dyke mom?"

Eric clenched his fists. He could envision swinging upward from his hip, smashing Cory's smug chin, shattering all his teeth, splitting his lips into red worms, watching his body fly back like it had been spring loaded. But instead he stood there, watching Cory and the girls smile, hoping they would just all go away and leave him alone, like he wanted to be. Like he deserved to be.

Cory stepped forward, so close that Eric could smell his breath.

"Did you forget how to speak, Marin?" Cory said. "Let me help you." Cory brought his fingers toward Eric's lips, like a pair of pincers.

But before Cory could touch Eric, a hand grabbed Cory's wrist, twisting it away, and an arm the size of a small tree trunk slammed into the middle of the boy's back, driving him face first into the row of lockers with a *whumpf.* Cory gasped and tried to wriggle free, but the enormous arm held him in place with ease.

The arm was attached to a kid. Not a kid. A *guy.* A guy Eric only knew from the way other kids avoided him in the corridors. They swerved around him like you might avoid a rattlesnake in the grass. He was the kind of kid new students were warned to stay away from. Including Eric.

Benjamin Ruddock. A senior. He was eighteen but could have passed for thirty. He was a head taller than Cory and Eric and out-weighed them each by about forty pounds. His sandy-brown hair fell across his forehead. He had the blue eyes of a calm lake, but there was a sparkle of menace behind them, as though a monster was hidden in the depths. Ruddock held Cory Stuber against the lockers almost effortlessly. Vanessa Jackson and Odette Meyers batted at Ruddock's arm with the effectiveness of paper airplanes flitting against the side of a Sherman tank.

"Let me go, asshole," Cory groaned, but his shaky voice belied the fact that he knew Ruddock would only let him go when he damn well pleased.

"Apologize to my friend," Ruddock said. Eric's eyes widened. He'd never spoken a word to Benjamin Ruddock.

"Go screw yourself," Cory spat.

Ruddock dug his palm deeper into Cory's shoulder, hard enough that his collarbone was likely beginning to bend. Cory cried out in pain.

"Apologize to my friend Eric," Ruddock said, "or I'll hide pieces of you in different lockers." Ruddock pushed harder. Cory again cried out in pain.

"I'm sorry," Cory whispered.

"I can't *hear* you," Ruddock said in a singsong tone.

"I'm sorry!" Cory said, loud enough for other kids to take notice.

"I'm sorry, *Eric*," Ruddock said.

"I'm sorry, Eric!" Cory wept. Ruddock let him go. Cory Stuber collapsed to the ground. The two girls knelt down to help him up, but Cory pushed them away and ran off, a neutered dog.

"You OK, kid?" Ruddock said to Eric.

"He was just being a douchebag," Eric said.

"Don't worry about idiots like Cory Stuber," Ruddock said. "In ten years he'll be pumping your gas."

Ruddock clapped Eric friendly-like on the arm and laughed. It made Eric feel good. People rarely laughed *with* him.

"Ben," he said, extending his hand. "Ben Ruddock."

Eric shook it. He could make out blue tattoo ink just under the right sleeve of Ruddock's shirt. "Eric Marin."

"Good to finally meet," Ruddock said. "I've had my eye on you, Eric Marin."

"Your eye on me?"

"Not in a creepy way. I want to talk about your future."

"My future?" Eric said. Penny's eyes narrowed, distrusting.

"Do you see yourself stuck in Ashby your whole life, dealing with troglodytes like Cory Stuber?"

"I . . . I haven't really thought about it."

"Don't you think it's time?"

"I don't know. I guess?"

Ruddock nodded. He turned toward Penny. "Listen, Ms. Wallace. Do me a solid. Let me have a chat with Eric. Then the two of you can catch butterflies until the end of time. OK?"

Penny looked at Eric.

He shrugged and said, "It's OK."

Penny nodded. "OK. See you, Eric. Text me later."

"See you," Eric replied. Penny walked away, quickly.

When she was out of earshot, Ruddock sighed. "I never thought we'd get rid of her."

"She's my friend," Eric said.

"You're right," Ruddock said. "I'm sorry. Sometimes I get a little impatient. But only for things I'm excited about. Like opportunities."

"Opportunities?"

"That's why I'm here. To give you an opportunity. You're a smart kid, Marin. I've seen you around. You're smarter than people give you credit for."

"What do you mean you've seen me around?"

"I keep an eye on all the younger classes. For recruiting purposes."

"Recruiting purposes? Recruiting for what?"

Ruddock ignored the question. "We're always looking for smart, capable, ambitious young men. Young men who have tremendous potential. But you're being pushed aside by others who are too blind to see it."

"I'm not being pushed anywhere."

"Sure you are," Ruddock said. "You're being pushed around by people at home. By people like Cory Stuber. People like your mom. They still see you as a kid. Only one person can change that, and I'm looking at him."

"You don't know the first thing about my mom," Eric said.

"Listen, Eric," Ruddock said, putting a heavy hand on Eric's shoulder. "I know your dad isn't around. Mine isn't either. I mean, he's still alive, but he's basically a living speed bump. Creates more problems than he solves. Hell, I'd rather have no dad than him. So same thing, if you think about it."

"That's not the same thing at all," Eric said. "So what the hell do you want?"

"It's not about what *I* want, Eric," Ruddock said. "It's about what *you* want, and what you're entitled to."

"And what do I want?" Eric said, sarcastically.

"Opportunity," Ruddock said. "You want people to hear you. And you want them to listen, because you deserve to be heard. I know you have a voice, a strong one. And that voice, plus your brains, can get you everything. You won't need to listen to anyone ever again, but they'll listen to you. Boy, will they listen to you."

"I don't understand."

"Just say yes. To opportunity."

"And what does that mean—opportunity?"

Ruddock smiled. "I'm about show, not tell. I want you to come to a meeting. Tomorrow. One a.m. Voss Field."

"The baseball stadium?"

"Yup. You'll *see* what I'm talking about."

"In the middle of the night? My mom—"

"If you really want something, you find a way to make it happen, and you don't let anything stand in your way. Definitely not a curfew, and definitely not parents. Trust me. This will be the best thing that's ever happened to you."

"I don't know . . ."

"As a show of good faith," Ruddock said, "I've been instructed to tell you that we're offering you a generous signing bonus. Just for coming."

"Signing bonus?"

Ruddock took out a cell phone. He typed in the URL of Cedar Bank and logged in. He tapped the screen a few times, then showed Eric the website.

"That's . . . that's my name," Eric said, shocked.

"This is *your* account. It belongs to you."

"There's ten thousand dollars in it."

"That's your money. *If* you come tomorrow night. If not, the account will be closed, and we'll just go on being strangers. Now put out your hand."

Eric hesitated.

Ruddock laughed. "Don't worry, I'm not going to read your palm."

Eric extended his hand, opened it. Ruddock placed something in his palm, then closed Eric's fingers over it.

31

"Don't show this to anyone," Ruddock said. "If you do, you'll regret it. We take it as seriously as death, and in time you will too. See you tomorrow."

Ruddock squeezed Eric's palm. As Ruddock walked away, Eric noticed another boy looking at him. Tony Vargas, a good-looking junior. He did not know Tony well, had no classes with him, and hadn't said more than two words to the kid in his life. Tony had a thick scar on his neck that was the subject of many rumors at Ashby High. Gang initiation, suicide attempt, et cetera. For some reason, Tony was staring at Eric in a way that suggested a familiarity. Tony nodded almost imperceptibly at Eric, then walked on, leaving Eric confused and unnerved.

When he was alone, Eric opened his hand. Sitting in his palm was a gold coin the size of a silver dollar. It was embossed with an image of four arms coming together, like a plus sign, their hands meeting in the middle. Shaking in unison. At the top of the coin was printed one word.

Fratres.

Eric had taken introductory Latin. He knew what the word meant.

Brothers.

CHAPTER 6

It took the Ashby Fire Department several hours to confirm the structural integrity of the remains of the Linklater home before they would permit forensics and investigating officers inside. As they waited, Serrano and Tally interviewed the crowd of onlookers and knocked on neighbors' doors, hoping someone could shed light on Matthew Linklater's death.

Rachel paced the driveway like a caged lion watching a limping zebra. She couldn't wait to get inside the house. Several months back, after she'd helped put a killer behind bars (nearly killing him in the process), the Ashby PD realized Rachel Marin could be a valuable asset to their overworked department. She had proven her abilities on the Constance Wright murder investigation—even if she'd pissed off the rank and file by doing their jobs better than they could. Serrano and Tally convinced APD brass she would be a boon to the squad, so Rachel was hired as a freelance forensics consultant. Serrano even dangled the possibility of a full-time position if she played her cards right and stayed out of trouble, but Rachel said that wasn't her goal. She didn't fully trust the legal system or law enforcement, and the Wright investigation hadn't given her much reason to change her mind. But solving crimes was far more satisfying than any other kind of work she'd ever done. And to move on with her life, Rachel had to feel competent. Needed. Able.

Rachel, Serrano, Tally, and Montrose carefully picked their way through the charred Linklater home. Ash and debris covered the floor. The formerly white walls were blistered and singed. What was a home yesterday was nothing more than a pile of cinder now. The real estate firm Linklater used to purchase the house had sent over the floor plans and schematics, and Rachel was mapping out each room in her mind as they went.

She opened what remained of the kitchen cabinets and examined the appliances. She could tell from the condition of the burners and stove that Linklater cooked frequently. The lack of glassware meant he wasn't much of a drinker and didn't host many dinner parties.

At the foot of what remained of the stairs to the second floor, Rachel stopped. She knelt down, ran a gloved finger over the floor.

"Detectives!" she shouted. Serrano and Tally came over quickly. "Look at this."

At the bottom of the staircase was a large, black burn mark, almost perfectly circular. Rachel traced her finger around the mark. "Look around the margins. See how in the center it's black and burned? But around that it's considerably lighter. Like someone poured lighter fluid in a pool and lit it. One of the fires was started right here."

Serrano motioned toward the staircase. "The staircase is singed in an almost perfect straight line. And the burn marks get thicker the higher up it goes."

Rachel said, "I'm thinking someone pooled an accelerant at the bottom of the stairs, then literally drew a line with it up the stairs."

"Gasoline?" Tally said.

"Most likely," Rachel replied.

"So let's see where the line goes," Serrano said.

They followed the burn mark up the stairs, one at a time, stepping gently, testing the wood. The black markings led to an open door at the end of the hall. The hardwood floors creaked beneath them, and they stepped gingerly. Despite the "all clear," none of them wanted to risk plunging through the floor and being impaled.

"It's the bedroom," Rachel said. There were remnants of several dressers, a reclining chair whose upholstery had burned to the metal, and a pile of molten plastic, twisted metal, and broken glass on the floor.

"Flat screen," Tally said, toeing the pile.

"Oh, that's awful," Rachel said, her hand going to her nose. The mattress was burned to a crisp, but Rachel could see small discolorations amid the char.

"Flesh," Serrano said. "They said Linklater was still in bed when they found him."

Tally looked at Rachel. "You OK?"

"Oh, yeah. My usual morning routine consists of coffee and then sifting through liquefied skin." She gulped down air. "The black line. The accelerant goes right up to the bed frame. Linklater was still in bed when the fire started, and whoever set it created something of a makeshift fuse. Accelerant leading all the way from Linklater's bed to the bottom of the stairs. Light the accelerant, flame goes up the stairs right to the occupied bed."

"That's dramatic," Tally said.

Rachel replied. "I bet it was purposefully so. Whoever torched Linklater's house didn't want it to even *appear* to be an accident. They wanted us to know beyond a doubt that it was arson."

Montrose appeared at the door. "I see you found the crematorium."

"Is there any way to tell what the accelerant was?" Rachel asked.

"We've taken samples from all over the house and sent them to the lab for testing. My hope is that it comes back as ethylene oxide, which has a very high flammability range but is also generally used for industrial purposes."

"Meaning the purchase could be traced," Rachel said.

"Potentially," Montrose replied. "But they could have also just used plain old lighter fluid, in which case it could have been purchased at any bodega in the Western Hemisphere."

"When you removed Linklater's body," Serrano said, "did you find any restraints? Anything that might have been used to tie him up?"

"Nothing," Montrose said. "No restraints. He was clothed, but all his clothing and some of the comforter fabric was seared into his skin."

"Even if the killer wanted us to know it was arson," Serrano said, "he or she still wouldn't want to get caught. So I'd be willing to bet it'll come back as plain old lighter fluid or gasoline. Untraceable, especially when half the city has stocked up for homemade BBQ."

Rachel said, "So they get into the house and subdue Linklater. They would have had to bring him upstairs without alerting neighbors. I'm guessing they knock him unconscious downstairs, then bring him upstairs. Then they set fires from multiple flash points. I'm guessing this one, by the stairs, was set first, to make sure Linklater was trapped. So my question is this: Why go to such lengths to murder a high school social studies teacher but also make it so damn evident that it *was* murder?"

As they looked over the remains of Matthew Linklater's bedroom, Montrose's cell phone rang. He put it to his ear.

"This is Montrose."

The big man stood still, listening. A look of confusion crossed his face, then his eyes widened. "You're not serious," he said. "Holy hell. I'll let them know."

He hung up.

"Who was that?" Serrano asked.

"Hector Moreno at the coroner's office," Montrose said. "They found something very, very strange in the victim's body."

"You mean on the victim's body," Tally said.

"No, Detective," Moreno said. "*In* the victim's body."

CHAPTER 7

When Hector Moreno removed the sheet from the body of Matthew Linklater, Serrano, Tally, and Rachel sucked in their breath like they were trying to prevent their breakfasts from escaping. The body itself was blackened, Linklater's features melted away into a ghoulish skeleton. The remaining dermis, the thickest layer of skin, was cracked and split, with cooked fat around the edges. His fingers were curled inward, like horrible claws, which Rachel knew was from the tendons shriveling and contracting from the heat.

Tally whispered a prayer. Serrano clenched his jaw. Rachel merely stood there, poring over the body of a man who, twenty-four hours ago, had been responsible for teaching her son.

Though the damage the fire had wreaked upon Matthew Linklater was horrifying, it wasn't what Rachel was focused on. She was staring at the soda-can-size hole that had been . . . burrowed . . . into the man's abdomen.

"What is that?" she asked Hector Moreno.

"That is where the rodent gnawed its way into his body," Moreno said, trying to keep his voice even.

"The what did what?" Serrano said.

"When I went to remove the organs, I found this hole with a number of very small bones inside the victim's cavity. I believe they're rodent bones. And based on the organ and tissue damage, I'm pretty sure Linklater was still alive when it was inside him."

"How exactly would that happen?" Tally said.

"It gnawed its way in," Moreno said.

"When you say *gnawed*," Serrano said, "do you literally mean . . ."

"I mean literally split the man's skin open with its claws and teeth," Moreno said. "A human sternum is pretty strong, with the breastplate. But from the bottom tip of the xiphoid process to the top of the pubis bone, people are pretty soft. Just skin and muscle and what lies beneath."

"What in the ever-loving hell . . . ," Serrano said.

Rachel said, "It's an infamous form of medieval torture. The Dutch used to put rats inside pottery, place it on a naked victim, then put hot coals on top." They all looked at her. She shrugged. "What?"

"I'm not sure I want to know how you know that," Moreno said.

"It was more commonly used as an interrogation technique," Rachel continued. "A prisoner would be restrained, bare chested. Then a rat was placed inside a metal bucket, and the open end placed on the person's abdomen. If the person didn't cooperate, a torch was held to the bottom of the bucket. As the metal grows hotter, the rat begins to cook, and it looks for a way out. And, well, people are softer than metal."

"Is that what killed Linklater?" Serrano asked.

"I haven't been able to determine the exact cause of death due to the degrading of most of the internal organs. But I did find something else." Moreno led them around to the corpse's head and traced a thin line by the right temple. "When bones reach an extremely high temperature, they begin to crack. This includes the skull, and they generally rupture along their suture lines. But I found one that is *not* along a suture line. A small fracture in the right temporal bone. It's not from the fire and appears to have been caused by blunt-force trauma."

"Could that be what killed him?" Rachel asked.

"I don't think so," Moreno said. "It wasn't a severe enough blow to have killed him, but it likely would have caused some cerebral bleeding or at least a concussion. Treatable with medical attention."

"Did it occur before or after Mighty Mouse began cooking?" Serrano asked.

"Again, it's hard to say, given the condition of the body," said Moreno.

"I'll bet the head wound happened before," Rachel said. "They had to get Linklater from downstairs to his bedroom without him screaming bloody murder. I'll bet they knocked him out, cracked his skull, then brought him upstairs."

Tally said, "If that holds up, then Linklater suffered the head wound at the front door. Which means he opened the front door for someone. Which means there's a good chance he knew his attacker."

Rachel nodded. "Literally opened the door to his own murder."

"So you think Linklater was tortured to give up information?" Serrano asked. "He was a teacher. Who would do that to a teacher?"

"I don't think he was tortured for information."

"Then why?" Serrano asked.

"To send a message. Whoever cracked his skull didn't care how badly the wound injured him. They knew he was going to die imminently anyway," Rachel said. "Head wounds aren't like they are in the movies, where someone gets walloped in the head with a sledgehammer, then they wake up an hour later with nothing a couple Tylenol can't cure. A head wound like this one on Linklater could cause a brain hemorrhage. Right, Dr. Moreno?"

The ME nodded. "As I said, the skull wound wasn't enough to kill him, but without proper treatment, it certainly could have presented major problems."

"So Linklater was dead either way," Rachel continued. "Now, there are six other homes on the same block where Linklater lives. The killer may have wanted us to know it was arson and murder, but they didn't want to actually get caught. Look there. At his mouth. You can see white fibers seared into the dermis. There was a cloth of some sort inserted into Linklater's mouth to prevent him from screaming. So the killer wasn't looking for a confession."

Tally said, "You're saying the rat was going to . . . eat into him no matter what."

Rachel nodded. "The killer wanted Matthew Linklater to suffer."

"A message rat for the cops," Tally said, rubbing her temples. "Just when you think you've seen everything."

Serrano said, "What if the message wasn't meant for law enforcement?"

"What do you mean?" Rachel asked.

"You might be an expert on medieval torture, Rachel, but obviously not movies. When a body is found with a rat, it's meant to scare other people from talking. Whoever did this knows the press will report the circumstances surrounding Linklater's death. Linklater wanted to say what he knew—hence the email to you—but before he could, somebody wanted to shut him up and scare others into doing the same."

"Obviously, Matthew Linklater knew something he wasn't supposed to," Tally said. "But there are no records of any criminal complaints filed by Matthew Linklater, no arrests, and no records of any 911 calls from his home or cell. The only thing that appears to be out of the ordinary was his email to Rachel."

Serrano said, "So here's what we know. Matthew Linklater knew something that unnerved someone so bad that they tortured and killed him to make sure he wouldn't talk and to scare anyone else from talking. Unfortunately, we don't know what Linklater knew, how he got it, or exactly who his death is meant to scare. But if this murder was a warning, it was directed at *somebody*. The big question is who."

"And remember," Tally said, locking eyes with Rachel, "Linklater's cell phone has not been found, which means the killer likely took it. And whoever has the phone also has access to Linklater's emails. Which means they know he contacted you and know you're going to be looking into this murder. So watch your back, Rachel."

CHAPTER 8

When Rachel got home, she tossed her clothes into a pile on the bathroom floor and spent the next thirty minutes showering in an attempt to cleanse the smoke, soot, and grime from her skin and images of the mutilated body of Matthew Linklater from her mind.

When Rachel moved her family to Ashby, she'd had every intention of disappearing into the unassuming, tree-lined, nod-at-your-neighbor-and-move-along background. She would work a menial job for menial pay, while her children would resume their educations that had been so mercilessly interrupted by fate.

And at first, she had kept to herself. But Constance Wright's murder had ignited a fire within her, a blaze of anger and passion that would not be extinguished. She was a *part* of this community now. That woman she used to be had remained in the home where her husband had been murdered, where her children had experienced terror beyond imagination. But finding Wright's killer reinvigorated Rachel. After so many years as a mother and widow, she finally had another purpose.

She put on a pair of jeans and a tank top, went downstairs, and made herself a cappuccino. Rachel didn't have many extravagances in their house, apart from the security systems, but she had splurged on a combination cappuccino/espresso maker. Other than marrying her husband and having children, it may have been the best decision she'd ever made.

At three thirty, Megan burst through the door. She wore a light-weight purple jacket with a neighing horse embroidered on the back.

Her long hair had darkened to a sandy blonde and was swept back into a long ponytail. Megan dropped her backpack on the floor, ran up to Rachel, and threw her arms around her. Even though her daughter was growing up, Rachel was glad she hadn't yet tired of afterschool hugs.

"Hi, Mom," she said. Rachel lived for these moments, especially since she knew the unashamed affection would dwindle as her daughter grew older and her mother's *cool* factor would drop to negative five thousand.

"How was school?"

"Fine. Did you know that Jordan Reese's family got a dog?"

"I did not know that."

"She showed me pictures. It's a bichon frizzy. *Soooo* cute."

"You mean bichon *frise*," Rachel said.

"Whatever. Can we get a dog?"

Rachel laughed. "Do you have time to train a dog, walk it, feed it, and take care of it?"

"Umm . . . no."

"Does your brother?"

"Sometimes Eric smells like he doesn't even have time to shower."

Rachel laughed. "So what you're saying is that you want a dog, but you want your mother to be the only one who actually takes care of Fluffy Marin."

"No, I'd want to take care of the puppy too," Megan said. "And we would *not* name it *Fluffy*."

"Let me think about it. OK?"

"So that's not a no?" Megan said, her spirits clearly lifted.

"It's not a no," Rachel said.

"I'll even pay for it! Once I get someone to publish my Sadie Scout books, I'll save up."

"It's not about money; it's about responsibility. I don't think you realize how much work dogs are."

As Megan began to pout, the door opened and Eric entered. Rachel and Megan both turned to look at him. His face was emotionless. Just a few hours ago, he'd learned his teacher had died, and it didn't appear to bother him any more than if he'd discovered a hole in his sock. It scared Rachel, seeing her son so detached in the face of such horrors.

"Eric," Rachel said, putting her hand on his shoulder. "I'm so, so sorry about Mr. Linklater. It's a terrible thing. If you need to talk, I'm always here for you."

Eric shrugged, like she'd told him they'd run out of cereal.

"It's OK," he said. "No big deal."

Rachel felt a flutter of worry in her chest. "It *is* a big deal. I don't expect you'd be able to process what happened so quickly. Did the school offer grief counselors?"

"Yeah. Principal Alvi scheduled a schoolwide assembly tomorrow morning. She was all vague in the announcement. Like, 'We need to talk about an important development facing the Ashby High community.' As though everyone doesn't already know that Mr. Linklater got microwaved."

"Eric, that's awful. That's a *person* you're talking about. Someone you know. Have some compassion."

"Was a person," he said. "*Was.*"

"I did not raise you to be cruel," Rachel said. "I think you need to talk to someone. Whether it's a grief counselor or a therapist. This isn't you."

He shook his head like he was casting off an errant piece of lint. "You don't get it," he said. "My dad was killed. Mr. Linklater was killed. The world is cruel and fucked up. I didn't make it that way."

He shouldered past her.

"Eric," she said, softly, but he ignored her and trudged upstairs to his room.

Rachel watched him go, unable to speak and unsure of what she would even say. She had witnessed Eric's struggles manifest themselves in so many ways since his father died. From terror to sadness to resentment to solitude to anger to cruelty in a heartbreaking, unending cycle. So many times he seemed to be pushing back against the negative thoughts and impulses, but they always came roaring back, stronger than ever, and Rachel worried that if he couldn't get a handle on the darkness, the poison would seep into his mind and his heart and never, ever leave. The thought of Eric growing up angry and unhappy felt like acid in her stomach.

She did not know how to stem his grief, calm his anger, cool his resentment. Those emotions still roiled in Rachel herself from time to time. But she was older and had two children who depended on her. She had to keep the darkness at bay, for their sakes. She had learned to hide her pain. Eric had not.

Rachel turned back to Megan, the dismay in her face becoming a plastic smile.

"What's wrong with Eric?" Megan said.

Rachel sighed and placed her hand on her daughter's cheek.

"Your brother has been through a lot," she said, softly. "He has memories that, thankfully, you are too young to have. What he's been through doesn't just go away. It takes time. A long time. All we can do is be there for him and let him know how much we love him."

"I *do*," Megan pleaded. "I tell him I love him. All the time. He tells me to stop. That he's not worth it."

Rachel rocked back on her heels. "He said that?"

Megan nodded.

"That he's not worth it?"

She nodded again. Rachel felt an ache in her chest, a low heat that rose into her cheeks and settled just below her eyes.

"As long as *we* both know he's worth it. He's worth all the love we have. We just need to keep showing him, and one day he'll realize it. Can you do that, sweetie?"

Megan smiled. "I can. I do love him."

"I do too. With all my heart. So, back to happier thoughts. Do you have any homework for tonight?"

"Homework is a happy thought?"

"Comparatively," Rachel said with a grin.

"Some math, but it's easy. And then I have to get back to my new Sadie Scout book. When I finished writing yesterday, Sadie was about to cross a dangerous river filled with poisonous snakes and allibators with huge teeth."

"Alli*gators*," Rachel corrected. "I can't wait to read it."

"When I'm done, I'm going to get it published," Megan said, confidently.

"I have no doubt you will."

Megan skipped off to her room. Rachel felt exhausted, a dull ache in her bones. She needed to focus on the murder. She booted up her laptop and began to review the file APD had collected on Matthew Linklater. He had never been married and had no children. He had a sister in Toledo, a married orthopedist, though they seldom communicated via phone or text more than every few months. His mother lived alone in a retirement community in Palm Beach Gardens. Both sister and mother were en route to Ashby for the funeral.

The closest Linklater came to a criminal record was a few scattered parking tickets, and those had all been paid in a timely manner. So how did an ostensibly ordinary, even boring man end up tortured and burned alive?

She checked her watch; it was five thirty. The kids would need dinner. Rachel had the ingredients to make a meatloaf with a side of mashed potatoes and asparagus. Cooking for children was like unrequited young love. Hours of effort, and you were lucky if they even acknowledged your presence. But she didn't want to be the mom who ordered pizza every time she had a long day.

Rachel took the ground beef from the fridge and stirred together eggs, ketchup, worcestershire sauce, bread crumbs, minced onion, milk, and parsley. Her ears pricked up at the sound of gunfire . . . only it wasn't actual gunfire. Eric was in his room obliterating an army of sprites at a decibel level that could cause an avalanche.

She took a bottle of merlot from the near-barren freestanding wine rack and poured herself a generous glass. She sipped as she assembled the meal. The smell of garlic was heavenly. She broke the beef apart with a spatula, stirring to make sure it didn't burn.

Then came a knock at the door. Her heart leaped at the prospect of John Serrano standing there with a smile and perhaps more wine. She laughed at herself. She felt like a teenager finally getting the text she'd been waiting all night for.

She turned the heat down, washed her hands, and went to the door. She was hoping to see Serrano holding a bottle of something dry.

But when she opened the door, Rachel's mouth dropped. Every muscle in her body tensed. A wave of panic ignited her synapses, as if an electric current had traveled from toe to head and back again.

Instead of John Serrano, a woman stood on her front porch. Her hair was different from the last time Rachel had seen her. Longer. It was now a dusky auburn, shoulder length, spilling over a brown leather jacket. She was about five eight, an inch shorter than Rachel. Her muscular arms and legs filled out her clothing. Her weight was shifted slightly to the side as though she might need to suddenly defend herself.

And in that instant, Rachel was reminded that the life she thought she was done with, the life she'd left behind—that life wasn't done with her. Not by a long shot.

The woman smiled. Big and warm.

"Hey, Blondie," she said. "It's been a while."

CHAPTER 9

Rachel stood in the doorway for what felt like a year. She'd recognized the woman before she opened her mouth to speak but was still stunned when the words came out, like the syllables were proof that she wasn't hallucinating.

The woman had aged, though Rachel could tell from her calloused hands, the triangular shape of her trapezius muscles underneath her jacket, that she was still someone you did not want to cross.

"Myra," Rachel said. "You look good."

"You mean Evie," the woman said with a sly grin. "And you do, too, Blondie. Though I guess it's Rachel Marin now, right?"

"And you're Evie Boggs. Guess you dropped 'Myra'?"

The last time Rachel saw Evie Boggs, she had prevented Evie from killing a man named Stanford Royce who had tried to rob them. Evie felt the man deserved to die. Rachel disagreed. It turned out Royce was a serial rapist, a career criminal. Had Rachel known that, she might have let Evie do what she wanted. Yet months later, Rachel was the one with the knife, hovering over a prone Stanford Royce.

"Not all of us need to hide from who we are," Evie said. "Anyway, it's been, what, five years? I'm so glad you took my advice." Evie spoke with the charm and casualness of an old college friend at a class reunion.

"Feels a whole lot longer," Rachel said. "Like a lifetime ago. And what do you mean, 'your advice'?"

"Ashby? Come on, don't pretend you don't remember."

Rachel did remember.

"So," Evie said. "Are you going to invite me in?"

Rachel looked over her shoulder. The kids were both upstairs. She turned back to Evie. She carried a tiny clutch. Too small for most handguns. Her pants were tight. Cloth tapered to her ankles. No weapons Rachel could see. And if Evie really wanted Rachel dead, the best time would have been right when she opened the door.

Rachel wanted to invite Evie into her home as much as she wanted to invite a leper into her bed. But she didn't need nosy neighbors asking about the woman standing on her front porch. *Was that a Jehovah's Witness? They do come around here quite frequently.* Besides, Evie was here for a reason. People from your former life didn't show up unannounced just for afternoon tea.

"Of course," Rachel said, sweeter than a sugar cookie. "Where are my manners? Come in, Evie. It's been far too long."

"It has," Evie said with an amused smile. Rachel led her to the living room. Evie sat on the couch, crossed her legs, relaxed. Rachel took the love seat. Feet on the floor. Anything but relaxed. Evie studied the decor. Too closely. Like she wanted Rachel to notice. It made Rachel wonder if she'd been casing her house and, if so, for how long.

"You have a lovely home, Rachel. You still go by Rachel, right?"

"Yes. But you already knew that," she replied.

"I did."

"So what the hell are you doing here?"

"I've been thinking a lot about the past," Evie said, ignoring the question. "You know, when we first met, you couldn't kick a can down the street. But look at you now. Taking down bad guys like you're Dirty Harriet. My little shin kicker. All grown up."

She knows about the Constance Wright investigation, Rachel thought.

"You haven't answered my question," Rachel said, impatiently.

"Aren't you going to offer me a drink first?"

"No."

"Well, you might be grown up, but your manners are worse than a teenage boy's. How is your teenage boy, by the way?"

"If you came here to comment on my manners or talk about my son, you can leave, or I can make you leave."

"Come on, you don't want to cause such a ruckus in your own home, do you?"

Rachel said nothing.

"You'd never believe it," Evie said, "but there was this horrible story on the news about a house that burned down in Ashby. With someone still inside. Video from the crime scene showed the cops skittering around like ants. And who do I see among all those cops? Acting like she might as well be one of the boys in blue?"

Rachel said nothing.

Evie pointed at Rachel and drew a circle with her finger. "Miss Rachel Marin. Your last name is Marin, right?"

"That's right."

"How'd you settle on Marin?"

"None of your business," Rachel said.

"I'd love to hear *that* story. But we don't need to get into it now. You changed your hair, changed your look, but I recognized you the moment I saw you on that TV. I don't forget a face. Especially after what we've been through."

"You tried to murder someone. I stopped you."

"You sure did," Evie said. "And I wonder where Stanford Royce is these days. You have any idea where he might be, Blondie?"

Evie's smirk made Rachel feel sick.

"So Stanford Royce holds a knife to my throat," Evie said, "and you prevent me from sawing him in half with his own blade. But then a few months go by, and Mr. Royce disappears off the face of the earth. Cops can't find him. No blood and no body. And pretty soon after that, you pack up and move to Ashby. Hell of a coincidence, wouldn't you say?"

"I would say."

"*Sure.* So when I saw my old friend Rachel on the television with the cops—"

"I'm not a cop," Rachel interjected. "But if you don't get to the point, I'll call the actual cops."

"No, you won't. Because then they'll ask who I am. And I'll have to tell them the truth. About me. About you." Evie paused and leaned forward. "About Stanford Royce. You don't want them turning over that rock, do you? The police would *love* to know what happened to him. All I have to do is point the finger."

"I don't know what you're talking about," Rachel said. "But if you threaten me again, I'll break you in half."

"Now *that's* the girl I remember," Evie said. She leaned back. Her voice softened. "Listen. Rachel. I'm not here to ruin your life. I don't want to mess with what you have. That's the honest truth. If I wanted to do that, I would have gone right to the cops. You'd do anything for your kids, right?"

Rachel nodded. "Yes."

"So would I. You know I'm a mom, too, right?"

Rachel nodded. "I remember you telling me that."

"But I'm not here to dredge up the past," Evie said.

"So then why are you here?"

Evie paused, then said, "Matthew Linklater."

Rachel felt her blood run cold.

"I know about the email he sent to you before he died," Evie continued. "I need to know why he chose you. I need to know what you know."

Rachel's mind was going a million miles a minute. She knew, at that moment, that Evie had come because somebody had sent her. Somebody knew about Rachel and Evie's past and was pushing on that pressure point *hard*. Somebody wanted Rachel to leave the Linklater murder alone.

"Evie, you know me well enough to know that I'm not going to say a damn word to you."

Evie sighed. "There's more at stake here than you realize. I know who you are, Rachel Marin. I know who you *really* are. You're a survivor. But a survivor with two kids. I know about Harwood Greene. I know he murdered your husband and that he's still out there somewhere. And I know that's why you killed Stanford Royce. Because you didn't want him to do to someone else what Harwood Greene did to you. Truthfully, I don't know how you sleep at night."

"I don't," Rachel said, both as a statement and a threat.

"But through all of it, you made it to Ashby and started over. Your children have a chance at life now, because of you. You need to protect what you have. Whatever you might know about Matthew Linklater, you need to stay away. Because trust me—I'm the good cop in this story. You don't want to meet the bad cops. When *they* knock on your door, they don't ask to come in for a drink."

"Mommy?"

Both women turned around to see Megan standing at the top of the stairs. She had a puzzled look on her face. Her hands were covered with blue ink stains.

"Hey, honey," Rachel said, keeping her voice even.

"I was writing my Sadie Scout book and heard you talking to someone." She looked at Evie and smiled. "I'm Megan."

"I'm Evie. It's a pleasure to meet you, Megan."

Megan came downstairs. Rachel wanted to tell her daughter to stay put but didn't want to let her know anything was out of the ordinary. "Evie is an old friend of Mommy's. Evie, this is my daughter, Megan."

"I don't remember you ever talking about an Evie," Megan said, skeptically.

Rachel took her daughter's hand. "There are a lot of things I don't talk about," she said. "That doesn't mean they didn't happen."

Evie held out her hand to Megan, very proper. Megan took it hesitantly. Evie gave it a firm up and down. Rachel watched the exchange like Megan was slipping her hand into a piranha tank.

"Miss Megan Marin," Evie said. "That sounds like a character from a book. Maybe a princess. Do you want to be a princess, Miss Megan Marin?"

Megan shook her head. "I want to be a detective or an adventurer."

Evie smiled warmly. "I bet you'll be great at both."

Megan beamed.

Evie turned to Rachel. "You have a beautiful family."

Rachel stared at Evie, wanting to leap across the couch and sink her fingers into the woman's neck. Instead, she said, "Thank you."

"Well, I've taken up enough of your time," Evie said, standing up.

"Really? Are you sure?" Rachel said with mock sorrow.

"Thank you for your hospitality, Rachel. Maybe one of these days we'll have that drink."

"I certainly hope so."

"I'll show myself out," Evie said. Rachel went to Megan, keeping herself between her daughter and the woman in her home. Evie opened the front door, then turned back.

"Miss Megan Marin?"

"Yes?" Megan replied, cheeks still red.

"If you're going to be a detective, be a good one. Everyone is afraid of the bad ones. And for good reason."

Then Evie Boggs closed the door behind her.

CHAPTER 10

Four and a half years ago

The two women sat on the bleachers inside the musty gym. They were alone. Sweat dripped from their chins, their arms, collecting in small puddles on the benches beneath them. It was a crisp fall evening, the kind ideally spent sipping a drink at an outdoor café or walking hand in hand with a loved one down a colorful, tree-lined promenade. But time stood still inside that gym. It could have been any day of the year.

The leaner woman wore yellow Lycra pants and a backless blue tank top. She was known simply as Blondie. The more muscular woman wearing black shorts and a white sports bra was Myra. Myra taught a self-defense class, which Blondie had learned about after moving to Torrington, Connecticut, with her two children. Blondie's family had endured an unimaginable crime, but one that had spurred her into action, in the most literal of senses. She had been training with Myra for nearly two years, unearthing long-forgotten muscles, sharpening her mind, learning how to protect herself and her children.

Since the death of her husband, Blondie had floated, aimless, unsure of how to piece her life back together. She felt unmoored. It was only in Myra's class that she regained some sense of control. The feeling that maybe, just maybe, if she punished her body enough, she could piece the fragments of her life back together.

Myra bit into a protein bar. Offered a bite to Blondie, who accepted it. The two women had been strangers at first. Myra maintained a distance from her students, both to protect them and herself. The "students" who took her class were broken men and women. No real names were allowed. No talking about personal lives once the gymnasium doors closed. Anyone who violated those rules was shown the door—quite literally. When it was learned that one student had found, and friended, another on Facebook, Myra put him in an *ude gatame* armlock, then tossed him across the parking lot like an empty coffee cup.

Myra always stayed at the gym after class ended. That was her private workout time, and the students knew better than to hang around. Once class was over, you were out of Myra's life and vice versa until the next class began.

But that night, after gathering up the courage, Blondie had asked Myra if she could stay late. Work out alongside her. To her great surprise, Myra said yes. And so they sparred, pounded the heavy bag and speed bag as if it had insulted their mothers, did burpees until their legs begged for mercy. And when they couldn't push any further, when every muscle felt like lead and even though their heads shouted *more* while their bodies pleaded *stop*, they called it a day.

"Remember, when you hit the heavy bag, it's not all about power," Myra said. "Don't punch *through* the bag. Snap your punches. And when the punch lands, don't pull your fist back. Let the rebound do it for you."

"Gotcha. Rebound," Blondie said. She looked around the empty gym. There were no clocks. No way to tell time other than dead limbs and pools of sweat. "Can I ask you something?"

"Shoot, Blondie."

"I know talking about ourselves is pretty much off limits. So you can tell me to shut up, and I won't take it personally, and I'll never ask you anything else not related to proper striking form."

Blondie waited. Myra said nothing.

"I ain't stopping you, kid," Myra finally said.

"Do you ever feel . . . trapped?"

Myra looked at Blondie and offered a slim smile. "Only every damn day. Why do you ask?"

"Because I don't know how long we can stay here. My family, I mean." Blondie took a pull from a sports bottle filled with an energy drink that tasted like sour grape juice mixed with formaldehyde. She didn't know why she had suddenly decided to share details of her personal life with Myra. For so long, since her husband had died, she'd had nobody to talk to. The children were too young to understand, and her friends had abandoned her.

"Thinking about moving? Or moving on?" Myra asked.

"Both. This city, it's too close to everything. I walk down the streets, and I swear I see ghosts. But I also don't think I can keep moving my kids. We need somewhere to settle. For good. Somewhere away from the ghosts."

"I know it might be kind of hard to see it right now," Myra said, "but the world is your oyster, Blondie."

"If you mean I'm stuck inside a small shell and can't move and could be eaten at any moment, then yes."

Myra laughed and clapped a strong hand on Blondie's thigh. Blondie winced. Tomorrow she would find a palm-size welt there.

"I feel for you. I do. But look at it this way. You can go anywhere you want. *Anywhere.* I mean, what the hell is keeping you here? Nothing. Go to New York. LA. Phoenix. Hell, move to Paris. What's stopping you?"

"Money, for one thing," Blondie said, droplets of sweat spattering onto the varnished wood. "We don't have any. I mean, we might. There's something in the works I can't really talk about. But even if I had money, I'd never move to a big city. We need to be somewhere quiet. Somewhere the kids won't feel crushed. We need a town, maybe a small city. Somewhere we can blend in and become a part of the surroundings without feeling like we're going to get run over. I want to do right by them."

Myra nodded. There was something beneath her eyes, a remorse. In that instant, Myra seemed like a different person. One consumed by sadness.

"You gotta do right by them," she said. "I screwed up my chance to do that. And I'm still paying for it."

Then her face changed. The sadness disappeared, like a mask had slipped back on. She laughed.

"Besides," Myra said, "look at the trap muscles on you. I feel bad for anyone who tries to run you over."

"You ever think about leaving?" Blondie said.

"All the damn time," Myra said. "I don't particularly like it here. But I have to stay."

"Why?"

"Reasons, Blondie. I made mistakes. And I'm paying for them. That's all you need to know."

"So if you did leave," Blondie said, "any ideas on where you'd go?"

"Ashby," Myra said. "I'd move to Ashby."

"Never been there. Why Ashby?"

"It's right up your alley. Western Illinois, a couple hours outside Chicago. I have some family there. Some people I don't see as often as I should. But it's the kind of place you'd love. Quiet. Folks mind their own business for the most part. Good school system for the kids. You could get a job, keep your head down. It's far enough from the bigger cities like Chicago and Springfield that real estate prices won't kill you, but close enough that if you need to travel, you have options."

"How do you know all this? You work in real estate in Ashby or something?"

"What did I say about asking so many questions?"

Blondie nodded. "So Ashby, huh?"

"If you do leave here, give it a look. It's a good place to disappear." Myra checked her cell phone. "It's getting late. Walk with me."

The women gathered up their belongings and left the gym. The cool air felt invigorating on their damp skin. Darkness fell over the city, but Blondie, for the first time in a long, long time, began to believe she just might have a future. She let the name sit on her lips. *Ashby.* If her settlement money came through, she'd look into it. Maybe she'd found her family's new home.

Several blocks away, a man walked toward them. His name was Stanford Royce. At that moment they were unaware of each other's existence. But their futures would soon be intertwined in blood.

CHAPTER 11

Today

Ten minutes after Evie Boggs left her home, Rachel received a text message.

Thanks for your hospitality. I'll be in touch. See you soon. ~E

She had never given Evie her cell number. And *See you soon.* The house could be under surveillance by Evie or someone else.

Rachel stood by the front door for twenty minutes, unmoving, to be sure Evie was not coming back. She spent the rest of the evening waiting, patiently, for her children to go to sleep. She tucked Megan in, marveling at the collection of pages from her new Sadie Scout book. She knocked on Eric's door, opened it after an irritated *What?* and told her son that she loved him. He nodded, and that was their final communication for the night. Then, when the house was quiet, she brewed a pot of french roast and went down to the basement.

The door to the lower level of the Marin home was protected by a three-inch-thick metal-framed door guarded by a keypad. Most families designed their basements for play. Thick carpeting for roughhousing. Toys and games scattered everywhere. Perhaps a man cave for the husbands who occasionally needed to escape their families and responsibilities, overstuffed La-Z-Boys opposite a home-theater system the size of a Range Rover.

Rachel had none of those amenities. Her basement was to work her mind and body. Her children were forbidden to use it. They had enough playthings.

On one wall, Rachel had mounted a rack of free weights, jump ropes, and plyometric equipment. She used these daily. The floor was covered with a rubber mat so her sweat wouldn't seep into a carpet or the floorboards. She cleaned it twice a week with water and mild detergent.

On the other side of the basement was her workstation, which housed several computer monitors and half a dozen external hard drives. Before they'd moved in, Rachel had installed closed-circuit cameras throughout the interior and exterior of the home. She stored the camera recordings on the hard drives. Over the past year, the cameras had recorded an armed man breaking into her home and another man abducting and trying to murder her. If Evie came back, Rachel would know.

Rachel booted up the computer. The first thing she did was look at the camera feeds around the outside of the house. She found nothing out of the ordinary. Then she ran a background check on Evelyn Boggs. She needed to know more about Evie. Damned if she would be frightened into silence.

Rachel had met Evie Boggs while she was living in Torrington, Connecticut. She had left her longtime home in Darien following the horrific death of her husband. A lawsuit against the city of Darien and its police department had garnered a several-million-dollar payout but left her with nobody to trust or turn to. In Torrington, Rachel began attending a self-defense class taught by a strong, boisterous woman who introduced herself as Myra. Everyone in the class used aliases to ensure privacy and security. Myra was the name Evie Boggs had chosen.

Myra's lessons had saved Rachel's life more than once. The woman she knew back in Torrington had dedicated her life to helping others. To helping women like Rachel. She would not turn on Rachel without a reason. She knew Evie was being used. Somebody was dangling a scythe over Evie's neck. Rachel needed to find out who.

According to her birth certificate, Evelyn Boggs was forty-two years old, born in Springfield, Massachusetts, adopted by Arnold and Estelle Boggs. There was no record of her birth parents. Serrano and Tally could potentially get that information unsealed, but not without a court order. Evie had graduated from Northeastern with a degree in communications and at twenty-two married a man named Charles Ford. They had one son, Benjamin, born at Yale New Haven Children's Hospital. She and Ford divorced, and Evelyn got custody of the boy.

She then married Javier Landau, and Landau officially adopted Evie's son. But Evelyn Boggs and Javier Landau divorced soon after, and records showed that despite Landau not being Benjamin Ford's biological father, the boy still spent a significant amount of time with his stepfather and had even attended school in San Luis Obispo, where Landau moved following the split. Strange, Rachel thought, that Evie's son was partially schooled in his stepfather's city.

Evelyn still lived in Torrington. Benjamin Ford was currently a student at Conn College, where he resided in Hamilton House. Javier Landau worked as an admissions officer at California State University.

Rachel could not find a connection between Evie Boggs and Matthew Linklater.

Putting Evie aside for the moment, Rachel thought back to the manner in which Matthew Linklater was killed. You didn't walk up to someone's home and happen to have the perfect arson materials *plus* a hungry rodent like you were a pet-store owner who'd gone off the deep end, as well as a can with which to commit an act of torture fit for one of the epic fantasy novels her son and boyfriend devoured like M&M'S. No, that kind of act required a healthy dose of both sadism and practicality. And as Rachel had learned firsthand, the most sadistic people also tended to be the most patient.

But planning that kind of crime took time. Meaning there had to be a trail.

She pored over Hector Moreno's autopsy notes, which he had sent via Dropbox. They had called in a local veterinarian, Dr. Walter Krecher, to analyze the rodent bones and teeth. Rachel's downstairs printer was out of paper, so she printed them on the shared inkjet upstairs, retrieved them, grabbed fresh paper, then headed back to the basement.

Per Krecher's notes, there were four types of rodents commonly found in Illinois: the house mouse, deer mouse, white-footed mouse, and Norway rat. Based on the larger size of the remains, Krecher believed the bones inside Matthew Linklater belonged to a Norway rat.

Rachel took a moment to reflect on the strange life journey that had led to her researching rat bones in a basement. From what she'd gathered, the Norway rat was the most common species, frequently used in lab experiments though even sold at pet stores. But this type of rat also tended to be most prevalent in places where there was an abundance of sewage or poor sanitation.

They also lived in colonies. Thankfully pest-control companies stayed open late. Rachel called the three closest to Linklater's home. None of them had a record of ever visiting the Linklater home, or any residence within a square mile, in the past several years. Which meant that whoever had done Linklater in had likely carried the rodent from somewhere else. Rachel wondered if there were laws against transporting filthy vermin across county lines but figured breaking those laws was the least of the killer's concerns.

She read the police reports. Serrano, Tally, and the forensics team had done a thorough job. They'd spoken to dozens of Linklater's neighbors, friends, and colleagues. He was not a loner, but he was not particularly outgoing either. He had friends but did not go out on a regular basis. He did not frequent local bars and only had two receipts from the nearby Loonie's Liquors in the past year—both for a single bottle of Belvedere vodka. He didn't seem particularly interested in other people, nor they him. He kept to himself but was not socially awkward or inept. He was just a man living an ordinary, contented life.

Rachel went back over the crime scene photos. Not the photos of Linklater's body. His charred, mutilated corpse would remain etched in her mind for a long, long time. She wanted to go back over photos of his house. Thankfully Montrose and the rest of his forensics team were professionals. There were dozens and dozens of photos of the Linklater home, taken from all conceivable angles. She tried to forget what she saw when she first arrived, in an effort to survey the scene through fresh eyes. What she saw in person may have been different than what the Ashby PD photographers captured. She was looking for discrepancies. Alterations. Clues. Clarity amid the rubble.

She printed all the crime scene photos and spread them out on the basement floor. She downloaded a PDF of the house's layout and photos used as previous sales material from a real estate brokerage site and printed them out as well. She then re-created the interior of Matthew Linklater's house using the crime scene photos, matching the photos up with the interior layout. Like a broker's listing after the apocalypse.

She put together each room, every corner and tile and floorboard. The living room. Bathroom. Kitchen. Closet. All burnt wood, melted plastic, and scorched metal. She looked at every beam. Every pipe. For something. Anything.

And then she saw it. At the very bottom of the grid. Ignored because it had been in plain sight.

The front door.

When Rachel, Serrano, and Tally were given access to the interior of the Linklater home, after it was declared structurally sound, they entered through the burnt frame of the front door.

The open front door.

But in the first responder photos, the door was closed. The PD had opened it when examining the structure. But after the crime itself, the door was closed.

Rachel examined photos of all the windows in Linklater's home. With few exceptions, the glass had been blown out by the fire. The frames still appeared to be intact. Linklater also had a home-security system. Had someone broken in through one of the windows, a call would have gone out to a security-monitoring station, and the murder-in-progress would have been interrupted. Not only did the killers need to prevent Linklater from alerting anyone to the crime, but they also needed to make sure no alarms had been tripped beforehand.

Which meant whoever killed Linklater had entered through the front door, then closed it upon leaving. Rachel looked at the photos. The doorframe was still intact. The chain was still attached to the wall. The wood had not been splintered in a way that would suggest the front door had been kicked in or tampered with. And if it had been, the security system would have gone off.

All of this meant one thing: Matthew Linklater had opened the front door for his killer.

It had to be somebody he knew. Someone he would open his front door for, without question, on a school night. Somebody he would not suspect. Somebody he believed was incapable of such a vicious crime.

Linklater did not come across to Rachel as a reckless man. He lived an ordered life. He did not fraternize with anyone outside a very, very small social circle. Which meant that whoever knocked on Linklater's door the night he died was someone he trusted. But what if Linklater was right? What if the person he trusted actually *was* incapable of such violence?

The answer was obvious. There were at least *two* people in Matthew Linklater's home the night he died. One of whom he knew and opened the door for. The other, Rachel surmised, was a stranger. Perhaps even someone Linklater did not see. Hiding just out of view. Waiting until Linklater opened the door before subduing him. Rachel rubbed her temples. Tried to picture the scene.

Linklater must have heard a knock at the door or the doorbell. He then went to answer it. He was a cautious man, so he looked through the peephole. He saw someone he recognized. Someone he trusted. Whoever had the gasoline, bucket, and rodent was out of view.

Rachel went over the case notes. Officers had interviewed many of Linklater's neighbors and every teacher in the school. Nobody claimed to have seen Linklater within three hours of his death.

Everyone in his small circle of friends had an alibi. Stu Bendix, an old college classmate who lived in Ashby, was confirmed to be at home with his wife. ATM footage showed Dinesh Pandit, a former colleague at Pemberly Middle School, entering a movie theater with his son in Peoria and exiting two hours and eighteen minutes later. There were a few others, and all had airtight alibis.

Rachel had to wonder: If it wasn't a fellow teacher or a friend, who else would Matthew Linklater have opened his front door for without hesitation?

She needed a break. Her eyes were bleary, and her shoulders ached from hunching over the computer. She'd drained the pot of coffee and felt jittery. Her tongue tasted like the underside of a carpet. She trudged upstairs to get a glass of water. She heard footsteps, grabbed a knife from the butcher's block, and spun around, expecting to see Evie Boggs standing in her living room.

"Mom! Stop!"

Eric stood there, terror in his eyes. Rachel immediately put the knife in the sink and took a step toward her son. He took a step back.

"Eric, I'm sorry, I . . . my head isn't right. I've been buried in paperwork."

"Who did you think I was?" he said.

"Nobody," she replied. "I'm just a little paranoid. I'm working on it. You can understand."

"Yeah. Sure. Whatever."

Eric held out a piece of paper. He did not come forward to hand it to her. It was a printout from her research. She'd obviously left a page in the machine. The printout was a picture of a large Norway rat.

"Why were you researching Midge?" Eric said.

"Midge?" Rachel said, confused.

"Yeah, isn't this Midge? Midge is the rat Ms. Genova keeps in the biology lab. She went missing the other day. We all figured she finally escaped. This is her, right? Are you trying to find Midge?"

Rachel's stomach did a flip. She knew where Midge was—at the Ashby City Morgue. She hadn't escaped; she'd been taken. By someone with access to the biology classroom. It wasn't a teacher, friend, or neighbor who knocked on Matthew Linklater's door the night he died.

It was one of his students.

CHAPTER 12

Per orders from their APD superior, Lieutenant Mazzera, Serrano, and Tally joined the assembly at Ashby High to answer questions from the grief-stricken students and faculty about the death of Matthew Linklater. Their aim was to help calm a community reeling from a horrific act of violence toward one of their own and assure everyone that the crime would not go unpunished.

The entire high school, a thousand strong, filled the Seymour J. Esch gymnasium bleachers. Those who didn't fit in the bleachers sat on the floor. The mood was somber. Serrano could not recall seeing so many children so eerily quiet all at once. He could hear soft whimpers from the bereaved, saw many of the students—and faculty—holding hands to give each other strength and solace.

Serrano and Tally sat on uncomfortable polyethylene steel-back chairs in the center of the gym, along with Principal Alvi and several other faculty members. Alvi wiped away tears and took the microphone.

Alvi's voice cracked as she spoke, fat tears spilling down her cheeks.

"It is with a heavy, heavy heart that I begin today's assembly with the news that Matthew Linklater, beloved teacher, colleague, and friend, has been taken from us."

Taken from us, Serrano thought. *Like someone came by and gently put him in a car and drove away, rather than being tortured and burned alive.*

After Alvi's remarks, Serrano and Tally gave a brief statement about the investigation and implored any students with information to come forward.

"We're not looking to get anyone in trouble," Tally said, to quell concerns about "narking." "We just want to make sure Mr. Linklater gets the justice he deserves. Some of you might be able to help us do that."

"Everything matters," Serrano said. "Something you saw. Something you heard. Even if you think it doesn't matter, maybe it does."

Principal Alvi informed the students that grief counselors would be available and that substitutes would be filling in for Mr. Linklater until the end of the school year. There was a murmur of disapproval from the students; Serrano wondered if a few cold hearts had hoped social studies might be canceled, those with poor grades being granted a morbid reprieve.

The detectives stayed in the gym for an hour following the assembly, hoping a student or faculty member might come forward, take a business card, or ask to talk in private. Nobody did. Either Matthew Linklater's death was a total mystery to Ashby High . . . or people were scared. They all watched the news, had access to social media. They knew how Linklater had died. The killer's message had come across loud and clear, and nobody else wanted to be next.

Walking back to their car, Serrano and Tally noticed a small memorial for Matthew Linklater outside the school's fence. Dozens of flower bouquets, framed photos of smiling students posing with Mr. Linklater, delicate votive candles, and prayer cards had been left in a neat, respectful circle. Taped to the fence was a large photograph of Matthew Linklater taken at the prior year's graduation ceremony. He was wearing a brown sport coat, his hair neatly combed and parted, his arms around two graduating seniors, all three of them caught midlaugh. Written in yellow chalk underneath the memorial were four words, encircled by a red heart: *We will miss you.*

"God, what a waste," Tally said.

"How do you think it went in there?" Serrano said.

"Unusual that not a single person came forward after the assembly," Tally said. "All these flowers and mementos, but apparently not one of the people in that building knows anything about what happened to Matthew Linklater. I don't buy it."

"He wasn't just killed," Serrano said. "That was some biblical wrath stuff that was done to him. Even if there are kids in there who *want* to talk to us, they've gotta be scared out of their minds. People won't come forward because they've seen what happens when they do. I don't think we'll get much help here."

Serrano and Tally drove back to the precinct and settled in at their desks.

"OK, let's start from the top. What do we know about Matthew Linklater?" Tally sipped a cup of coffee and grimaced. "Ugh, I'm starting to think they use washing machine runoff in the pot."

"Other than the fact that he died in a way that should be reserved for pedophiles and telemarketers?" Serrano said. "Matthew Linklater was a single, Caucasian male, forty-eight years old. No prior arrests, no marriages, no children. He worked at Ashby High for the past thirteen years, and prior to that was on the faculty at Pemberly Middle School in Chicago. I spoke to his former headmaster at Pemberly, who recalls Linklater as an exemplary educator with no known legal or personal issues. No reprimands or warnings in his file. He was Mr. Freaking Rogers."

"I pulled his bank statements and got his employment records from Principal Alvi," Tally said. "Linklater was making a shade over sixty-seven grand a year, paychecks deposited biweekly. No deposits out of the ordinary. The only thing that raised my eyebrows was a onetime deposit of eleven thousand dollars on March eighteenth of last year, but we were able to trace it to a horse racing bet at Fairmount Park. Linklater nailed a trifecta. Lucky, but not illicit. He even declared the winnings on his tax return."

"Nobody on the faculty had an unkind word to say about him," Serrano added. "But none of them seemed to know him all that well either—you know, quiet, kept to himself, seemed nice, et cetera, et cetera. Principal Alvi said there were absolutely no hints of any sort of impropriety."

"But somebody went to a whole lot of trouble to kill him," Tally said. "He did something or had dirt on someone. But he was scared enough of the potential repercussions to keep it quiet. Until he emailed your girlfriend."

Tally drained the rest of her mug and set it on her desk. Photos of Tally's three stepchildren covered the sides of the mug. It was last year's birthday present from Claire's children. Serrano remembered the day she brought it into the office. Tally's face glowed like someone had turned on high beams behind her eyes. Serrano's partner always had purpose, but that day she had passion. The mug was proof that Leslie Tally was no longer just somebody's wife but part of somebody's family.

Claire's ex-husband, Alonzo, the father of her children, had been out of their lives for several years. He lived in Baton Rouge with his new wife, a Pilates instructor fifteen years his junior. Serrano had heard Claire wonder how Alonzo might even *meet* a Pilates instructor, given the extent of his physical exertion was lifting nachos into his mouth. Serrano knew it had taken a long time for the Wallace children to come to terms with Claire's admission of her sexuality and even longer to accept Claire and Leslie's relationship. That mug was a symbol. *You're one of us now.* The Wallace children approved. Tally drank from it every day, washed it diligently, and when she left for the night, always placed it on her desk with the kids' pictures facing out.

It made Serrano burst with happiness for his partner. But her good fortune reminded him of the hole in his own heart that would never mend. Even though Rachel had brought him into her life, he was not her children's father. Unlike Alonzo Wallace, Rachel's husband did not abandon his family. He was torn from them, a page ripped from a book that could never be replaced.

Tally's cell phone pinged. She opened her email app. Smiled.

"We might have something," she said.

"Go on," Serrano replied.

"Linklater's cell phone hasn't been found yet. More than likely it was taken or destroyed by the killer. But we got the carrier to send over Linklater's cell data, including texts and emails from the weeks leading up to his death."

"Anything interesting?" Serrano said.

"Mostly work-related emails. A few calls and texts to his sister, debating whether to move their mother into an assisted-care facility. But there are over a hundred texts to and from a woman named Gabrielle Vargas. Their most recent communication was confirming a dinner date from last Monday. Ms. Vargas is an accountant, forty-six, divorced, and lives with her sixteen-year-old son, Antonio, in North Ashby. Antonio also happens to be a junior at Ashby High."

"Looks like somebody had a girlfriend," Serrano said. "None of Linklater's colleagues mentioned him being in a relationship. He obviously kept things with Ms. Vargas under wraps since it's dicey to date the parent of a student. Think their relationship could have something to do with him getting killed? Jealous ex?"

"Let's talk to Ms. Vargas and find out," Tally said.

"Be gentle," Serrano said. "Her boyfriend just got killed like he moved into the wrong house in a Stephen King novel. Go easy. But get answers."

"Gentle is my middle name."

"That's a lie."

"Maybe so, but it should have been."

Serrano laughed. "You have an address for Ms. Vargas?"

"421 North Grove Street."

"All right," Serrano said. "Here's hoping Ms. Vargas knows what information the good professor was keeping to himself."

Serrano and Tally went to the lot outside the precinct and got into their Crown Victoria.

A woman sat at a bus stop across the street. She held a cell phone. She nervously chewed the thumbnail on her other hand, caught a cuticle in her teeth. Peeled it off, tasted her own blood. When the detectives pulled out, Evie Boggs snapped a dozen pictures of the car, zooming in on the make, color, and license plate. She then sent a selection of photos via text message. A minute later, she received a text message back.

Moonlight diner. Two hours. In person. Come alone or we hurt someone you love.

Evie had to stop herself from crying out. She wiped an errant tear from her eye, slipped the phone into her purse, and walked away.

CHAPTER 13

Gabrielle Vargas lived in a modest two-bedroom apartment covered in wood-paneled floors and decorated floor to ceiling with poorly assembled IKEA furniture. Drawers that didn't close fully, dressers tilted at a slight angle.

Detectives Serrano and Tally sat on one end of an L-shaped green microfiber sofa. Gabrielle sat on the other end holding a cup of tea that she had not sipped from. Her eyes were bloodshot from crying, lack of sleep, or both. She was an attractive woman with shoulder-length hair, brown speckled with hints of gray, tied in a ponytail. She wore a thin gray cashmere sweater over a white tank top. She held her face over the full cup of tea, even though it was no longer hot enough for steam to rise.

"The truth is I didn't know Matthew that well," Gabrielle said softly. "We only went out a handful of times. And whenever it seemed like we were getting closer, he would stop responding to my texts. I think the kids call it being ghosted. But then he would pop up again a few weeks later. My friends all thought it was because he wanted to see other people, but he always struck me as kind of lonely. I've dated players, and Matthew wasn't that. It was more like he didn't know how to be in a relationship or handle going steady." She laughed wistfully. "Do people even use that term anymore?"

"I wish kids today were that old fashioned," Tally said. "Now it's all hookups and apps. Technology has made dating so complicated."

"That's the truth," Gabrielle said. "When did emojis replace phone calls and actual conversations?"

"I don't know," Tally said, "but I never agreed to those terms."

Serrano said, "Again, we are sorry for your loss, Ms. Vargas. Now, just to confirm. You did see Matthew Linklater last Monday evening. Is that correct?"

She nodded. "We hadn't talked in a few weeks. It wasn't the first time he'd disappeared. I didn't take his reluctance as malice. As I said, he just didn't seem to really know how to function in a relationship, how or when to take the next step. But he was always kind."

"That must have been hard," Tally said, "trying to parse the mixed messages."

"Especially from a scheduling perspective, making sure my son is fed. I don't go out all that often, and when I do, if I don't cook before I go, Antonio will just order in and eat an entire meatball pizza."

"That would be your son. Antonio."

"He was Antonio until about twelve years old, and then he insisted on going by Tony. But I kept calling him Antonio, and eventually he gave up trying to correct me."

"And Antonio is a junior at Ashby High."

"That's right. He didn't have any classes with Matthew. They didn't know each other."

"Did Tony know you were seeing Mr. Linklater?"

"He knew I was seeing someone," Gabrielle said. "But I make it a point not to introduce men to my son until I know they're going to be around more. That I can count on them. I never got to that point with Matthew."

"After all the headache," Serrano asked, "and with Linklater being so unreliable, why did you agree to see him again?"

"Do you know how it feels to be lonely, Detective?"

Serrano's eyes met hers, and he nodded. "I do, Ms. Vargas."

"Most nights I come home, take my makeup off, cook for Antonio, then read or watch TV. I'm asleep most nights by nine thirty. Sometimes it just feels good to have a reason to dress up. To do my hair. To stay up late, to have someone to talk to about your life, where you've been and where you want to go. Who will share theirs with you. And I guess I hoped one day I'd meet someone who could share my loneliness. So that neither of us would be alone."

"What about Tony?" Serrano said.

"I love my son with every drop of blood in my body, but teenage boys aren't exactly known for their conversational skills."

Tally jabbed her thumb at Serrano. "Adult men aren't always known for their conversational skills."

Serrano shot Tally an annoyed look, but it was for show. He knew Tally was using him as a whetstone so she could sharpen her rapport with Gabrielle Vargas.

"What was your relationship with Matthew Linklater like?" Tally said.

"I'm not sure if you could really call it a 'relationship,'" Gabrielle said. "I knew after the second time we went out, we might not have been what you'd call 'destiny.' He was so uptight. It was like dating a pair of corduroys."

Tally laughed. Serrano said, "What's wrong with corduroys?"

Tally locked eyes with Vargas, and they shared a sly smile.

"So why did you continue to see him?" Tally asked.

Vargas shrugged. Her arms unfolded just the slightest bit. She was loosening up. Times like this, Serrano couldn't help but think that his partner was a remarkable detective. She was one of the toughest people he'd ever met, but when the situation called for it, she had the bedside manner of a doctor putting an anxious patient at ease before a risky procedure.

"I'm going to sound awful saying this, but he was there," Vargas said. "He wasn't a *bad* man. I've dated those. Too many and for too long."

"Haven't we all?" Tally said.

Gabrielle said, "Despite his oddness—is that a word?—he was kind. He was gentle. And he listened, and most importantly, he asked questions. Most men don't do that. You can finish a bottle of wine and an entire charcuterie board and realize the person sitting across from you hasn't asked you a single question other than 'Are you going to eat that?'"

Tally laughed. Gabrielle continued.

"At my age, it's all divorced dads who bring their baggage to dinner, or the older men who would rather date girls the age of their granddaughters. And then there are the cubs who have mommy hang-ups. And don't get me wrong. You can have fun with younger men. But Matthew . . . he didn't have any baggage. No moaning about an ex-wife or alimony payments during dinner. No catching him scrolling through a dating app when you get back from the bathroom. Matthew wasn't the kind of guy who would sweep you off your feet. But I think as you get a little older, your priorities change. The men who say they'd die for you are the ones who assume every text message is from an ex-lover. Give me kindness, decency, and stability over grand, emotionally volatile gestures."

"You and Matthew met online, right?" Serrano asked.

She nodded, closed her eyes, and smiled as though conjuring up a memory. "My son convinced me to try the apps," she said. "I told him they were for high schoolers and pervy middle-aged men. But my friend Marjorie met her boyfriend on one, and they just got back from Cabo, so I figured, What's the harm? But if I had a dollar for every 'U up?' or unwanted picture of a man's junk, I could sail to Cabo on my yacht."

"So Matthew was different," Tally said.

"Let's just say sometimes a follow-up question is the biggest turn-on," Gabrielle said with a sad laugh. She wiped tears from her cheeks. "When I told him I liked nature documentaries, the next day Matthew sent me a link to ten of them on Netflix that we could watch together. When I said I'd had a rough day, he told me to tell him about it and sent me his list of his favorite nature-sound playlists. Sometimes it's nice to know you can still be surprised."

"Ms. Vargas, I hate to ask, but I have to. Did you and Matthew Linklater have a sexual relationship?" Tally asked.

Gabrielle nodded. "Planning a romantic evening when you have a teenager is like planning a wedding, only more complicated. I would have to organize a sleepover for Antonio at his friend Peter Lincecum's house at least three weeks in advance. Antonio always fought me like hell, said Peter lived in a dump and his father was an asshole and why couldn't they just stay here. You only get to play the 'because I'm your mother and I said so' card a few times. But I guess it's better than getting a cheap motel room."

Then it seemed to hit Gabrielle Vargas all at once. Her eyes grew red and watery, and she held her hands against her face as she began to sob. Tally held a tissue out to her before she even knew to ask.

"Thank you," Gabrielle said, wiping her face. "What happened to Matthew . . . I have a hard time believing that kind of evil exists in the world. The only ones who deserve that kind of pain are those who do terrible things to children."

"We agree," Serrano said.

"And that's why we're here, Ms. Vargas," Tally said, leaning forward, taking the woman's hands in hers. "You were one of the last people to see Mr. Linklater. We've spoken to his colleagues at the school, his neighbors, and his friends, and outside of his classes and the occasional jog, nobody saw him in a social setting."

"See what I mean about being surprised?" Gabrielle said. "I didn't even know he ran. Now I can't help but picture Matthew ambling down the street in a pair of silly Lycra jogging shorts. He had the palest legs."

"When you saw him on Monday," Tally said, "did Matthew say anything that stood out? Anything out of the ordinary?"

"Like what? What do you mean by out of the ordinary?"

"Anything that he might have been concerned about. Or upset about," Serrano continued. "Or something he said that might have concerned you. Was he nervous? Did he seem distant or distracted? Or even scared?"

"Definitely not scared," she said. Her eyes went to the ceiling as she thought. "He talked a lot about his job. About his students. There were a few of them he really seemed to have high hopes for. One in particular . . . what was her name . . . Penny Wallace. He said she was absolutely brilliant. Some people just go to work for a paycheck. I could always tell Matthew took his work home with him."

Gabrielle didn't notice the smile that spread across Tally's face. She couldn't have known that Penny Wallace was Detective Tally's stepdaughter. But Serrano could practically feel his partner's heart swelling.

"It sounds like Matthew was truly a devoted teacher," Tally said.

Vargas nodded. Serrano sensed a twinge of regret in Gabrielle Vargas's face, a measure of remorse that things never quite gelled between her and Matthew Linklater. Serrano knew firsthand, though, that you could admire, respect, even *want* to love someone, without being able to fully lose yourself to them.

"Back to my question," Serrano said. "Can you recall anything Mr. Linklater said that struck you as odd or memorable?"

Gabrielle Vargas recrossed her arms. "I honestly don't know," she said. "He talked mostly about work. Papers to grade, tests to score, things he still had to finish before the end of the school year. I . . . I really don't know, Detective."

"Please think," Serrano continued. "Anything at all. Sometimes it's the smallest things that lead to the biggest breakthroughs."

Gabrielle sat there. Serrano could tell she wanted to say something but, for some reason, hesitated.

"Gabrielle," Tally said. "For Matthew."

She looked up at Tally, her eyes soft, filled with sadness and remorse. Finally she spoke.

"Something was under his skin at dinner," Gabrielle said. "But he seemed more annoyed and angry than scared or upset. I didn't think much of it because being a little ticked off about your job is hardly something to call the FBI over."

"What was it?" Tally said.

"He was talking about how teaching was so different now than when he first started. Mainly about how expectations were different than reality. That sometimes he felt like he had to be both a teacher and prison warden at the same time and that the system was broken for these kids. That there were higher expectations for teachers than parents. Parents could screw up their kids in any number of ways and never get called on it. But if a teacher made one mistake, no matter how small, their livelihood could be in jeopardy."

"What brought this on?" Serrano asked.

"He said he hated having to step in for absentee parents. Parents treating school like it was just taxpayer-funded day care. That too many kids were being left behind. Parents letting their kids get exploited."

"Exploited? How?" Tally said.

"He said over the years he'd come to be able to tell which kids came from bad homes. They had this empty look in their eyes, like the fighting and cruelty they saw on a daily basis had made them numb. Made them angry. And that anger made them vulnerable. Susceptible to people who could . . . take advantage of it."

"Ms. Vargas," Serrano said, "I get the sense there was something specific that put this on Matthew Linklater's mind that night. We need to know exactly what he was referring to."

Gabrielle's lower lip trembled. "I'm sorry. It's just, when I hear you say the word *was*, it's hard to talk about Matthew in the past. We held hands the other night. He kissed me right outside this building and said he couldn't wait to see me again. That he wanted to do things right this time. How do you grieve for someone you could have loved but never got a chance to?"

"There's no right or wrong way to grieve," Serrano said. "Sometimes the grief itself honors their memory." Gabrielle Vargas looked at him, her eyes practically begging for some sort of understanding. Serrano could tell she'd responded to the gravity and tenor in his voice, and it made him believe that she had also known this kind of sadness.

She nodded. "I like the sound of that." She paused, then said, "Matthew talked about a boy. Benjamin something. Riddick or Rudder."

"Ruddock?" Tally said.

"Ruddock, that's it. Benjamin Ruddock."

"What did he say about Benjamin Ruddock?" Serrano asked.

"He said he didn't like the kid. Which was odd for him to say. I'd heard him talk about a lot of the students in his classes but never heard him flat out say he didn't like one of them."

"Did he say why he didn't like Benjamin Ruddock?"

"I asked him that. He said the Ruddock kid was smart. But not book smart. Smart in the way a Mafia captain or drug dealer might be smart. Like he knew how to manipulate people. Get kids to follow him. Make them do what he wanted them to."

"Did Matthew elaborate on that?"

"No," Gabrielle said. "I asked him to. He said, 'Trust me, you don't want to know.'"

"So he obviously had a legitimate reason to be concerned about Benjamin Ruddock," Serrano said. "He wasn't just airing petty gripes about his students."

"Whatever it was, it wasn't petty. And when I pried, he just changed the subject." She paused. "After what happened to Matthew, maybe it was to protect me."

Tally and Serrano looked at each other.

"It's strange," Gabrielle said. "I'm remembering all these things he said more clearly now than when he actually said them."

"That's not uncommon with grief," Serrano said.

"You sound like you've experienced your own," Gabrielle replied.

"I have."

"How did you get past it?"

Serrano offered her a warm smile. "I'll let you know when I do."

CHAPTER 14

Evie Boggs sat in the northwest corner of the Moonlight Diner, on the corner of Willowbrook Place and Daunton Road. The outside of the diner looked like a detached retro railway car, covered with artificially rusted, curved metal. A sign in a pink 1950s-era font read **DINE HERE** atop the entrance. The interior was lined with red padded stools and a stained wooden countertop. The booths were fitted with cherry red Naugahyde vinyl. Evie found a small tear in the seat of her booth. She stuck her finger in, pulled, and ripped it open a little wider.

Evie's waitress had offered a tip-friendly smile when she ordered. Over the next forty-five minutes, Evie had received five coffee and two water refills. She had gone to the restroom twice. She was so hungry her stomach hurt, but she did not want to eat in front of these men in fear that she might vomit. One of the men she was waiting for she had never met. She had once held a knife to the other one's neck in his own home. To this day, she wished she had followed up on the threat and swiped the blade across his fleshy throat.

Finally, two men entered the diner. They both smiled when they saw Evie. She took a breath and placed her trembling hands beneath the table where the men could not see them. Evie did not fear the men because of what they could do to her. She feared them because of what they had promised to do to people she loved.

The one approaching on Evie's left was about five foot seven, 240 pounds, with shoulders so wide and thick a skateboard could rest across them. His walk was more of a side-to-side lurch, like a wrecking ball at the end of a wire.

The one on her right was six foot five, willowy thin, his gray-brown hair parted as if by machete. He moved with a kind of grace that reminded Evie of shades rustling near an open window. Viewed from behind, you would assume the men were strangers, perhaps having struck up a friendship after having met by chance at a bar. But from the front, one look at the sharp, intelligent yet malevolent hazel eyes, the thin noses, and the pursed lips, and you would know immediately that despite the difference in size, they shared the same blood.

The tall man slid into the booth across from Evie. She felt his knees press up against hers. The shorter man slid in next to her, his meaty arm forcing her uncomfortably into the side of the booth. The tall man's knees held her in place from one side. The shorter man's bulk held her from the other. She was trapped.

"Long time," the shorter one said.

Evie said nothing.

"Ms. Boggs," the tall man said. "Thank you for coming."

"It's not like you gave me a choice," Evie said. "Besides, you're late."

"No. We arrived exactly when we meant to," the tall one said. "My name is Randall. I know you've . . . *met* . . . my brother, Raymond."

The shorter man, Raymond, took Evie's coffee cup, swallowed the dregs, then placed it back in front of her.

"Too much cream," he said.

"You're free to get your own," she said. "On me."

"I like my coffee the way I like my money," Raymond said.

"How's that?" Evie said.

"Taken from someone else," Raymond responded, taking a sip of Evie's water.

"You guys should go on tour. But I really hope you didn't ask me here just to take my beverages. They do have Uber Eats in Ashby."

"I like her," Raymond said with a smile, a dribble of water leaking from his mouth and sliding down his chin.

"You shouldn't talk with your mouth full," Evie said. "If you recall, I almost gave you another mouth, about six inches below that one. Maybe I should have."

Raymond smiled. "I was wondering if she would still be feisty."

"And if you don't give us more information," Randall said, "the next thing in your mouth will be a palm full of your son's hair after I tear it from his head."

Bile rose in Evie's stomach. She tasted it in her throat.

"You don't need to make threats. I'm here. I'm cooperating." Evie dug her nails into her knuckles, anger and fear and adrenaline coursing through her.

"So cooperate. What have you learned about the current predicament?" Randall asked.

"I've only been in town two days," Evie replied. "I've told you everything I've learned."

"And that is not nearly enough. We cannot have people looking into our business."

"They wouldn't be looking into your business if you were better about keeping your business quiet."

Randall ignored the comment and said, "Have you learned who is investigating the untimely death of our friend Mr. Linklater?"

Evie took out her cell phone, opened the photo app, and scrolled through seventeen photographs.

"Detectives John Serrano and Leslie Tally of the Ashby Police Department. They're officially working the Linklater murder. They've been interviewing all of Linklater's colleagues and associates."

"Are they capable?" Randall asked.

"Seems so," said Evie.

Raymond frowned and looked at his brother. Something seemed to pass between them that did not require words.

Randall shook his head.

"No. Disappearing the detectives will only draw more suspicion and law enforcement participation."

Raymond seemed disappointed by his brother's response.

"What do you know about these particular police?" Randall said.

"A bit," Evie replied. "It's a small enough city that people talk. I've put together files from public documents—newspapers, city council meetings."

"You can send it to Mr. Brice," Randall said.

Evie nodded.

"You really shouldn't use so much cream in your coffee," Raymond said. "It masks the natural flavor of the beans."

"This is a joke, right?" Evie said. "You came to lecture me on coffee prep?"

"She's very combative," Randall said.

"Very combative," Raymond added.

"She does not have very much foresight," Randall said. "Given what we know about her."

"No, she does not," Raymond said.

"Enough," Evie said, sighing. "Sitting with you two is like watching *Gossip Girl* with a brain injury. Anyway, digging up dirt on cops is not easy. Make too much noise and people notice, word gets around, and the cops circle the wagons. And if I get on the cops' radar, then guess what? You guys are on their radar. I would assume you'd prefer to stay beneath their radar."

"That would be preferable," Randall said.

"Most preferable," Raymond replied.

"Highly preferable."

"Ugh. I need a Xanax and a crowbar to the face talking to you two," Evie said.

"In the event that you cannot get much closer to the police," Randall said, "what is your plan to stay ahead of this?"

"The woman Matthew Linklater wrote the day he died."

"Rachel Marin," Randall said.

"Right. I know her. I mean I *know* her."

Raymond raised his eyebrows.

"Not in that way, you stubby trouser stain. But we have a past."

"Is Mr. Brice aware of this?" Randall asked.

Evie nodded. "Apparently she does some work with the police, but she's not actually police."

"And why would she speak with you?" Randall said.

"Let's just say I have some leverage over her."

"Leverage?"

"I know certain things she would prefer to keep quiet."

"This sounds like an ideal situation," Randall said. "Leverage can be more powerful than an army."

"Yes, it can," Raymond replied.

"So you can squeeze this Marin woman."

"It's not quite that simple. She's not a cop, but she's not just some regular civilian. She's dangerous. And if I don't play it careful, she could be even more dangerous than the cops."

"In what way?" Randall asked.

"They're sworn to uphold the law," Evie said. "Rachel Marin is not."

"I see," Randall said.

"She sounds scary," Raymond said, with an amused smile.

Randall said, "We expect you to glean information from whatever sources are available to you, whether it is this Marin woman, Detectives Serrano and Tally, or any peripherals that might possess knowledge of Mr. Linklater's death or our business with Mr. Brice. I expect you to then turn over any and all information you come across in a very timely manner."

"Very timely," Raymond said.

"Quite timely," added Randall.

"I'm going to stick sharpened pencils in my ears if you guys don't stop that," Evie said. "Trust me: whatever I find out, you'll know."

"I'm sure your son will be happy to hear that," Raymond said.

Evie's heart began to thud in her chest. She dug her nails deeper into her skin.

"Speaking of which," Randall added, "you should know that we are constantly monitoring your son to ensure his complete and total happiness. Nothing is more important to us than your son's well-being."

"Stop talking about my son," Evie said through gritted teeth.

Raymond took a cell phone from his jacket pocket, tapped a few buttons, then turned the screen around for Evie to see. A video began to play. Evie watched it, her eyes widening in terror. Her hand flew to her mouth, and she bit down on her flesh to keep from screaming.

"Is that . . . *at his school?*"

"Yes. We have a close friend keeping an eye on your son at this very instant. He's a good-looking kid. Smart, from what we hear. And with that kind of smile, he'll make a lot of friends and break a lot of hearts. I promise you, Ms. Boggs, we would prefer not to hurt him. Blood only leads to more blood. But if blood can resolve a problem—or prevent one—we will not hesitate to remove your son's lips with rusty scissors and mail his smile to you in a plastic bag."

Raymond took another sip from Evie's glass and spat a stream of liquid into her face. She recoiled and wiped the saliva from her face with one hand, the other clenching into a fist. She had no doubt that she could beat either one of these two men to death. But she would be sentencing her son to death if she did.

"If we feel for a moment that you are withholding information from us," Randall continued, "we will open every vein in your son's body and send every ounce of his blood to you in a nice container for posterity."

86

"We might need more than one container," Raymond said. "Bodies contain a lot of blood."

"Enough, you goddamn psychopaths," Evie said. "If you touch him, if it takes my whole life, I will kill both of you. And I'll make it slow."

"I have no doubt you would try," Randall said.

Evie said, "What would Brice say if he knew you were threatening my family like this?"

Randall said, "Mr. Brice knows that we are men of our word. We genuinely have no desire to see any further bloodshed. We are businessmen. If we feel that our business is safe to operate, we have no need or desire to upset the delicate ecosystem we have created. And neither does he."

"In other words," Raymond said, his lips moist, "you make sure we're well fed, your kid's insides get to stay on the inside."

"You'll get everything," Evie said. "I swear."

"This Marin woman," Randall said. "She seems like a combustible element. The fact that Mr. Linklater contacted her means he believed she could work outside the law if necessary. It concerns me. Does it you, brother?"

"It does, brother," Raymond said.

"We need to know that you will deal with this element should it become truly combustible. Remove it, if necessary. Can we be assured you will do that?"

Evie thought about her son. The video they had just shown her. She thought about all the mistakes she had made in her life. Mistakes she was still paying for. But she still had time to make things right. To make it up to her son. But none of it would matter if they were both dead.

"If it becomes a problem," Evie said, "if *she* becomes a problem, I will deal with it."

Randall and Raymond looked at each other and smiled.

"Good," Randall said. "Mr. Brice has a contingency plan just in case."

"Contingency plan?" Evie said.

"Let's just say you're not the only mom with a messed-up son," Raymond said.

Evie felt the saliva in her mouth dry up. It was one thing for them to threaten Rachel, a grown, strong woman who could look out for herself. It was another to threaten people's children.

Randall slid out of the booth, leaving a dent in Evie's leg where his kneecap had pressed into her.

"Don't be a stranger," Raymond said. When he slid out, Evie could practically feel her lungs regain their shape. The two men left the diner side by side without looking back. The bell above the door jingled twice: once when they opened it and once again when it closed.

Then Evie Boggs buried her face in a soiled napkin so the other customers wouldn't see her cry.

CHAPTER 15

Thankfully for Rachel, Ashby High had begun digitizing yearbooks, class photos, sports rosters, and curricula fifteen years ago. It wasn't hard for her to cull a complete catalog of Matthew Linklater's students dating back to his first year at Ashby. Rachel figured that whoever was involved in Linklater's death was someone he'd seen on a regular basis and interacted with, and he would've had at least a cursory knowledge of their day-to-day activities. Linklater also would have been much more likely to open his front door for a student he still taught. Which would also correlate to someone who currently had access to the biology lab for the snatch-and-grab job on Midge.

She texted Serrano.

May have a lead

She watched three dots blink as he replied.

Ditto

You first

Met with a woman named Gabrielle Vargas. On-and-off paramour of Matthew Linklater. Mother of a student, kept on the DL, which is why Principal Alvi wasn't aware of it. Vargas

said Linklater was concerned about a student named Benjamin Ruddock. May be nothing, but it's a thread.

Rachel opened her laptop and did a search for a Benjamin Ruddock in Ashby. She found various social media accounts belonging to Ruddock, including Twitter, Instagram, and Facebook, but they were all set to private. His avatar was curious, though. No photo. Simply the word *Fratres* in gold lettering against a black background. *Brothers.*

Ruddock was eighteen, set to turn nineteen in the fall. He was old for a senior. He'd been held back. She wondered whether it had been educational or behavioral. Ruddock had been tagged in several public photos, which Rachel saved to a folder she created on her desktop. While most high school boys struggled to grow patchy beards and wispy mustaches, Ruddock had a five o'clock shadow. Most of his baby fat had melted away, revealing high cheekbones and a sharp jawline. He had intelligent eyes and an easy, dimpled smile. He had the kind of slightly dangerous look that teenage girls swooned over. But the slightly malevolent look in his eyes warned Rachel it wasn't just hearts he was capable of breaking.

His mother, Danielle, had died seven years ago from ovarian cancer at just thirty-eight years of age. His father, Timothy, fifty-six, owned a two-bedroom home on Needlepoint Lane that he purchased seventeen years ago for $147,000. An image search for Timothy Ruddock produced only a photo from the website of a local bar, McSwiggan's, holding up a glass of brown liquor in one hand and an empty beer in the other. He had his son's sandy-blond hair and the same look in his eyes that said he'd just as soon hit you with a beer bottle as serve you one.

Everything about Benjamin Ruddock screamed trouble. But trouble was one thing. Killing and torturing a man to death was a whole different universe.

Rachel texted Serrano her suspicions that one of the people at Linklater's door the night of his death was a current Ashby student. He wrote back:

You think Ruddock killed him?

I don't know. I don't like what I'm seeing about the kid. But that doesn't mean he's a murderer. What does Tally think?

We both think that given what Vargas said, it's at least worth talking to him.

He's 18. That's over the age of parental consent for questioning. You can bring him in.

We just might.

What's the holdup?

The holdup is making sure that if/when we bring him in, we know what buttons to push and how much leverage we have (or don't have) on him.

Give me five minutes. I'll find out what he knows.

Don't even go there, Rachel.

Fine. But no reason you can't bring him in for questioning.

Remember which one of us is an actual member of the law enforcement community. You follow our lead. Not the other way around.

And remember that if not for me, Constance Wright might have been chalked up by the Keystone Cops as a suicide.

A minute passed. No dots to indicate that Serrano was typing. Finally she wrote:

Too far. I'm sorry. Let's not fight. Same team, right?

No response.
After what felt like eons, Rachel texted,

See you tomorrow?

Five minutes later, Serrano replied.

Sure

She hated that word. *Sure.* It conveyed no enthusiasm. Just a perfunctory statement of acceptance.

Just then, Rachel saw a small light go on in the live stream of Eric's room. She enlarged the video box to full screen. The light came from Eric's cell phone, which was charging on his desk. It looked like an incoming text message. Eric paused his game, then picked up his phone and looked at the screen. His thumb hovered over the keypad, as though debating whether to respond. Then he put it back down and resumed his game.

Rachel watched him, desperate to know what was inside his head. When she'd first had the cameras installed, she worried she would feel guilty for spying on her children without their knowledge. But she got over it. Some parents installed keyloggers on their kids' computers or checked cell phone email and text logs regularly. Rachel knew that if her kids learned about the video surveillance, there would be hell to pay.

But Eric didn't know what it felt like, as a mother, to have a psychotic man with a gun just steps away from her children's bedrooms.

She would never forget the sight just a few months ago of the deranged man, loaded gun in hand, approaching the stairway leading to where her children slept. The cameras were an invasion of their privacy. Of that Rachel was acutely aware. But if there was even a small chance they might save them from harm, which she knew there was, they were worth any potential fallout.

Rachel opened the feed to her son's room and scrubbed back on the video until she saw the light appear on his cell phone. She watched it again. Eric clearly knew the texter—he simply chose not to respond. Why?

Rachel scrubbed it again, zoomed in on the cell phone, then used imaging software to enhance the pixelated screen. When the light blinked on, Rachel paused the video. She could just make out the ID on the text message.

Penny Wallace.

Detective Tally's stepdaughter. Rachel knew Penny and Eric were in the same class in school, and at family dinners they seemed friendly. Teenagers texting at odd hours was hardly uncommon. Not to mention that Penny was a straight A student, beautiful, and ambitious. If any girl was texting her son late at night, Rachel was OK with it being Penny Wallace.

But then Rachel enlarged the text itself. She felt her heart rate speed up.

Hey Eric, u ok? Worried about u. I've heard weird rumors about BR. Just be careful.

BR. Benjamin Ruddock. It had to be. Why was Penny Wallace warning Eric about Benjamin Ruddock, the same kid who was a person of interest in Matthew Linklater's death?

Rachel felt dizzy. Like she had a blind spot for her son. She shut down her computer and went upstairs. She knocked on Eric's door.

There was no answer. She knocked again, this time harder. She was ready to knock again when a voice came from the other side:

"I'm busy. *Go. Away.*"

Rachel felt like a dagger had been placed against her heart, cold and sharp. She needed to find a way to reach her son. Because now it wasn't just his nightmares that could harm him. There was something very, very real.

CHAPTER 16

Eric Marin knew that nobody had ever definitively escaped from Alcatraz. There was that movie where Sean Connery was an old dude who'd escaped, like, thirty years ago and managed to sneak back in. But the only real people to ever get out of Alcatraz itself—Frank Morris and the brothers John and Clarence Anglin—presumably died in the frigid waters of San Francisco Bay.

Eric had never been in prison. He hoped he would never know what it felt like to be behind actual bars. But living with his mother, Rachel, often didn't seem all that different from being trapped in a prison. If Rachel Marin had been in charge of Alcatraz back in 1962 when Morris and the Anglins were there, they never would have made it out of their cells.

Eric was tired of feeling like a prisoner in his own home, his own life. Ever since his father died, Eric had been a sidecar, pulled along by his nightmares, his mother. He never had a say in anything. Tonight that would change. He wasn't sure if he could trust Benjamin Ruddock. But he also knew that if he didn't do something, he would go through life a doormat. Maybe Ruddock was the key to finding out what he was truly capable of.

Tonight, he would find out.

Tonight, he would escape from Rachel Marin's Alcatraz.

From the day they'd moved to Ashby, Eric had known there was something different about the Marin home. But he hadn't been able to put a finger on it until the night a deranged man broke into their home, armed with a loaded gun and a knife that would have made Rambo flinch. Until that night, Eric's mother had forbidden her children from going downstairs. She'd made up some ludicrous story about asbestos. But that night, Eric's mother had sent him and his sister down to the basement to hide from the crazed gunman in their home. And when Eric finally saw what was *really* downstairs, he'd understood why his mother had been so secretive.

The entire Marin home was wired. Not the way most families wired their home, with outside-motion detectors, alarms, floodlights, and all that good stuff. No, the Marin home was wired the way the freaking Batcave was wired. The basement had surveillance equipment that would make James Bond jealous, with enough training equipment to open up her own gym. Given how much hardware his mother kept downstairs, Eric guessed there had to be cameras installed all over the house: inside *and* out. In a way, he understood his mother's paranoia. If Rachel had been this paranoid when Eric's father was alive . . . maybe he would still *be* alive.

Sometimes all Eric could feel was anger. Like heat wrapped around his body. He wanted to scream, punch the walls, punch *somebody*. But there was nothing. Nobody. Collected energy that never got released. Sometimes he hated his mother but then hated himself for hating her because he knew she didn't deserve it. Still, he needed an outlet. Some way to release all that bubbling anger and energy, or one day he would just explode.

Maybe Benjamin Ruddock was that outlet. He thought about the way Tony Vargas had looked at him after he'd spoken to Ruddock. Tony had nodded at him. Like he respected him. Tony Vargas had never given him the time of day before. But now, he seemed ready to befriend him. It felt good. It felt *good* to feel good—a cracked window in a room filled for so long with smoke and ash.

And the money—$10,000. Many of Eric's classmates earned coin on the side. A babysitting job, helping old folks set up their Wi-Fi networks. Eric's mother had never permitted him to do any of it. Eric knew $10,000 wasn't going to change his life. But it was a sign of respect. A sign that Ruddock wasn't full of it. And that there could be more—a *lot* more—if he put his nose to the grindstone. He'd been waiting so long to prove his worth. And now, it was time.

Eric turned off his bedroom light at nine forty-two. It was around the same time he went to bed every night. He did not say good night to his mother, because if he had, she would've known something was up.

But when he climbed under the covers, Eric was still wearing the same clothes he'd worn that day. He tucked his blanket up tight around his neck to hide his collar. He was tired but could not let himself fall asleep. He didn't want to play on his phone, because it might draw her attention. He simply lay there and waited. And waited.

When he finally heard the telltale sound of his mother's footsteps going down to the basement, Eric made his move.

Making her think he was asleep was the easy part. Getting out of the house—and then back in—without being seen . . . that was the part that would have made Sean Connery jealous. But if she ever found out, she'd lock the house up so tight a mouse fart would be stuck inside forever.

Whatever the hell Benjamin Ruddock is talking about, this "fratres" thing, it had better be worth it.

Ruddock had approached him for a reason. Not Cory Stuber. Not Ronny Welch or Avery Johannson or Suresh Taneja. Ruddock went to *him*. Eric had never heard anyone at Ashby talking about whatever the hell "fratres" was. It was a secret, a low whisper. It was meaningful. Eric *had* to know why.

Neither his mother nor his sister seemed to have noticed the stuffed animals missing from Megan's room when she went to bed. Hell, she had a million of them. He'd sneaked them out of her room, one at a time. His mother was distracted by Megan's droning on and on about the "book" she was writing. Sadie something. Talking about how one day she would get them published. So lame. But it kept his mother and sister busy.

Stealth and speed and cunning. Eric had all that. He knew it.

When all the stuffed animals were under the covers, Eric sat up slowly; then, still covered, he gently assembled the dolls to loosely form the outline of a human body. It didn't need to look perfect. Just enough bulk to fool his mom at a glance. He put a baseball glove on the pillow. His father had given it to him years ago. One of the last things Eric's father did before he died was promise to help break it in. But now, years later, the leather was still stiff.

Eric didn't even know why he'd kept it. Just looking at it made him queasy. But he couldn't throw it out. It felt wrong.

Eric drew a deep breath. This was it. The riskiest thing he had ever done. That in and of itself was sort of sad, but he swore he would make up for all the days he'd moldered inside the cell of his mother's making. This was his chance. No more Eric Marin, son of a dead man. Wallflower, weirdo, ghost. Ruddock had called tonight an opportunity. Eric would not let this opportunity pass him by. After all, Eric's mother herself hadn't exactly obeyed the rules the last few years. Why should he?

"Let's see what you got, kid," he whispered. Then Eric Marin slid out from under his covers, crossed to the other side of his room, opened the window, and climbed out onto the second story roof hanging over the freshly mowed lawn. He looked down. Looked around for nosy neighbors. He was alone.

It was a ten-foot drop. The grass was soft. Eric landed without a sound. He felt a sharp pain in his knees from the jolt, but it went away as soon as he began to run.

CHAPTER 17

Two Years Ago

Rachel opened the door. She had a pleasant smile on her face, because she knew the ensuing conversation would be far from pleasant.

"Mr. Roberson," she said, sweetly. "Please, come in. It's so nice to meet Albie's dad. Would you mind taking your boots off?"

Ed Roberson complied. He left his boots by the front door and followed Rachel into her home. Ed was six foot even, with thinning black hair, a graying goatee, and a slight midsection paunch that a few weeks on the treadmill could remedy.

"This is a lovely home, Ms. Marin," he said. She offered him a bright over-the-shoulder smile as she led him into the living room. She took a seat on the sofa, and he on the love seat across from her.

Albie Roberson was in Eric's seventh-grade class. He had come over after school to study, but an hour into their "studying" session, Rachel could hear the familiar bleeps and blorps of digital alien hordes being slaughtered. She didn't much mind, though. She could not remember the last time Eric had had a friend over. It saddened her to think it may have been the first time since they'd moved to Ashby. Eric needed friends. But he also needed to be protected. Which made the conversation Rachel was about to have with Ed Roberson that much more difficult.

"Can I offer you a drink?" she said. "Water? Iced tea?"

"I'm good, thanks. I hope Albie hasn't behaved too badly."

"On the contrary, he's been a total joy. I brought the boys some snacks, and when Albie was finished with his plate, he brought it downstairs, washed it, and put it in the drying rack. I wish some *other* kids who lived in this house did that."

Ed laughed. "I'll give my wife all the credit for teaching him manners," he said. "So, should we get the boys?"

"Not just yet," Rachel said. "Let me just say, Mr. Roberson, that it's been a pleasure having Albie over. Eric mentioned that he and your son were getting close, and I'm glad I finally got to meet him. He's a delight."

"Call me Ed," he replied. "Albie said Eric was one of the smartest kids he knows. My wife always tells him, 'Hang out with people smarter than you, and they'll rub off.' So thanks for letting your boy lend ours some of his smarts."

"I'm sure your boy will rub off on Eric too," she said. Ed Roberson nodded and looked around, as though waiting for something.

"So, um, can we grab Albie? My wife will have dinner ready soon, and I hate to have her slave over a meal and let it go cold."

"In a minute," Rachel said, with a firmness that seemed to catch Ed Roberson by surprise. "Mr. Roberson, I need to ask you something."

"All right," he said, crossing his arms over his chest. "Shoot."

"It's personal."

Ed Roberson sat back, now looking suspicious. "I'm not sure how to respond to that."

"Well, I'm afraid I have to ask it anyway. What exactly happened the night of October eleventh, 2015?"

Ed's arms went down. He leaned forward, pleasantries evaporating from his voice. "What the hell are you talking about?"

"You know exactly what I'm talking about. October eleventh, 2015."

"I *don't* know what you're talking about, and so I won't answer your question. Now, Ms. Marin, I'm going to get my son, and we're going to leave."

Roberson stood up.

"Sit *down*, Ed."

He looked at Rachel. Something in her eyes, her tone of voice, convinced him to sit back down.

"On October eleventh, 2015," Rachel said, "you and three other men—Stan Vrychek, Lawrence Duns, and Anderson Billingsley—were arrested in the basement of Mr. Vrychek's home on Moss Street in Carltondale. I don't have to ask if that is true because I've seen the arrest report."

"How—"

"It doesn't matter. What matters is that the four of you were arrested for possession of cocaine with intent to sell. Five kilos. That's about a hundred and fifty *thousand* dollars' worth of coke."

"That was a long time ago," Roberson said through gritted teeth. "I'm a father."

"You were a father then too," she replied. "Now, what's strange is not the arrest itself. What's strange is that you were the only one of the four who wasn't charged with any crimes. Your buddies Vrychek, Duns, and Billingsley all did time. You did not. That's pretty strange, don't you think?"

Ed Roberson sat there, unmoving.

"I'm willing to bet," Rachel said, "that you didn't get any jail time because you testified against your friends. And maybe you gave up who-ever supplied you with the powder in exchange for immunity."

"What do you want?" Roberson whispered, the edge gone from his voice.

"What I want is for you to know that as long as our sons are friends, which I hope is a very, very long time, I will be watching you every moment of every day. See, if you *did* flip on your friends, you never really paid a price for your crime. Hell, I wouldn't be shocked if you're still distributing—just got a little smarter about hiding it. But I will not—and I hope I make this as clear as a plastic baggie—will *not* allow my son to be anywhere near crimes like that. I know, legally, you're off the hook with the black-and-whites. So consider me your gray shadow."

"Just let us leave," Roberson said, pleading. "I'm not in that life anymore."

"Maybe not. But if I get wind that you're dealing, snorting, or even watching a *movie* where people do drugs, I will make sure you serve every second of that time you should have back in 2015. Do you get me, *Ed*?"

"I do," Roberson said. He stood up and shouted. "Albie! We gotta go. *Now.*"

A moment later, Albie and Eric came downstairs. Albie Roberson was a sweet-looking gangly kid, twelve years old, with a mop of red hair and a face full of freckles.

"Hey, Dad," Albie said. "Thanks for the pickup."

"Not a problem," Ed Roberson said quickly, watching Rachel as he spoke. "Come on. Let's go."

"Thank you, Ms. Mari—"

Ed dragged Albie out the front door before the boy could finish thanking Rachel for her hospitality.

"Everything OK?" Eric said. Her son was standing at the top of the stairs, a confused look on his face.

"Absolutely," Rachel said. "Did you guys have fun?"

"Yeah," Eric said. "And before you ask, *yes*, we did actually get our work done."

"I knew I didn't even need to ask."

"Albie is going to come over again next Tuesday," said Eric, with genuine enthusiasm in his voice. "Is that OK?"

"Of course it's OK," Rachel said. "I'm really glad you're making friends."

Albie Roberson did not come over the following Tuesday. That afternoon, Eric got home from school. He was clearly upset from the moment he walked in the door.

"Everything all right, hon?" Rachel said. She was sitting on the floor with Megan, helping her glue sequins to a dress they were making for her Halloween costume.

"No," he said. Eric walked over to Rachel and Megan and looked down at his mother. "Mom, what happened last week?"

"What do you mean?" Rachel said, keeping her eyes on the dress.

"Albie Roberson didn't speak to me this whole week. Every time I saw him, he walked the other way like he didn't want to even be near me."

"That's odd," Rachel said. "Maybe he's just distracted? Or he has a big test coming up?"

Eric shook his head. "He doesn't. Today I managed to get him alone in the locker room before phys ed. I asked him what was going on. He told me we couldn't hang out anymore. I asked him why. He said he just couldn't and to leave it alone." Eric paused. "Why would he say that, Mom?"

"I really don't know," she said. "You'd have to ask Albie."

"I don't know. I feel like somebody isn't telling me something," Eric said. Then he went upstairs and slammed his door.

Rachel never saw Albie Roberson alive again. The following spring, Albie was diagnosed with chronic lymphocytic leukemia. Due to his treatments, he did not go to school for the final three months of the semester. He passed away that fall.

Eric and Rachel attended his memorial service at Saint Bartholomew's Church on a cold, rainy November morning. Friends and family gave eloquent, emotional remembrances for Albie. Rachel sat in a pew next to her son and listened to every word. She expected Eric to cry. Since she had spoken to Ed Roberson, no other friends had come to the Marin house to see Eric. He came home every day, marched right to his room, and closed the door. The light inside him seemed to have dimmed.

Rachel saw Ed Roberson in the front pew. He had lost the extra ten pounds, and another twenty on top of it. His wife, Delilah, and his daughter, Annie, had their heads on his shoulders. Rachel could see their shoulders trembling as so, so many people came to the pulpit to speak of the boy.

At one point, Ed stood up to greet a mourner. They shook hands and hugged. Ed turned around, and for a moment, his eyes locked with Rachel's.

"I'm sorry," she mouthed.

Ed Roberson did not respond. Then Rachel noticed Eric looking at her. He had seen the interaction. Something in her son's eyes, a mixture of sadness and anger, made Rachel feel like a cold spike had been driven into her stomach.

She wanted to say to Eric, *I'm sorry. I didn't know. I couldn't possibly have known.*

But she said nothing.

The priest said, "Give Albert Wendell Roberson eternal rest, O Lord, and may your light shine on him forever."

Rachel saw a single tear slide down her son's cheek. He wiped it away quickly.

CHAPTER 18

Today

Rachel Marin watched the entire masquerade from her computer with a mixture of horror, anger, and perhaps the smallest twinge of amusement and pride. She debated putting an end to the silliness, then installing state-of-the-art motion sensors in Eric's room that would let her know every time her son burped.

But she didn't want her children to grow up afraid of her. The death of Rachel's husband had locked Eric in an emotional prison, but rather than beat against the bars, he had retreated into a corner, sullenly living out his sentence with no possibility—or interest—in parole. She had tried to pull him out but instead had seen him recede further. Her once-buoyant son was drowning, and it tore her up. She'd *wanted* him to lash out, to flout the rules. Anything to prove he had some fight in him. So as Rachel watched her son slip out the window, leaving behind a bed full of fluffy animals like some sixth-rate illusionist, Rachel couldn't muster the anger most mothers would have. For years she'd wanted Eric to act like a boy. To test her boundaries. To venture into the unknown, to take risks, just like she had. Well, Eric had finally called her bluff.

That said, Matthew Linklater's killer was out there. And the evidence pointed to one of Eric's classmates. She wondered if tonight's escape had anything to do with Penny Wallace's text. Was Eric going to see BR—Benjamin Ruddock? She had to know, but she couldn't follow him. Not with Megan fast asleep in the other room. As much as she loathed asking for it, Rachel needed help.

Lucky for you, you've been shacking up with a cop.

John Serrano picked up on the third ring. She'd clearly woken him, but he didn't seem particularly put out.

"Hey, Rach," he said. "Calling for some late-night action?"

"You should be so lucky. Actually, I have a favor to ask."

There was a pause.

"Rach, it's one in the morning."

"So you're willing to get up for sex but not for a favor?"

"Totally bizarre, I know. Like you're above a booty call."

"I certainly am not. But that's not why I'm calling."

"So you want me to drag my tired ass out of bed in the middle of the night?"

"That's why it's called a favor. It ipso facto inconveniences the person being asked."

"Lucky for you I'm turned on by Latin. So what's the favor?"

"Eric just sneaked out of the house. Well, at least he *thinks* he sneaked out of the house. I don't know where he's going, but thankfully he forgot to turn off the GPS on his phone."

"Why don't you just keep him on a literal leash? Would save you the anxiety and save me the sleep."

"You're hilarious. He's currently heading east on Foster Lane. With Linklater's killer still out there, I don't like not knowing exactly where he is. I need to know where Eric is going, and I can't leave Megan alone. Will you follow him for me?"

Rachel heard a sigh and a scratching sound on the other end. She preferred not to know what body part Serrano was picking at.

"So you want a cop to follow Eric," Serrano said, "but not *the* cops."

"Exactly."

"And you don't want me to just find him and bring him home?"

"I don't even want him to know you're there. Eric has been through hell, and half the time I feel like he's slipping away from me. I want him to trust me, but I also know what's out there. And it scares me. I think this might have something to do with Benjamin Ruddock."

There was silence on the other end. "You're dancing on a thin wire, Rachel."

"I'm aware of that every second of every day."

"He could just be going to see a girlfriend."

"He doesn't have a girlfriend."

"Are you sure?"

"He's fourteen years old, John."

"I had a girlfriend at fourteen. Two, if I remember right. Carmen Fay and Daisy Strahovski."

"Congratulations to your teenage dick," she said. "But I think I'd know if Eric was seeing someone. Now, are you going to do me a favor or not?"

"There are different levels of favors," Serrano said. "'Can you pass the half-and-half' is level one. 'I'm going to wake you up in the middle of the night so you can put on a pair of pants and then go follow my teenage son around' is level ten."

"I'll make it up to you."

There was a pause. "How so?"

"You were hoping for action, right? Let's just say your level-ten favor is different from mine. And I'll owe you a favor."

There was a pause, then Serrano said, "Let me find those pants."

Serrano threw on a pair of moderately clean jeans and a dark-blue sweatshirt. He turned his phone to silent, got in his car, and clipped his cell to the hands-free mount. It lit up with a text from Rachel.

> Eric just turned left on Foster, approaching Whippoorwill Drive

He enabled the dictation function on his phone and spoke a text back to Rachel.

> On my way

Serrano pulled out and headed south. The intersection of Foster Lane and Whippoorwill Drive was about three and a half miles from his house. Few cars were on the roads at this hour, and Serrano had been at the Marin home enough times that Eric might recognize his silver 2012 Ford Edge. He'd have to be cautious when he got close.

Serrano could understand why Rachel was concerned. Teenagers sneaking out of their parents' homes in the middle of the night was hardly an uncommon occurrence. Hell, when he was a kid and his dad had passed out on the couch surrounded by tall boys, Serrano could have sneaked out and come home with a marching band and his old man wouldn't have noticed. But Eric Marin sneaking out in the middle of the night was different. Especially if it involved Benjamin Ruddock. There was something eating at the boy, and Serrano knew if Rachel couldn't help him, Eric would waste away.

At first, Serrano had been able to crack Eric's hard exterior. He'd seen the boy without his protective shell. They shared a love of fantasy and science fiction, traded well-worn books, spent hours comparing their favorite authors and iconic characters, and debated which films had been most faithful to their source material. (Though they both loved the *Lord of the Rings* films, they agreed J. R. R. Tolkien might have been unnerved by the CGI elephants.)

But the walls had soon gone back up. Getting Eric Marin to crack a smile was like pushing a boulder up a hill coated with Vaseline.

Serrano yawned, lowered the window a crack, and let the cool breeze in. He didn't have time to stop for coffee and had no idea how long this night would last. Anything to keep him awake.

As he approached Whippoorwill, Serrano texted:

Where is he? Don't want to get too close

He stopped

Where

Serrano slowed the car down as the three dots blinked on his cell phone. When the words appeared, his pulse quickened.

Voss Field

The baseball stadium where the Ashby High teams played. Where his own son had once played. John Serrano had terrible memories of Voss Field. He hoped tonight would not add another.

Serrano parked two blocks away from Voss Field and jogged in the shadows toward the stadium. The massive LED lights towering above the field were dark, abandoned sentries keeping watch. When he reached the field, he crept toward the chain-link fence separating the infield from the stands. The moonlight cast a faint glow on the field. Serrano was able to make out around twenty people standing near the pitcher's mound. They were all young. High school age. All boys.

This field held ghastly memories for John Serrano. It was here, almost ten years ago to the day, where he watched a baseball game on a gorgeous spring afternoon, unaware that it would mark the end of his life as he knew it. Within hours, his son would be in a coma from which he would never wake, and two years later the wedding ring he'd promised to wear until the day he died would be tossed in a box and shoved into a twenty-dollar-a-month storage unit alongside other assorted bric-a-brac. The faint white dent circling his ring finger was more painful than any wound he'd ever received on duty.

Serrano felt dizzy. He was looking at a group of boys standing around a baseball field, and in every one of their young faces, he saw a resemblance to his dead son. He knelt down in the gravel and took slow, steadying breaths.

Compartmentalize, he thought. *They're not Evan. They're not Evan.*

He blinked away the image of his son and focused on what was in front of him.

There were nineteen of them, all seemingly between the ages of fourteen and eighteen. High schoolers. Kids. He recognized several of them from the assembly at Ashby High. What the hell were they doing here in the middle of the night?

Then Serrano saw him. Eric Marin, hands in his pockets, eyes downcast as he shifted his weight from side to side. Fidgeting. Nervous.

"So is someone coming or something?" one of the boys asked. "My mom is at her boyfriend's, but she doesn't usually stay the whole night. If I'm not home by five, she's gonna whip my ass."

"Be patient," one of the other young men said. He was short and thin, and his voice did not waver. "He'll be here."

Serrano turned the brightness on his cell phone all the way down, opened the Notes app, and began entering his observations.

19 boys. No girls. Mostly caucasian. All appear to be between the ages of 14–18, but not 100% certain. Eric here. Waiting for someone?

A text came in from Rachel.

What's he doing at Voss Field?

Don't know yet. Will keep you posted.

Make sure he's safe. Let me know what's going on.

I will when I know.

Thank you John.

One of the boys stepped into the middle of the group. He was big and red cheeked, around six one, two-hundred-plus pounds, with both muscle and fat competing for space beneath his sweatshirt. He appeared agitated. He pointed at the short, thin boy who'd told them to be patient.

"Yo, Ronnie, I think this is all a bunch of bullshit. Tell us why we're out here in the middle of the night, or we walk."

Ronnie did not appear fazed. "Take it easy, Darren. He'll explain everything."

"How about you explain it *now*, Ronnie?"

The big kid, Darren, approached Ronnie. He towered over him by a good six inches and outbulked him by a whole third grader. If the situation turned violent, Serrano would have to step in. It would ruin Rachel's desire to keep Eric in the dark, but he couldn't allow blood to be shed. Darren looked like he could squash Ronnie's head like an edamame pod. Serrano had a canister of pepper spray in his pocket and hoped he would not have to use it.

"I'm waiting," Darren said. Ronnie began to shake.

"I told you, he'll be he—"

Darren grabbed Ronnie's wrist and twisted it. The thin kid cried out in pain. Serrano grabbed the pepper spray from his key chain and stood up.

Just then, a voice called out.

"That's enough."

Darren and Ronnie turned. A man of about forty approached the group, having seemingly materialized from nowhere. Another young man walked alongside him. Serrano recognized him immediately. He was bigger than Darren and walked with a controlled swagger. His eyes alone looked like they could win most fights. Benjamin Ruddock. The other boys did not appear to recognize the older man. Ruddock walked around the circle, shaking hands, clapping kids on the back like he was running for mayor. The older man just stood there watching, like an owner proud of his prize racehorse.

Ruddock's companion had silvery hair despite his relatively young age. He was clean shaven, a severe part in his hair, about five foot eleven, maybe 190 pounds. His face was emotionless as he watched the group. Then he stepped into the middle of the circle, and the kids went silent.

Serrano took out his cell phone. He snapped numerous pictures of the silver-haired man, Benjamin Ruddock, and each of the kids in the group. Ruddock continued around the circle, shaking each boy's hand, clapping them on the back. "Glad you're here. You won't regret it."

Ruddock stopped in front of Eric Marin. Eric looked nervously at Ruddock, as though unsure of what to expect. Ruddock raised his right hand and closed it into a fist. Eric instinctively took a step back. Ruddock laughed and held his fist out. Slowly, Eric raised his. Ruddock gave him a fist bump and clapped Eric hard on the back. Serrano saw Eric smile, like he'd been let in on a joke. A chill ran down Serrano's spine.

Serrano texted Rachel:

Benjamin Ruddock here

What's going on?

Don't know yet.

John talk to me.

I will. Patience.

The stranger approached Darren and Ronnie, the larger boy's hand wrapped around the smaller one's wrist like it was a drinking straw.

"Let go of him," the man said to Darren. Darren eyed the man. The man leaned in toward Darren and whispered something that Serrano couldn't hear. Darren's eyes widened, then narrowed. Then he let go of Ronnie's wrist but pushed the smaller boy to the ground. The silver-haired man sighed and shook his head.

"Was that necessary?"

"You need to tell us what the *hell* is going on here," Darren said, "and you need to do it now. We came 'cause your boy Ruddock told us to. Now you need to tell us all why we're out here in the middle of the damn night."

"That's a fair request," the man said. "But one thing I do not tolerate is bullying. Bullying is the sign of a weak mind, and violence is a tool of the simpleminded. In business and in life, you do not get a second chance to make a first impression."

"What does that even mean?" Darren said. The man sighed again, looked at Ruddock, and shook his head sadly. Ruddock nodded and shrugged as if to say, *We gave him a chance.*

The man walked slowly and deliberately around the circle. He stopped in front of Eric, looking him up and down as though sizing the boy up. The man nodded and said something to Eric that sounded like, "I'm glad you came."

Then the man walked into the middle of the circle and spoke to the entire assembled group.

"You're each here because you have been identified as extraordinary young men with tremendous potential. But so far, your potential has remained untapped. Either due to circumstances beyond your control, parental or societal interference, or plain old bad luck. Gentleman, you have been held back."

He let the words sink in. Serrano noticed several of the boys nodding in agreement.

"You have been held back by your parents. Your friends. Your teachers. A culture that has written off young men. Society wants to leave you behind. How do you feel about that?"

The boys murmured.

The man continued. "How many of you have been told you're not good enough? Not smart enough? How many of you have been pushed to the outside, forced to watch as other kids get ahead while you get nothing? You've all been told what to do your whole lives, by selfish people who want to control you because they themselves are afraid of your potential."

Serrano felt a chill as he saw Eric nodding along as well.

"Young, strong, intelligent men like you are being left in the dust. I can give you the tools to ensure you are never left behind again."

The boys were silent. Serrano had a sick feeling in his gut.

Darren broke the silence. "Listen, you whack job. I want to know why you dragged us out of bed in the middle of the night to stand around like assholes to listen to you preach like some second-rate used-car salesman. Who the hell are you, anyway?"

The man's expression didn't change. He approached Darren. The boy had a significant size advantage over the older man and stood his ground.

"Darren Reznick," the man said. "Benjamin told me you had an attitude. He told me you were too volatile, too unreliable, and that we shouldn't have invited you to join us. I disagreed. I told him that your kind of energy, if focused, could make you a valuable asset."

"'Valuable asset.' What does that mean? I'm gonna twist you into a pretzel if you don't speak English," Darren said. "Why. Are. We. Here?"

"Clearly you have proven Mr. Ruddock right," the man said. "Maybe you should not have been invited. All right, everyone. Since Mr. Reznick is so impatient, let me tell you exactly why I'm here and why you're here. My name is Bennett Brice, and I am a simple businessman. That's all I am. Nothing fancy. But I make more money in a month than your parents have made in their lifetimes."

Again, he let his words sink in.

"But I also consider myself a philanthropist," Brice said. "I like to give back to my community. But not by giving my money to organizations that would squander it. I give *opportunities*. But I don't like to work with trust fund babies. I don't give opportunities to people who have had good fortune handed to them. I expect you to *work* for me. Work *with* me. And if you join me and live up to your potential, you can earn a future brighter than you could ever imagine, bigger than your parents could ever provide you, and far more than your so-called friends would ever expect from you."

Brice continued.

"Imagine asking the girl of your dreams to the prom with a glittering diamond necklace that you paid for with your own money. Or maybe the bank is about to foreclose on your parents' home. Imagine paying off their mortgage yourself—or even moving out and buying your own place. Want to go to college? Imagine showing up for your first day of orientation in a brand-new Alfa Romeo 4C Spider, paid for in full. Or maybe you want to run a business. Like me. Imagine having the seed money to start your own firm, to hire people from your own brotherhood. Your fratres."

"What do you mean by opportunities?" one of the boys asked.

Serrano recognized the voice. It came from Eric Marin. Brice turned to Eric and smiled.

"Eric Marin. I've had my eye on you. I'm very, very glad you're here."

Serrano saw Eric puff up his chest slightly, flattered.

"Mr. Ruddock," Brice said, "would you show my friend Eric here what might come of the opportunities I'm referring to?"

Ruddock nodded and walked over to Eric. He lifted his right arm and held it out for Eric to inspect. Even from a distance, Serrano could see the sparkle of metal on Ruddock's wrist. He zoomed in with his phone and took a picture. It was blurry, but there was no doubt Ruddock was wearing a watch that probably cost more than Serrano's monthly take-home. Ruddock walked around the circle, showing off the gaudy accessory. The boys gawked.

"Is it real?" one said.

"Real as my daddy's drinking problem," Ruddock responded. The boys laughed. They were laughing *together*. The whole spectacle gave Serrano an uneasy feeling.

"But it's not all just about the so-called *bling*," Brice said. "When I met Mr. Ruddock, he was directionless. Untalented boys get ahead due to advantages they have at birth. Money. Connections. Mr. Ruddock had no such advantages. I helped him gain that edge. And now Mr. Ruddock is the man every girl wants and every boy envies."

There was a murmur among the boys. They were being swayed by the man's shiny promises and Ruddock's shinier watch. Serrano could smell a con a mile away, but these were impressionable kids. Still, nothing illegal had taken place. All he could do was watch.

"If you'd like to cease being spectators in your own lives, you will start tomorrow as trainees. Just like how medical students will accompany doctors on their rounds to learn the profession. That is what you will be doing after your classes end tomorrow."

"I'm always home by four," one said.

"You are young men," Brice said. "You are not babies. If an afternoon curfew is the obstacle that proves insurmountable, then you will have a slim chance at success in any sort of business or in life."

The boy nodded. "I'll figure it out."

"Good," Brice said. "You will each be paired off with one of my employees, to learn. Mr. Ruddock will assign you one of my trusted men. Members of your fratres. Now, if you decline this opportunity, no hard feelings. I'm sure you'll be very happy changing wiper fluid for the next sixty years. But if you want to become men, all you have to do is choose your destiny."

"How about you just tell us how we go about getting one of your boy's Rolexes," Darren Reznick demanded. "Enough of this cloak-and-dagger crap."

"Mr. Reznick," Brice said, his voice growing irritated. "Part of the reason I'm good at what I do is because *I* know that information is more valuable than money. All will be relayed to you at the appropriate time, and not a moment sooner."

"I've decided this is the appropriate time," Reznick said. "Otherwise I tell everyone in school about this little circle jerk, and we'll see what happens."

Brice nodded at Benjamin Ruddock.

Moving so fast Serrano could barely believe it, Ruddock lunged at Darren Reznick's legs, taking him down to the ground. Reznick was strong and struggled, but Ruddock knew how to fight. Within seconds, Ruddock had Reznick's face in the dirt, his arm pinned behind his back. With every breath Reznick took, dirt blew out from his face in a brownish spray.

"Get the hell off me!" Reznick shouted. Serrano could see the rest of the boys watching the scuffle, their eyes wide, unsure whether to step in. Eric took a step forward but stopped. Ruddock had a wide smile on his face, knowing that no matter how much Reznick struggled, he had the boy at his mercy. Serrano could feel his heart pounding. This was getting out of hand.

"When someone offers you a life-changing opportunity," Ruddock said, twisting Reznick's arm until the boy cried out in pain, "you say *yes*."

Brice simply stood there, his face blank. He did not seem to be taking any enjoyment from the scuffle, but he made no move to stop it.

"Stop, please!" Reznick yelped.

"I will," Ruddock said. "But I invited you here, and this is how you repay me? You need to show a little gratitude, son."

Ruddock twisted Reznick's arm farther back, and the boy screamed. Serrano stood up and walked toward the infield.

"Ashby PD!" he shouted. "Benjamin Ruddock, get off that boy *right now*."

The badge in Serrano's outstretched left hand reflected the moonlight, shining silver in the dark.

Half the boys skittered into the night as soon as they saw Serrano. The other half, including Eric Marin, stood rooted in place.

Benjamin Ruddock turned his head to face Serrano but kept the pressure on Darren Reznick's arm. Dirt caked the boy's face and hair.

"I said get off him, Ruddock," Serrano said. "Detective John Serrano. APD."

"You gonna shoot me, cop?" Ruddock said as the detective approached.

"You have until the count of three," Serrano said, standing over Ruddock. "One . . ."

"Twothree," Ruddock said, quickly, with a smile.

"I wasn't bluffing," Serrano said. Before Ruddock knew what was happening, Serrano shot a stream of pepper spray into the boy's face. Ruddock rolled off Reznick, coughing and clawing at his face. Reznick leaped up, holding his tender arm.

"I had that under control," Reznick said.

"Sure you did," Serrano said. He looked down at Ruddock, panting in the dirt.

"Don't rub your eyes. You'll just make it worse," Serrano said.

"You're way out of line, Officer," Brice said, his voice even.

"It's Detective," Serrano said.

"There's no crime here, *Detective*. All these men are here of their own volition."

"I don't see men. I see kids. You're the only one I'd call a man. And there's a name for the kind of man who hangs around young boys in the middle of the night."

"Call me all the names you want, Detective, if it makes you feel good. But there is still *no crime*. And given that you're a detective, you're not here responding to a 911 call. Which means . . . what—you just happened to be in the area?"

Serrano ignored the question.

"Assault is a crime," Serrano said.

"There was no assault," the man replied. "These were just boys having a tussle. There are no broken bones. No torn ligaments. Nothing happened that an ice pack can't cure. For that, you shot pepper spray point blank into the face of a high schooler. I'm sure your lieutenant will love to hear about this."

"That high schooler could break you over his knee," Serrano said. "I'm going to need to see some identification."

"By all means," the man said. He took out his wallet, removed a business card, and handed it to Serrano.

Serrano kept an eye on Ruddock and scanned the card. It was plain white with black lettering. It read, simply:

Bennett Brice

YourLife

For a Better Life

There was no phone number or email.

"I'm going to need your contact information," Serrano said.

"I'm afraid you don't have the right to ask me for that," Brice said. "As I pointed out, no crime has been committed here, though I'm sure Mr. Ruddock's parents and legal counsel may claim you violated his rights with that vicious and unprovoked assault. I have no doubt, as an officer of the law with all the resources afforded you, you can find out everything you wish to know about me via legal means. But you cannot demand that I provide you with it. And if you press, I have lawyers who would make the devil himself piss his pants."

Serrano laughed. "You're a piece of work, Brice. And you're right. I'm going to know everything about you before you've had your morning coffee."

"I assure you, Detective, any efforts to discredit me will be a complete waste of your time."

"Yeah . . . let's just say after this little *Children of the Corn* performance, I think I trust your assurances as far as I can throw this stadium."

Brice laughed dismissively. "Have a good night, Detective. If you contact me for any reason other than to apologize for your abhorrent behavior tonight, you'll be hearing from my attorneys." Then Brice addressed the boys. "I'm afraid we will have to end tonight prematurely due to the authorities. As usual, overstepping their bounds and trampling on our freedoms. I look forward to seeing you all again soon. Have a good night, gentlemen."

Brice walked off the field.

The rest of the boys eyed Serrano warily, then began to depart. Benjamin Ruddock had gotten to his knees. His eyes were red and watery. He spat at Serrano's feet, got up, and walked away.

Serrano offered Darren Reznick his hand. Reznick looked at it, shook his head, and got to his feet.

"No need to thank me," Serrano said sarcastically. Reznick had been a hair away from having his rotator cuff ripped to shreds, but a cop having to save his shoulder from permanent damage had likely bruised his ego worse than his joints. Reznick walked off without giving Serrano as much as a second glance.

Then Serrano saw Eric standing to the side of the pitcher's mound. He was holding back tears, his face twisted into a look of pure hatred and shame that made Serrano's blood run cold. He could see anger, confusion, and worst of all, humiliation. But not at the hands of Bennett Brice. At the hands of John Serrano. Eric knew Serrano was there to follow him. And that Eric's own mother had sent a cop to spy on her son.

Before Serrano could say anything, Eric Marin ran off into the darkness.

CHAPTER 19

Rachel stared at her cell phone. It was nine o'clock in the morning. Both children had already left for school. Megan had woken up her usual cheery self. She was almost finished with the first draft of a new Sadie Scout book. She wanted Rachel and Eric to read it and critique it (i.e., tell her how much they loved it) when they got home. Rachel told her there was nothing in the world she would rather do, and she meant it. And her brother would read it when he got the chance, she said—school has just been so busy—but she knew the hesitation in her voice would let Megan know her brother would not be diving into Sadie's adventures anytime soon.

"That's OK," Megan said. "I don't care if he reads it or not. I still love him."

The first part, Rachel knew, was not true. The second, she knew, was. But it broke her heart that Megan couldn't have both.

Rachel had not slept. She'd seen Eric climb back through his window at 3:13 a.m. She'd gone to his door, hand ready to knock, but realized she did not know what to say. Should she be angry that he'd left? Thankful that he hadn't been hurt? Both? In the end, she'd decided to let him sleep, though she lay awake staring at the ceiling, wondering what kind of mother she had become. Since her husband's murder, Rachel had dedicated her life to controlling and protecting her family in every conceivable aspect. But when it came to the most important part of her life, her children, she felt like she was failing.

Eric had left for school without saying a word. Rachel's "I love you; let's talk when we get home" went ignored. She watched him go, a lump climbing her throat. She went back into her house and sat at the dining room table, not remembering the last time she'd felt so alone.

Megan's new Sadie Scout pages sat on the dining room table, next to the case file on the Matthew Linklater murder. One set of pages had sprung from the boundless imagination of her daughter. The other contained nearly unimaginable horrors. Rachel felt like this had become her life: wonder adjacent to evil.

She had begun to page through the Linklater file when she received a text from John Serrano.

We need to talk. About Eric and last night. Come to the precinct at 10am.

Rachel took a quick shower before throwing on a pair of jeans, a white T-shirt, and a lightweight leather jacket. She then drove to the police station, showed her ID to the desk officer, and headed to the detective bureau. Detectives Serrano and Tally were sitting at their respective cubicles. They were having a conversation but stopped when they saw Rachel.

"Oh, don't you dare do that," Rachel said.

"Do what?" Serrano said, looking puzzled.

"That thing where you're talking about someone behind their back but then see them and pretend you weren't. Spit it out."

Tally replied, "Rachel, we weren't talking about you."

"Bull," she said. "I would never lay a finger on you, Detective Tally, but I will choke my so-called boyfriend out quicker than you can blow out a match if you don't start talking."

Serrano looked at his partner. She shrugged.

Tally said, "We were talking about how last night Claire tried to have the talk—you know, the sex talk—with Penny, and Penny bolted from the room so fast you'd think she'd joined the track team, then spent the rest of the night blasting music so loud I'm pretty sure they could feel the bass in Beijing."

"But, you know, keep on assuming we were talking about you," Serrano said.

Rachel felt her cheeks flush.

"I'm sorry. It's been a morning."

"I'll bet," Serrano said. "Last night was a night."

Rachel said, "What happened at Voss Field, John? What happened to my son?"

Tally pulled a chair over for Rachel and said, "Sit."

She did. "OK. Now talk."

Serrano said, "Does the name Bennett Brice mean anything to you?"

Rachel shook her head. "No. Should it?"

Tally opened up a tab on her computer. On the screen was a professional-looking photograph of a man in his early forties with silvery hair and an attractive, easy smile. He wore a sharp gray suit, and his gleaming white teeth were either expensive veneers or had never been sullied by a drop of coffee or puff of tobacco.

Rachel said, "Who is he?"

"Bennett Brice. President and CEO of a company called YourLife. He lives in a seven-bedroom, six-bathroom house in a gated community on Randolph Lane that he purchased for seven-point-two million dollars five years ago."

"Well, good for him. What does that have to do with my son?"

"Last night, at Voss Field," Serrano said, "there were nineteen young men. All high schoolers. Some are current students at Ashby High—I recognized them from the assembly following Matthew Linklater's death, but some I'm guessing attend nearby schools as well."

"OK," Rachel said. "And?"

Serrano said, "Eric was there because he'd been recruited by Benjamin Ruddock."

"Recruited? For what?"

Tally replied, "YourLife is, for lack of a better term, a legal Ponzi scheme. There are companies like it all over the country. They sell everything you could possibly imagine. People at the top, like Brice, recruit others to work as 'captains.' They then recruit teams to work below them. Think about it like Girl Scout cookies, only instead of cookies, they're selling top-of-the-line kitchen ranges, stereo equipment, even cars. One person can have as many as a dozen 'teams' under them, and for every product the team sells, the person at the top gets a cut."

"Sounds like the mob," Rachel said.

"If the mob sold fifty-inch plasmas and laundry detergent, then yes," Serrano said. "The idea is that the person at the top fronts the money to purchase the goods. The captains take a cut of the markup, then pass the rest up top. Brice buys his products wholesale. All those teams sell them at retail, or even a little less, since they don't have to deal with distribution or warehousing. And that red meat profit between the wholesale and retail is split between the teams and the people at the top. Like Brice."

"OK, I get the business model. But why was my son there last night?"

"Presumably, Eric was one of the young men recruited to join one of Brice's teams. To work for YourLife."

"That cannot be legal," Rachel said.

Tally replied, "Unfortunately, as long as the goods being sold have been purchased legally, and Brice obeys child labor laws and pays taxes, he's not breaking any laws."

"But Eric was there in the middle of the night," Rachel said.

Serrano nodded. "Also not illegal. Sketchy? Sure. But Eric didn't appear to be coerced or threatened into being there. No money exchanged hands. Brice didn't even formally make an offer for any of the boys to work for him. It was more of a sales pitch."

"Did it work?" Rachel said.

"Benjamin Ruddock showed off a watch that looked like it cost more than my car," Serrano said. "If I'm a stupid young kid, I'd pull my intestines out through my mouth to get to have one of those."

"Stupid young kids?" Rachel said.

"Bad choice of words," Serrano said. "Impressionable. Malleable. Vulnerable. Brice said if the kids want in, their training starts today."

"And Benjamin Ruddock was there too," she said. "Why?"

"Ruddock seems to be Brice's link to the kids. Brice can't recruit in the schools himself, so he gets guys like Ruddock to recruit for him."

"It's likely that Brice has kids like Ruddock recruiting in other local schools as well," Tally said.

"You're telling me," Rachel said, "that the kid who's a person of interest in Matthew Linklater's murder is recruiting my son to join some shady business venture?"

Serrano nodded.

"Did he see you last night? Did he know you were following him?"

Serrano nodded. "I had no choice. Two of the kids started to mix it up, and one of them could have been seriously hurt. I had to stop it before it got bad."

Rachel said, "You just told me this asshole Brice was on the up-and-up. Now you're telling me there was violence last night?"

Serrano said, "Brice wasn't personally involved in the altercation. It was between another boy and Benjamin Ruddock."

"This same Benjamin Ruddock who might be involved in the murder of his own teacher and also recruited my son into this . . . cult."

Serrano nodded. "The same one."

"Well, this is a *fantastic* start to my day. Thank you, Detectives. I don't care if it's not five o'clock here yet. I need a drink."

"Rachel, you need to talk to your son," Tally said. "We were able to use the photos Detective Serrano took last night to identify some of the other boys who were there. Most of these kids come from troubled homes. They've either been suspended or have warnings in their student files, and a few have even had social services step in due to suspected physical or emotional abuse."

"What are you saying, Detective?" Rachel said, her eyes narrowing.

Serrano said, "Brice preys on troubled kids. Kids who are susceptible. Kids he can manipulate. Kids looking for an outlet. They're very specific about who they've targeted and why they're only targeting young men. There's a reason they went after Eric. We both know the trauma he's experienced."

"You're saying Bennett Brice exploits young kids like my son because they're . . . unhappy?"

"Not necessarily unhappy. Vulnerable. More susceptible to emotional manipulation," Tally said.

Rachel thought about what Evie Boggs had said.

I'm the good cop in this story. You don't want to meet the bad cops.

Eric hadn't been recruited by Ruddock and Brice just because he was vulnerable. He was recruited to keep Rachel in line.

Rachel stood up. "I appreciate you doing me a favor last night," she said to Serrano. She turned to leave.

"Where are you going?" Serrano asked. Rachel said nothing. "Don't even think about it. As far as we know, he hasn't broken any laws. We're working on this, Rachel. Don't get in the way. You're not a cop."

"I'm not going as a cop," Rachel said. "I'm going to see Bennett Brice as a mother."

CHAPTER 20

Eric Marin got off the bus with a swarm of confusion and anger clouding his mind. He hated that his mother had sent her cop boyfriend to watch him, like some puppy who couldn't be trusted off his leash. He couldn't shake the image of John Serrano walking out of the darkness, holding up his badge. When Eric's eyes had met Serrano's, they'd exchanged a knowing look; they both knew why Serrano was there.

He thought about what Bennett Brice had said. *Opportunity.* Opportunity had never presented itself to Eric Marin. It evaporated the day he found his father butchered on their doorstep. So why shouldn't he see what Brice and Benjamin Ruddock had to offer? It wasn't even about the watch. It was about pride. Eric couldn't remember the last time he'd truly felt like he'd accomplished something. If his mother could be so proud of those stupid little books his sister wrote, Eric would give her something else to be proud of, whether she approved or not.

Then he saw Penny Wallace, and the anger dissipated like steam.

Her dark hair was tied up in a topknot, and she wore a crisp white-collared shirt over a black skirt. She was talking to Amanda Dubuque, and they were laughing about something. Then Penny saw Eric, and her smile widened. He could read her lips as she said to Amanda, "Catch you later." She wanted to talk to *him*.

Penny walked over to Eric with a quickness in her step that made his heart feel like it might burst from his chest and go skipping across the parking lot.

A thousand words raced through his head as she approached. Things he wanted to say. Things he desperately wanted to *avoid* saying. And when she stopped in front of him, the only thing that came out of his mouth, thankfully, was, "Hey, Penny."

"Hey, Eric." She examined his eyes. "You look like you haven't slept in a decade."

"Long night," he said.

"I know. I was up super late studying for Ms. Jenkins's algebra quiz. You too?"

"Yeah. Up late studying."

"Well, aren't we talkative this morning?" she said.

He heard a tapping sound, looked down, and saw her tapping the heel of one shoe with the toe of another. Was she . . . nervous? Were those same thoughts and feelings speeding through her mind as they were his, a locomotive of unsaid words tumbling through Penny's head like a double-decker bus going ninety down a steep hill?

"Her quizzes are no joke," Penny said. "I don't think she got the memo that quizzes and tests are *not* the same thing."

"I know, right?"

"Right."

Penny laughed. It was nervous but genuine. He knew Penny was averaging an A minus in algebra (Eric was holding a steady B plus). Penny wasn't one to sing her own praises, but whenever Eric's family had dinner with the Wallaces, every time there was a lull in the conversation, Claire would boast about the accolades her daughter was racking up. Her mom probably thought that college admissions offices were listening in, Penny joked, but given what Eric knew about his own mother, he wondered if Penny might be serious.

"What time did you go to sleep?" she asked.

"I don't know. Eleven? Midnight? What about you?"

"Twelve thirty."

"Wow. That's late."

Eric remembered checking his cell phone when he got home from Voss Field. It read 3:13 a.m. He hadn't slept in over twenty-four hours and had completely forgotten that they even had an algebra quiz today. He'd read the material and was reasonably sure he could wing it.

"How are your mom and sis?" Penny asked.

"They're OK. Megan is writing these little books. Adventure stories. About a kid named Sadie Scout who solves mysteries and jumps over crocodiles."

"Your kid sister is writing books?" she said. "That's so cool. We can't get Elyse to read anything longer than a tweet."

Eric laughed. "I read a couple of her books. They're OK, I guess."

Penny gave a sly smile. "You're her brother. Saying they're 'OK' probably means they're awesome. She should try to get them published. You and your mom are, like, geniuses. I bet you could help her."

"I doubt it," he said. "Maybe I'm not as smart as you think."

"Don't put yourself down," Penny said, the lightness leaving her voice. "You're better than that."

"Am I?"

She paused, then said, "Are you OK? You don't return my texts, and now you're acting like if you say more than two words, you're going to get expelled."

"I'm sorry," Eric said. "My head . . . it's just overstuffed right now."

"Like a mushroom," she said with a smile.

"Like a mushroom," he replied.

"I have an idea," Penny said. "We have Ms. Jenkins's final exam coming up. I'm fuzzy on chapters thirteen to sixteen. We can go over them together. Unless, you know, you're fully prepped for it."

Study partner. Study partner. Is she asking me to be her study partner? Is that even a thing these days?

His mouth dried up. But he felt his head nodding as if it had a life of its own.

"I'd like that," Eric croaked. Penny smiled. He wanted to reach out and take her hand. Gently. And just go off with her to talk. Tell her about everything. His father. His mother. Last night. How his childhood had been ripped from him, the wounds still bleeding. How he felt trapped in his own life. He saw Penny's pinkie finger twitch and wanted to jump inside her head, read her thoughts, know everything she wanted to say but did not.

"When . . . ," she began.

"Tomorrow? After school?"

Penny smiled. "It's a study date."

Before Eric could reply, he heard a deep voice say, "Pretty sure my man here has plans."

Suddenly there was an arm around Eric's shoulder. A big beefy arm thicker than his neck. He knew without looking that it was Benjamin Ruddock.

"Sleep well?" Ruddock said, jovially.

"Not particularly," Eric said.

"Excuse us," Penny said, "but we were in the middle of a conversation."

"I know. Sincere apologies for my rudeness," Ruddock said. "Just let me borrow my boy here for a minute, and you can get right back to it."

"I'm nobody's boy," Eric said.

"Only a figure of speech," Ruddock said. "But you're right. You're nobody's boy. Penny, let me borrow my friend here for a minute."

Penny turned to Eric, waiting for him to respond.

"Penny . . . ," Eric said.

"It's all right," Ruddock said. "She'll be here when we're done. Right, Penny?"

"Maybe," she said. "Maybe not."

"Ooh, keeping us in suspense. I like a girl who likes some mystery. I promise, Ms. Wallace, he'll catch up with you soon."

"It's OK, Penny," Eric said. "I'll text you."

Penny nodded, sadly, and walked away.

Eric watched her enter the school. Then he turned to Ruddock. "What the hell, man?"

Ruddock held out his hands in an apologetic gesture. "Whoa, calm down. I just wanted to see if you'd given any thought to last night."

"I've given it a *lot* of thought," Eric said.

"And?"

"And I need to know more before I say yes."

"All right," Ruddock said. He held out his wrist. Eric's eyes widened. "This, my friend, is an Omega. Cost a little over five grand. It was a birthday present to myself for my eighteenth birthday."

"Holy crap," Eric said.

"I know your mom isn't broke ass like my dad. You live in a nice place."

"How do you know that?"

"Me and Mr. Brice, we do our homework. We don't invite people into our fratres unless we know how they are, inside and out. I bet your mom tells you what you can and can't buy. When you can and can't leave the house. She has you on a leash. Am I right?"

Eric said nothing.

"If you want to be able to make your own rules, buy what you want, go *where* you want, then say yes. If you want to wear a collar the rest of your life, the school is right there. We won't ever have to talk again."

Eric looked back at the school.

Ruddock seemed to know what he was thinking. "Penny Wallace is a hell of a girl. Smart *and* pretty. That kind of girl wants to be with somebody who's a *somebody*."

Eric knew that Ruddock was selling him. But at the same time, everything he said made sense. He thought about how many restrictions his mother had placed on him over the years. Without even asking how he felt about them. How their house felt like a gilded cage. Eric knew what his mother had been through. But that didn't give her the right to treat Eric like an egg she had to carry in a blanket to keep it from cracking. He was smart. He was ambitious. And if Benjamin Ruddock and Bennett Brice were a means to an end, so be it.

"Let's do it," Eric said.

Ruddock smiled. "You won't be sorry."

Eric took out his phone and texted his mother:

Home late

Seconds later, she wrote back:

Where will you be?

Eric did not respond. He put the phone back into his pocket, and he and Ruddock walked toward the school entrance.

Just then, Eric heard an anguished scream of pain and a snapping sound like a tree branch breaking. He turned to see a guy wearing an Ashby High shirt writhing around on the asphalt by the school buses, his face a mask of agony. Two people wearing Michael Myers Halloween masks were sprinting across the road, a backpack swinging from one of their arms. The guy's voice. Eric could swear he recognized the injured kid's voice.

"They stole his bag!" a girl yelled. Eric could see the two husky school security guards—who didn't look like they could catch a dough-nut if it rolled off a table—shuffling after the assailants. But they'd disappeared into the nearby woods before the rotund guards had made it ten feet in the direction of the injured boy.

"Did anybody see anything?" one of the guards huffed, hands on his knees, trying to catch his breath from the ten-yard dash.

A girl wearing a red shirt and black skirt was kneeling next to the boy. She held his head in her arms, trying to calm him. She said, "Those assholes just came out of nowhere and threw him to the ground. One of them held him down while the other one grabbed his bag. They twisted his arm. *Hard.* They didn't need to. They already had his bag. I think it's broken."

That was the snapping sound, Eric thought. *Not a tree branch. His arm.* The boy was holding his wrist, howling in pain. One of the guards was speaking into a radio. At least a dozen kids were dialing 911. Several were recording the aftermath on their cell phones. Then the boy rolled over. Eric saw his face. A wave of nausea rose from the pit of his stomach into his throat. The injured boy was Darren Reznick.

Eric turned to Benjamin Ruddock. The boy shrugged.

"Hate to see such nice guys get hurt," he said. "See you after school, Marin."

CHAPTER 21

Rachel ignored the calls from John Serrano. Her phone was snapped into a hands-free mount on her dashboard, and every time the screen showed an incoming call from *Detective John Serrano*, she grew irritated. It occurred to her that in the months since she had first met John Serrano, when he was the investigating officer on Constance Wright's death, she had never bothered to change the ID on her phone, even when they began dating. It was not "John Serrano," or even "John." He was still listed as "Detective John Serrano."

Serrano had shared meals with her, shared laughs and tears with her, watched movies with her children, slept in her bed, and touched her in ways she had missed and longed for. But he was still "Detective John Serrano." Rachel wondered if that meant something.

The YourLife headquarters was in downtown Ashby, a twenty-minute drive from the station. Bumper-to-bumper traffic doubled that time, and all the while Rachel was barely able to contain the sparks of rage glowing hot within her. She wasn't sure if she wanted an explanation from Bennett Brice or an apology, or if she simply wanted to toss him out a window into oncoming traffic.

The YourLife office was in a commercial office complex off Pimpernel Road. She pushed through the glass doors and entered an atrium with the letters *YL* spotlighted on polished black tiles that covered the floor. A man of about twenty-five sat behind a sleek marble security desk. He wore a gray suit and had slicked-back blond hair and a clean-shaven face. Reddish razor burn poked out above his shirt collar.

He smiled at Rachel and said, "Welcome to YourLife, where we help you find your best life. What can I do for you?"

Rachel strode to the desk with a purpose.

"I'm here to see Bennett Brice."

"Your name?"

"His head shoved so far up his ass he'll be able to pick his nose with his incisors."

"I'm . . . sorry?"

"That's what Bennett Brice is going to get if he doesn't come out of his hole right now."

The young man's mouth moved, but no words came out. Rachel took a breath.

"I'm sorry. This has just been . . . a morning. Tell Mr. Brice that Rachel Marin, Eric Marin's mother, is here to see him."

The young man nodded, seemingly relieved that he didn't have to relay Rachel's first answer. He picked up the desk phone and dialed. "There's a Rachel Marin here to see Mr. Brice." He nodded, then hung up and said, "One moment."

Thirty seconds later another young man entered the lobby. He was about six feet tall, solidly built, in his late twenties, wearing a smile that had been practiced in a mirror.

"Ms. Marin," he said, his voice pleasantly condescending. "We're so happy you're here. Mr. Brice will see you now."

Rachel looked at the new guy, then back at the other. "Is this like a Stepford Boy recruitment center?"

Neither one responded. The one at the desk looked hurt. The one who'd just come in continued to smirk.

"This way, ma'am," the new one said.

"After you, Abercrombie."

Abercrombie led Rachel through the door into a waiting room, then went back behind his desk. Abercrombie was obviously Bennett

Brice's secretary. Abercrombie pressed a button, and a pair of frosted-glass double doors opened. He motioned for Rachel to enter.

"Mr. Bennett Brice," he said.

"Thanks, kid. Now you can go back to modeling sweaters."

Rachel stepped into Brice's office. Abercrombie closed the doors behind her.

"Ms. Marin. Thank you for stopping by."

Bennett Brice sat in the center of a massive U-shaped granite desk. The desktop was lined with computer monitors, a phone, and several metal in-boxes with papers neatly stacked in each. There were no photo frames, no personal touches. Behind Brice, a massive *YL* was etched on the light-gray-painted wall in three-dimensional cursive, the lines of the *Y* and *L* seeming to wrap and dance around each other: solid yet playful. It was a sleek, modern office, but to Rachel it felt empty and soulless.

Brice stood up and said, "Ms. Marin. Please. Have a seat."

There were two black leather chairs in front of Brice's desk. Rachel walked up to the desk but did not sit.

"I'm fine like this," she said.

"Can I get you anything? Water? Coffee? A morning aperitif?"

She ignored the question and said, "You will never speak to my son again."

Brice's brow furrowed. He looked hurt, but fake hurt.

"Now why would you say that? I barely know Eric."

"So then never speaking to him again should have very little effect on the rest of your life. And that's the last time I ever want to hear his name come from your lips."

Brice stood up and walked around to the other side of the desk. He took a seat on the edge and crossed his arms. His movements were effortless, like he was gliding on ice.

"You're right," Brice said. "If I never spoke to Eric again, my years would continue unabated. But what effect would it have on *his* life?"

"What effect would never seeing you again have on his life? About the same as if I told him he would no longer be able to turn water into grape soda. Absolutely none."

"I don't believe that's true. I think it would negatively affect him tremendously."

"You think awfully highly of yourself."

"It's not about me, Ms. Marin. It's about Eric. If I were to vanish today—"

"I'd be a happy woman," Rachel interrupted.

Brice sighed dismissively. "If I were to vanish today, Eric would lose the greatest opportunity of his life."

"Oh, is that so?"

"That is so. I've given many young men just like Eric incredible chances. Chances to earn self-respect. Chances to earn pride."

"And money."

"Money only comes with the attainment of both confidence and ambition. I can help him attain both."

"That's *my* job," Rachel said.

"Is it? I think you're overdue for a performance review, then."

It took all of Rachel's willpower not to grab Bennett Brice by his fashionable blue tie and strangle him with it. She took a deep breath.

"My son is not for sale," she said.

"I haven't bought your son, or anybody else, for that matter. I pay competitive wages based on performance. Nothing more. My employees are not expected to give anything more than their time and effort. And they can walk away whenever they like. That certainly doesn't sound like I 'own' anybody, does it?"

"So what would you call gathering a whole bunch of teenagers together in the middle of the night?" she said, voice rising.

"A test of commitment," Brice replied curtly. "The most successful young men all have one thing in common: sacrifice and commitment.

The ones who made it their mission to be there last night are the ones who seem willing to offer both."

"Why all men? Why no women? Let me guess: young girls are smart enough to not go near you."

"On the contrary," Brice said. "My office fields a dozen calls from prospective female employees every single day. Brilliant, talented young women. But one thing I've learned in this troubled day and age is that young men feel like they're missing something—or that something has been taken away from them. Their needs are not being met. They are being emasculated. Lobotomized. I give them a chance to reclaim their pride, to embrace their natural ambitions and abilities."

"I'm sure the Better Business Bureau would love to know about this gender parity."

"Don't even try to threaten me, Ms. Marin. All our workers are considered independent contractors, from a legal perspective. We are not subject to the same scrutiny as, say, the police department where your boyfriend works."

Rachel's breath left her. "How do you . . ."

"I'm in the relationship business, Ms. Marin. I have relationships with my customers as well as my employees. And if you don't know everything about the people you're in a relationship with, you're as good as dead. I knew everything about you before I ever met your son."

"Not *everything*," Rachel said. "I'm warning you. Stay the hell away from my family."

"Or what?" Brice replied. "You'll strangle me in the snow? You crushed a man's larynx. Nearly killed him. I heard he even had to petition the courts to be allowed to use a voice box in prison."

"He deserved every ounce of pain he got," Rachel said.

"And do I *deserve* it, Ms. Marin? To be strangled in the cold dirt?"

"I haven't known you for very long. I'll let you know."

"You've got a sharp sense of humor. I bet Eric appreciates that."

"I'm only going to say it one more time, Mr. Brice. Don't speak to my son again."

"And I'm only going to say it one more time, Ms. Marin. My company is legitimate. We pay wages and report our revenues to the IRS. Our workers *choose* to be employed by us."

"I can assure you my son doesn't want anything to do with you."

Brice nodded, looking skeptical. "Maybe you should let him decide that. Or you can decide for him and see how well that goes. I'm not a psychologist, Ms. Marin, but I don't think troubled young men respond well to being given orders."

"My son is not troubled."

"Then maybe I just know your son better than you do."

Rachel took a step toward Brice. He flinched slightly but remained seated on the edge of the desk.

"If so much as your breath touches me," he said, "I will have you arrested and prosecuted to the fullest extent of the law. My lawyers get paid a retainer larger than the down payment on that three-bedroom house you own."

Rachel took a step back.

"Everything I know about you is in the public record," Brice said. "You purchased that house several years ago, and given the market, I'd bet it's gone up in value. But it's strange . . . I cannot find any records of a 'Rachel Marin' from any time before you moved to Ashby. I have a feeling *you're* the one hiding something, Ms. Marin. You should be far more frightened than I am about the truth coming out."

"The only thing I'm hiding is how badly I want to beat you half to death with your keyboard."

"Charming. Now I think it's time for you to leave, Ms. Marin; otherwise I will call security. Everything in this office is being videotaped as we speak. You are the aggressor here. Not me. I have evidence of you threatening an innocent man in his place of business. Something tells me you wouldn't want to see your face and name all over the evening news."

Rachel looked around the room. She'd been in such a rush, her vision so colored by anger, that she had not cataloged her surroundings like she usually did. Of course Brice had cameras. How could she have been so stupid?

"Just stay away from us," Rachel said.

"I will ask the same of you," Brice said. "Now please leave, Ms. Marin. Oh, and say hello to Eric for me. He's a fine young man with limitless potential."

Rachel could feel the blood pounding in her temples. She merely pointed at Brice, an empty gesture, and went to leave his office. He knew too much. She'd been caught off guard, her anger getting the best of her. Her threats were baseless, and he knew it. She needed to learn everything there was to know about Bennett Brice, and she needed to know it *now*.

Just before Rachel reached the office door, it swung inward.

"Your noon appointment is here," Abercrombie said.

"Show her in," Brice replied.

Abercrombie stepped to the side. Brice's next appointment entered the office. Rachel's mouth opened, and she took in a sharp breath. She felt an ache in her head but couldn't tell if it was real or imagined.

"We have to stop meeting like this," said Evie Boggs.

CHAPTER 22

When Rachel exited the YourLife offices, two things greeted her. She was not pleased to see either one.

The first was a blaring, intense yellow sun that pierced her eyes like needles, making it feel like her skull had been squeezed inside an iron maiden.

The second was the sight of John Serrano getting out of his Crown Victoria with a look on his face that said they were probably not going to fool around that night, or any night in the near future.

He opened his mouth to speak, but before a word came out, Rachel said, "I don't want to hear it."

"Tough," he said. "Because you're going to."

She didn't need to ask Serrano how he'd found her. They both knew where she was headed when she left the precinct.

"Eric is my son," Rachel said, putting on a pair of sunglasses. "There's only one person who gets to decide how to raise him, and it's not you."

"I would never tell you how to parent, Rach. And I care about Eric too. You know I do. But as of right now, the worst thing Bennett Brice has done is chat with some kids at a baseball field well past their bedtime. Trust me, if I told you some of the things I did on that field past my bedtime, you wouldn't think what Eric did was so bad."

"Eric wasn't just there hanging out with some friends, smoking a joint or drinking some beers or making out with some poor chick who doesn't realize I'd be the mother-in-law from hell. Brice is exploiting these kids."

"It's not exploitation if it's legal," Serrano said.

"Legal as far as you know," Rachel replied.

Serrano nodded. "As far as we know."

"Well, I can't take the chance that 'as far as we know' isn't actually as far as it goes."

"I understand that. But right now, Bennett Brice is not a suspect in any crimes and as far as we know has nothing to do with the murder of Matthew Linklater."

"There you go again with the 'as far as we knows.'"

Serrano said nothing.

"Benjamin Ruddock is a person of interest. Ruddock was there last night. *My son* was out in the middle of the night with a boy who may have tortured a man to death."

"Easy, Rachel," Serrano said. "We have no proof that Ruddock was actually involved in Linklater's death."

"But we don't know he wasn't. And Ruddock is intertwined with Bennett Brice. Which at the very least makes Brice tangentially involved in Matthew Linklater's death."

"Careful. That's a lot of hearsay. You don't do your best thinking when you're angry, Rach."

"Actually, I do my best thinking when I'm angry."

Serrano stepped forward and took Rachel's hand. She hesitated but gripped it back. He leaned down and kissed her gently on the lips. A warmth spread through her. She pressed back on him, her hands finding his waist.

"That's not fair," she said. "Cops aren't supposed to be good kissers."

"I was born with a gift," Serrano said.

Rachel took a step back. "Let me ask you something," she said. "Does the name Evelyn Boggs, or Evie Boggs, mean anything to you?"

Serrano said, "No. Should it?"

"How about Myra?"

"Myra what?"

"There's no last name. It's an alias. Can you do me a favor? Run the name Evelyn Boggs through the criminal records database. She has, or had, a residence in Connecticut, possibly in or near Torrington."

"You want to tell me why?"

Rachel looked back at the YourLife office. She remembered what Brice had said about the recording devices.

"Not here," she said.

"All right. I'll call Tally and see what she can dig up for us while we head back."

"Thanks, John."

They got into their separate cars and drove back to APD. Tally met them outside.

"I'd have an easier time training a squirrel to salsa than training you not to make terrible impromptu decisions," Tally said to Rachel. "So, has Bennett Brice filed any complaints against Ms. Marin yet for trespassing?"

"We just left Brice's office. Give it half an hour," Serrano said dryly.

Tally nodded, obviously finding no humor in the conversation, then said to Rachel, "One of these days you're going to go after the wrong person the wrong way and make a mess that even we won't be able to clean up."

"Good thing I'm handy with a broom," Rachel said.

"I hope it's some magical Harry Potter–ass broom that can sweep away lawsuits and criminal complaints. Because if Bennett Brice makes a stink to the right people—or wrong people, in your case—it's going to be harder for the department to justify keeping you on the payroll."

"I don't need the money," Rachel replied.

"That's not the point, and you know it."

"Let's get back to what's important here," Serrano said, playing peacemaker. "Leslie, what did you find on Evelyn Boggs?"

Tally showed Rachel a printout with a photograph of Evie Boggs in the upper-right-hand corner. "That her?"

"Yup," Rachel said. "That's her."

Rachel took the page from the detective. It was an arrest report. Dated five years ago. Which was a little over two years after Rachel had met Evie Boggs. The report had been filed in Litchfield County in Connecticut, charging Evelyn Marie Boggs with one count of felonious assault, one count of trespassing, and one count of possession of a deadly weapon, which was noted in the report as a folding pocketknife. Rachel read the report.

On the night of October 12, five years ago, Evie Boggs had gone to the Bethlehem home of a man named Raymond Spivak. Bethlehem, Rachel noted, was just a few towns over from Torrington.

When Spivak answered the door, Boggs apparently threatened him with the folding knife. Spivak locked himself inside his bedroom. He then made two phone calls: first, to his brother, Randall Spivak. The second to 911. When the responding officers arrived, Boggs was sitting in Spivak's kitchen, sipping a mug of peppermint tea. Evie was taken into custody and booked at the Torrington Police Department on Main Street.

A photo of the "victim," Raymond Spivak, accompanied the report. He was big and bald, with a thick neck and thicker eyebrows, and given the size of his shoulders looked like he could pry the door off a car.

"Evie Boggs showed up at *this* guy's home and threatened to filet him," Tally said. "He looks like a rhino, only less cuddly. Why the hell would he be scared of her?"

"You don't know Evie Boggs," Rachel said. "Besides, rhinos don't move all that fast, and a good knife cuts through muscle quite nicely."

"I don't want to know how you know that," Tally said.

Rachel pointed at the report. "It says that all charges against Evie Boggs were dropped. Why?"

"That, I don't know," Tally said. "I can contact Torrington PD to find out."

"Great," Rachel said.

"But I won't."

Rachel blinked. "Come again?"

"I said I won't," Tally replied. "Unless you tell me what this is all about and what your relationship is to Evelyn Boggs. Otherwise I have enough on my plate with the Linklater murder to be doing you blind favors. And I'm sure Torrington PD has things they'd rather be doing than to go digging into half-decade-old arrests that led to no convictions."

Rachel said, "I know Evie Boggs. She came to my home the other day and threatened me."

"She did what?" Serrano said. "Why?"

"Let's just say we have a history."

"All right," Tally said, crossing her arms. "I did you a favor by running this report. You return the favor by telling us the truth about you and this Boggs woman."

Rachel looked at Serrano. After the Constance Wright case was closed, she had told him more than she'd ever thought she would tell anyone ever again. The death of her husband had made Rachel push everything inward. There was nothing to be gained by emotionally flaying herself. She'd thought she could never trust anyone again. Until the night John Serrano told her about his son.

Serrano's son, Evan, had died following a freak accident during a baseball game. It had ripped apart Serrano's life, destroyed his marriage, and sent Serrano into a tailspin of alcohol and depression. It had taken him a long, long time to pull himself out of the muck. But when he told her the truth, sitting next to her at the very field where his son had been fatally wounded, Rachel felt she could trust someone for the first time in a very, very long time.

Since she'd befriended Evie Boggs.

"When I first met Evie," Rachel said to the detectives, "I knew her as Myra. She taught a self-defense class in Torrington that I joined after . . . my husband died. It was free and open to anyone who had been victimized and wanted a way to defend themselves. To fight back. To feel like their broken pieces could be mended. I needed that. In a lot of ways, Evie saved me."

The detectives listened in silence.

"Evie . . . Myra . . . she and I grew close. That class was my salvation. I was so scared and angry and just terrified of everything. She helped me to focus my negative energies. To channel them into something positive and use them to protect myself and my children. Evie Boggs—Myra—saved my life."

Rachel looked at Serrano. He was listening intently, but there was a glint of hurt behind his eyes. Rachel had not told him any of this. She had accepted him into her home, into her bed, and into her children's lives but had not allowed him one of her deepest truths.

"Go on," Tally said. "I have a feeling this doesn't end well."

"It didn't," Rachel said. "One of the rules in Myra's class was that everyone used an alias. So they could feel protected. That's why Evie went by Myra. But Evie and I, we grew closer. Closer than she told the rest of the class we were allowed to get. We trusted each other. We told each other the truth. About our pasts. About who we were. Who we were *really*. She told me her actual name. I was the only one in the class who knew it. Anyway, one night we trained late and walked out together. A man assaulted us and held a knife to Evie's neck."

"I have to say, if I was going to mug two women, you and this Evie person would not be at the top of my list," Tally said.

"This man was a stranger. Evie turned the tables on him. She broke his arm. Took his knife. Then she got this crazed look in her eye and held the knife like she felt his insides needed some fresh air. It reminded me of those nature shows where a lion takes down a zebra, and there's this split second before the lion tears the helpless animal to shreds. Evie was going to kill that man. But I stopped her. I saved the man's life . . ."

Rachel trailed off.

"And what?" Serrano said.

"And after that, we never spoke again. I prevented her from killing a man. She felt that he deserved to die. I did not. And because of me, he got away. That was the last time Evie and I spoke. Until the day Matthew Linklater died, when she showed up at my door."

"Why didn't you tell us about this?" Serrano said.

"Because she knows things about me. Things I'd rather not be public." Her eyes pleaded with Serrano. "You know what I'm talking about."

"So why show up now?" Tally asked. "After all that time?"

"She told me to back off the Linklater case. She knew about the email he sent me. I'm positive that's why Brice and Ruddock went after Eric as well. Insurance. To keep me in line."

"How did Evie know about the email Linklater sent you?" said Tally.

"When I was leaving Bennett Brice's office today, Evie Boggs was going in. I think Ruddock killed Linklater. That would explain how Brice knew about the email. There's a connection between Brice and Evie Boggs. And she's using her leverage against me to protect him."

Rachel caught Tally giving Serrano a look that said *She's not telling us everything*. Rachel stayed silent because Tally was right. She was not telling them the whole truth, or even something close to it. She left out the name of the man who assaulted them that night, Stanford Royce, and the truth about what Rachel had done to him after she learned he was a serial predator. The truth was dangerous. The truth could not be controlled once it was set loose. Rachel saw distrust in Serrano's eyes.

"So you wanted to look into Evelyn Boggs as a personal favor," Serrano said.

"No," Rachel replied. "She's connected to this. I'm sorry for with-holding information from you. But if you'd been through what my family has been through, you'd be careful what you share."

A crackling sound came over Serrano's radio.

"10-23, arrived at Ashby High School. Investigation ongoing. Victim has been transported by EMTs to Mackenzie North Hospital."

"Ashby High?" Rachel said, her pulse quickening. *Eric. Something happened to Eric.* "What's going on there?"

Serrano took the radio and said, "This is Detective Serrano. Dispatch, what's the 10-101 at Ashby High?"

"Already have a detective en route, Detective Serrano. Appreciate your enthusiasm, but it's under control."

"Glad to hear it. But can you give me the details anyway for my slam book?"

The dispatcher chuckled. "Sure thing, Detective. There was a mug-ging just as the kids were getting off the morning school buses. Witnesses say two perpetrators jumped the vic and stole his backpack. They broke his wrist in the process. Vic is out of surgery and stable. Witnesses are being questioned. We have suspects, but both fled the scene. They were wearing horror-movie masks. No IDs have been made. We have officers canvassing. A few students caught the aftermath on their cell phones, but so far nothing usable has come up."

Rachel took her phone from her purse. There were no messages or texts.

My kids.

"Who was the victim?" she said, grabbing Serrano's arm and speak-ing into the radio. He pulled away from her, with force.

"Dispatch, do we have an ID on the victim?"

"One second, Detective Serrano."

Every second felt like an eternity. She could feel sweat dripping down her lower back. They stared at the radio, waiting.

"Detective, the victim is one Darren Reznick, aged seventeen."

Rachel closed her eyes and allowed herself to breathe.

When she opened them, she saw Serrano gritting his teeth. He cursed under his breath.

"What?" she said. "What's the matter?"

"Darren Reznick was there last night at Voss Field. He mouthed off to Brice. Reznick is the kid Ruddock attacked."

"And this morning Reznick gets 'mugged' and has his arm broken," Tally said. "You think . . ."

Serrano nodded. "Brice sent a high school kid a message. Matthew Linklater gets burned alive as a message. No wonder nobody would talk to us after the assembly. Having your arm broken means you got the easy way out."

CHAPTER 23

Rachel drove home, parked, then called an Uber. Serrano and Tally were going to look into the Reznick assault. Rachel felt bad for Reznick. He had no idea what he'd gotten himself into. Which meant Rachel needed to find out.

Seven minutes later, she was picked up by a sixty-five(ish)-year-old man wearing a red flannel shirt and an old tan-colored cap with a bass fish embroidered on the bill. According to the app, his name was Stan, and he had 584 rides under his belt. Given his age, Rachel guessed Stan had been laid off and was now driving to make ends meet. Stan seemed far more upbeat than Rachel felt, whistling as he drove off.

Fifteen minutes later, Stan pulled up at the destination Rachel had entered into the app. "You have a good one, Miss."

"You too, Stan."

Stan waved and drove off. Rachel opened the ride-sharing app. When prompted, she gave Stan a five-star rating and added a $500 tip. At least she could make *somebody*'s day. Then Rachel entered the building, strode up to the desk, and said, "I'd like to rent a car."

She left the rental-car lot with a Toyota Camry the color of soaked wood. It was a hideously unattractive ride but also the kind of vehicle you would notice only if you had a waterlogged timber fetish. Popular make, popular model, no noticeable scratches or dents.

She looked at Eric's text. **Home late.** She gripped the steering wheel so hard her knuckles turned white.

At 3:00 p.m., Rachel drove to Ashby High and parked her turd-colored rental a block and a half from the school entrance. She had a clear view of the school bus lanes. She noted two police cars parked in the school lot, likely investigating the Reznick assault.

As she sat there waiting for the school day to end, Rachel thought about all the people who had tried to help Eric after his world was upended. So many teachers and counselors and therapists that she had forgotten their names. Rachel had gone with him to innumerable appointments, watched in pain as he cried, his body shaking with fear, wondering just what kind of salve could heal those kinds of emotional wounds.

"I see my dad at night, in my dreams, when I go to sleep," she remembered Eric saying to one counselor. *"I know it's not real, but I try to stop it. I go into my room, and I see him on my bed. But he's in pieces. There's no blood, but it's like . . . everything was taken apart and just put there neatly. Even though I know he's dead, I try to talk to him. 'Dad,' I say. He doesn't answer. I don't want to touch him, because all the pieces might fall apart. 'Dad,' I say again. Nothing. But then he looks at me. His mouth opens, and blood comes gushing out like a river. And I start screaming. And then I wake up, and I'm screaming for real."*

How a child could move past that, Rachel did not know. She used to have nightmares of her own. But hers had largely subsided. Her only nightmares now were about things that might befall her children. Things she could not prevent. Which is why she'd gone to Evie Boggs in the first place. Why she became obsessed with honing her mind and body to knifepoints. She needed to control everything humanly possible. Leave as little to chance as she could. Maybe she had suffocated Eric. But it was for his own protection. She knew that, even if he did not.

Being a parent meant keeping your children safe at all costs. Even if they hated you for it.

At three thirty, the first wave of students began to file out of the school. She could see kids skipping, running, chatting joyfully with friends. A sadness lanced her heart. Rachel had not seen that kind of carefree smile on her son's face in a long, long time.

As the kids spilled out of the school, Rachel watched from behind the dashboard, waiting for a glimpse of either her son or Benjamin Ruddock. The exodus began to thin. There was still no sign of them. It was possible Eric had gone to the bathroom. Stayed an extra couple of minutes to ask a teacher about an assignment. But then the trickle of students dried up. It was nearly three fifty. No way Eric would have stayed in school an extra twenty minutes. Once that bell rang, kids shot out of school like cannonballs. But not her son. Where was he?

Three fifty turned to four and then four ten. Her heart was thumping. She texted Eric:

How was school? When will you be home?

She waited five minutes. There was no response. Panic began to set in. It was unlikely she had simply missed him. Rachel trusted her instincts and had scanned every student like the Terminator. Eric had not left the building.

At least not through the front door.

She pulled out her phone and opened the GPS-tracking app. Lucky for her, Eric had forgotten to turn tracking mode off. The little blue dot indicated that Eric was a good mile from the school. He must have slipped out a back exit. She cursed under her breath.

Rachel pulled into traffic, watching Eric's location on her cell.

The blue dot was currently stopped on Sycamore Lane between Indigo and Beechwood. It took Rachel four minutes to get there. Lush, green dogwood trees lined the streets in front of family dwellings, all with two-car garages and manicured front lawns, many with metal basketball hoops mounted in their driveways. Rachel idled on the corner of Sycamore and Beechwood. According to the app, Eric was halfway down the block. She waited.

She refreshed the app every thirty seconds. Finally Rachel saw her son. He left a house on Sycamore, walking with another boy. But this was no more a boy than Rachel was a squirrel. He stood around six one, considerably north of two hundred pounds. He was solidly built, with broad shoulders and a trim waist. He walked with a swagger, arms swinging by his sides. He looked like the kind of kid—broad shouldered and confident—that college football coaches would roll out the red carpet for during recruiting season. She recognized his face from the school directory. Benjamin Ruddock.

And then there was Eric. Fourteen, looking like a salad fork next to Ruddock.

Eric walked quickly to keep pace with Ruddock's long strides. Rachel snapped pictures of the home and jotted down the house number—52 Sycamore Lane. Then she noticed something else.

Nestled into the crook of Benjamin Ruddock's right arm were several thin manila envelopes. When they reached the end of the driveway, Ruddock took the envelopes, unzipped his backpack, and slid them inside. Then he clapped Eric on the back and said three words, which Rachel could read on his lips. *You did well.*

The boys walked down Sycamore and made a right on Indigo. Rachel eased to the corner and followed the blue dot as it continued down Indigo for three blocks, then made a left onto Murtagh Lane. After a right onto Mackey Drive and another left onto Riggs Way, the dot stopped.

Rachel drove slowly. It appeared that Eric and Ruddock had entered a house at 415 Riggs Way. She pulled up across from the house and did a background search on her phone. The home was owned by a woman named Tabitha Pike. Before she'd had a chance to find out more, Eric and Ruddock had exited the house. Once again, Ruddock was holding a stack of manila envelopes, which he transferred to his backpack. Ruddock was smiling. Eric's face was devoid of emotion.

That was quick, Rachel thought. *YourLife is all about selling products, but they weren't inside long enough to do that. They weren't there to sell anything. They were dropping something off.*

What was in those envelopes?

Rachel stayed three-quarters of a block behind the boys. They did not give off any signs that they knew they were being followed. When they turned right onto Ivyhill Drive, Rachel waited two full minutes and then followed.

She wondered how many houses were on their route. Rachel was OK time-wise until 6:30 p.m.; then her part-time nanny had to leave. She prayed Eric would be done by then. And once he got home, she would pry the truth out of him. What were they doing in those homes? What was in the manila envelopes? *How can I help you?*

This was not the first time Rachel had surveilled someone. But it tore her heart out doing it to her own child.

"We're being followed," Ruddock said, as calmly as if he were commenting on the weather. Eric's eyes widened. "Brown sedan. Don't look. Don't turn around."

Eric felt fear. More fear than he'd felt so far that day. Even though he did not fully trust Benjamin Ruddock, he felt oddly safe while with the older boy. Ruddock's confidence was contagious. Every home they visited, he was in complete control. He shook hands, then introduced Eric as a YourLife trainee ("Handpicked by Mr. Brice himself!"). Then he would hand over a manila envelope. Eric did not know what was in the envelopes. And he knew well enough not to ask.

He did find it odd that at each home, Ruddock was invited in without hesitation. And the thin smiles the owners gave him had the faintest traces of fear. As though they didn't feel they had a choice but to invite him into their homes.

Ruddock took a cell phone from his pocket and dialed. After a moment, he said, "Sorry to call, but we have a tail. I'm on Violet Road heading to see Mr. Meyerson. You can track me. It's a brown four-door. Don't know make or model. Let me see what I can do."

Ruddock opened the phone's camera app and switched it to a front-facing view. Then he held the camera up until the brown car was in the viewfinder and snapped a photo burst. Ruddock then texted the photos to a number Eric could not see.

"Just sent you some pics of the car. You'll send help? OK, cool."

Ruddock ended the call, put the phone back in his pocket, and smiled at Eric.

"All taken care of. On to the next one."

Eric quickly glanced behind him and wondered who Ruddock had called. He thought about the sound of Darren Reznick's arm breaking and wondered just what this "help" was going to do to the person in the car.

Rachel watched Ruddock take a cell phone from his bag and make a call. She felt a sneeze and quickly ducked beneath the dashboard so she wouldn't draw their attention. When she came back up, Ruddock was putting the phone back into his bag.

She followed them for several more blocks until they entered a driveway at 98 Violet Road, a three-story colonial painted a light gray with white trim. Half a dozen redbrick steps bracketed by wrought iron railings led to the front door, which was adorned with Corinthian-style columns. The lawn was trimmed to a neat emerald green. The bricks had been power washed and treated. The limestone columns looked like they had been recently washed with stone cleaners and microfiber.

Rachel parked down the street and pulled up the GPS app. And waited.

And waited.

She pulled up a property listing for 98 Violet Road. The owners, Harold and Wanda Meyerson, had purchased it seven years ago for $3.2 million. They obviously had money—why would they need a couple of teenage boys to come to their home to sell them trinkets?

After fifteen minutes, Rachel began to grow concerned. The boys had spent no more than five to ten minutes in each of the previous homes. Could she have lost them? The GPS tracker still marked the blue dot at the current location, but something about this didn't feel right.

She texted Eric:

Hey hon, can you let me know when you'll be home? Ballpark ETA?

Nothing. Not even the three dots letting her know a response was coming.

Five minutes passed. Ten. Fifteen. It was nearly five thirty. She needed to see if the boys were still there. She needed to be home for Megan in an hour but couldn't leave without knowing for certain what was happening to her son.

Rachel killed the engine and stepped outside. The street was quiet.

She walked toward the home at 98 Violet Road. Then Rachel heard a sound behind her. It registered in a millisecond, the crunching of foot-steps on dried leaves, with a pace that suggested the person was running rather than walking. She reacted instantaneously.

Rachel whipped around to see someone wearing a Michael Myers Halloween mask and holding a black Smith & Wesson M&P pistol.

And it was pointed at Rachel's head.

A high-pitched voice said, "Don't mo—"

But Rachel moved faster than his words could come out.

Rachel did three things almost simultaneously. The first thing she knew to do when a gun was pointed at your head was to get out of the line of fire. She ducked slightly down so that the top of her head was well below the muzzle.

At the same time, she brought both of her hands up lightning quick, gripping the gunman's wrists. She pushed them upward so the gun was pointed at a forty-five-degree angle into the sky, ensuring the line of fire was not directed at her or any bystanders.

Concurrently to that, she stomped her left foot into the side of the assailant's knee.

Hard.

The gunman howled and collapsed to the ground, holding his injured knee. Rachel was able to rip away the Smith & Wesson without a shot being fired. It was over in less than two seconds.

Rachel drew the slide back and ejected the cartridge from the barrel chamber, then removed the magazine. She put the gun, cartridge, and mag into her purse, took out her cell phone, and zipped the bag back up. Then she approached the downed man as she dialed 911.

A wave of horror hit her like a slap. The gunman was small. Too small to be an adult. And the scream . . . it was not the scream of an adult male.

What had she done?

Rachel knelt down and ripped the mask off. Then she gasped, stood up, and took a step back.

Staring back at her from the ground was a boy, barely older than her own son. He had dirty-blond hair, freckles, and the wisps of a teenage mustache. His eyes were wide and terrified. Tears streaked down his cheeks as he clutched his injured leg.

"My knee," he said. His voice was high, so high. She had injured a boy. A boy who was aiming a loaded weapon at her head, but still . . .

"Who are you?" she said. Then the 911 dispatcher picked up.

"911, what is your emergency?"

She said, "My name is Rachel Marin. There's an injured boy who needs medical attention. We're at 98 Violet Road, and . . ."

With her attention fully focused on the downed boy, Rachel did not hear the other man come from behind.

All she felt was a hard thump against her temple, and everything went dark.

CHAPTER 24

Years Ago

"Mommy, Daddy, look!" *the young girl said. Her voice was an excited whisper, trying to properly convey her unabashed excitement while not scaring her incredible discovery away.*

Twenty feet in front of her, a small rabbit had bounced onto the stone path. Its fur was gray, with a hint of brown speckled throughout like cinnamon. The girl immediately held out her hands, warning her parents not to take another step lest they frighten the wondrous creature.

The family had spent the morning wandering the nature preserve, stopping every few feet to match the flowers, fauna, and animals to their descriptions in the guidebook. The girl bounced around the park with pure joy as her parents held hands, basking in their daughter's happiness. She careened from discovery to discovery, blonde hair trailing behind her in a tangled mess, as her parents watched her, hearts swelling. A year earlier they hadn't known if they would ever travel as a family of three again. They were going to sop up every moment and not leave until the sun went down.

"Mommy, lookit," she whispered, pointing again to the tiny creature.

"It's beautiful," her mother said. She knelt down next to the girl and pressed their cheeks together. The girl took her hand, and her mommy squeezed it, gently, as she did not have the strength she used to.

"It's so small," the girl said, her voice fearful, as though something might happen to the bunny as she watched.

"I think it's a baby," her mother replied.

"Looks like a jackrabbit," her father said. He knelt down with them. Her daddy was tall, and the girl could hear his knees creaking. She could feel his stubble scratch against her cheek, and she giggled.

"That tickles, Daddy," she said. He put his arm around her and pointed.

"Look at that coloring," he said. "Beautiful, right?"

"It's so, so cute," the girl said, looking at her mother with pleading eyes. Her mommy smiled, knowing exactly what was coming next.

"That's a wild rabbit, sweetie," she said. "We can't take it home."

The girl lowered her head.

"Please?"

"Sweetie, not every animal is meant to be kept inside. Some need to be free, so they can run around out in the wild."

"Like that rabbit?" she asked.

"Like that rabbit," her mommy replied.

"Is it a girl rabbit, Daddy?"

"I'm not sure," her father said. "I forgot to renew my veterinary license."

They watched the small bunny, the girl transfixed. The father took out his camera, a bulky, cumbersome thing.

"Shh, Daddy, don't scare it!"

"I won't, hon."

He put the camera to his face and clicked a button several times. The girl held her breath, praying her dad wouldn't scare off her new friend.

"There. All done. I got some good ones."

"Can I see?" the girl said.

"Not yet, silly," he said. "I have to get them developed. I think there's a Fotomat near the hotel with twenty-four-hour service."

"But I want to see the pictures now," she whined.

"I just took them, hon," her dad said. "You can't expect to take a picture and get to see it right away."

The girl made a hmph *noise, irritated she would have to wait so long to see the photos.*

"You don't need pictures," her mother said. "Look. It's right there in front of you. In real life."

"I know. But it won't be there forever."

The bunny turned, as though noticing the family's presence for the first time. The girl smiled and waved at it.

"Hi, bunny!" she said. The bunny's nose twitched. The girl took a step toward the bunny, and it sprang off into the brush. "Bye, bunny," she said dejectedly. "Mommy, where do you think it went?"

"I think the bunny went to go spend time with its own family," her mother said. She stood up and lifted the girl into the air. She giggled and thrust her arms out like a soaring airplane. Daddy laughed and took more pictures. The girl could hear Mommy breathing heavily.

The girl remembered how, not so long ago, her mother had been sick, so sick, thinner than a Popsicle stick, sleeping all day and all night. But her mommy promised that as soon as she got better, they would take a vacation as a family. And when Mommy started to get better, they booked the trip to the Bay Area. For months they talked about how they wanted to go hiking along nature trails and lie on sandy beaches, feeling the water nip at their toes. They couldn't wait to fill every moment with new experiences and tastes and joys. To feel like a family again.

And now here they were. The girl marveled at the woods, wonders all around her, like she had been taken from her former life and plunked into a magical world where there were no cares, nothing to be afraid of, no doctors or smells of medicine—just beauty occupying every inch of her horizon.

The girl was happier than she could ever remember being in her whole life.

The girl knew her parents would take her even if she didn't ask, but she had to be a hundred, a thousand, a million percent sure.

"Can we go to the gift shop?" she said, pleading, as though they had already turned her down and she had to make a case for it.

Her father smiled and took her hand.

"We wouldn't miss it. I need a snow globe for my collection."

"Daddy, why do you have so many snow globes?" she said.

"They remind me of everywhere I've been," he said. He squeezed his daughter's hand and then his wife's hand. They both smiled. "And they remind me of all the places I haven't been yet but want to go to. With both my girls."

He gazed lovingly at his wife. She leaned over, and they kissed ever so gently. The girl made an ick face and stuck her tongue out.

"Ew, gross. Neither of you have brushed your teeth since this morning."

"One day you'll understand," her mother said.

"I don't think so," the girl replied. She looked into her mother's face. The hollows under her eyes were starting to fill in. The gray was leaving, pink hues spreading over her skin like the final moments of a sunset. When she was sick, she had lost so much weight the girl wondered if it would ever come back. But even though her mother looked better than she had in a long time, the girl could tell how much energy she had expended just walking through the preserve. She looked tired, her legs beginning to buckle under her. More than once, she'd had to stop and sit, then sip from a bottle of water before continuing on.

"Let's go back to the hotel," her father said. "I don't want you to push yourself too hard. We have more days here."

The mother nodded remorsefully, as though she wanted to continue but knew her body would resist.

"Still getting my strength back," she said. "I'll be OK tomorrow."

The girl's father looked at her. "You OK with heading back, sweetie?"

The girl saw concern in her father's eyes. It scared her.

"OK, Dad," she said. "Let's go home."

"Not just yet," the mom said. "We said we'd go to the gift shop, and so we're going to the gift shop."

The mother walked off in a hurry, then turned around and said, "Well, am I the only one who wants to buy something at the gift shop?"

The girl and her father looked at each other, smiled, and jogged to catch up.

The gift shop was small and spare but lovingly curated. Barrels of petrified tree bark. Glossaries of all the animals and plants that could be found in the preserve. Magnifying glasses, rubber insects, maps, and books and books and more books.

Then the girl saw it, and her heart nearly burst with delight.

In a small basket in the corner by the exit was an assortment of stuffed animals that could be found in those woods. Birds. Frogs. Deer. And more.

The girl ran over and plunged her hands into the collection, fingers kneading the plush fur, the button eyes. An instant was all it took for her to fall in love with every single animal in the basket. She looked up and saw her parents watching her, joy in their eyes that nearly made her cry.

She didn't even need to ask.

"Pick one," her father said.

Her eyes widened.

"Really?" she said. "Please don't be messing around, Daddy."

"I'm not messing around. You can have one. But just one. So pick one that's really, really special. That you'll want to keep forever."

The girl nodded. This was a big responsibility. There were so many stuffed animals in the basket, and she could love each and every one of them.

But she knew which one she wanted as soon as she saw it. The other animals she could love. This one was beyond love.

The girl brought the animal up to her father and held it out to him.

"This one," she said.

"Are you sure?"

She nodded like she'd never been more sure in her life.

"OK, then."

He brought the stuffed animal to the cash register. A skinny, bespectacled teenage boy rang it up. Her father paid and plucked the price tag from its fur. Then he handed the girl her new pet.

It was a small bunny, with gray and brown fur and delicate, inky-black glass eyes. The girl could see herself in their reflection, her smile wide as a canyon. A single tear fell onto the bunny's fur, and her heart felt full. In that moment she wasn't sure if she'd ever loved anything else as much as she loved that small furry bunny.

"Thank you, Mommy. Thank you, Daddy," she said as she nestled the baby bunny in her thin arms.

As they went to leave the gift shop, her mother said, "What's its name?"

The girl looked at her, confused.

"Every pet needs a name," she said.

"Can I name it whatever I want?" the girl replied.

"Whatever you want. It should mean something."

The girl looked around, as if for inspiration. Her eyes settled on a big coffee-table book next to the cash register. The title was The Wonders of Marin County.

"Marin," the girl said. "Her name is Marin."

Her mother smiled, leaned in, and petted the bunny's head gently.

"Hello, Marin. My name is Wendy Powell. This is my husband, Alan, and you've already met our daughter, Olivia. It's very, very nice to meet you. Welcome to our little loving family."

The girl hugged her bunny so tight that for a moment she thought it might explode. Then she kissed its soft nose and said, "I love you, Marin."

The girl did not know it then, but it was the last trip her family would ever take together. Her mother would pass away in six months. Her father five years after that.

But in that moment, hugging Marin the rabbit, her mother's and father's adoring eyes gazing down upon her, the girl had never been happier in her whole, entire life.

CHAPTER 25

Today

Rachel knew she was in a hospital room before she opened her eyes. The smell was unmistakable: a mixture of antiseptic, soiled sheets, illness, and body odor.

She opened her eyes. Tried to focus. The world appeared to her behind a gauzy film. Blurry and distant. She blinked, over and over, trying to will it away. Slowly her eyesight returned, the blurs taking hard-edged form.

Rachel took inventory of her body. There was a sensation of tremendous pressure on the right side of her head, like her skull was being held under a panini press, but dulled, thankfully, by pain medication.

She tried to think of the last thing she remembered. She recalled tracking her son and Benjamin Ruddock, waiting for what seemed like an eternity at the house on Violet Road. Then she got impatient. She got sloppy. She left the safety of the vehicle without checking her surroundings. Her instincts dulled by concern and fear.

She'd barely taken a step before . . .

The gun.

The gun. The boy. Oh God. She'd hurt a boy.

She couldn't have known. A gun was pointed at her head. It was a reaction, immediate and uncontrollable. It was self-defense, she told herself. If she'd waited a millisecond longer, she could have been dead.

But then someone hit her from behind, while she was calling 911. She didn't see the second person. Again, she was too distracted. She was vulnerable. And that momentary lapse had landed her in the hospital, with her head on fire.

Her kids. Where were her kids?

"Mom?"

She knew that voice. Megan. Oh, thank God. Megan.

Rachel opened her eyes wide, the world taking shape. She could see chairs. And on one of the chairs was a large blur that appeared to be in the shape of her seven-year-old daughter.

"Megan . . . ," Rachel croaked. Her voice was raspy; her throat burned. She had no concept of what time it was or what day it was.

Megan slid off the chair and walked to Rachel, tentatively. She put her hand on Rachel's leg.

"Mommy?"

"I'm OK, baby," she said, fighting through the haze. "Everything is fine."

A lie could be forgiven if it calmed her child.

Rachel felt Megan place her head on her hip. Her daughter was shaking and trying not to cry. Rachel stroked her hair.

"It's OK, sweetie. I'm all right. I'm here."

"You were saying our name," Megan said softly, like she was concealing a secret. "In your sleep."

"Our name?"

"Marin. You kept saying the name Marin. And something about a rabbit. But you were kind of mumbly, so I might be wrong. Were you dreaming, Mommy?"

"I was, baby."

"What were you dreaming about?"

Before Rachel could respond, a doctor entered the room. He was tall and thin, in his early sixties, with kind eyes, a crown of white hair circling his bald head, and a gray goatee peppered with black.

"Ah, glad to see we're awake."

"That depends how you define *awake*," Rachel said.

"Well, forming full sentences is a good start. I'm Dr. Copeland. How are you feeling, Ms. Marin?"

"Water," Rachel said. "Need water."

"Of course."

He took a pitcher from a tray and filled a plastic cup. He handed it to Rachel. She drank, slowly. The burning in her throat began to ease.

"The good news is you have a concussion," Dr. Copeland said.

"That's the *good* news? I'm guessing you didn't get this job because of your impeccable bedside manner."

He laughed. "I say that's the good news because there is only a very minor skull fracture and no cerebral bleeding. A concussion and a pretty deep laceration. I'd say you should be thankful it wasn't worse."

"It was a gun," Rachel said. "Someone hit me with a handgun."

"We don't know for certain what the weapon was . . . but a metal firearm would explain the fracture and laceration. Police have been in and out of your room. One cop in particular seemed pretty upset. Almost as if he took your injury personally. He refused to leave. Even when his partner told him they needed to go." Copeland paused. "I have a feeling you know the cop I'm talking about."

Rachel smiled wearily. "I do."

She looked around the room. Other than Megan and the doctor, it was empty.

"Megan," Rachel said softly. "Your brother . . ."

Megan looked up. "I don't know where he is. We tried to call his phone, but he didn't answer."

Rachel saw her purse on a chair. "Cell phone. In my purse. Give it to me."

Megan rummaged around in Rachel's purse and handed her the phone. She opened the GPS-tracking app and tapped Eric's name.

Searching. Searching. Searching.

There was no blue dot.

Rachel tried again.

Searching. Searching. Searching.

Still nothing. He must have turned the tracker off. Which meant he'd found out she had followed him. But had he known before the attack or after?

She dialed Eric's number. It rang several times and then went to voice mail.

"Eric, it's your mother. Please call me. I . . . I don't care about anything else. I just need to know that you're safe. You're not in trouble. So just call me. Text me. Anything. Please. I love you."

She pressed the end-call icon. Her face felt hot, pressure forming behind her eyes.

"Mom?" Megan said. "Is Eric OK?"

Rachel looked into her daughter's eyes. "I think so. I hope so."

The first part was a lie.

"I love him so much," Megan said. "I want him to be OK."

"I do, too, baby."

Suddenly Rachel felt a stabbing pain blaze along her head, like a match had been struck on her scalp, and she cried out in pain. She brought her hand up to touch the wound, but the doctor took her wrist gently.

"Best leave that alone for now. You have half a dozen staples in there."

"Staples. Great. Now I'm getting office supplies stuck into my head."

The doctor smiled and looked at Megan. "Is your mother always this funny?"

Megan's concern eased. She smiled back. "No."

"Maybe getting bonked on the head improved my sense of humor," Rachel said. "Silver linings."

"Always look on the bright side of life," Dr. Copeland said.

"Let me ask you a question, Doctor," Rachel said. "The pain seems to be coming from the area of my parietal bone. Is that where the staples were put in?"

The doctor appeared impressed. "That's correct. I didn't know you had medical training."

"I don't. Well, not exactly. So, based on the location of the wound and my height, the weapon would have to have been swung at a downward angle toward my head."

Rachel made a diagonal swinging motion with her fist.

"I'm no criminal-forensics expert, but that would seem to be a possible scenario."

Rachel thought about the boy who'd pulled the gun on her. He was thin as a cane, and maybe five foot five wearing sneakers. Rachel was five nine. There was no way he could have hit her on the top of her head unless Rachel was ducking or he had a stepladder. Even Eric was about five six. The wound meant she'd been injured either by an adult or a much taller kid. Rachel had spent enough time at Ashby High to know that the number of boys significantly taller than her was minimal.

Benjamin Ruddock was certainly tall enough to crack Rachel at that angle from a standing position. So was Bennett Brice.

She tried to sit up, but a wave of nausea swept through her, forcing her back into the hospital bed.

"Take it easy," Dr. Copeland said. "Remember, you literally have bruising on your brain. There won't be any long-term damage, but you need to rest. Take it easy for a few days before resuming normal activities."

Megan let loose a snort.

"What's so funny?" Rachel said.

"Thinking about you taking it easy," Megan said. "It's funny."

Megan's voice did not make it sound like she thought it was funny.

"Somebody call for a stripogram?"

Rachel looked up to see John Serrano standing at the door. He looked to Megan, who was sitting by the bed.

"I meant candygram," he said.

"You said *stripogram*," Megan said. "What's a stripogram?"

"It's when you strip the wrapping off a piece of candy and give it to someone so they feel better."

"Ooh, I want a stripogram," Megan said. Serrano's face turned red.

Rachel mouthed the words "Good save."

Serrano walked to the bed, knelt down, and gently kissed Rachel's hand. He placed his hand on her cheek. It felt like home. She put her hand on his and gave it a firm squeeze.

"How are you feeling?" he said.

"Like someone drove an SUV into my head."

"How are *you*?" he said to Megan.

"I'm OK," Megan said softly. She smiled at Serrano, and Rachel felt her heart warm.

"They're going to keep you overnight for observation to make sure there's no cranial bleeding," he said.

"Thank you, John. Hey, Dr. Copeland, is there a vending machine around here? I'd kill for a soda."

"Down the hall. Out this door, make a left, and then another left."

"Hon," Rachel said to Megan, "can you go get me a soda?"

"I didn't know you drank soda," she said.

"I don't. But it's more polite than asking you to leave the room for a minute so I can talk to John."

"Ooohhh. You need to have a *grown-up* talk?" Megan said.

"Exactly. Grown-up talk."

Megan nodded. "You could have just said that. I'm not a little kid, you know."

"I know you're not. You're right. That's the last time I ever treat you like one. I promise."

"And . . . Mom?"

"Yes, hon?"

"Next time, let Sadie Scout do the dangerous stuff."

She took a few crumpled dollar bills from Rachel's purse and disappeared.

"I'll come back later to check on you," Dr. Copeland said. "Remember what I said. Take *care* of yourself. Rest. Your brain needs time to recover."

Then he left Rachel and Serrano alone.

"OK. Now tell me exactly what happened," Serrano said.

She told him how she'd followed Eric and Benjamin Ruddock. How when she got out of the car, a kid young enough to be dreaming of a learner's permit pulled a gun on her. How she injured his knee, got belted in the head, and then woke up here.

"We'll need the addresses of all the homes your son and Benjamin Ruddock stopped at," Serrano said. "We've already begun canvassing Violet Road, but so far we haven't turned up any witnesses to the assault. You're lucky you'd already dialed 911, or you could have lain there unconscious until someone found you bleeding in the street."

"What about the kid?" Rachel said.

"The kid?"

"The one I hurt. The one who pulled the gun on me. I messed up his knee pretty bad. That's why I called 911. Where is he?"

"When EMTs arrived, there was nobody else there. Just you."

"I felt his knee buckle, maybe a torn ligament or two. He would have needed medical treatment." She thought for a moment. "Someone took him away before the ambulance came. You need to check all hospitals in the area. Look for a boy between the ages of thirteen and sixteen who may have been admitted with a dislocated kneecap and possible damage to his ACL and PCL. I'm sure it will be reported as a sports injury or some other fake accident."

Serrano noted all of this. "We're on it."

Rachel said, "My son. I don't know what he's involved in. But YourLife is as legitimate a business as Monopoly money is a legitimate currency."

"You think your assault is connected to your following Eric and the Ruddock kid?"

"I *know* it was. That's why they waited in the house on Violet Road for so long. Ruddock must have made me tailing them and called for backup. Then all they had to do was wait for the cavalry to arrive. Ruddock is smarter than I thought. He knew I'd get out of the car and come looking for Eric."

"Do you think . . ." Serrano trailed off.

"No. I don't think Eric knew I'd be attacked."

"I called Eric," Serrano said. "It went straight to voice mail. But we're looking for him."

"Thank you, John."

Serrano nodded solemnly. "You're lucky this didn't end worse. A lot worse. Either for you or someone else."

"My husband always told me I was hardheaded."

Serrano didn't laugh.

"Guess it's a weird time to bring up my dead husband, huh."

"Yeah, just a little weird. This is serious, Rachel."

A wave of nausea sluiced through her body. She closed her eyes and took deep breaths until it passed. Then she sat up.

"I need to get out of here," she said.

"You're kidding, right?" Serrano said. "The doctor just said they're keeping you for observation. You don't mess around with brain injuries."

"Until I know where my son is, I can't just lie here like a breadstick."

"Rachel . . ."

She pressed the call button on her hospital bed.

"I need to find Eric," she said. "Everything else can wait."

"No need to get up. Found him."

Rachel's head snapped to the doorway. She recognized that voice. Standing just outside her hospital room door was Evie Boggs.

And standing beside Evie was Rachel's son.

CHAPTER 26

Rachel told Serrano that if he took his eyes off Eric, she would stick his badge so far up his ass you'd be able to see its reflection behind his eyes. Serrano complimented her on her clever, if disgusting, turn of phrase and took Eric and Megan to the cafeteria.

"All right. Talk," Rachel said to Evie. Evie took a seat on a chair across from Rachel's bed. "My head hurts and it feels like I got hit by a truck, but if you don't tell me what the hell you're doing here with my son, I will levitate out of this bed and squeeze it out of you."

"First off, take it down a notch," Evie said. "Even on a good day, I'd use you for a punching bag. Second, you need to know that Bennett Brice had absolutely nothing to do with what happened."

"So it's just a coincidence that I get a gun pulled on me while following his YourLife flunkies?"

"Right there. Think about what you just said. You were following two children. *Children.* Do you know how that's going to look if you take this any further?"

"One of those children was my son."

"So you rented a car to follow him. Yeah. That sounds sane."

"How did you know I rented—"

"I talked to your cop friends. They said you were found near a brown Camry. I've been to your house. Didn't see a brown Camry. If the media gets word of this insanity, they're going to dig."

"Bennett Brice threatened to sic the media on me too," Rachel said. "You're not very original. If he doesn't cut my son loose, this is going to end badly for him."

"Are you threatening Bennett Brice?" Evie said. "Because that's not the first time."

Rachel said nothing.

"Mr. Brice gives at-risk children incredible opportunities. They can earn money—a lot of money—working for him. He helps troubled teens. What he's doing is noble."

"I don't see anything noble about it," Rachel said. "I see him exploiting vulnerable kids."

"You are wrong," Evie said.

"Rarely," Rachel replied. "Why are you defending him? How much is he paying you?"

"See," Evie said, "even your guesses are so far off the mark they're in the woods. Look at what you've become, Rachel. Didn't you come to Ashby to get away from violence? But since you came here, you've found violence at every turn."

"I help bring criminals to justice," Rachel said. "Criminals can be violent."

"Didn't you shoot a man inside your own home not too long ago?" Evie said. "That sounds to me like a criminal bringing violence to you. Into your home, where your children sleep. Don't bring any more violence into your life, Rachel."

"Is that a threat?" Rachel said.

"Not in the least. Bennett Brice did you a favor. He told our friend Benjamin Ruddock to bring Eric to me to bring to you as an olive branch. To let you know that he's not the bad guy. That we care about your family."

Rachel thought for a moment. "Tell me about Raymond Spivak. Why did you try to kill him?"

Evie's eyes widened.

"How do you—"

"Like I said. I investigate criminals. And you have a criminal record. What did Raymond Spivak do to you that made you go to his home with a knife? And why were the charges dropped?"

Evie leaped out of her chair. She looked at Rachel with a mixture of anger and pity.

"That was a long time ago and has nothing to do with Bennett Brice or why I'm here. Besides, Raymond isn't the Spivak brother to worry about."

"You're referring to his brother. Randall Spivak, right? Talk to me. *Tell me* what this is all about, Evie. Because even though I'm the one who just had a gun pulled on me, you're the one who looks scared."

Evie stood there for a moment, as though measuring whether to say something to Rachel, then turned around and left the room.

CHAPTER 27

Megan slept in a chair beside Rachel's bed. Eric sat in another chair, but from what Rachel could tell, he didn't sleep. Rachel tried to talk to him, but she had a hard time focusing, and Eric refused to give more than one-word answers. A constant faint glow from his cell phone illuminated his face. His thumbs tapped away incessantly. Rachel couldn't tell if he was playing a game or sending a text. *What if he's texting Ruddock? Or Brice? Or Evie Boggs?* She prayed it was something as simple as him texting Penny Wallace. If only things were as simple as a teenage crush.

She wanted so desperately to look inside his head, to see the wiring, to understand how to relieve him of his anger and sadness. She missed the carefree young boy she once knew. It destroyed her to think he might be gone. There were some pains that never subsided. There were some fractures not even a mother could mend.

Rachel flitted in and out of semiconsciousness. Doctors came in and out to check on her. Eric stayed in the room, next to Megan. She did not know if he slept.

At one point, Rachel looked at Eric, only to find that he was staring at her. His face was a mask. Emotionless. She smiled at him, drowsily.

"I love you," she said.

Eric did not respond.

In the morning, John Serrano took the children to school. Megan gave Rachel a hug and said, "Mommy, come home." It took everything she had not to cry.

"I should be able to get out of here today, dear," she said.

Eric went over to the bed. His face gave no evidence of what he was thinking.

"I'll see you later today," she said. "I love you, Eric. No matter what."

Eric simply nodded. He leaned down and placed his arms around his mother, but there was no weight or emotion behind the gesture. He may as well have been fastening a seat belt. Then they left Rachel alone.

By late morning, the wooziness had begun to subside. Her head still felt like she'd been kicked by a mule, but physical pain she could handle as long as her equilibrium returned. At ten o'clock, she was discharged with acetaminophen, with clear instructions not to take ibuprofen due to the increased risk of cranial bleeding.

She threw the pain meds in the garbage before she got to the parking lot.

She hailed a ride share from her app and went home. Rachel took a long, hot shower, turning the temperature down slightly when she began to feel dizzy. She traced the swollen wound beneath her shower cap. When she got out, she texted Serrano:

Kids get to school ok?

Yup. Megan told me the plot of her next Sadie Scout novel.

Tell me it doesn't involve Sadie getting bonked in the head.

Ha, no. I told her they'll make a great movie one day. She almost asked me to adopt her.

Thank you John. For everything.

No worries. Just glad Eric is ok, at least on the outside. Even if Brice is denying involvement, I'm going to keep an eye on things just to be sure.

Rachel almost wrote back *I will too* but decided against it.

I appreciate it.

When you're ready, let's all reconvene on the Linklater murder.

You got it. One more thing: Evie mentioned Raymond Spivak's brother. Randall. She seems scared of him. Does he have a file?

I'll pull up whatever we have

She responded with a thumbs-up emoji, then put on a fresh pair of jeans and a dark-green tank top, put her hair up, and collected her thoughts.

It had all started with Matthew Linklater's death. His murder had led to the emergence of Evie Boggs, the recruitment of her son, and her head being nearly cleaved in two. She did not think Evie had killed Linklater herself—it just seemed too much of a stretch for the killer to literally knock on Rachel's door herself—but she had been wrong before. Rachel felt in her bones that Benjamin Ruddock was one of the people at Linklater's house the night he died. It would make sense: Linklater would have opened the door for one of his students, obviously unaware he was facilitating his own death. Even if he was wary of Ruddock, he couldn't possibly have known just how dangerous the boy was. She needed to know if Linklater had ever met Bennett Brice or Evie Boggs. And there was only one person who might know more about Matthew Linklater.

Gabrielle Vargas.

CHAPTER 28

Gabrielle Vargas seemed unsurprised when Rachel Marin knocked on her door.

"Ms. Vargas," Rachel said. "My name is Rachel Marin. I'm working with the APD on Matthew Linklater's murder. I know you've had a hell of a week, and I hate to impose even more, but I was hoping I might ask you a few questions about Matthew. Can I come in?"

Gabrielle sighed and said, "You know, I've seen enough movies to know that if you date a murder victim, cops are going to come in and out of your apartment like you're handing out free coffee." She held the door open to allow Rachel inside.

"I'm not a cop," Rachel said. "More like cop-adjacent."

"I know you're not a cop. You actually asked if you could come in. So far none of the cops I've spoken with have had the decency to ask."

"For once, I'm not the one who needs to work on their manners."

Vargas smiled and led Rachel to the living room. She walked around her apartment with her arms folded in front of her, uneasy, like she was protecting herself from something unseen.

"I understand you already spoke with Detectives Serrano and Tally," Rachel said.

"That's right, among others," she said. "I haven't had this much company in years. They were mostly pleasant enough. In my experience, that hasn't always been the case with cops."

"In your experience?"

"My ex . . . I had to file a restraining order against him. After I threw him out, he kept showing up at the apartment. He tried to kick in the door. And when I called the cops, the responding officer asked why I was being so mean to him. Why hadn't I just tried to patch things up? Talk it through? I showed him the bruises on my arm in the shape of his fingers, and he shut up pretty quick. The next day, I get a call from the landlord saying if I can't keep the noise down, he'll evict me. Funny how that works. Men cause trouble, and women take the blame."

"I'm so sorry," Rachel said. "I hope your ex is far, far out of the picture."

"He's in Pinckneyville," Vargas replied. "Doing eight years for felony distribution of narcotics and armed robbery."

"Well, then," Rachel said. "Here's to assholes ending up where they belong."

"He gave me my son," Vargas said. "Antonio is the only good thing that came out of that bad decision. He has his father's smile but thankfully not his heart."

Rachel's eyes went to a large photo album on the glass coffee table. "May I?" she asked.

Gabrielle smiled. "Of course. Nowadays everything is digital, but I still like to be able to hold an actual album. Feels more permanent than the cloud."

"You're absolutely right. I haven't filled out an actual album in, I don't know . . . years? Maybe it's time to start again."

"There's always time," Gabrielle said.

Rachel picked up the thick leather-bound album and opened it. Each page held four photos inside plastic sleeves. The photos on the first page looked several decades old. She recognized a younger Gabrielle Vargas as a toddler, three or four, sitting in an inflatable kiddie pool filled with plastic toys: a water pitcher, a shovel, a garden hoe, a seahorse. She had a sunburn and a toothy grin and appeared to be the happiest kid in the world.

"Where were these taken?" Rachel asked.

"Maricopa County, Arizona," Gabrielle said. "I grew up in Mesa."

"How did you end up in Ashby?"

She laughed.

"A boy. I know. Such a cliché, right? But I was a kid and didn't know any better. How did you end up in Ashby?"

Rachel thought for a moment, then said, "A boy too. In a very roundabout way."

"Mine lived in Phoenix. We met at Moonlight State Beach, in Encinitas. I had taken a spring break road trip there with some girlfriends. He was playing volleyball, and he gave me this look that just made me shiver in the heat. He was twenty-nine and I was eighteen, and I should have been wary of a guy almost thirty hitting on a teenager. But that's the kind of thing I only know with hindsight. I had just graduated high school, and he was mature in a way that all the boys I grew up with weren't. He *knew* things. I was young and stupid and didn't realize what I considered maturity was actually the opposite. They don't know anything, so they go after girls who don't know any better."

"I'm sorry," Rachel said.

Gabrielle nodded solemnly and continued.

"I wanted to start a family right away. He didn't. Which I'm thankful for now, because if I'd become a mom by twenty and *then* had to deal with everything he put us through, I don't know how we would have survived. So we waited ten years. He got a job as a foreman in a construction crew in Ashby, and neither of us had obligations keeping us in Mesa. So we came here. I got my CPA and a decent-paying job as a comptroller at a local car dealership. So at least when he got sent away, I had an income. I could pay our bills, and we could say good riddance without being destitute. We didn't need him."

"I'm a mom too," Rachel said. "Two kids. I have a son around Antonio's age at Ashby High. It sounds like you've set up a pretty good life for you and your boy. Against the odds."

Gabrielle smiled. "I'd do anything for Antonio. I'm sure you understand that."

"I do," Rachel said. "But sometimes *anything* doesn't feel like enough."

"No," Gabrielle said, with an underlying sadness in her voice that Rachel picked up on. "It never feels like enough."

Rachel continued flipping through the album. She watched as Gabrielle Vargas grew older, a flip-book showing her journey into womanhood. Grade school. High school. Her quinceañera. High school graduation. Then a man came into the picture.

He was tall and tanned, with shoulder-length dark hair, blue eyes that looked like sapphire, a mustache, and the faintest hint of muscle definition. He wrapped around her like a blanket, enveloping her, obscuring her. When she was around him, her shoulders always appeared to cave inward, like she was waiting for the next bad thing.

Gabrielle had had that same look when Rachel entered her home. Gabrielle was usually smiling, but there was something hidden beneath the smile. Her eyes were just a little too wide, her teeth just a little too visible. Like she was putting on a show for the camera. For the man she feared.

The deeper into the album Rachel got, the more Gabrielle Vargas's smile faded. It came out occasionally, a star in a dark sky, but only in photos alone with Antonio.

"What's he drawing?" Rachel said.

Gabrielle came over. She looked at the photo Rachel was pointing at. She smiled, wistful yet sad.

"That was Antonio's first comic book," she said. "'Mr. Mutant and Octopus Boy.' He wanted to write comic books. He was—is—so talented. He could create these stories out of thin air. I don't know how he does it, how his brain can just work like that. He wrote so many stories. He had piles and piles of comics and—what do you call them—graphic novels. Posters and artwork covering his room like a museum."

Rachel said, "My daughter wants to be a writer. She's only seven, but she has this series she's been writing about a girl named Sadie Scout who goes on adventures. I don't know how to judge those things or what it will lead to, but sometimes I wish I could just climb inside her head for a little while. I bet I'd be overwhelmed with pride."

"That's how I always felt. Antonio had boxes and boxes of stories. He created so many characters. He wanted to put together a portfolio to send to the companies that publish comics."

"What happened with them?" Rachel said.

Gabrielle took a step back. Sipped her drink. "He stopped writing them," she said. "I guess he outgrew them. You know how kids are. Always moving on to the next thing."

Rachel's eyes narrowed. Gabrielle wasn't telling the truth.

"I don't look at this album very often, to be honest," Gabrielle said. "Hidden in plain sight, I suppose. I have all the happy memories I need stored up here in my own cloud. I keep this mainly for Antonio. Even if I've pushed his father from my mind, it's not my place to do it for him as well. He's old enough to know the truth."

"I'm trying to figure all that out myself," Rachel said, solemnly. "If we only share half the truth with our kids, they'll learn to never trust us."

Gabrielle breathed out and uttered a nervous laugh. "This is getting serious. I could use a refreshment. Do you drink bourbon?"

"Any other day I'd take you up on that in a heartbeat. But I got clonked in the noggin, and my doctor made me promise to take it easy until they know how many brain cells I lost."

Gabrielle laughed and went to a china cabinet. She took a bottle of Bulleit from a shelf and poured herself a finger. She raised the glass. "To your brain cells."

Rachel raised an imaginary glass and pretended to clink. "To our sons."

"Our sons." Gabrielle raised her glass again and took a sip.

Rachel returned to the album. She watched Antonio grow up before her eyes. He was tall like his father and had inherited the man's deep-blue eyes and dark hair. But his nose and chin were his mother's. And she recognized his smile. It was the same one Gabrielle had when she'd toasted to him just now. In every photo he was wearing the costume of a different superhero. Batman. Superman. Captain America. Wolverine. Daredevil.

But then, as she kept turning pages, Rachel noticed something odd.

Antonio disappeared. Not from the earth, but from the album. At least for a while.

After he was born, there were photos of Antonio on every single page. He was the focal point of the album. But suddenly, he vanished. There were pictures of Gabrielle, pictures of Gabrielle with her friends, but strangely none of Antonio. It was as if he'd ceased to exist.

Until he reappeared. Many pages later and a gap of what looked like at least a year. He no longer wore superhero shirts, opting instead for monochromes. Black. White. Gray. As though the color had been drained from his life. Rachel studied the photos. It wasn't just his fashion sense that had changed.

"Ms. Vargas?" Rachel said. "What happened to Antonio's neck?"

There was the briefest hesitation from Gabrielle, a sharp intake of breath that would have gone unnoticed by most. But not by Rachel. To her, the millisecond-long passing of air over Gabrielle Vargas's front teeth might as well have been a fusillade of cannon fire.

"What do you mean?" Gabrielle asked. She was a terrible liar.

I guess we're going to play this game, Rachel thought.

Rachel held up the album. "In this photo, there's a scar on Antonio's neck. Right here. The scar is not present in any photos before this page."

Rachel drew her finger across a faint red line that ran underneath Antonio's jaw, from his earlobe nearly to his chin.

"But if you look here," Rachel said, flipping back several pages. "Antonio disappears from this album for what I'm guessing, based on the changes in seasons, a year, maybe eighteen months. I think he got that scar, and you took him out of the album while it healed. You didn't want to see it."

"I don't know what—"

"How did he get that scar, Ms. Vargas?" Rachel's politeness was gone. Now she needed answers.

Gabrielle came over. She responded without looking at the photo. "I'm sure it's just a trick of the light or something."

Rachel nodded. "Right." She flipped forward. "It's here too. And here. And here. If it was the camera's fault, why didn't you get a new camera?"

"I don't know," Gabrielle said, and finished her drink.

"Listen, Ms. Vargas. You kept Antonio out of this album for a reason. Because you didn't want him to remember. You didn't want *yourself* to remember. What happened to him?"

"It's none of your concern," Gabrielle said. She went to the cabinet and took out the bottle of bourbon. Rachel stood up, bracing herself against the arm of the sofa as dizziness overwhelmed her. Rachel walked slowly over to Gabrielle Vargas and gripped the bottle before she could pour another drink.

"Actually, Ms. Vargas, it *is* my concern. Your boyfriend was brutally murdered. I think my son is involved with the people who did it. Your son clearly suffered a terrible wound that you literally tried to erase from your life. These people are capable of heinous violence. I need to know what happened to your son."

"Please . . . ," Gabrielle said.

"Ms. Vargas, I'm on your side," Rachel said. "I'm on Antonio's side."

A tear spilled down Gabrielle Vargas's cheek. It dropped onto her hand, slid down to her pinkie, stayed there for a moment, then fell to the floor. Then she mouthed two words.

"I can't."

Rachel mouthed, "Why?"

Gabrielle Vargas began to shake her head. More tears came. Rachel took her hand, held it strong.

"Ms. Vargas," she said. "I need to know who you're protecting."

"My son," she said. "I'm protecting my son. Just like you're protecting yours."

"Who are you protecting him from?"

Gabrielle looked around her apartment, as if she'd heard a strange noise and was suddenly frightened of an intruder. But Rachel hadn't heard anything. Gabrielle went to the kitchen, took a cell phone from her purse, opened the Notes app, and typed two words.

BENNETT BRICE

Then she deleted the words and said, firmly, "Thank you for coming, Ms. Marin. Now I need to ask you to leave."

CHAPTER 29

When Rachel arrived home, she had two missed calls from John Serrano. She called him back.

"Hey, John."

"We need to talk," he said. "I'll be there in fifteen."

Rachel checked her watch. She had two hours before the kids would be home from school. Whatever Serrano needed, it had to be done before they got home. She needed to be with them, alone, just the Marin family.

While she waited, Rachel thought about Gabrielle Vargas and the two words she'd typed and deleted. *BENNETT BRICE.*

She thought about the lengthy scar on Antonio's neck and wondered how he'd gotten it. Gabrielle was clearly terrified of Brice. She had a feeling that Brice was in some way responsible for her son's wound. Rachel considered approaching Antonio, but she knew full well as a mother herself that she would flay and disembowel anyone who approached her children without her permission. Maybe disembowel and *then* flay. She could cross that bridge when she came to it.

Rachel was brewing a cup of decaf tea when Serrano knocked on the door. She led him into the living room, took a seat, put her feet up, and sipped her drink. Serrano sat down across from her.

"You're not sitting next to me," she said. "So you're here on official APD business."

"In a way," Serrano said. "The department received a letter from Bennett Brice's attorneys this afternoon."

Rachel put her cup down. "And?"

"They've officially filed a restraining order against you. If you come within a hundred yards of the YourLife offices, or if you were to speak to Bennett Brice or any of his employees without a warrant or their having a lawyer present, they will sue you and the department for harassment."

"Well, that went to DEFCON one fast," Rachel said.

"They have video of you threatening Bennett Brice in his office. Then you freely admit to following Benjamin Ruddock without any cause."

"No," Rachel said. "I was following my son."

"Be that as it may." Serrano paused. "There's something else."

"That's a loaded statement. What's the 'something else'?"

"I pulled Randall Spivak's file."

"And?"

"And it's clean. No convictions of any kind. Not even a parking ticket."

"OK . . . why does that make me nervous?"

"Because Randall Spivak has also been questioned in half a dozen murders over the past ten years. Never arrested, never charged, and never convicted. Every case fell apart when witnesses refused to testify against him. Look."

Serrano handed Rachel a folder. She opened it. The first page was a photo of Randall and Raymond Spivak. They were brothers by blood but looked as identical as a celery stalk and a tomato.

Raymond Spivak was compact, muscular, solid, like a potato with deltoids. Randall was tall, lean to the point of malnourishment. He towered over his brother by at least nine inches, maybe more.

"Experience has taught me that if someone is questioned in that many crimes but never convicted, they're a psychopath but a cautious psychopath," Serrano said. "They're the scariest kind, because they're smart enough to cover their tracks."

"So Bennett Brice is the legitimate face of YourLife," Rachel said, "but the Spivak brothers are the cudgel."

"It's a possibility," Serrano said.

"But then there's the Evie Boggs situation," Rachel said. "Evie is working for Brice. But she despises the Spivaks. If Brice is working with the Spivaks, why would Evie go to such lengths to defend Brice against Linklater's murder?"

"I don't know yet," Serrano said. "But if the department has its hands tied legally, or if you get arrested, none of that helps us bring Matthew Linklater's killer to justice."

"It's my son, John. My *son*. What am I supposed to do? I can't back off."

Serrano sighed. "I don't know. I really don't. In a way, this job is easier without kids. It's one thing to face danger on your own. It's another thing entirely to see someone you love threatened by it. Because they're always your priority."

"I would go to jail if it meant my kids were safe," Rachel said. "I would let a psychopath do whatever they wanted to if it meant my children would wake up every morning. I want Brice and the Spivaks and Evie to be scared of what the police might do to them. But I want them to be *terrified* of what I might do to them."

Rachel paused. Then she said, "I know that at one point, you would have felt the same way."

Serrano looked at Rachel, sadness washing over his face.

"I would have," he said. "Before Evan died. I would have done everything you just said. I just wish I'd had the chance."

"I know you would have."

"I wish you'd met him," Serrano said. "I wish Eric could have met him."

"I do too."

Rachel got up, took Serrano's hand, and pulled him to the couch.

"Sit next to me," she said. Serrano eased himself down next to Rachel. She put her hand on his knee. He placed his on top of it. They interlocked fingers.

"When our family broke," she said, leaning in close to him, "part of me wanted to just disappear. Completely. Move to the Gobi Desert, or some ranch out in Montana—somewhere I could see the mountains, where the nearest neighbors were miles away, and I would never have to talk to anybody. I wanted to be alone. To get away from everything. But I didn't. I didn't want to force my kids to live my life. But sometimes I wonder if I should have."

"It's easy to judge every decision you've ever made," Serrano said, "because now you have perspective and time. At the time you make them, you don't have those. But you can't change the past, or the decisions that brought you where you are. And it doesn't mean the bad things are necessarily your fault. I don't really believe in fate. But I believe we do our best."

"I try. I try so goddamn hard."

Serrano rested his head against Rachel, gently.

"Does that hurt?" he said.

"Never."

"What happened to your husband wasn't your fault," Serrano said.

"And what happened to your son wasn't yours," Rachel said. "But I still walk around every single day with guilt weighing me down like an anchor."

"Sometimes you have to let it go," Serrano said. "For your loved ones if not yourself. Because when you let those things weigh you down, they drag down people you care about. I know that from experience."

She looked down at their intertwined hands. She rubbed Serrano's thumb, felt the roughness of his skin. She wondered how many times he had drawn his gun. How many times he had fired it. How many lives he had taken.

"I want you to tell me the worst things you've ever done," Rachel said.

Serrano looked at her. "I'm sorry?"

"I want to know the worst things you've ever done. Things that rip you apart from the inside every time you think about them. Things you've pushed from your mind."

"Rachel, I . . ."

"Please."

He looked down. Nodded. He took a long breath.

"After Evan died, I was out of control. I drank every day until I couldn't feel. My wife threatened to leave me every night, and every night I convinced her to stay. That I would get help. Looking back, I wish I'd let her go. I would have saved Deirdre so much pain."

Serrano stopped.

"Please, John," Rachel said. Serrano nodded.

"One night, after my shift ended, I went to Hinsky's Pub on South Main. I ordered a shot and a beer. And then another shot and a beer. They refilled my glasses so many times I lost count. Suddenly I'm in the bathroom and . . ."

He stopped.

"Go on," Rachel said.

"And my pants are around my ankles. I'm leaning up against a dirty stall, and a girl I went to high school with is going down on me. Becky Albertelli. We used to call her the Beckinator. I don't remember why. I don't even remember seeing her at the bar before that moment. When I realized what was happening, I apologized and ran out with my pants still halfway down. When I checked my phone, I had a dozen missed calls from Deirdre. Somehow I managed to drive home without killing myself or anyone else. I should have been suspended from the force for that alone. When I got home, Deirdre was a mess. Her mother had had a stroke, and she'd been trying to reach me for hours. And I was bare assed in a grimy bathroom in a dive bar, looking at the top of the head of a girl I hadn't seen or thought about in fifteen years. I think about that a lot. I don't know if our marriage would have survived anyway after Evan died, but . . . if there was anything solid left in our relationship, I broke it that night."

"That's pretty bad," Rachel said. "Did you ever talk to the Beckinator again?"

Serrano shook his head. "I remember seeing a wedding announcement a year or two later. She seemed happy. Your turn. Quid pro quo."

"All right," she said. She thought about the worst thing she'd ever done. Images flashed in her mind. A knife. Blood. So much blood. A bracelet with Tiger Eye beads locked in a safe in her bedroom upstairs at that very moment.

Don't tell him that. It will change everything.

"After Bradley died," Rachel said, "I moved the kids to Torrington. We couldn't stay in Darien. Not after what happened. And every night for I don't know how long, Eric would wake up screaming. He had nightmares where he would see his father and relive what happened to him. I cannot imagine reliving that moment every night as a child. Every night I would go into Eric's room and climb into his bed and hold him until the crying and shaking stopped. But it didn't always stop. Sometimes his screams woke Megan. She was just a baby back then. And then I had two crying children in the middle of the night, and I felt so . . . helpless. I was still grieving myself at that point. I was an emotional wreck. But I didn't have anyone to talk to. Nobody was there to hold me. I had nightmares, too, but mine had to be ignored because I had two children who took precedence. I don't think I slept for six months."

Rachel paused.

"Anyway, one night after a session with Evie, I was just completely and utterly spent. I'd worked out for half the day. My muscles felt like meat sliding off a smoked rib. That night, when the kids went to bed, I opened a bottle of wine and put on a movie. Something mindless, just to take my mind off things. Half an hour into it, Eric began to scream. But I didn't move. Then ten minutes later, Megan began to scream. My children were screaming for their mother. They needed me. But I still didn't move. I couldn't. I couldn't do it another night. I needed one evening for myself. So I turned the volume on the television up and sat there and drank wine for an entire hour while my children cried for their mom. And I ignored them. I ignored my *children*. It was only one night, but I think about it every day. There is no guilt on this earth greater than that of a mother who could have prevented their child's pain and didn't."

She felt Serrano put his hand on her cheek. She turned to him.

"I can *be* alone. I can *be* strong." She turned to face him. "But sometimes I don't want to be."

Rachel slipped her hand behind Serrano's head and pulled him toward her, her lips finding his as she closed her eyes and kissed him hard and deep. He pressed back against her, his hand resting on her rib cage. She felt an electric current flow through her, rushing through her body in a torrent, warming her blood in an instant. She felt dizzy, heated, but ignored it.

She took his hand and placed it on her breast, and she gasped when he pressed on it, gently. He moved against her, and she could feel him growing hard. She couldn't remember the last time she'd ached for him, or anyone, so desperately. She had willed herself to not feel, to conceal her desires, but now she let everything go and lost herself in his touch. Rachel unzipped his fly. Serrano stood up and slid his pants down, his lips still pressed against hers, his hand still sending electric currents through her. She gripped him and heard him moan. Her head pounded, but she didn't care.

While still holding him, Rachel undid her jeans and slid them to the floor. Next came her tank top and his shirt. When they were both naked, she pushed Serrano onto the couch and straddled him. She kissed him passionately, then helped guide him inside her.

Her body felt like she'd been plugged into an electric socket. As she lowered herself on Serrano, over and over, she could feel the hairs on his chest tickling her skin. She moved faster and faster, their movements in sync. She could feel his heart beating against her chest, their bodies growing slick with sweat. Finally she grew close, her body bucking, Serrano holding on for dear life as a bolt of lightning shot through Rachel. She slowed and came to a stop, their lips finding each other, hands intertwined once again.

And then she lay there, still atop him, letting their breathing return to normal, their hearts slowing down, finding a rhythm. Serrano kissed her neck gently.

His eyes were closed. Hers were open.

Then she sat up, placing her hands on his chest. He opened his eyes.

"You OK?" he said, gently tracing her head, skirting her wound. Rachel nodded and kissed him.

"If I ever catch you texting with Becky Albertelli," she said, "I'll kill you both."

Serrano laughed and kissed her forehead. He ran his hands along the sides of her torso, his right thumb resting just below the thick, red scar. A reminder of the true worst thing she'd ever done. The one thing she'd kept to herself. The only thing she would never tell him.

CHAPTER 30

Serrano left before the school buses arrived. Rachel didn't want Eric to see them together, not after what had happened at Voss Field. Before he stepped out the door, Serrano kissed Rachel, deeply and passionately, and then he left.

At three thirty-two, the grade school bus pulled up, and Megan climbed off. She waved to her friends and skipped to the front door. Rachel gathered her into her arms and held her tight.

"My baby," she said.

"How's your head, Mom?"

"It's all right. Just a little bonk. I'll be fine."

"I wish Sadie Scout had been there to help out," Megan said. "She's very good at stopping bad guys. And crossing dangerous rivers."

Rachel laughed. "The next time I have to cross a dangerous river, I'll be sure to give Sadie a call. How was school?"

"We learned about indig . . . again . . . indigenous people in geography. They're kind of like people who stay who they are, even if everything around them changes. They don't change at all. There are, like, a hundred indi . . . gus tribes left in the world."

"Sound it out, hon. In-Dig-E-Nous."

"In-Dig-E-Noose."

"Close enough."

Megan looked around. "Is Eric home yet?"

Rachel shook her head. "Soon."

"Do you think he still loves us?" she asked.

"Oh, Megan, I know he does."

"OK," she said. "I have to get back to the new Sadie Scout book. Maybe I'll have her meet some In-Dig-E-Nous people. They can learn from each other."

"That sounds like it would be an amazing story. I can't wait to read it."

"Oh, it will be," Megan said with the confidence of a Pulitzer Prize–winning writer. "Love you, Mom."

"Love you, too, hon."

Megan bounded up the steps to her room, leaving Rachel alone. Half an hour later, she received a text message from Eric.

Be home late

It took all her self-control not to throw her phone against the wall. She knew exactly why he would be late. He'd be following Benjamin Ruddock around as he delivered whatever the hell was in those envelopes.

She checked her GPS app and tapped on Eric's name.

Person not within range or app is turned off

This time, she actually wound up to chuck the phone before catching herself. She took a breath. Without GPS to track him or any concept of when he might be home, Rachel felt powerless. She texted him back:

Please keep me posted. Do you have an idea of when you might be home? We need to talk. I love you. Always and no matter what. Mom.

She did not receive a response. She sat on the couch. Poured more tea. She didn't particularly even like tea but felt tea was the sort of drink you drank while you waited.

And waited.

And waited.

She made Megan a frozen veggie burger with Minute Rice, the Mom Guilt of being unable to focus enough to cook her daughter a decent meal kicking in fast and hard.

At eight o'clock, she called Eric's cell phone. She tried the GPS app again, but it was still off. Her heartbeat was hummingbird fast. Her head hurt like a cracked dam, her brain trying to leak out. She paced around the house. Cleaned the kitchen. Paid some bills. Backed up her laptop. Still no word from Eric.

At ten o'clock, she debated calling Serrano again to ask for another favor. The police had resources to find a cell phone's GPS signal and track its location. But Eric had been gone from school for less than seven hours. And Serrano might feel just a little used after an afternoon of sex followed by yet another favor. She did not want him to feel like their relationship was transactional.

There was one person she could call. And thankfully, that person picked up on the first ring.

"You know this isn't your boyfriend's number, Rachel," Detective Leslie Tally said. "I'm too old and too married to be getting booty-called at night anymore."

"Thanks for picking up, Detective."

"It's Leslie. When I'm off the clock, it's Leslie."

"Leslie. I know this is weird. But I have a favor to ask."

"Is this an official favor?"

"Sort of."

"Is it going to get me fired, divorced, or killed?"

"None of the above."

"All right, then. You still make that amazing Thai chicken casserole?"

"When the occasion calls for it."

"OK, Marin. Here's the deal. You bring a dish of that casserole over for dinner one night, with enough to feed a family of hungry Wallace children, and you got yourself *one* favor."

"Deal. But there's a catch."

"Oh, fantastic. What is it?"

"The favor I need isn't actually from you. It's from your daughter."

There was silence on the other end. Then Tally said, "Then you'd better plan to bring two casseroles."

At 1:46 a.m., Eric Marin returned home.

Rachel was sitting on the couch watching an infomercial. She had already purchased a new cutting board, a fishing pole (she had never fished in her life), an adult onesie (with pockets), and the world's best (alleged) eye cream. Her head throbbed like someone was using a pogo stick on it. But the moment she heard footsteps coming up the driveway and recognized the gait and shuffle of her son, she ran to the door, pulled it open, and hugged him.

"I'm not going to ask you where you were," she said. "I'm not going to ask who you were with. I'm just glad you're home. And I want you to know that when you want to talk to me, I will be here for you no matter what."

She hugged him so hard she could feel his shoulder blades beneath his jacket. He did not return the embrace. But he also did not try to escape it.

Finally she let her arms fall to her sides.

"G'night, Mom," Eric said. Then he hung up his coat, took off his shoes, and went upstairs. Rachel watched him, thinking that even last year, when she had been drugged and thrown into the back of another man's car, his intention to murder her and bury her in a ditch, she had never felt so helpless.

CHAPTER 31

Penny Wallace sat on a low brick wall outside the entrance of Ashby High, wondering just what the hell she was going to say to Eric Marin. She had known Eric for only a couple of years, but she felt herself to be a decent judge of character. So in that time, she'd learned that he was very smart, very funny, very talented, and very, very troubled. She knew Eric's father had died six or seven years ago under mysterious circumstances, and she knew the loss ate at him. Eric refused to talk about his father, and Penny did not ask.

Eric joined Ashby Middle School in seventh grade, one of only two new kids in the class. The other one was Darcy Perriman, and she was gorgeous and rich and outgoing, and those made making friends easy. Eric would sit alone in the cafeteria, his face buried in books thicker than his head, tattered paperbacks with dragons and wizards on the cover. Penny wasn't the most popular girl in her class, but she didn't need to be. She had enough friends and never felt the desire to step on others just to climb the Mean Girl ladder.

Her hardest moment had come when her mother, Claire, had left Penny's father. She'd sat her three kids down one night and told them that she was attracted to women and had been for a long time. That she couldn't keep the truth from the people she loved. And she *did* love them—their father too—with all her heart. But she needed to pursue happiness and love on her terms. They did not understand it. They were too young and too emotionally volatile, and just like any family, they did not want to see theirs break up, under any circumstances. But it was not their decision.

So their father had moved out and moved away and made no attempt to fight for custody (*that* jabbed at Penny like a splinter that had never been removed). After that, the Wallace dinner table became much, much quieter. Her mother had spent weeks and weeks crying. She'd confided in them. Had she done the right thing? Had she ruined her family's happiness for her own? Was she selfish? But eventually the crying slowed, then it stopped, and to Penny's surprise her mom actually *did* seem happier. One day she introduced Penny and her siblings to Leslie Tally—*Detective Leslie Tally.*

"You're dating a cop?" Penny had said.

"No," her mother replied. "I'm dating a wonderful woman."

Penny had never seen her mother so happy.

But for the Wallace kids, at least at first, it had opened a door to mockery. Their classmates reveled in shockingly gleeful cruelties that had shattered Penny. First, it was "Your mother's a dyke." Then it was "Your mother's a dyke who's married to a dyke cop." The words lanced. Penny held the tears in, then unleashed them in never-ending torrents the moment she got home.

She told her mother she was upset about a boy. They both knew she was lying.

"One day," Penny's mother had said, "and I don't know when that will be, but it will come, you'll feel bad for all those sad, shallow people. Because they have hate in their hearts. And only unhappy people have hate in their hearts. One day their hate will wash off you like water because you can live a happy life despite their ignorance. But they'll always be hateful, and they'll always be unhappy."

Eventually, the cruelty had subsided. Penny was just another kid—happily. Every now and then, some ignoramus would make a snide remark, and Penny would just smile and say, "I hope being an asshole works out for you one day."

She had not chosen to become friendly with Eric Marin. He was not part of her social circles, and frankly, her friends thought he was weird. They weren't wrong, but he was also more.

Their friendship had been thrust upon them by circumstance. Leslie Tally and John Serrano were not just detectives in the Ashby Police Department; they were family. Penny and her siblings loved him and cried for him when his son died. And when Serrano began dating Rachel Marin, they had no choice but to spend time with Eric. Megan was far easier; the girl could tell stories like she didn't need to breathe.

But eventually, Eric had opened up. He was smart. Funny. And clearly desperate for someone to talk to. But he was also guarded. As fast as he could open up, he could shut down just as quickly. So she'd always had a bit of a soft spot for Eric. Maybe more than she let on. She'd known he was hurting. But it wasn't until last night that she knew how much trouble he was in.

Penny lived only a few blocks away from school, so she usually waited until the last moment before walking over. But that morning, she'd surprised her mother by leaving fifteen minutes early. Leslie had taken her aside the night before and passed along a favor from Rachel Marin. She'd agreed in a second, but it meant getting to school before the buses began to arrive. She needed to beat Eric.

Penny watched intently as each bus drove up and coughed up its collection of students. Finally, the one with Eric Marin pulled up, and he got out.

He was wearing blue jeans and a black polo shirt. His eyes were red rimmed, like he hadn't slept in a week. And maybe he hadn't. He didn't so much as make eye contact or speak to anyone as he ambled toward the entrance.

"Hey, Eric!" she called out. He turned. A smile came over his face instantly.

"Oh, hey, Penny," he said. "What's up?"

Eric's voice was unenthusiastic but almost purposefully so, as though he was trying too hard to play it cool. That was one of the things she liked most about Eric: he couldn't even try to play it cool. He was just him.

"I have no idea what I'm going to write for my term paper for Ms. Stern's class," she said. "I feel like the night before I'm just going to narrow it down to two topics, flip a coin, and pull an all-nighter. Have you decided?"

He nodded. "I'm writing about Lennie from *Of Mice and Men.* How he guards George and the animals. How he's a protector but doesn't understand that he's capable of killing the ones he loves. He's not evil—he just doesn't know better."

Penny nodded. "That sounds really good," she said, earnestly. "I was thinking we could go over some of the material later. Maybe after school? You could come by. My mom made peanut butter brownies."

She said the words *peanut butter brownies* with a lilt in her voice. She remembered after one family meal, Eric had eaten at least four of them. Eric perked up.

"I think I could do that," he said. "I'd just have to—"

"Eric Marin. The man of the hour."

Penny closed her eyes and cursed under her breath. She knew that voice.

"Hey, Ben," Eric said. Benjamin Ruddock came up, smiling. He loomed above them like a tank over two dachshunds.

"Hey, Penny," Ruddock said. "Good to see you again."

"Sure. You too."

Ruddock laughed. "Not a lot of sincerity there. But that's OK. You'd just think that after all the incredible things I'm doing for Eric here that his friends would be a little nicer to me."

Penny looked at Eric and said, "You know, maybe I'll write my paper on Narcissus. How he fell into despair when he realized that nobody could ever love him as much as he loved himself."

"Listen, *Miss Wallace*," Ruddock said. "Go run along and play with all the other little girls. The grown-ups need to talk."

Penny stood her ground. She needed to get Eric alone. That was the plan. She'd already been concerned about Eric even before hearing it from Rachel Marin. Plus, rumors were flying around school that Ruddock had had something to do with Darren Reznick's compound arm fracture. Even before the last few days, every kid with a brain in Ashby had been scared of Ruddock—and the people Ruddock knew. Now, they were absolutely terrified.

"You got my text, right?" Ruddock said to Eric.

Eric nodded. "Yeah."

"So you'll be there?" Eric nodded again. "Good. 'Cause our friend needs to address a few things. Rumors. But I'm meeting with him one on one later, and I can't wait to tell him how great you were the other day."

She needed to know what they were talking about. What was in the text messages Ruddock was referring to. Thankfully, Penny and Eric had homeroom together.

She had an idea. Penny took out her phone and texted Eric:

So is he like your douchy bodyguard or something? Do you pay him in Axe body spray?

She heard Eric's cell phone buzz, and he slipped it from his pocket. She watched as he entered his PIN: 33078.

He read Penny's text, smiled, and wrote back:

I'm sorry. I can't study with you. Please understand. And yes. He wears a LOT of Axe.

Eric slipped the phone into his pocket. Penny sped up and said, "Hey Eric, if you can't study, then I need to ask you one more thing about Ms. Stern's paper—"

Then Penny tripped, her shoulder clipping the back of Eric's knees. He fell to the ground, and Penny landed in a heap on top of him.

Penny apologized profusely. Ruddock watched with morbid amusement as they disentangled themselves.

"I'm so sorry . . . stupid tree root came out of nowhere," Penny said.

"It's OK," Eric said, brushing the dirt from his pants. "Are you OK?"

"Yeah, I'm fine. Just embarrassed," Penny replied.

"One day I'll introduce you to girls who know how to walk," Ruddock said. "Come on, Marin. Someone belongs in the dirt, and it isn't you."

Eric and Ruddock walked off. She waited, then looked down and smiled. She held Eric Marin's cell phone in her hand. When they were out of sight, Penny used the stolen PIN to unlock the cell. She found a text message thread between Eric Marin and Benjamin Ruddock. She used her own phone to take screenshots of the entire conversation, then texted them to Rachel Marin along with a note:

Please find out what's going on. I have a terrible feeling that Eric is going to get hurt. Or worse.

CHAPTER 32

Rachel scanned the screenshots Penny Wallace had sent her. She asked how Penny got them, and when Penny wrote back, she gave the girl credit for resourcefulness. Not that she would advocate the semiviolent tripping of her own son, but Penny had found a way to get information without being detected. She was a girl after her own heart.

Penny had sent five screenshots of a text exchange between her son and Benjamin Ruddock. Most of them were big nothings. It was clear Ruddock was being very careful about what he sent via text. Though it was very possible he had other means of communication beyond the cell phone he used to communicate with Eric. There were three exchanges in particular that caught Rachel's eye. The first was sent the afternoon of the initial meeting at Voss Field.

Ruddock: Glad you're coming tonight. You won't be sorry. Time to change your life, Marin.

Eric: I still feel like I should know what this "meeting" is all about.

Ruddock: Don't sweat it, big guy. It'll be worth your time. Emphasis on 'worth'.

Eric: What do you mean?

Ruddock: I mean just be smart, work hard, and treat my man with respect. Soon enough people will be asking YOU for favors.

Eric: Who is 'your man'?

Ruddock: See? There you go asking questions. Let's just say he's like if Jesus, Bill Gates, and Donald Trump had a baby and that baby grew up and said "Hey Eric Marin, let's do business." You'd be stupid not to.

Eric: I don't know what any of that means.

Ruddock: You will. And if you miss this meeting, you'll regret it for the rest of your life.

Eric: Why does it have to be in the middle of the night?

Ruddock: A test, my friend. Before soldiers go off to war, the squad leaders need to know if they're capable of handling the battles. If you can't even hack a late night meet, how can you be expected to do anything else?

Eric: My mom. You don't know what she's like.

Ruddock: Trust me, my man. We know all about your mom.

Rachel looked at the last text from Ruddock. *We know all about your mom.* Brice had looked into Rachel even before he'd met Eric. Which confirmed her suspicions that they were using Eric as a way to get to her. If things went bad, they could claim she was emotional, had a vendetta. They knew Rachel had pressure points. And they were pressing on them. *Hard.*

She read the second text exchange between the boys. Based on the time stamps, they appeared to have been sent while Rachel was recovering in the hospital.

Eric: My mother got attacked.

Ruddock: Sorry man.

Eric: Sorry man? You're saying you didn't know? That you didn't have anything to do with it?

Ruddock: You kidding me bro? Absolutely not. Had no idea that crazy bitch was anywhere near us.

Eric: Don't call her that.

Ruddock: You're right. I apologize. This is a violent town. Hell, your mom nearly got herself killed last year.

Eric: I'd better not find out that you or Brice had anything to do with it.

Ruddock: First, if you threaten me again, I'll rip your legs off and beat you to death with them. I'm a reasonable guy, but I have limits. Second, I. Had. Nothing. To. Do. With. It.

Eric: What do I say to her if she asks? She's smarter than you think. She's not going to believe that it's a coincidence that she got attacked while following us.

Ruddock: It is a total coincidence. Just tell her that and you'll be golden.

Eric: You'd better be telling me the truth.

Ruddock: And what exactly would I gain from lying to you? You're going to be a star, Marin. Just keep your eyes on the prize. Fratres now and always.

Eric did not respond to the last text.

The final text that Rachel took an interest in was one line, and one line only. It had been sent that very morning, after Eric had left for school and before Penny Wallace stole the phone. It read:

Tuesday. 1:30. VF.

Tuesday. One thirty in the morning. Voss Field. The next meeting with Bennett Brice. It had to be.

Rachel texted Penny Wallace:

Great job. Thank you. I owe you.

Penny wrote back three minutes later:

No biggie. U owe me nothing. Just help Eric.

I'll do whatever I have to do. What about his phone?

Slipped it in his bag during homeroom.

Smart. Now put your phone away. You're in school. Thank you Penny. You're a heck of a snoop.

You ever need an apprentice, you know where to find me.

It was accompanied by an emoji that Rachel suspected was supposed to be a detective holding a magnifying glass but for some reason looked more like a proctologist.

Rachel knew where she had to go next: 98 Violet Road. The house Eric and Benjamin Ruddock stopped at right before her head was split open.

Rachel drove to Violet Road. It was midmorning, a calm, bright day. Rachel parked on the street in the identical spot she'd parked the rental. Before she exited, she checked her surroundings. Every mirror. Every blind spot. Peered behind every bush and tree where somebody could hide. She saw nothing.

She'd slipped a pair of TigerLady self-defense safety grips into her purse that morning and now gripped one as she exited the car. They were palm-size plastic handles that with a squeeze released three short retractable claws. Each claw held a narrow channel inset meant to scrape skin and blood from any assailant for DNA testing.

Once the door was closed, Rachel backed up against the car and did a 360 turn, looking for any sign of life. She could hear her own breathing, feel the blood thumping in her temples. She saw an elderly woman walking a regal-looking poodle. Rachel wasn't a fan of poodles—give her a golden retriever or a black Lab—but the woman's taste in pets appeared to be the most dangerous thing about her.

Rachel waited. Listened. Gripped the claw in her hand. She heard nothing but the faint rustling of leaves, car horns from far away, and the steady chirping of birds among the trees.

Nothing.

Still, she had to be cautious. She approached the house at 98 Violet Road slowly. When she got to the curb, she stopped again. Looked around. Still alone, as far as she could tell. She put her hand to her head and felt the staples in her scalp, the skin still tender. Somebody was going to pay for those.

Two cars were parked in the driveway at 98 Violet Road: a silver Prius and a black Range Rover. As though the owners couldn't decide whether they wanted to save the planet or destroy it. Rachel approached the front door, still scanning her environment. She rang the bell. She could hear a shuffling sound from behind the large oak door.

The door opened, revealing a sixtyish woman wearing a faded yellow terry cloth bathrobe. Her hair was in curlers. She looked perturbed by the interruption.

"May I help you?" OK, perhaps more than slightly perturbed.

"Yes, hi. My name is Rachel Marin, and I work with the Ashby Police Department. Are you Wanda Meyerson?"

"I am." The woman's eyes narrowed as she looked Rachel up and down, her curlers bobbing. "You're a police officer? You don't look like a police officer."

"I work *with* the Ashby police," Rachel said. "I'm not police myself."

"I'm confused," the woman said. "What's the difference?"

"Sometimes I ask myself the same thing," Rachel replied. "But from your perspective, it means that I'm just here as a courtesy. I just have a few questions for you. I don't need to bring in the actual police. Unless I find it necessary."

"Necessary for what? What kind of questions?"

"The other day, two young men—teenage boys, actually—came to this house. They were here for over half an hour. Did you see them or speak to them?"

"Two boys? What did they look like?"

Rachel took out her cell phone. She heard a clanking noise behind her and whipped around. A toddler across the street had tipped over her tricycle and was propping it back up.

"Sorry," Rachel said. "A little jumpy."

"I'll say," the woman replied.

Rachel showed the woman a photo of her son.

"He doesn't look familiar."

Rachel felt a sinking feeling in her stomach. She pulled up a photo of Benjamin Ruddock.

"Him either."

"So neither of these boys came to your house?"

"Oh, I wouldn't know about that. I had my weekly cribbage game and then saw a movie with my sister. I was out all day."

Rachel kept her irritation at bay. "Why didn't you just tell me you weren't home?"

"Didn't seem pertinent."

"Didn't seem . . . . OK. Let's step back. Is it possible these boys have been to your home but you weren't aware of it?"

"I suppose so? My husband was home. He has to feed and walk the dog. And he doesn't go out much. Said we paid enough for this house that folks can come here if they really want to see us. But I have friends I like to see. I'm not a hermit, even though Harold can be. He's more than content to sit on the couch and watch television all day. But those shows he watches—utter crap. Personally I like baking shows. Do you ever watch a baking show and think they must do some creative editing? Because once I tried to make one of those cakes, and—"

"Is your husband here now, Mrs. Meyerson?" Rachel asked, interrupting the woman's meandering soliloquy.

"No. He goes away every few weeks for business. He flew out yesterday morning."

Flew out yesterday morning, Rachel thought. *He's visited by Ruddock and Eric, given an envelope, then flies out the next day.* There was no chance it was a coincidence.

"Can you recall any other instances of young boys, again around high school age, coming by your house?"

"Like delivery boys?"

"In a way. Only they would have been invited inside."

Wanda Meyerson thought for a moment. "I do recall—and this would have been a few years ago at least—a time when a young man used to come around fairly regularly. Maybe every other week? He would disappear into the study with Harold for a bit."

Rachel showed Wanda Meyerson the photo of Benjamin Ruddock again. "Could it have been this boy, perhaps a few years younger?"

"Oh no. Most certainly not. The boy who came over had—I'm not supposed to say *fat* these days—a *metabolism* problem. And he was short . . . er, vertically challenged. My grandchildren always give me a hard time for being politically incorrect. These days you never know *what's* going to offend people. I say live and let live; everyone should stop being so sensitive, because back when I was a young girl, I—"

"So the name Benjamin Ruddock doesn't ring a bell?"

"No. This boy's name was . . . hold on . . . Alex. Yes, Alex."

"Do you know his last name?"

"I'm afraid not. We were never properly introduced. Harold doesn't have the best social skills. And the boy seemed like he wanted to get in and out as fast as possible."

Alex. Teen. Was younger than Ruddock is now. Chubby.

"And where did you say your husband was flying to today?"

"Where he always goes for some rest and relaxation," Wanda said. "I just wish he'd invite me sometimes."

"And where would that be, Mrs. Meyerson?"

"Oh, why, the Cayman Islands."

CHAPTER 33

"John," Rachel said, "you're not going to believe this. Or maybe you are. Anyway, I went to the home of Harold and Wanda Meyerson on Violet Road and—"

"Wait, slow down," Serrano said. Rachel was driving to the Ashby PD station at speeds that could have gotten her license revoked. The skies were beginning to darken, a grayish pall descending from above, blotting out the sun. Patters of rain hit Rachel's windshield. Within moments, she heard thunder, and the skies opened, a sheet of rain hitting her car like a slap. "Did you say the house on Violet Road? The one where you were assaulted?"

"That's the one."

"The one you followed Ruddock and Eric to?"

"You have quite the memory. Anyway . . ."

"Rachel, are you kidding me? If Brice finds out you went to the home of one of his clients—"

"Listen, *Detective*, I spoke to Wanda Meyerson, and she told me her husband, Harold, left for the Cayman Islands. For some 'R and R.' *Without* his wife. I thought it was too much to be a coincidence that he left the country the very day after Ruddock came by his house. So I also checked out the other homes the boys visited."

"Rachel, I can't hear you over the rain. Did you say you went to more people's homes?"

"Yep. And get this: at least *four* other people Ruddock visited flew out of Peoria airport *the next morning*. Wanda said Harold Meyerson's return flight comes in tomorrow. Two days in the Caymans. That doesn't really sound like much of a vacation, does it? And going without his wife? Sounds to me like he's going down there for business. I'm guessing it's Bennett Brice's business. And he's not the only one."

Serrano paused on the other end. Rachel could tell he was weighing his anger at Rachel's flouting Brice's legal threats versus the fact that she may have legitimately uncovered information worth investigating.

"Get here fast, but get here safe. If I know you, you're driving at speeds that might challenge the sound barrier."

They hung up. Rachel put the wipers on full speed but could still barely see through the monsoon. Her head swam. From the concussion, the staples she could feel biting into her scalp, but also the many, many tendrils the murder of Matthew Linklater seemed to have sprouted. And every time she felt she had a hold of one, three more grew in its place.

She parked in the visitors' lot at the Ashby PD station and ran inside, not fast enough to avoid getting drenched. She showed her ID, and the officers manning the security desk buzzed her through. She found Serrano and Tally waiting for her at their desks. Tally handed her a wad of tissues, which Rachel used to dab at her face.

"You look like the rat that the drowned rat dragged in," Tally said.

"You only get away with that because you helped me," Rachel said. "Thank you, Detective. And thank Penny again for me."

"Just for the record, if I'd known you were asking for Penny Wallace's help," Serrano said, "I would have told you no."

"That's why I didn't tell you," Rachel replied.

Tally said, "You know I care about your kids. But this *is* starting to sound like a bit of a vendetta. And if that's the case, I won't do anything that could jeopardize this investigation. Or violate a restraining order."

Serrano pulled out a seat and motioned to it. Rachel sat down.

"Tell us everything you found out," he said.

"Four homes," she said. "I started with the Meyersons on Violet Road. Harold Meyerson flies to the Cayman Islands the day after he's visited by Benjamin Ruddock and my son. Wanda Meyerson says he's going on a vacation but will be back in two days. Sounds fishy, right? So I backtrack. Go to the other houses Ruddock and Eric visited before the Meyersons' that I know about. At each house, the owner or co-owner flew out to the Cayman Islands *the very next day*. I'm thinking that these good ol' folks are laundering money and hiding it overseas for Bennett Brice."

"Laundering how?" Serrano said.

"Brice could wire the money to the Caymans himself. But it would leave an electronic trail. By having these people act as couriers, he's off the hook. At every house, Ruddock delivered a manila envelope. I'm thinking they contained financial documents. Bank account numbers. Then Harold Meyerson and the others fly to Grand Cayman and deposit the funds, and Bennett Brice is free and clear."

Tally said, "But why would Harold Meyerson agree to do that? Brice might be clear, but if it looks like Meyerson is squirreling away money to avoid paying taxes, he's liable for either a hefty fine or jail time. So why risk all that for Bennett Brice?"

"I don't know yet," Rachel said.

"I don't doubt there's something hinky about this," Serrano said. "But at the moment, all we're doing is looking for a crime. It's not a crime to fly to the Caymans. We need something more tangible."

"More tangible?" Rachel said. "Matthew Linklater was murdered. Darren Reznick's arm was broken in the school parking lot. I nearly had my brains scooped out and deposited on Violet Road. My son is—"

"Your son is preventing you from thinking straight," Tally said.

"Brice went to my son because he wanted the cops to think I had a vendetta. It scared him that Linklater was on to him, so he's trying to discredit me since I'm the one Linklater reached out to. Brice knew if I found any dirt on him, he could claim I had a personal vendetta against him because of Eric. He's using my son to shield himself."

"But right now you have no proof that Brice is connected to Matthew Linklater's murder," Serrano said. "And as of right now, we don't know any laws he's broken regarding your son. We have a crime. Linklater's murder. All of this is tangential."

"Tangential," Rachel said sardonically. "Sometimes I can't believe I let you inside of me."

Serrano's cheeks reddened.

"I'm going to pretend I didn't hear that," Tally said. "But if you two want to turn a murder investigation into couple's therapy, take it outside."

Rachel felt anger bubbling within her. These were the moments she saw John Serrano not as a partner or a lover but as an obstacle. Still, she had to temper her emotions. She was acting as a mother. A protector. Serrano was a cop. He had to stay within the confines of the law. Rachel had no qualms about tiptoeing outside the law. And if that's what it took, she would simply keep the detectives out of the loop.

"I do have one thought," Serrano said.

"That's a record," Tally said.

"Look, I don't need both of you on my case. Anyway, Rachel, the kid who pulled the gun on you. You said you disarmed him and hurt his leg."

She nodded. "Dislocated kneecap, ACL and PCL injuries."

"There were no police reports of any injuries on Violet Road that day. Rachel had the idea to check with local hospitals to see if any kids in that age range were admitted with leg injuries that line up with what you're telling me."

"And if there are none?" Rachel said.

Tally replied, "We can check with local schools. You said the kid pulled the gun on you within half an hour of you staking out the Meyerson place. That gives us a half-hour radius, at most. I'm guessing there are about a dozen schools in that area with kids between the ages of twelve and sixteen enrolled. It wouldn't take long to call up the principals, nurses' stations, see if they've seen any students with noticeable new injuries or restricted activities."

"It's a start," Serrano said. He looked at Rachel, his voice bordering on contempt. "*That* is an actual criminal investigation. Finding the kid who assaulted you."

"Thank you," she said. "I probably don't need to say it since, you know, you spend a fair amount of time with me. But I don't always work well with others."

"I hadn't noticed," Serrano said.

"I will tell you this, though," Rachel added. "If I can prove that Bennett Brice was behind these attacks, or that he's involving my son in criminal activities, I'm going to bury him so deep they'll find oil in Ashby before they find his body."

CHAPTER 34

Benjamin Ruddock had been in Bennett Brice's house only twice before. The first time was when he had been promoted, the circumstances of which had never been discussed again. He'd only met the boy—Alex something—once. And the next week, Alex and his family had moved far, far away from Ashby. The second time was three weeks ago, when he and Brice met to go over the latest group of YourLife recruits. At the time, the list of recruits did not include Eric Marin. Marin's inclusion was a last-second decision, due to special circumstances.

Always be ready to adapt, Brice had told him. And so far, Benjamin had.

Brice had invited him over for lunch. *Invited* was too nice a word. You didn't refuse an invitation from Bennett Brice.

Ruddock watched as Brice took the gleaming steel sharpening tool from the walnut knife block, then slid out an eight-inch chef's knife. He looked at the blade, admired its craftsmanship, then gently placed the tip of the tool on the quartz countertop. He held the knife at a fifteen-degree angle to the sharpening tool, then, with a swinging motion, slid the length of the blade across the metal.

Brice repeated this five times, then switched to the other side of the blade and gave it five strokes. He then held the blade up to the light, nodded, and placed the sharpening tool back in the block. Brice was wearing a thin linen shirt with sleeves rolled up to his elbows, olive-colored chinos, and a pair of light-blue slippers. He looked comfortable yet classy.

First, he sliced the garlic thin enough to be translucent. He then set a nonstick pan on a burner and dropped in a pad of unsalted butter. When the butter melted, he added the slivers of garlic. As they began to sizzle, a pleasant aroma wafted up from the pan. To the cooking garlic, he added the sliced white tops of several scallions, then a dozen sea scallops, which he'd had dry-packed and overnighted from a fishery near the Canadian border. As he stirred, he took a sip of Catena Zapata chardonnay.

Then he turned around and said, "Benjamin. Have a seat." He looked at the Omega watch on his wrist. Ruddock knew that watch ran a cool $18,000. "Lunch will be ready in twenty minutes. I'm willing to bet this tastes better than whatever gruel they serve you in that school cafeteria."

Benjamin Ruddock approached the kitchen island tentatively. "I definitely don't remember them ever serving scallops," the boy said.

Brice's home was spotless and white, all marble, quartz, and white tile with state-of-the-art appliances and first-rate cutlery. The spacious living room was adorned by a white-brick fireplace, its mantel covered in framed pictures. The ornate, expensive furnishings included a floating wood coffee table, two rust-colored iron floor lamps, and four pristine white bookshelves made from reclaimed wood. The shelves were overstuffed with books several rows deep, spines dangling precariously over the edge. They contained old volumes with cracked leather spines, biographies of world leaders and business luminaries, several classics in their original languages (according to Brice these included *Anna Karenina* in Russian, *Les Misérables* in French, *The Tin Drum* in German). Plus a selection of popular mystery novels and science fiction thrown in for good measure. Ruddock had no idea if Brice had read all, or any, of the books, but they looked fantastic in his home, and Ruddock supposed that was partly the point.

The entire home gave off a vibe that Bennett Brice was smarter, cleaner, and more worldly and could cook a better dinner than you. If there was such a thing as modest conceit, Brice's home was a perfect example of it.

Brice washed and dried a bunch of asparagus, placed them in an aluminum tray, and seasoned them with salt, pepper, and a sprinkle of freshly shaved parmesan. He put the tray into the oven, set the timer for fifteen minutes, and turned to Ruddock.

Ruddock took a seat on a padded wooden kitchen stool. He absently picked at a scab on his hand.

"The rest of the drop-offs went without a hitch?" Brice said.

Ruddock nodded, still focused on the scab.

"Benjamin? Please do not be distracted when you are a guest in somebody else's home. It's rude."

Ruddock looked up as though he suddenly realized where he was.

"I know. Sorry, Mr. Brice. The Meyersons were the last on the list. So once we got out of there, we were done."

"It's very fortunate you noticed the Marin woman following you," Brice said. He spooned melted butter over the scallops. "That's part of the reason I liked you right from the start. You're perceptive. Aware of your surroundings. Anyone can follow instructions. Or a recipe. Not everyone can improvise."

"Harold Meyerson . . . he really didn't like that we hung around the house for so long. He said it drew attention to him. He was worried that if the neighbors saw us, they'd ask questions. I guess they like to snoop. He said they already ask questions about his trips, and he's running out of excuses."

"We may need to cut the Meyersons out for a while," Brice said. "When a client gets skittish, their decision-making can no longer be trusted. Let's cut him out until this dies down."

"You got it," Ruddock said. "One more thing. Eric Marin."

"What about him?" Brice said, attention focused on his cooking.

"He kept asking why we couldn't leave. He's in, but he's questioning things. I don't think he's as reliable as some of the other guys."

Ruddock paused. "Speaking of which . . . I think we need to drop Eric Marin."

Brice nodded and continued to spoon. After a moment, he said, "Keep Marin in. Under ordinary circumstances, I'd agree. But these are extraordinary times. We need the leverage the Marin boy gives us. Keep him close. Is he coming to the next meet?"

"He said he was."

"Good. Keep the pressure on, but keep it gentle."

"You got it." Ruddock paused. "How's Peter Lincecum? Sounds like Rachel Marin hurt him pretty bad. Busted his knee."

A splash of butter flew from the pan and landed on the floor. Brice ripped a paper towel from a roll and sopped it up, then tossed it in the trash.

"Mr. Brice? How's Peter?"

"Peter will be fine," Brice said. "I spoke to his father. I apologized for any harm that came to Peter and said he would be compensated for the injury."

Brice was acting strange. Ruddock felt like he'd touched a nerve.

"But aren't you worried?" Ruddock said. "If Peter needs medical attention, they'll ask what happened. I like Peter a lot, but if he tells the truth, it's a big problem, right? With the brothers?"

"You let me handle the brothers," Brice said angrily. "They are not your concern."

"Pete's a good kid," Ruddock said. "I told him we'd take care of him. He and Tony Vargas are tight. Maybe I could talk to Tony. Get word to Peter that we have his back."

"You will do no such thing," Brice said. "We do not need this Linklater situation getting any more fragile than it already is."

"Not to argue, Mr. Brice, but it's my reputation out there too. I tell kids like Peter and Eric Marin that if they work hard and put themselves on the line, they'll be taken care of. If one of the kids gets hurt and then gets ignored, or worse, the others might start to ask questions. If there really is a chance of the brothers going after Peter, he needs to know. We need to protect him."

"Benjamin," Brice said. He left the spoon in the pan and turned to his protégé. "I have done more for Peter Lincecum than you could ever know. I will handle the brothers. And I will address any concerns regarding your perceived loss of reputation."

"Thank you, Mr. Brice."

"Now onto Eric Marin. One thing you will learn over time is that leverage in the right hands is more powerful than any firearm. Any man can hold a gun. But the right leverage will make him afraid to fire it. Eric Marin provides us with leverage."

"Like Elliot Pine," Ruddock said. "One of the newbies. I know his dad, Willis, owes money, like a hundred K, to the brothers. And that Elliot is working for us to help pay off his dad's debts. We have leverage on Willis Pine and motivation for Elliot. Either one of them turn on us, Willis either goes to jail or gets done up."

"Done up?"

"Whacked."

"This is not the mob, Benjamin. Violence is never the preferred tactic. But to answer your query, yes. Elliot Pine has a great deal to fear from people who might do him harm."

"People. You mean the brothers."

"You have answered your own question," Brice said.

"I have to ask," Ruddock said. "You're working for them too. And if I'm going to *progress* in this field, I need to know the full story. What leverage do they have over you?"

Brice stopped cooking. He turned to face Benjamin Ruddock. The boy stood his ground. A look came over Bennett Brice's face that Ruddock had never seen before. The man's voice cracked as he spoke. Ruddock felt a shiver of fear run up his spine.

"What I owe," Brice replied, "is something money cannot buy."

Just then, the doorbell rang.

"Answer that, please," Brice said. Ruddock went to answer it.

He opened it to find a woman standing there. She wore a dark-brown tank top and jean shorts. Her hair was tied back in a ponytail. She was forty or so, with toned, trim arms and shoulders. For some reason, Ruddock knew she could handle herself. The woman smiled at Ruddock.

"So you're the apprentice," the woman said. "Nice to meet you. Evie Boggs."

She extended her hand, and Ruddock shook it. "Ben Ruddock," he said.

The woman sniffed the air.

"Let's see: buttered scallops and asparagus. Am I right?"

Ruddock nodded. The woman smiled.

"One thing you can say about my brother: he knows how to cook."

CHAPTER 35

It took eleven schools before Serrano and Tally hit pay dirt. They'd spent the morning calling every junior high and high school within a thirty-mile radius of Ashby, inquiring about any recent notable injuries to students. Two hours into their calls, Tally snapped her fingers to get Serrano's attention. He had just hung up on the school nurse at Macadam High, who informed him of three cases of lice, one broken nose suffered during an apparent highly competitive game of dodgeball, and one case of hives when sophomore Sally Watkins had an allergic reaction to a shrimp po'boy served in the school cafeteria.

Serrano put down his phone and listened as Tally spoke. When she hung up, she turned to him and said, "Got it. Let's go. I'm driving."

Tally merged onto the parkway and said, "Peter Lincecum. Sixteen years old, about to finish his sophomore year at Toni Morrison High. Homeroom teacher noticed him walking with a bad limp and sent him to the nurse. The teacher, Carol Lyons, said she practically had to fight with Lincecum to get him checked out. When Peter got to the nurse, she took one look at the knee and knew he had ligament damage that would require medical attention. She said when she went to examine it, Peter Lincecum screamed like he'd been gored by a bull. Principal Sloane Barker told me the nurse reported the injury to her. Teachers and nurses are required to report any suspicious or out-of-the-ordinary injuries or illnesses to the head of school."

"In the event the injuries occur at home and social services needs to get involved," Serrano said.

"Exactly."

"Did Lincecum say how the injury happened?" Serrano asked. "Or why he hadn't seen a doctor? And what about Lincecum's parents?"

"That's where it gets hinky," Tally said. "Principal Barker told me the nurse stepped away for a moment to get some ice to try to reduce the swelling, but when she got back, Lincecum was gone."

"Gone? Is he still at school?"

"Barker doesn't know," Tally said. "He didn't show for his AP calculus class."

"Something about this isn't right," Serrano said.

"You mean less right than a teenager putting a gun to your girlfriend's head, getting his knee kicked in, keeping the injury quiet, then disappearing from school once people start asking questions?"

"Yes. Less right. Far less right. The boy is scared of something. To not report the injury means he doesn't want it made public. You get the feeling I'm getting?"

Tally nodded. "That Peter Lincecum is scared to death about something. And that his injury might be connected to the Linklater murder."

"That's the feeling I was talking about," Serrano said.

Tally said, "I got Peter Lincecum's home address from Principal Barker. Maybe we'll get lucky and he went home."

Twenty-two minutes after they'd left the precinct, Tally pulled into the driveway of 119 Kennesaw Lane in the town of Carltondale, just outside Ashby. The mailbox read "Lincecum." The ranch-style house had a dated yellow paint job, and the overgrown lawn looked like it hadn't been mowed in months. Weeds sprouted between cracks in the cement walkway leading up to the distressed-brick front steps. A thin layer of grime covered the windows, and the peeling paint exposed rotting wood beneath. The entire property looked ignored—with the exception of the brand-new blue BMW 5 Series parked in the driveway.

"Not too often you see a car worth more than the home it's parked in front of," Serrano said. "That's a fifty-five K ride, easy."

Serrano ran the plates. The registration came back to a Mr. Lloyd Lincecum at the current address.

"So they can pay for the car but not a lawnmower?" Tally said.

"Bennett Brice," Serrano said. "Recruiting vulnerable kids to make money. I'm willing to bet Peter Lincecum works for YourLife and bought his dad a new car."

"Maybe your girlfriend was right to go after Brice from the beginning," Tally said. "Stay sharp. Bad things have been happening to people looking into Bennett Brice."

They got out of the car. Serrano had begun walking toward the front door when he heard Tally say, "John. *Stop.*"

He halted in his tracks. It took less than a second for him to see what had caught Tally's attention. Serrano could see four small windows inset in the front door, each about ten inches by ten inches.

The glass in the lower-left window had been broken inward.

Serrano's hand went to his Glock. The detectives crept to the front door and took positions on either side. Tally pointed at Serrano. He nodded.

"Lloyd Lincecum?" Serrano shouted. "This is the Ashby Police Department. If you're inside, make yourself known. If there is anyone else inside, come out now with your hands above your head."

They waited. They heard nothing but silence.

"I don't like it," Serrano mouthed to Tally.

"Me either."

"Lloyd Lincecum," Tally said, banging on the door with her fist. "Peter Lincecum. We are going to enter your home. If you are inside your domicile, make yourself known."

Still no response. The detectives looked at each other. They were sweating, controlling their breathing, guns drawn. Serrano reached up and tried the doorknob. It was unlocked. Tally nodded. Serrano turned the knob and pushed the door open. They both waited on either side of the doorframe. Serrano could see inside the home, at an angle. Furniture was overturned. Papers were strewn about. Serrano crossed his wrists in an X to let Tally know to be careful. She nodded.

Serrano moved slightly to his left, preparing to enter the home. Then a gunshot boomed from somewhere inside the house, the bullet sizzling past Serrano's head close enough for him to feel the brief gust of wind.

Serrano dived backward, away from the door. Tally grabbed her radio and shouted, "Shots fired at 119 Kennesaw Lane. Officers need backup. One shooter, maybe more."

Another shot rang out, and the doorframe directly above Tally's head exploded into a shower of wood chips.

Serrano inched closer to the door. He had a poor angle. He couldn't tell where the bullets had come from. The acrid smell of gunpowder laced the air. Both gunshots had sounded the same. Serrano heard footsteps from inside the house.

He mouthed to Tally, "You OK?"

She nodded.

Serrano made a circular motion with his finger and mouthed, "One shooter."

"Going around back. Keep him busy."

"Be careful."

Serrano crouched so that his head was lower than the first-floor windows and duckwalked through the grass around the side of the house. There was a side window, but the shades were drawn. He heard Tally shout, "Backup will be here in seconds. Put your weapon down, and come out with your hands above your head. There is no way out of this. Nobody needs to get hurt."

Another gunshot rang out. Serrano stopped. *Tally.*

He heard Tally shout, "Active shooter! Get back in your homes!"

Tally was trying to clear the street of civilians. Serrano moved around to the back of the house. His heart was hammering in his chest. Sweat had pooled at his lower back. Behind the house he found a small unkempt yard, a rotted wooden table, three rusted metal chairs on a chipped and weather-worn concrete patio . . . and a back door.

Serrano tried the knob. It was locked. There was a small inset quartet of windows in the back door, similar to the front. All the panes were intact. Serrano stood to the side and peered in. A thick layer of grime prevented him from seeing much. He looked at the doorframe. The wood around the lock was moldy and weak. Small favors.

Serrano took out his cell phone and texted Tally:

Count down from 5. On 0, fire one round into the house. Respond with YES to confirm and that will start the countdown.

Four seconds later a reply.

YES

Serrano began counting down. He took a step back from the door. *Five. Four. Three. Two. One.*

Serrano kicked in the back door at the same moment that Tally fired a shot, masking the sound of the doorframe crunching inward.

Serrano ducked inside, around the broken door. He found himself in what could charitably be described as a living room. An old television sat atop a dusty metal stand, and the tangled black wires from the set and cable box looped around the room haphazardly. Food, cigarette butts, and even small shards of broken glass were embedded in the dirty gray carpeting.

Serrano saw one door, off to the right. He held his gun out and walked slowly to the doorway. He heard a creak. About fifteen feet in front of him. Somebody walking on warped wood. Footsteps. As far as he could tell, just one set.

The doorway led to a galley kitchen. The countertops were all old laminate, the appliances caked with dried food. He proceeded through the kitchen. At the end, he could see a foyer.

Another creak. This time closer.

Then he saw a figure move across the room in front of him. It was a man, thickly built, bald, about five seven, with a neck thicker than his head. The man's back was to Serrano, but the detective could see a gun in his left hand. He was peering through the window, waiting for Tally to show herself.

Serrano raised the gun and aimed at the man's spine.

"Police! Freeze!"

The man did freeze. But he held on to the gun. He slowly turned around, gun still aimed at the floor. He looked at Serrano, eyes wide, panicked.

What in the hell is he doing here? Serrano thought.

"Raymond Spivak!" Serrano shouted. "Drop your weapon!"

Spivak's eyes grew even wider. His mouth opened as if to say, *How . . .*

Suddenly Tally appeared out of nowhere and tackled Spivak with the kind of form an NFL linebacker would have applauded. She drove through his knees, avoiding a steer's worth of upper-body muscle. Spivak crumpled sideways, his large head thudding off the floor.

The moment the big man hit the ground, Serrano launched himself into the room and kicked Spivak's gun hand. Spivak cried out as several of his finger bones cracked. The gun skittered away.

Spivak reached for the gun, but Serrano pointed his Glock at the man's head and said, calmly, "You can take your brain with you or you can leave it here. Your call."

Spivak stopped moving. Tally rolled Spivak onto his stomach, pulled his wrists behind his back, and snapped a pair of handcuffs on him. He squealed as she squeezed his broken fingers, then made a grunt-ing noise as she cinched the cuffs tight around his massive wrists.

They heard sirens outside. Backup.

Serrano and Tally stood beside Spivak, breathing heavily.

"Nice tackle, Detective," Serrano said.

"'You can take your brain with you or you can leave it here'?" Tally said. "Not exactly 'Go ahead, make my day.'"

"Cut me some slack—I didn't have time to think of anything snap-pier," Serrano said.

A dozen officers flooded the house. Serrano and Tally hauled Spivak to his feet.

"John," Tally said. "Look."

She pointed at Spivak's pants. There was a splotch of red by the right cuff. It looked fresh.

"That's not his own blood," Serrano said.

CHAPTER 36

Raymond Spivak sat in an interrogation room inside the Carltondale Police Department. His thick wrists were manacled to the metal table in front of him. A plastic cup of water sat untouched just out of reach of his right hand. Detectives Serrano and Tally stood on the other side of a two-way mirror, observing Spivak. He seemed simultaneously nervous, agitated, confident, and angry.

A tall black man, six five or six six, wearing a brown suit and wire-rimmed glasses, approached the detectives, hand outstretched.

"Lieutenant Graysworth Allen," he said. "Which one of you Lawrence Taylored him?"

Tally raised her hand. "It's all about leverage, sir."

"Nicely done, Detective."

"Just wish we'd gotten there sooner," Serrano said.

"Do you have an ID on the vic?" Tally added.

Allen nodded. "The body was found in the den, next to the couch. Ligature marks around the vic's neck match the blood-coated piano wire we found in a plastic bag in Spivak's pocket. Safe to say after forensics and our blood-spatter team are done in that house, we'll have enough to send Raymond Spivak to prison for several lifetimes."

"So Raymond Spivak garroted Lloyd Lincecum," Serrano said.

"That's a hard, brutal way to kill someone," Tally said.

"Look at the size of Spivak's forearms. He could asphyxiate a cave troll," Serrano said.

"Sorry? Cave troll?" Allen said.

"Ignore him—his brain is swimming with weird fictional creatures," Tally replied. "So Spivak kills Lloyd Lincecum on the same day we begin to investigate his son Peter's knee injury and disappearance from school. What about Peter's mother?"

"Stefanie and Lloyd Lincecum divorced eight years ago," Allen said, "but she's not Peter's biological mother. There's no mother listed on Peter Lincecum's birth certificate, but we're working on it. Stefanie has been arrested five times for possession and possession with intent to sell. Currently serving eighteen months in Pinckneyville after she tried to buy a rock from an undercover. We'll talk to her, but as far as I know, she's been out of the picture for some time and wasn't a target."

"Have you found Peter Lincecum yet?" Serrano asked.

Allen shook his head. "We found the boy's cell phone in his locker at school. He obviously abandoned it so he couldn't be tracked. We're trying to unlock it as we speak. I miss the days when unlocking a cell phone was easier than programming a VCR."

"Does the name Evie Boggs, or Evelyn Boggs, mean anything to you, Lieutenant?" Serrano said.

"No. Should it?"

"How about Myra?"

"Got a last name?"

"Fraid not. But this Evie Boggs was arrested five years ago at Raymond Spivak's home with presumed intent to harm."

"Harm . . . him?" Allen said with a doubtful snort. "I could park my F-150 on this guy's shoulders."

"I hear you," Serrano replied. "But we read the arrest report. Raymond Spivak ran from *her*. This Boggs woman is skilled and dangerous."

"So what does Evelyn Boggs have to do with Raymond Spivak murdering Lloyd Lincecum?"

"Boggs is a person of interest in a murder we've been investigating in Ashby. A schoolteacher named Matthew Linklater. We believe

Spivak's killing Lloyd Lincecum is related to matters surrounding the Linklater murder."

Allen's eyes narrowed. "How?"

"A woman named Rachel Marin does some investigative and forensic work for us," Tally said. "The other day, she was following a pair of teenagers working for a man named Bennett Brice, who has a connection to Evelyn Boggs. Peter Lincecum attempted to kill Rachel Marin, or at the very least scare her off, we believe at the behest of Bennett Brice. Marin injured Peter Lincecum while defending herself but was then knocked unconscious by another assailant. Then Lincecum disappeared. We believe Peter can provide information on Brice and his organization, and it all ties in to the murder of Matthew Linklater."

"Raymond Spivak was not at that home looking for Lloyd Lincecum," Serrano said. "He was there to kill Peter Lincecum. Lloyd got in the way, so Spivak killed him. We think this murder, Evelyn Boggs, and the Linklater homicide are all connected to Bennett Brice."

Allen looked through the mirror at Raymond Spivak, his manacled bulk locked to the table, then back at Serrano and Tally. "Just what in the hell did you bring to my town, Detectives?"

Spivak hardly seemed nervous, which disturbed Serrano. Either he knew he was going to prison, in which case he could relax, or he was confident he *wasn't* going to prison, in which case he likely had a hell of an expensive lawyer en route who was probably also kept on retainer by the devil himself.

Then the interrogation room door opened, and a man of about fifty walked in. He wore black shoes that looked expensive and were polished to a gleam and a suit that likely cost more than Serrano's car. He sat down next to Raymond Spivak and put an arm across the man's broad shoulders, like he was consoling a child whose pet goldfish had just died.

"Freaking Chester Barnes," Tally said. "Figures."

"He charges two grand an hour," Serrano said, "and has defended enough cold-blooded criminals to populate Martin Scorsese's entire filmography."

Tally looked at Serrano. "What in the hell *did* we bring into this town?"

Forensics found a pair of nitrate-coated Firm Grip workman's gloves at the Lincecum house, matched Lloyd Lincecum's blood type to the stains on the gloves, and confirmed that dirt from underneath Raymond Spivak's fingernails matched dirt found inside the glove's fingers. With that, Raymond Spivak was formally charged with first-degree premeditated murder in the death of Lloyd Lincecum and remanded to the holding cells in Carltondale to await arraignment.

Serrano called Rachel as they drove back to Ashby and put the call on speaker.

"John," she said, "what's going on? Did you find Peter Lincecum?"

"Not exactly. We hit a snag."

"A snag? Define snag?"

Tally said, "We got to the Lincecum house and found Peter's father, Lloyd, murdered."

"Oh my God. What about Peter?"

"He skipped out of school and hasn't been seen since," Serrano said. "His cell was found in his locker. Carltondale police are searching for him. We think the man who killed Lloyd Lincecum was really there for Peter."

"Well, this just keeps getting worse," Rachel said.

Tally added, "Also, the man we arrested for Lloyd Lincecum's murder was Raymond Spivak."

There was silence on the other end.

"Rachel?" Serrano said.

"You're kidding me, right? The same guy Evie Boggs tried to kill murdered Peter Lincecum's father?"

"Yup. Spivak was formally charged about fifteen minutes ago."

"Where the hell is Evie Boggs?" Rachel asked. She sounded worried. Serrano and Tally exchanged a glance. Neither had ever heard Rachel so unnerved before.

"We might ask you the same question," Tally replied.

"There's no way Evie can know that Spivak is in town," Rachel said. "Or if she does know he's here, they're not on the same team. She would have carved out his guts and gone Hannibal Lecter on his sweetmeats."

"Do we know *why* Evie wanted to kill Raymond Spivak in the first place?"

"Evie despises the Spivaks," Rachel said. "Raymond Spivak knows why. I need to speak with him."

"Not gonna happen," Tally said. "We've already had to cede jurisdiction on the Lincecum murder to the Carltondale PD. They won't even let *us* question him, let alone you. And there's another thing."

"I'm not sure I can take another thing," Rachel said.

"Spivak's lawyer is Chester Barnes."

"Chester Barnes. Oh, fantastic. He would represent Charles Manson if the check cleared. But it also tells us that Spivak has money. A lot of it. Or he's bankrolled by someone else who does."

"You think it might be Brice?" Serrano said.

"I don't know. I don't see Bennett Brice being shortsighted enough to call Peter Lincecum to attack me, then immediately try to have him killed. He would know we'd point the finger right at him. I think Spivak is acting independently of Brice."

"So whose side is Evie Boggs on?" Tally said.

"I don't know. But if the other Spivak brother, Randall, is really as dangerous as you say, my guess is he's looking for Peter as we speak. We need to find Peter Lincecum *immediately*, because if we don't, Randall Spivak is going to make sure nobody ever sees him alive again. And I will *not* see any more kids hurt by these psychopaths."

CHAPTER 37

After hanging up the phone, Bennett Brice went to his wine cabinet, studied the bottles, then settled on a 2014 Domaine Leroy Vosne-Romanee. He held it, turning it over until he could see the faintest reflection of his own face in the glass. Then he gently placed it back, opened a cabinet, and took out a bottle of Johnnie Walker Blue. He poured three fingers into a crystal tumbler, sniffed it, and took down half the portion in one swallow.

Benjamin Ruddock had gone home after lunch, stomach full and questions sated. For the time being. Brice sympathized with the boy, having to spend his nights at home with *that* father. But Ruddock was smart and ambitious and, above all, a fighter. He would be on his own soon enough and would never look back.

"Don't tell me you're not going to offer me one," Evie Boggs said, gesturing to Brice's drink.

She sat on a cream-colored sofa, cell phone next to her thigh, right foot absently tapping the floor. Brice refilled his glass, then poured another one, a larger one, for Evie. He handed it to her.

"I suppose there's not much to toast to at the moment," she said.

"Unfortunately not," Brice replied. "It's been a very difficult week. Those impetuous . . ."

"Monsters," Evie said. "You can say it. They can't hear you right now."

Brice said nothing, just sipped his drink. He took a seat in a chair across from Evie. He took another sip, then set the glass on the coffee table.

"Peter Lincecum is gone," he said.

Evie's face turned white. She shook her head, liquor spilling from her tumbler onto the carpet.

"Oh, no. Bennett. Don't say that. What happened? Where is he?"

"I don't know. We work with one of the teachers at the boy's school. He alerted me that Peter was injured, likely by the Marin woman when they confronted her. But Peter disappeared after the nurse questioned him about his injury."

"Bennett. This is out of hand."

"You know I would have never sent Peter into harm's way," Brice said.

"I know," Evie said. "The brothers. I should have slit Raymond's throat when I had the chance."

"That's not all," Brice said. "Raymond went to the Lincecum home to find Peter."

Evie leaned forward. Her cell phone slid onto the floor. She did not move to pick it up.

"Bennett . . . ," she said through gritted teeth. "What happened?"

"Raymond killed Lloyd Lincecum. I have a cop in the Carltondale PD who told me Detectives Serrano and Tally went to the house to find Peter and found Raymond there right after he'd finished off Lloyd."

"Serrano and Tally? From the Ashby PD? So the Spivaks *and* the cops are looking for Peter."

"That is the situation," Brice said. "Everything with Matthew Linklater got far, far out of hand."

"Oh God." Evie swallowed the rest of her drink. "Nobody else was supposed to die."

"You know I don't approve of violence either," he said.

"That's not entirely true," Evie said. "You sent the boys to hurt Darren Reznick, didn't you?"

"He will heal," Brice said, "and will have learned a valuable lesson."

Evie stared at Brice's hand. The Johnnie Walker was rippling; Brice's hand holding the drink trembled.

"Bennett," Evie said. "Talk to me. What's going on?"

Brice swallowed the rest of his drink, then placed the glass down, making a clink-clink sound as he struggled to keep his hand even.

"I thought getting to Eric Marin would keep his mother in line." He took another drink. "I was wrong."

"Rachel Marin is not someone who is 'kept in line,'" Evie said. "I told you what she did back in Torrington. She killed Stanford Royce. I know it."

"Maybe if it ever came to it, we could get the Torrington PD to reopen the Royce investigation. But right now, my concerns aren't a trial. They're Peter Lincecum and Randall Spivak."

Evie said, "I know this family. Randall started hunting Peter the moment the cuffs were put on his brother. I need to find Peter before Randall does."

"You'll have to move fast. Randall is psychotic. And with his brother locked up, he could be even more volatile."

"I need a lead. Somewhere to start," Evie said. "Lloyd Lincecum is dead. I can't just walk into Peter's school and start questioning his friends and teachers. Either the Carltondale PD or Serrano and Tally will be all over me in five minutes."

"I'm less concerned about the cops being all over you," Brice said, "than about what happens if you cross paths with Randall Spivak. And if Spivak gets to Peter Lincecum before you do . . ."

"He'll never be seen again." Evie rubbed the bridge of her nose and stood up. She wiped away a tear and headed toward the front door.

"What are you doing?" Brice asked.

"I need help. Someone who knows this town better than I do. Someone else who doesn't want to see any more children hurt," she said. "I'm going to find Rachel Marin."

CHAPTER 38

Randall Spivak sat on a park bench beside a still pond, holding half a bagel in his hand, tossing crumbs to a small gathering of pigeons. With each crumb tossed, he watched joylessly as a phalanx of feathers fought over the morsel like starving children over a loaf of bread. It was late afternoon, the sun hanging low over the horizon. The park was bustling with children just let out of school. They were oblivious to the tall man. Had they known what he was capable of, they would have run screaming. Randall watched a pigeon nip and swallow a piece of bagel, then turn and squawk at an adversary, declaring the prize for itself alone.

Spivak's hair was nicely parted down the left side; at forty-eight he had a sprinkling of gray amid the brown. Crow's-feet had just begun to set in at his eyes, which gave his face a look of both intelligence and calm. The former he had. The latter he did not.

He wore a pair of pleated brown slacks, a periwinkle-blue dress shirt buttoned to the top, and a tan blazer. He looked like an accountant, perhaps, or an appraiser, someone whose job was not marred by stress or action. This was also false.

He did not look like a man who had murdered five people, if there was even such a consistency to that kind of violence. Four of the deaths were premeditated. Only one, the first one, had been impetuous. That was the only killing he regretted. Not the killing itself, but the manner in which it had been done. Sloppy and emotional. He had been just thirty-three at the time, and a woman had spurned him following a date. He had mistaken her politeness for romantic interest and then beaten her to death with a meat tenderizer in her own home.

The first killing was the only one that bothered him. Again, not because of the action itself, but because it was the only time he had allowed his anger to get the better of him to such an extent. It had taken three days of careful planning to dispose of the body in such a way that it would never be found. The next four killings were barely even memories. They had left no more of an imprint in his mind than would a mediocre dinner from several months ago. There was knowledge that they did, in fact, take place, but they had no bearing on his current life and were not memorable enough to warrant any further thought.

Randall had not wanted to be there that afternoon. He was not sloppy, but the same could not be said of the people he worked with and depended on. Despite the red on his résumé, his brother, Raymond, tended to handle the dirty work. But his brother was careless. He loved Raymond like he loved his hands, his arms, his head, his eyes, his heart. Raymond was a part of him. But he also harbored a constant annoyance at his brother the same way you would be irritated with a bad back or a bum knee that ached during the cold months. More of a nuisance than anything, but Randall tolerated him with a resigned, exasperated understanding that there was no permanent corrective to Raymond's impetuousness.

He had grown tired of cleaning up Raymond's messes. But this time, Raymond had gone too far and let things get out of hand. And Randall did not see a way out.

Randall did not say a word when the lawyer took the seat next to him on the bench. He simply kept tossing crumbs to the birds. The lawyer seemed to be waiting for the man to speak. Then, realizing the taller man would not, he began the conversation.

"I don't see your brother getting out of this, Randall," Chester Barnes said. "They have blood on his clothing that matches Lloyd Lincecum; gloves with small tears that match the piano wire found at the scene, covered in blood and with embedded glass particles from the broken front-door window; a gun with his fingerprints on it that was used to shoot at two detectives; and a positive GSR test. If this goes to trial, we could be looking at life. In fact, I'd say Raymond is lucky this state abolished the death penalty."

Randall remained quiet. Then he picked up a palm-size rock from the ground, brushed off a layer of dirt, and flung it at one of the flocks of pigeons. The birds scattered, wings beating the air as they quickly realized their meal ticket had turned on them.

"You could have hit one of them," Barnes said, after the last bird had disappeared over the nearby buildings.

"I was trying to," Randall replied. "I don't accept that there's no way to fix this."

"Accept it or not, this is what's happening," Barnes replied. "They have your brother, pardon the phrase, dead to rights. I could try to make a case that he stumbled upon the murder scene by accident, that the reason he had blood on his hands was because he was trying to resuscitate Lloyd Lincecum and only shot at the police because they didn't properly identify themselves. But it raises the question of what he was doing in Carltondale in the first place. It will open up a line of questioning about the Lincecum boy and likely more. And I don't think you want to go down that road."

"What did my brother say when you spoke to him?" Randall asked.

"He's willing to plead guilty," Barnes said. "And frankly, that's likely his only chance for parole."

"Is the insanity defense an option?"

"Given the premeditated nature—again, he arrived at the scene wearing heavy-duty gloves and carrying piano wire—that would be incredibly difficult."

"What if they ask why he was in Carltondale to begin with?" Randall asked.

"If he pleads guilty to first-degree murder, they won't ask for circumstantial details. Lloyd Lincecum is dead at Raymond's hands, end of story. I may even be able to get it down to second degree if he pleads guilty and avoid a life sentence. The DA is willing to go with that if he can get a murder conviction without wasting months and millions on a trial. There's just one problem."

Randall Spivak nodded. "The boy."

Barnes said, "Peter Lincecum never came home. Raymond says he wasn't at the house. He's in the wind. He could be next door. He could be in Texas by now. But as long as he's out there, someone knows about you, your brother, and Bennett Brice and could testify against all of you. With Lloyd Lincecum dead, we don't have any leverage over him. If the police find him and he testifies . . ."

"He won't," Randall said.

"I envy your optimism," Barnes said. "One more thing. The DA told me that the Lincecum boy is injured. That the Marin woman may have dislocated his kneecap, torn a tendon or two. And to the best of our knowledge, he has not received medical attention. There are no records of any hospital admission, and he has not been back to school since he vanished. He's alone. He's hurt. And he's scared."

"You should have warned my brother," Randall said. "He should have confirmed the Lincecum boy was home before he got there. This all could have been avoided."

"Your brother is a grown man," Barnes said. "He can make his own mistakes."

"He has a history of being sloppy. He should have handled the Boggs situation differently too. Instead she comes to his home? He invites conflict. That's why he's sitting in a cell right now. He got bad advice."

"You're his brother," Barnes said. "Doesn't that make you his keeper?"

"Brothers don't always listen to brothers. Sometimes you need a third party to cut through the biases of blood. Raymond is a bull. Strong, yet often mindless. Bulls can be a necessary evil when a display of force is needed to achieve your goals. But they have a hard time slowing down once in motion. They react without thinking. Raymond should have cased the Lincecum home before thinking of entering, and he should not have harmed Lloyd Lincecum until he knew where Peter was. Now the boy has every incentive to turn on us."

"I have enough on my plate dealing with Bennett Brice and the mess at YourLife. But if the cops or this Marin woman get to Peter Lincecum before we do, it all comes down. *Hard.*"

"Peter Lincecum is an injured boy afraid for his life," Randall said. "He's probably terrified out of his mind. Scared people make mistakes. I'll find him."

"You won't be the only one looking for him," Barnes said. "The detectives from Ashby are already suspicious of Brice and surely know how valuable Peter Lincecum's testimony could be. And that Marin woman, she's a wild card. You have competition."

"And Evelyn Boggs?"

"As long as we have our leverage over her, she can be controlled. Find the boy. Loose threads have a way of being unraveled by the wrong people."

"The only proper way to deal with a loose end is to cut it and burn the thread," Spivak said. Then he got up and walked away.

CHAPTER 39

I'll be home late

Rachel looked at the text from her son and this time tamped down the desire to do catastrophic harm to her cell phone. She checked his GPS. Still off. She called him. Nobody picked up. Was this the rest of her life? Spending each and every day petrified about what her son might be doing, whom he might be with, and whether or not he would ever actually speak to her again?

Her head ached. She took two aspirin, unsure if the headache was from the dent in her skull or the dent in her relationship with her firstborn.

She went into Megan's room, knowing that her daughter's loving presence would soothe her mind, at least temporarily.

"Shh, Mom," Megan said. She was hunched over her desk with a pen. "I'm at a *really* important part in this Sadie Scout book, and I don't want to lose it."

"Well, don't let me interrupt Sadie's latest adventure," she said. Rachel went over, kissed her daughter's cheek, and exited the room.

She heard a faint *I love you* from her daughter just as the door closed, and her heart swelled.

She heard a knock at the front door, and Rachel ran to it.

Eric. It had to be Eric.

But Eric has keys.

Rachel opened the app on her phone linked to the camera mounted above the front door.

"You've got to be shitting me," she whispered.

Rachel went into the kitchen and took a screwdriver from a drawer. She held it in her left hand, hidden, flush against her wrist, then opened the door.

"Hi," said Evie Boggs. "Can I come in?"

"Can I rearrange your face with my foot?" Rachel replied.

"That . . . uh . . . no. We need to talk. I promise this will be more pleasant for either of us than you . . . doing that." She paused. "It's about Peter Lincecum."

Rachel's eyes narrowed. "You can talk to me from there."

Evie looked around the neighborhood. There was no shortage of people within earshot of Rachel's porch door. Rachel saw her neighbor, Monique Weatherly, walking her Pomeranian, Yippy. Monique waved. Rachel unenthusiastically waved at her. Yippy yipped and promptly peed on a shrub.

"You sure you want to talk here?" Evie said. "Lot of people can see us."

"Empty your purse," Rachel said.

"Rachel . . ."

"Do it."

Evie sighed and emptied the contents of her purse onto the doormat. Her wallet, a tube of lipstick, Tic Tacs, a tampon, keys, a cell phone, a small hairbrush, mascara, face wipes, a granola bar, a portable phone charger, hand sanitizer, and a canister of Mace.

"See?" Evie said. "Nothing nearly as dangerous as whatever you've got hidden in your left hand."

"Screwdriver," Rachel said. "Phillips head."

"So you plan to stab me and then assemble some furniture?"

"Turn your cell phone off," Rachel said. Evie held down the power button until Rachel could see the "Power Off" message flicker. "Now put everything back into the purse and give it to me."

"This is the most polite mugging ever."

"Shut up and do it."

Evie tossed her belongings back into the purse and handed it to Rachel.

"You haven't confiscated these," Evie said, holding up her hands. "They're registered as deadly weapons."

Rachel paused. "Is that true?"

"No. I've just always wanted to say that."

"Come on in. But my boyfriend is a cop, and I know half a dozen ways to cut off the blood flow to your brain."

"I taught you at least three of those," Evie said.

Evie stepped through the door, and Rachel closed it behind her.

"Living room is that way," Rachel said. "Sit."

"You're not going to show me in?" Evie said.

"I'm not turning my back on you," Rachel said. "And take your shoes off in my home. We're not animals."

Evie took her shoes off, left them by the door, went into the living room, and sat down on the couch. Rachel sat across from Evie and placed the screwdriver on her lap.

"All right," Rachel said. "I have questions. And you give straight answers, or you leave."

"How's your head?" Evie said.

"Oh, we're doing pleasantries now?" Rachel said. "It's dandy. If I need to staple some pages together, I can just borrow one from my scalp."

"I'm sorry about that."

"You didn't hit me. Or did you? I still don't know who to thank for the little boo-boo on my head."

Evie flinched. "You might not believe this, but I don't want to see anyone hurt. Not you. Not your son. And most certainly not Peter Lincecum."

"How do you know about Peter?" Rachel said.

"Bennett Brice is my brother," Evie said.

Rachel sat back. She eyed the screwdriver. "You're serious."

Evie nodded.

"And you neglected to tell me that before because . . ."

"It wasn't important," Evie said.

"So when you told me, all the way back in Torrington, that you had family in Ashby, you were talking about Bennett."

Evie said, "That's right."

"So the real reason you're here in Ashby is because of your brother?"

"Yes and no," Evie said.

"You're not very good at this straight-answer thing, are you? So answer me this. You're a mother. Why put up with Bennett when he's exploiting children to make himself rich?"

"It's more complicated than that."

"Then uncomplicate it," Rachel said.

"I don't know everything," Evie said. There was shame in Evie's voice, which suggested to Rachel that she was telling the truth. And that perhaps she didn't know everything because she had chosen not to ask.

"Then tell me what you do know."

"I need to be certain you're not going to involve your boyfriend or his partner," Evie said.

"If Bennett is committing a crime, the police have to be notified."

"And if they are notified before we can fix things, people will die. Matthew Linklater should not have died. Lloyd Lincecum should not have died."

"They did not *die*. They were murdered, in part because of what you and your brother are involved in."

"I don't want anyone else to get hurt," Evie said. "And neither does Bennett. You might think he's exploiting those kids, but he *does* care about them. He *is* giving them opportunities. Bennett has been doing this for a long time. Three years ago, a man named Derek Burbank donated five hundred thousand dollars to Saint Jude's Children's

Research Hospital. Derek came from nothing. He was orphaned at three years old. But he worked for Bennett and learned how to harness his talents."

"I bet that helps Bennett sleep at night," Rachel said.

"Actually, it does." Evie looked around. "Do you have anything to drink?"

Rachel gave her a *You've got to be kidding me* look. Then she got up, went into the kitchen, opened the freezer, took out a bottle of Ketel One, poured a shot, and handed it to Evie.

Evie downed it and held the glass out. "Double or nothing?"

"If you're thirsty you can lick the sink."

Evie put the glass down.

"Bennett is a smart man. But he's made some bad business decisions. Poor investments. He was loaded up with debt. And if you know my brother, he's willing to find any way to succeed. Even if they're ways most people wouldn't consider. And that includes working with people you shouldn't work with."

"Let me guess," Rachel said. "That's where the Spivak brothers come in."

"That's right. Bennett knows Chester Barnes from way back in the day. And Chester knows everybody in this town," Evie said. "He can help you within the law or outside of it. Bennett reached out to Barnes, looking for a way to get back on his feet. Barnes knew a man named Raymond Spivak. The Spivak brothers are two of those people you don't want to get into business with."

"But your brother did," Rachel said.

Evie nodded and stared longingly at the empty shot glass. "The Spivaks started out as loan sharks. Bill collectors for some bad people. But they had one thing most loan sharks don't: ambition. I don't know all the ugly details; they may have had mob connections, but they were making millions and couldn't actually use any of it. You can't put it in banks because you would need to declare it, pay taxes on it. And there are only so many mattresses you can hide cash under."

"So they needed a way to launder their money," Rachel said. "And when Bennett Brice reached out to Chester Barnes, the opportunity presented itself. He connected Bennett with Randall and Raymond Spivak."

"My brother represented an opportunity for them," Evie said. "Bennett could launder their cash while also expanding their base of operations. So they made a deal with Bennett. They agreed to bankroll him with a new venture. Something where cash flow was erratic. They would buy a nice house for him to live in so he could keep up the mirage of a man who got rich running a successful business. Bennett would filter the Spivaks' money through YourLife."

"What about the Caymans?" Rachel said.

"Once YourLife was set up in Ashby," Evie said, "the Spivaks were able to get their hooks into local residents. There *is* money here. And the Spivaks knew where to look. And it wasn't just loan-sharking. They hired PIs to find out everything about everyone. Rich city councilman having an affair? They'd hack into his phone and find the dick pics. Hedge fund manager with a predilection for young boys? They'd show up at his house with a thumb drive full of photos taken at a local motel."

"That's what was in the manila envelopes I saw Benjamin Ruddock delivering," Rachel said. "Money from the Spivaks to be deposited into offshore accounts. But why use kids like my son?"

"They're smart. Well, at least Randall is. They don't just go after any kids. They find kids from broken homes. Kids whose parents are in prison. Kids on the fringe. Kids whose parents are about to be evicted. Kids who are vulnerable and desperate." Evie pointed at Rachel. "Kids whose parents have something to hide."

"This is evil," Rachel said.

"It was a means to an end," Evie said. "Bennett *did* offer these kids a lifeline. It wasn't all about money. They became fratres. A brotherhood.

This has been going on for a long time. Bennett has helped a lot of kids find better lives."

"But how was he able to target the right children?" Rachel said.

"The Spivaks would pay off school psychologists, social workers, even parents. In turn they were given leads. Kids with a chip on their shoulder. Then Bennett would follow up. He didn't recruit everyone. Kids with emotional problems, violent tendencies. He went after good kids in bad circumstances."

"I still don't buy that all these kids were willing to work for him," Rachel said.

"You're so naive, Marin. You're a kid. Your parents are useless. Maybe drunks or addicts. You live in squalor. A good-looking businessman offers you *real* money and a chance to change your life. A way out. Who's going to say no to that?"

"Eric doesn't need the money," Rachel said. "He doesn't have to want for anything."

"The most valuable things in the world can't be bought," Evie said. "Like self-esteem. Pride. You know that as well as I do. Anger is a valuable commodity. It's the same way drug cartels get kids to work for them. It's why eleven-year-olds end up dealing on a Baltimore street corner. You make them feel like it's their only way out, and they'll follow you until it's too late for them to realize there *is* no way out."

"So then why are you here?" Rachel asked. "You and Bennett have a nice little gig destroying people's lives while convincing yourself you're Robin Hood."

"Because it's one thing if a pedophile gets swindled or a crooked politician gets blackmailed. I can live with all that. Gleefully. But Peter Lincecum is going to die if we don't do something. And I can't live with a kid being put in the ground."

"Can your brother live with that?" Rachel asked. "If saving that boy's life means tearing down YourLife? Are you willing to trade the possibility of your brother going to prison to save a life?"

Evie paused. She said softly, "I just know I can't let a boy die because I did nothing. You know this town better than I do. You're willing to do whatever it takes. I need your help."

Rachel nodded. "OK. I can work with that. But I need you to agree to two things."

"What?"

"First, I'm going to need you to come with me tonight."

"Where?" Evie asked.

"It doesn't matter. You're going to say yes without asking any questions."

"All right. Yes."

"Second . . . I need to call my boyfriend."

Evie stood up and shook her head. "No way. Uh-uh. You told me you weren't going to call the cops."

"I'm not," Rachel said. "This cop also happens to be my babysitter. We have work to do."

CHAPTER 40

It took slightly more convincing to get John Serrano to agree to come over to Rachel's house this time. The simple "favor" wouldn't cut it.

Whose girlfriend asks him to come over at night to watch her daughter—who's already asleep, by the way—so she can go out and do God knows what?

By the time they'd hung up the phone, Rachel had promised to cook him a four-course meal, watch any movie of his choosing (even those involving trolls and/or elves), and participate in half a dozen sexual acts, some of which Rachel had to google. In the end, given that most of the acts sounded like more fun than her usual Tuesday night, Rachel agreed.

But when Serrano knocked on the front door, only for Rachel to open it, revealing Evie Boggs standing in the foyer, Rachel had to make Serrano swear not to ask any more questions. She promised to explain everything tomorrow.

"There's only one way I'm going to agree to any of this," Serrano said.

"You want me to do—what was the last one—the turducken tantra?"

"Well, yes. But I'll need a few days to stretch to make sure I'm limber enough for it. No, I was going to say a pint of ice cream and a cold beer."

"I have a low-fat yogurt pop and a handle of Ketel One in the freezer."

"Guess that'll have to do," Serrano said. He took Rachel's hands, leaned in, and kissed her. Rachel felt a heat spread through her body, and she thought about how they'd made love the other day, needing each other. She hadn't known how much she'd been craving that warmth and intimacy until they had returned to her life with John Serrano. There'd been many times over the past few months when she'd questioned the relationship. Questioned whether she could trust anyone. Commit to anyone. But feeling him inside her, feeling her body shiver as she climaxed, she knew she'd have to see it through. She deserved that. She didn't know if she loved him. But she knew she didn't want to be without him.

"I have a feeling I know where you're going," Serrano said. "Just be careful, Rachel."

"I always am," Rachel said, slipping on a blue windbreaker.

"If you were always careful, I wouldn't have to remind you."

She smiled at Serrano, blew him a kiss. Then Rachel and Evie walked out the door.

"Where are we going?" Evie said.

"To get my son back."

"In the middle of the night?"

"Yup."

Voss Field loomed ahead of them, a monument in the void, the massive LED lights hanging overhead casting a pall over the darkened field. Evie walked alongside Rachel, her hands in her pockets.

It was 1:15 a.m. when they arrived. Rachel had no idea how punctual these people were. The field itself was lit only by the moon, but even in its soft glow she could make out a number of kids toeing the dirt around the infield. All boys. All young. They were fidgety, and there was a palpable sense of unease. They knew about the murder of Peter

Lincecum's father and were understandably anxious about what it meant. And after the Linklater death and Reznick assault, the fratres kids were justifiably on edge. One of their own had lost a parent—possibly because of his ties to the very man they had come to see.

"This is a YourLife meeting," Evie said. "What the hell are we doing here?"

"Like I said," Rachel replied, her voice steel. "Getting my son back."

"Please don't do anything rash, Rachel. There are lives at stake."

"Including my son's. You want me to help you?" Rachel said. "Then first I need to burn your brother's business down."

"Rachel . . ."

Rachel saw Eric. He was standing by himself near the pitcher's mound. He was on his phone and appeared to be texting. Rachel would have cut off a toe to see what he was writing.

She recognized Benjamin Ruddock. He was talking to a boy much younger and smaller than Eric. Ruddock towered over the boy but leaned in close, his hand on the kid's shoulder, appearing to reassure or console him about something.

Rachel saw Bennett Brice approaching from the right field bleachers. Brice walked quickly. He appeared agitated, moving with a purpose. As soon as the boys noticed Brice, a hush fell over them.

Benjamin Ruddock went to meet him. Ruddock extended his hand. Brice gave it a perfunctory shake and kept walking. He stopped when he got to the pitcher's mound. The boys encircled him.

"Gentlemen, thank you again for coming," Brice said. "I have a number of important things to discuss. You may have some questions of your own, and I need to set the record straight on a few issues."

Rachel's heart began to beat faster as she walked onto the field. Evie followed her. The boys were still focused on Brice. But then a hefty boy of about sixteen saw the women approaching. His mouth dropped and he pointed at them. He said something Rachel could not hear. Brice turned around.

"Evie. Ms. Marin. What the hell are you doing here?"

Rachel looked at Eric. His eyes were wide. He took a step back, as though afraid his mother was there to scold him, or worse.

"Tell these kids the truth, Brice!" Rachel shouted. "Tell them about Peter Lincecum. How his father is dead and Peter is missing because of you. About the gangsters and killers you're in business with."

"Rachel . . . ," Evie said, softly yet urgently. "This isn't what I agreed to."

Rachel ignored her.

"Gentlemen," Brice said, his voice overconfident, trying to keep a rein on the meeting as the boys started to fidget. "My sister and this woman have nothing to do with our business, and this crazy person is lying."

There were murmurs from among the group of boys. Rachel wanted to reach out to Eric, to grab him, to take him away. But first he needed to understand why she was there. That she was protecting him. And she would do that even if he hated her for it.

Eric seemed utterly confused by what was going on. Ruddock was going around the circle, trying to keep control, reassuring the other boys that this intrusion was nothing to be alarmed over.

"Ms. Marin, if you don't leave, I'm going to be forced to call the authorities," Brice said. "This woman has threatened me numerous times. She is completely unhinged and emotional."

"Go ahead," Rachel replied. "Call the cops. Tell them the truth. Tell them—"

And then a crack of thunder interrupted Rachel. Not thunder. It took less than a second for Rachel to realize what the sound was.

That was a gunshot.

Red began to blossom underneath Bennett Brice's clean white shirt. His hand went to his chest. It came away coated in blood. He looked up, in shock. Then one of the boys screamed.

"Evie?" Brice said as he fell to a knee.

"Bennett?" Evie cried. "Oh my God, Bennett!"

Another crack filled the air, and this time the screams multiplied. Another crack. And another. The boys began to flee, running in all different directions away from the field, cries filling the air like something out of a horror movie.

Three shots, Rachel thought. *But only one hit the mark. The gunman is an amateur.*

"Eric, run!" she shouted. Then she saw her son sprinting away from the field. Rachel ran after him, her legs churning as fast as they ever had in her life.

Then Eric's legs buckled under him, and he collapsed to the ground with a cry. Rachel's eyes widened. She saw a trickle of red dripping down his leg, and for a moment, Rachel's heart felt like it had stopped. But then she saw the culprit: he hadn't been shot—he'd just tripped and shredded his knee on a rock.

But it also meant he was stationary. And given that Rachel had no idea if the shooter had any targets in mind other than Brice, she dived on top of her son, tucked him under her body, and shielded him. Her wounded head thrummed as she hit the ground, a bubbling sensation like seltzer in her brain.

"Mom," Eric said, struggling to break free from her grip. He was strong, but Rachel was stronger.

"Just stay here," she said, her arms around his head. "Just stay here."

He stopped moving. She could feel Eric's heart beating so fast, jackhammer fast, as he gulped down air, trembling beneath her.

Take me, she thought. *Please don't hurt him.*

Then Rachel heard another shot and looked up in time to see Bennett Brice knocked forward from the force of the bullet. Rachel saw a puff of grass and dirt kick off the ground about twenty feet in front of Brice. The bullet had entered and exited cleanly through Brice's arm, the bullet burying itself in the turf. Five shots. One in Brice's chest. One through Brice's arm. The rest had missed.

Brice got to his knees and began to crawl. Blood dripped from his shirt, from his sleeve. Evie was next to him, on the ground, crying. Both were covered in blood and dirt. One hand was around her brother, trying to help him get away. The other held a cell phone.

"My brother has been shot," Evie said between gasps. "Voss Field. He's been hit twice. The shooter is still here. You need to send cops and an ambulance *now*."

Brice managed to stagger to his feet. Evie threw his arm around her shoulder. He tried to limp off the field but collapsed to a knee. Rachel watched them in horror, still covering her son.

"It's OK," she said to Eric, hoping the words would comfort him, even if she didn't believe them.

"Come on, Bennett," Evie said, her voice desperate, terrified, pleading. She tried to pull her wounded brother along. "We have to get you out of here. You're going to be OK."

Brice got back to his feet. He staggered forward. Rachel heard a siren in the distance. But it was far away—too far.

Suddenly five shots rang out in succession—*BOOM BOOM BOOM BOOM BOOM*.

Rachel heard two soft thuds. A red splotch appeared on Bennett Brice's stomach, and a gout of blood sprang forth from the side of his neck.

Evie screamed as Brice fell forward. He twitched once and then did not move again. Rachel watched Evie Boggs wail as she rolled her brother over and tried to administer CPR. But the man was dead. Evie was trying to resuscitate a corpse.

"It's over," she whispered to Eric. "It's over, baby."

Her son replied with three words.

"No, it's not."

CHAPTER 41

Ten shots. Four hit the mark. And Bennett Brice was dead.

Rachel was sitting in her living room. It was six thirty in the morning. A cup of cold coffee rested on the table in front of her. Dirt and grass covered her jeans. Her shirt was torn and caked with mud. The sofa cushions had grime all over them, detritus that had fallen from her body, pieces of the field that had stuck to their clothes.

I'm going to need to get these cushions professionally cleaned, she thought absently, a buzzing in the back of her skull as she struggled to make sense of the night's violence.

Serrano had stayed at their home. Leslie Tally had joined him as soon as she got word of the shooting. Once Rachel and Eric returned home, APD Officers Chen and Lowe took over so Serrano and Tally could begin the work of tracking down the shooter.

As soon as Rachel and Eric stepped through the door around three in the morning, covered in dirt and tears and blood, Serrano embraced them. To Rachel's surprise, Eric hugged Serrano back. Hard. Her boy's hands clung to the man's back, fingers gripping his shirt so hard they turned bone white. Serrano put his hand on Eric's head and said, "It's going to be OK. You're safe."

Rachel joined the embrace. It was the first time in a long time she could remember having her arms around her son without him struggling to break free.

"Thank God you're both OK," he said.

"Are we?" Rachel replied.

"In the most important sense of the word, yes," Serrano replied. "We'll work on the rest of it."

Once the other cops arrived, Serrano and Tally left to work the case. Serrano was no longer a babysitter, a boyfriend, or a friend. He was on the job. They had nearly twenty kids who'd witnessed the shooting to interview, complicated by the fact that their ages necessitated having guardians present for questioning, plus forensics having to scour the entire interior and exterior of a baseball stadium.

Lowe and Chen took statements from Eric and Rachel. They asked Eric about his relationship with Bennett Brice. How he had come to be at Voss Field that night. If he knew anyone who wanted Brice—or Matthew Linklater—dead.

Eric sat on the couch next to Rachel while the cops peppered him with questions. His hands were folded in his lap. His eyes downcast as he responded. Rachel kept her hand on his knee, not firm enough to make him feel like he was being guided but with enough pressure so he would know she was there for him. With him.

"So you met Bennett Brice through Benjamin Ruddock?" Chen said. He was sitting on the love seat across from Rachel and Eric.

Eric nodded. He said nothing.

"And you met Brice in person two times, both at Voss Field. Both times in the middle of the night, around one thirty a.m. Is that correct?"

Eric nodded again. Megan sat at the dining room table, scribbling on a notepad, seemingly oblivious to the circus in their home.

"What did Bennett Brice say in each of those meetings?" Lowe asked him. Lowe's voice was sympathetic, understanding that Eric was still in shock. The boy stayed silent.

"Eric," Rachel said. "I know this is hard. But we need to find out exactly what happened tonight and why. You can help us find the truth."

Eric shook his head, tears streaming down his face. "I can't," he said.

"Yes, you can," Rachel replied, giving his knee a gentle squeeze. "We need you, hon. *I* need you."

"No. I can't talk anymore. Just leave me alone. Forever. Just let me go somewhere I can be by myself. I have to get away from you and Megan."

"Eric," Rachel said, taken aback. "Why would you say that?"

Then Eric looked at Rachel, eyes red and wet. "Because everyone around me dies," he said softly. "Mr. Linklater. Albie Roberson. Mr. Brice. Dad. *You* almost died. I don't want that to happen to you or Megan or Penny. I lose everyone I care about. What's wrong with me?"

Rachel felt her heart tear open. "Oh, baby, none of those were your fault. Terrible things happen that none of us can control. You are a *good* son. And I am blessed to be your mom."

He looked at her and said, "Should I leave? So you and Megan will be safe?"

Rachel gathered Eric into her arms and held him and said, "Don't you dare. It took me a long time to realize this, but you're like me. You *are* me. The way you've felt, that anger and helplessness—that's how I've felt, too, since your father died. But I found an outlet for it. I never let you find yours, and I'm so, so sorry. You have courage and compassion, but we also live with incredible guilt. And that's not fair. Because that guilt doesn't belong to you, just like it doesn't belong to me. These things *happened* to us. They were beyond our control. That doesn't mean it doesn't hurt. It *should* hurt. It just means we can't blame ourselves for the pain."

She knew the officers were waiting, patient, but they could all go to hell while her son was hurting.

"I would follow you to the ends of the earth to protect you," Rachel said. "If you went up in a hot-air balloon, I would build a plane out of gum and paper clips to go get you. But soon enough you won't need it. Because you're strong on your own. You're like mithril armor times a million."

Eric laughed, and Rachel felt the tear in her heart close ever so slightly. She ached for that laugh like a drowning woman ached for air.

"How do you know what mithril armor is?" he said.

"Maybe if you weren't too busy playing *Warfare Brigade Zombie Platoon Seventeen*, you would have noticed that I read one or two of those fantasy books you and John always talk about."

Eric nodded, seemingly impressed. "They're good, right?"

"I never thought I'd ever be so invested in elven culture," she said.

Eric laughed, and Rachel felt it in her heart.

"Listen, all I want is you here with us," Rachel said. She repeated herself. "Here. *With us.* And I'll do whatever I need to do to help you stay that way. I'm sorry if I've been too much, too suffocating. If I didn't let you be *you*. But I'll do better."

"I will too," he said.

At that moment, Megan came over and draped her arms around her brother's shoulders. She kissed him on the back of his neck and said, "I will too."

Eric choked out a mixture of a sob and a laugh and squeezed his sister's arms tightly. "I love you so much, Megan."

"I love you, Eric."

"I want to read every Sadie Scout story."

She stepped back, her face now deadly serious. "Do you mean that?" she asked.

"I mean it."

Megan jumped up in the air and said, "I'm writing a brand-new one just for you." Then she ran off to her room.

"That's a lot of reading you just committed to," Rachel said to Eric.

"I know. I owe it to her."

"You do," she said.

Eric turned back to the detectives and said, "OK. What do you need to know?"

He gave them the names of all the kids he knew who were at Voss Field both nights he attended meetings. Rachel paid attention to what Eric said as closely as the cops did. Because she prayed Peter Lincecum was still alive. If he was out there somewhere, hiding for his life from Randall Spivak, the clock was ticking. And while Serrano, Tally, and the rest of the APD officers had to cede jurisdictional authority to the Carltondale police, Rachel had no such limitations.

Rachel had also lost touch with Evie Boggs. She had texted Evie several times but hadn't heard from her since the first gunshot hit her brother. Evie was her best link to Brice, to YourLife, and to getting a lead on Peter Lincecum.

"Why don't you go take a shower?" Officer Chen said to Eric. "Feel good to wash the night off a bit. Let your mom and I catch up."

"Go ahead, hon," Rachel said. She rubbed Eric's back. He stood up, wobbled as if in a stupor, then righted himself. Then he planted a kiss on Rachel's cheek and left. Rachel beamed.

Once Rachel was alone with the officers, she sighed and ran a dirt-streaked hand through her hair.

"Any line on the shooter?" she asked the cops.

Chen shook his head. "Shots came from outside the stadium, so no footprints in the outfield grass. No debris in the parking lot. We're going over it, but given the size of the crime scene, it will take time."

"What about the weapon?"

"No sign of the gun or the spent shells," Lowe said. "The shooter collected them."

"There were ten shots," Rachel said. "But only four hit Brice. That means either the shooter was far away or was an amateur . . . or wanted to make it *look* like he was an amateur."

Lowe gave Chen a look. Like he wanted to say something but dreaded the consequences.

"OK, what did I miss?" Rachel said.

"We have an official complaint from the YourLife office," Lowe said. "There was no love lost between you and the victim. I have to ask, Ms. Marin. Did you kill Bennett Brice?"

"You can give me a GSR test right here and now," she said. "And twenty people can testify that I was at the field in plain sight and never drew a weapon. Plus ballistics will tell you that the shots came from nowhere near where I was standing when he got hit."

"Wouldn't prove anything conclusively," Chen said. "We know how smart you are, Ms. Marin. There's no way you'd do something as careless as fire the weapon yourself. But you obviously knew when the meeting was taking place, where it was taking place, and the layout of the field so that your entrance and exit wouldn't be seen. Information that could have easily been relayed to a third party."

"You think I arranged for Bennett Brice to be murdered?" Rachel said with genuine surprise in her voice. "That I hired a hitman or something, like I'm a jilted wife who caught her rich husband diddling his secretary?"

"I'm not saying you did," Lowe said. "But you were also injured while following YourLife employees, including your own son, in violation of a court order."

"You have means and motive," Chen said. "And you clearly don't think the law applies to you. We've heard this song before, Ms. Marin."

"Check my phone records," Rachel said. "Check my bank statements. I'll email them all to you this afternoon. If you can find any evidence that I set this up, I bet you'll also find records of me cooking the perfect cheese soufflé while getting busy with George Clooney. Am I a suspect?"

"We're not at liberty to discuss an ongoing investigation," Chen said. "But if you plan on leaving the state, let us know."

Rachel could feel the blood pounding in her head, stinging the still-healing wound. She took a few deep breaths to settle her nerves. Antagonizing the cops wouldn't solve anything. She knew full well there was nothing to connect her to Brice's murder. But the person who killed Matthew Linklater and Bennett Brice was still out there—and a young boy's life was in danger. Rachel wouldn't be able to help anybody if she kept the microscope on herself.

"Anything you need, Officers. For what it's worth, I can assure you I had nothing to do with the death of Bennett Brice. And I'm willing to provide any information that will aid in your investigation. I'm on your side."

Lowe looked at Chen, as if to say, *That's good enough for me.* Chen appeared more skeptical. But he stood up and said, "We're glad you and your son are safe, Ms. Marin. If you can remember anything else from last night, you know where to find Detectives Serrano and Tally."

"I do."

"Just one more thing," Officer Chen said. "We never found Bennett Brice's cell phone. Certainly possible he didn't bring it to the field. But any idea where it might be?"

"I don't. I'm sorry, Officer."

"Figured I'd ask. Thanks, Ms. Marin."

She stood up and shook the officers' hands. Chen made sure to let his gaze linger on Rachel for an extra moment before they left.

Cell phone.

The police never found Matthew Linklater's cell phone either. She doubted Brice would leave his cell unguarded, but it was entirely possible that in the commotion someone took it. But why?

Once the police were gone, Rachel went upstairs. She could hear Eric showering. She poked her head into Megan's room, finding her furiously scribbling in her Sadie Scout notebook.

She went to her bedroom, peeled off her soiled clothes, and placed them gently in a pile on top of the laundry basket. Her shoulder ached where she'd hit the dirt to protect Eric. She was still in good shape, but the bruises hurt a little more; the aches and pains took longer to fade away. It was beginning to feel like she wasn't merely burning the candle at both ends but taking a blowtorch to the middle simultaneously.

After she got dressed—and confirmed that neither of her children had left the house while she was in the shower—Rachel texted Serrano:

Any line on the shooter?

It took twenty endless minutes for him to respond.

Still interviewing the kids from Voss. Most tell the same story. Shots came from somewhere beyond the outfield fence. Nobody saw anyone. The list of people who wanted Bennett Brice dead is just slightly longer than the Magna Carta.

What about Peter Lincecum?

The Carltondale PD is on it

We need to be on it too

It's outside our jurisdiction Rachel

For some reason, the final *Rachel* irritated her. As if Serrano was scolding her about trying to prevent the death of a young boy.
Then Serrano sent another text:

I know what you're thinking

Is that so? Then you'll be at my door imminently with a bottle of Rioja and some dark chocolate with sea salt

Just be careful Rach. As dangerous as you think Bennett Brice was, he was a businessman. A shady one, but I don't think he ended any lives himself. But Randall Spivak is still out there.

Then he should hope he doesn't run into me in a dark alley.

That's exactly what I was hoping you wouldn't say.

CHAPTER 42

John Serrano watched as forensics technicians clad in white latex suits scoured Bennett Brice's empty office at YourLife. What was just yesterday a workstation was now a mausoleum. Brice's office, the security desk, and all surfaces had been wiped down thoroughly by the cleaning crew the previous day. They'd fingerprinted the security guard and Brice's secretary for exclusionary measures—both had alibis that checked out—but so far had turned up barely a fiber. They had warrants waiting to be approved to gain access to Brice's phone calls and text messages.

They had not found Brice's cell phone at the office or at his home. They'd found several chargers and cords, so they knew he had one. And wherever it was, it was turned off, so they couldn't track it via GPS or a phone-finding app. Serrano had a very good idea who might have it. But until she turned up, they had to continue scouring the remnants of Bennett Brice's life.

Serrano and Tally had left several voice mails for Evelyn Boggs. Evie had kept her past well guarded, but she was officially Bennett Brice's next of kin. Boggs had gone with the ambulance to the hospital, then disappeared after Brice was pronounced dead at 2:42 a.m. She was not a suspect, but Serrano hoped she could narrow down the grocery list of people who might want to see Bennett Brice dead.

Tally finished speaking with Isaac Montrose from forensics and walked over to Serrano.

"Clean as my stepson's hard drive after he found out Claire installed spyware," she said. "YourLife itself *is* a legitimate business. They pay taxes, have all their W-9s on file, and even pay an HR department in India. Freaky middle-of-the-night meetings and the odd murder aside, there's nothing here that would incriminate Bennett Brice or give us a lead on who killed him."

"Let's see what the phone company gives us," Serrano said, knowing full well he wasn't expecting to find much of anything in Brice's phone records. "In the meantime, Brice is the victim here. We need to remember that."

"If you had to venture a guess," Tally said, "who'd you peg for this?"

Serrano thought for a moment. "Randall Spivak. With his brother being held for the murder of Lloyd Lincecum and the Carltondale PD looking for Peter, Brice and Peter Lincecum were the two people most willing and able to send him away. And if they could pin a murder or two on him, with Brice's help, he'd never see the light of day. And if the CPD finds Peter Lincecum before Randall can, Lincecum could bury YourLife. Brice is a businessman. White-collar guys would give up their mothers if it meant avoiding jail time. But with Brice dead, a jury would have to convict Randall based only on the word of a traumatized teenage boy."

"That's if it ever even made it to trial," Tally said. "After what Raymond Spivak did to his father, Peter will be put into protective custody immediately. That would mess with a grown man's head, let alone a kid's. With Brice gone, the number of people who would and could testify against the Spivaks is pretty small."

"People like us, we screw up, we suffer the consequences," Serrano said. "But when kids are forced into a fate they never signed up for, it rips your heart out. Kids like Peter Lincecum, Eric Marin, and . . ."

"Evan," she said softly. "I know, John. I *know*."

"Thanks, partner. We didn't have much religion in my house growing up. My dad believed in the word of his bookie more than the word of God, and my mother never tried to change his mind. I can't say I think about spirituality all that much. To me it feels like leaning a ladder against air and hoping it'll stay put. But last night I prayed for those kids. And if there is someone up there, I hope they're listening."

"I hope so too," Tally said. "So let's consider finding Bennett Brice's killer your path back to the light."

"Kind of like when Indiana Jones had to find the cup of Christ after his dad got shot by the Nazis and found some old dude who'd apparently lived in a cave for a few hundred years and ate nothing but dust bunnies, right?"

Tally rubbed her eyes in exhaustion. "Whatever medication you're on, I think we need to triple it."

"Detectives." Montrose waved them over. They joined Montrose, who was in front of a desktop computer home screen. "We're in."

"Nice work." Serrano slipped on a pair of latex gloves.

Brice's hard drive was neatly organized. He had valid receipts, tax statements, employment and payment records, and inventory data from hundreds of products sold by YourLife. It would take a week to go through it all, but at a glance it looked remarkably detailed, organized, and most likely legal.

"I don't buy it," Tally said. "Zero chance this company was on the up-and-up."

Serrano replied, "Brice was obviously careful enough to make it *appear* to be that way. Benjamin Ruddock worked as Brice's recruiter in Ashby. He was able to get to Eric Marin because of proximity. They saw each other in school every day. But Peter Lincecum lived several towns away. I doubt Benjamin Ruddock was recruiting in Carltondale. So the question is: Who was?"

"This feels like the mob," Tally said. "Brice at the top, captains like Ruddock designating responsibilities to soldiers lower on the chain. Money flowing to the people at the top like Brice and Spivak."

"Any chance one of the kids took out Brice? You know, kill the king and take over his kingdom?"

"You're thinking Benjamin Ruddock orchestrated it," Tally said.

"The thought crossed my mind."

"I considered it," Tally said. "But Ruddock and Brice seemed tight. Brice was Ruddock's golden goose. Maybe one day he saw himself at the top of the food chain, but not as a high school student. Just feels like too much of a stretch."

"So you're still thinking it was Randall Spivak?"

"It makes sense. Raymond kills Lloyd Lincecum while looking for Peter because Peter is a loose end. But since Peter is missing and a threat to testify, Randall would have motivation to eliminate anyone else who could flip."

"Speaking of which, any word on Evie Boggs? I'm guessing she knows more about Bennett Brice's dealings than the Spivaks are comfortable with."

"Nothing yet," Tally said. "Voice mails and texts unreturned. You should tell Rachel too. Those two have a past, and if Randall is really tying up loose ends, he'll come looking for Evie. And we both know Rachel has a tendency to be a lightning rod for violence."

Serrano nodded and tapped out a text to Rachel.

"Now let's find Randall Spivak," he said. "I want to bring him in for questioning."

"If I'm Randall Spivak," Tally said, "I'm hiding under a rock. He's a person of interest in two different murders involving two different police departments. I wouldn't be surprised if he's in Scandinavia by now."

"Maybe so, but if he's still after Peter Lincecum, he isn't lying low. Speaking of which, I think we need to aid our friends at the Carltondale

PD. Lloyd Lincecum's murder might be outside our jurisdiction, but it's clearly connected to Brice's death and likely Matthew Linklater's. We find that connection, we tie all those murders together into one big conspiracy."

"You think the same person who killed Linklater killed Brice?"

"I don't know. Linklater clearly knew something about Brice that imperiled Brice's operation. I doubt Brice himself lit the match. The Spivak boys seem more likely to do that. But Brice may have orchestrated the blaze."

A young officer approached Serrano and Tally. She looked nervous, maybe a year or two out of the academy at most. Given the large police presence at the YourLife offices, she was likely there for crowd control. Serrano remembered his first few years on the job, walking into every crime scene like you could lose your job at any moment, wanting to impress the veterans but not wanting to come across as brash or cocky. It was a thin line rookie cops had to walk, and nobody taught you how to walk it. Serrano always tried to be helpful, understanding. Those rookie cops would become detectives, lieutenants, chiefs. Hell, he could end up working for this girl in ten years.

"Detectives?" the officer said.

"Name, Officer?" Serrano said.

"Cutrone. Shelley Cutrone. Deputy Shelley Cutrone."

"Deputy Shelley Cutrone, what can we do for you?"

"There's someone outside who'd like to speak with you," Cutrone said.

"Does this person have a name?" Tally said.

Cutrone handed Tally a business card. She looked at it, frowned, and passed it to Serrano like it had lice. He read it and cursed.

Chester Barnes. Attorney at Law.

"Once you start turning over logs, the insects come out," Serrano said. He sighed. "Let's see what brings the esteemed counselor to our crime scene."

Serrano and Tally went outside. The sun was high in the sky, baking the streets and turning Ashby into a dry sauna. The YourLife building was cordoned off with police tape. Officers kept a small group of onlookers behind a row of barricades. Many had cell phones out, taking pictures and recording videos. Serrano knew some of those recordings would be shared on social media and possibly picked up by local or national news organizations covering the Brice murder. Citizen journalism at its finest.

There was no such attention paid to the death of Matthew Linklater. Money and publicity tended to go hand in hand, even after death. But at the same time, it meant the detectives had to be even more careful about what they did and said at all times. Citizens had a right to know law enforcement was on the up-and-up, but single images could be taken out of context, and videos could be edited deceptively.

The detectives slipped on sunglasses. Cutrone pointed them toward a black Cadillac Escalade down the block, away from the police activity. Through its open window they could see a man sitting in the back seat. The other windows were tinted to the edge of legality. The passenger was facing forward, motionless, almost bored, as though waiting patiently for a drive-through order.

"Assume we're being recorded," Tally said. Serrano looked at the mob of people rubbernecking Brice's office. Most of them held out cell phones. Some were taking selfies with the crime scene in the background.

"Always do," he said. "I'll bet that Cadillac has more cameras and mic setups than a Spielberg movie."

At the car, Serrano put his elbow on the window and leaned down. "The honorable Chester Barnes," he said. "Please, don't get out."

Chester Barnes was forty-nine years old but, depending on the light, could look either a decade younger or a decade older. He had garish, unnatural golden skin that looked like he'd been locked inside a tanning booth for an entire presidential administration and veneers the size of pocket squares. His hair color lay somewhere between pumpkin orange and muddy brown, and his face looked like it was continually moisturized. Serrano wasn't much of a clotheshorse and couldn't tell offhand how much his suit cost, but the fine cloth and subtle pinstripes didn't look like they'd been taken off the rack. He wore cologne that smelled to Serrano like a generous mixture of grapefruit and mildew. Chester Barnes was the most successful and notorious defense attorney in Ashby, and everything about how he presented himself seemed to be done with the express intention of making him very, very hard to forget.

"Detective Serrano. Detective Tally," Barnes said.

"So what brings you to our humble crime scene?" Tally said.

Barnes reached into his suit-jacket pocket and took out a cell phone.

"I already have an unlimited LTE plan," Serrano said. "But I'm glad to know AT&T was willing to hire you."

Barnes sighed wearily. "I've been working with police departments for over twenty years on the side of the law, and it will never cease to amaze me how unfunny cops can be. It is almost as though God decided to make a percentage of people on this earth inherently unlikable and put them all in law enforcement."

"I don't know—I still think I have a shot at a career in stand-up," Tally said. "But nothing will ever be as funny as you pretending to be on the side of the law."

"I'm on the side of my clients, Detective, as is any good legal representative."

"I'll ask again," Tally said. "Why are you here? We're investigating two different murders, plus we can't get the thermostat at the station to work, so we don't have much time for you."

"Then I'll make it quick," Barnes said. "As you investigate the untimely death of my client, Bennett Brice—may he rest in peace—I will be looking after his interests, both legally and financially."

"By interests, you mean his family," Serrano said. "I assume you're referring to Evelyn Boggs."

"Mr. Brice had a not-insignificant amount of assets," Barnes said. "He expected all disbursements to occur as he wished. I will be making sure that none of Mr. Brice's assets are unduly . . . *penalized* or frozen as a result of your investigations."

"Right now we just want to know who killed your client," Serrano said. "If our investigation proves that his finances were obtained through illegal means, we will do with those monies as the law sees fit."

"And as the law's representative, if one penny is withheld, I will rain hellfire on you and your sad, small bureau that will leave the Ashby Police Department in a crater the size of Illinois."

"Hear that?" Serrano said. "He's going to rain hellfire down upon us."

"I love barbecue," Tally replied. "I'll bring the A.1."

"No A.1.," Serrano said. "Too sugary. Nothing I hate more than drowning a good steak in goopy sweetness."

"If you're finished, Detectives," Barnes said, a slight flush creeping into his cheeks, "I have something you need to see."

"Need to see?" Tally said. "I *need* to see my wife in dark-red lingerie. I don't *need* to see anything you have to show me."

"This is growing tiresome. If you choose not to watch it and then act without having done so, you'll have to answer to the courts. And the media."

"Both scary," Serrano said. "OK, Attorney Barnes, let's see what you've got. But if it's a cat GIF, I'm going to be really ticked off."

Barnes unlocked the phone with his thumbprint and opened the video tab. He swiped to a file, then pressed the play arrow. Serrano and Tally both leaned in. Serrano took Barnes's wrist and tilted it slightly to reduce the glare on the screen.

The clip began to play. It lasted a total of fourteen seconds.

The video appeared to be security-camera footage from inside a pub or bar. Serrano couldn't tell the exact location without being able to pause or zoom in. The paneling was dark wood. The ceiling was covered in soccer flags and jerseys. There were ten to twelve people at the bar and in booths dining and drinking. That was all. Nothing out of the ordinary. And then the video ended.

"That's it?" Tally said. "I've seen more action in my garden."

Barnes restarted the video, then paused it at the seven-second mark. He zoomed in on a man sitting alone at the bar. The patron wore black chinos and a crisp white long-sleeve button-down shirt. He was slim, his back straight, one hand in his lap and the other on a pint of dark beer. The time stamp on the video was 1:46 a.m. the previous night.

But it was the man's face that got their attention. Serrano heard Tally curse softly under her breath.

"It's Randall Spivak," she said.

"That's correct," Barnes said. "This video was taken at the Cask and Dragon pub on Northwest Tenth Street. It is authentic, so feel free to have it reviewed by your technicians. I know that due to the unfortunate demise of Mr. Brice, your police department, always quick to act without proof or wit, might in its haste falsely accuse my client, Mr. Spivak, of a heinous crime of which he is completely innocent."

Barnes handed Serrano a thumb drive.

"The full video is on this drive. You'll be able to see that Randall Spivak was at the Cask and Dragon for one hour and twenty-two minutes. He is visible for the duration of the video, except for one minute and forty-three seconds in which he goes to the restroom. His time at the bar overlaps with the time of Mr. Brice's death. Not even your second-rate AG would have the balls to claim that Mr. Spivak was able to leave the bar, kill Mr. Brice, and be back on his stool in under two minutes."

"We'll review the file," Serrano said.

"I expect nothing less. Mr. Spivak enjoyed two pints of ale and an order of potato skins. To my knowledge, neither of those actions breaks any laws."

"If he got potato skins without sour cream, that is considered a crime in many states," Tally said.

Barnes did not smile. "I hope you catch Mr. Brice's killer, Detectives. I knew Bennett for a long time. He was a friend and a good man. Once again, I expect you to leave any and all of Mr. Brice's assets untouched. And now that you have proof that Mr. Spivak was not the perpetrator of this terrible crime, I expect you to leave him be."

"Maybe we will, maybe we won't," Tally said. "Depends whether there are any other crimes he's the perpetrator of."

"You went to a lot of trouble just to make sure your client—who has not even been questioned—has an alibi for this murder," Serrano said.

"I've been around this city for a long time, Detective. Longer than both of you. I've seen cops come and go, and I've seen a lot of innocent people's names smeared due to shoddy police work. To the extent that I can lessen my clients' exposure to your hostilities, I will do that. Now, if you approach my client, or impede in any way the disbursement of his assets, I will make sure you're both guarding a soybean farm in Nebraska within the week."

"That sounds like a sweet gig," Tally said.

"I bet you get an employee discount on popcorn," Serrano added.

"Have a good day, Detectives," Barnes said as the Escalade window closed. "I hope you are more skilled at finding this killer than you are at comedy."

The Escalade sped off, leaving Serrano and Tally in a cloud of dust at the curb. Serrano looked at the thumb drive in his palm.

"What do you make of it?" Tally said.

"We'll get the lab to authenticate the video," Serrano said, "but I highly doubt Barnes would have brought it to us if there was even the slightest chance it was faked. He *knew* we'd be looking into Spivak. But he's also planting seeds. If we go after Randall, he can send this video to the media and claim police harassment. Chester Barnes is a whole lot of things, but he is not someone who sets himself up to fail. We have to consider the very real possibility that Randall Spivak didn't kill Bennett Brice."

"So what now?"

"We'll have the contents of Brice's hard drive analyzed and his bank records subpoenaed. But right now, I want to talk to perhaps the only person on earth who's definitely *not* a suspect in Bennett Brice's murder."

CHAPTER 43

Evie Boggs sat on a rumpled comforter atop a hard mattress inside a dirty motel room that she'd paid thirty-three dollars for, in cash. Her clothes from the previous night were inside a plastic garbage bag on the floor. She wore a clean white T-shirt and cheap yoga pants, which she'd purchased for twenty-one dollars total at a bargain clothing store next door to the motel. She stared at her cell phone. She couldn't keep up with the barrage of text messages and calls. The Ashby PD. Rachel Marin. Mackenzie North Hospital. She was trapped inside a hurricane. Still grounded, but so close to being blown away.

One number among the missed calls terrified her. She ignored it for the time being.

Her brother was dead. Gunned down by some coward in the dark. She'd lain in the dirt of the baseball field, watching Bennett's life spill from his body, powerless to do anything other than wail.

The ambulance had arrived quickly. The police soon after. By the time the EMTs had loaded Bennett's pale, blood-soaked body onto a gurney, all the boys had disappeared. As had Rachel and Eric Marin. Evie was left alone to ride with her brother's desecrated body to the hospital. They pronounced him dead upon arrival.

Evie felt like she was trapped in a balloon, the air being sucked out of it, the walls collapsing inward around her. She couldn't breathe. She had to go. She had a vague memory of stumbling outside the hospital, still covered in gore, getting into a cab, and telling the driver to *take me somewhere I can sleep.* She supposed that's how she'd ended up in a grimy hotel room looking like an extra from a *Saw* movie.

Bennett was not a saint, yet deep down Evie truly believed he'd given these boys an opportunity they never would have received otherwise. People had gotten hurt along the way, but she and Bennett could both say that the ends justified the means. Evie knew, though, that the Spivaks were demons deep down. Volatile and vicious. Any peace would be short lived. She just wished Bennett had known that as well as she did. To Bennett, the Spivaks were merely unorthodox business partners. At the worst, they were necessary evils. Evie knew that was bullshit. They were just evil.

Linklater's death ate at her, but she'd agreed to try to quash the investigation because the other option was her brother spending the rest of his life in prison.

She had come to Ashby to try to contain things. Prevent her brother's company from crumbling, and keep him out of jail. Try to keep the police and Rachel Marin away from YourLife. But things were out of control. Too many people had died. And more lives were still at risk. She no longer had to look out for her brother. There was only one person she needed to protect.

From her pocket, Evie pulled a cell phone covered in bloody fingerprints. She ran her finger over the screen, then pressed the "Home" button. A picture appeared on the home screen. She recognized the person in the photo and had to stifle a cry.

She entered six numbers into the password screen, and the phone unlocked. Then she opened the contacts app and scrolled down to the *R* section. Once she had the information she needed, Evie texted Rachel Marin.

CHAPTER 44

Rachel's cell phone lit up with a text. She checked the ID and laughed out loud both from surprise and a complete lack thereof. The text was from Evie Boggs. It was the first time she had heard from Evie since Bennett Brice was killed.

There was no message. Just an address.

1362 Wambaugh Street. Now.

Rachel did a quick search to find the owner of the home at that address. She let out a breath when she saw who owned the property. *Here we go.*

Rachel looked out the window. Two police cars were parked out front. She could see Lowe and Chen having coffee in one of them. Lowe appeared to be singing along to something on the radio, to Chen's great annoyance. Rachel went upstairs. Eric was lying on his bed, reading a worn copy of *Dune*, by Frank Herbert.

"I've never been so glad to see you living in other realities," she said. "I've never read it. Should I?"

"Should you?" Eric said, incredulously. "It's, like, a classic. Detective Serrano gave it to me a few months ago. This is the third time I've read it."

"You know, when I see you with your head in other worlds," Rachel said, "somehow it lets me know you're a little closer to this one. And that makes me happy."

Eric smiled. "Everything OK?" he said.

"I have to go out for a little bit."

Eric sat up. Folded the top-right corner of the page to hold his place.

"I thought treating books like that was a sin," she said.

"The more you love something, the more it shows," he replied.

That is truer than you know, she thought.

"Are the police still outside?" he said. Rachel nodded. Eric gave a sly smile. "I bet you can get out of here without them noticing. You're way sneakier than I am."

"I'm not sure if that's a compliment. But I am glad you have faith in my sneaking abilities."

"I'm sorry if you ever lost your faith in me."

"Eric," she said. She sat down next to her son. "I *would* never, *could* never lose faith in you. I will love you no matter what, for every single day I'm lucky enough to be your mother."

She kissed him on his forehead, and he squirmed. "Hey, come on, Mom."

"Sometimes you're just going to have to put up with those," she said. "But I promise not to do it in public. Or around Penny Wallace."

She playfully punched his arm.

"Mom, stop."

"Am I going too far?"

"When you're super old, and not like a ninja anymore, I'm going to steal your dentures."

Rachel laughed. "That's fair."

"OK, go do what you need to do. I'll watch Megan. She asked me to start reading her Sadie Scout books. I think she wants me to read all of them." He paused, concerned. "How many are there?"

"I think at least twenty. You'd better get to it."

Eric's jaw dropped, and he sighed. "Fine."

His tone had the irritated petulance of a teenage boy. At that particular moment, though, it brought Rachel immense joy.

"I want a book report on each and every one of them," she said.

Eric began to protest, but then he stopped. "You're not serious."

Rachel winked at him. "Maybe. Maybe not. Love you, hon. No matter what."

Evie Boggs was standing on the corner of Wambaugh Street and Oakmont Terrace, smoking a cigarette, a nasty curl to her lip that could have been the taste of the cig or just the general disgust with how the last few days had left her life a pile of rubble. When Evie saw Rachel Marin coming, she tossed the cigarette into a pile of leaves. Rachel rolled her eyes at Evie, pressed the toe of her shoe into the pile, and ground the butt until the tip was snuffed out.

"All it takes is one leaf to catch fire and get blown into someone's lawn," Rachel said.

"Who are you, Smokey the Bear?"

"He's a distant relative," Rachel said. "I didn't know you smoked."

"It took me a long, long time to quit," she said. "Lucky I never got sick or got anyone else sick. Today was the first craving I've had in years. Do you know how much they charge for a pack these days? I could put a down payment on a house or buy some avocado toast."

Rachel laughed, then said, "How are you holding up?"

"How am I? Let's see. My brother was murdered last night, I slept on a mattress probably stuffed with roach carcasses, and now I'm here with you and giving myself cancer. I feel like a freaking human rainbow. How are you, Rach?"

"I'm sorry," Rachel said. "I am. Last night . . . I just wanted to find Peter Lincecum and prevent anyone else from getting hurt. I had no love for your brother, but I never wanted to see him dead."

"Yeah, well, that doesn't make me feel any better."

"I lost someone close to me before too. You know that. And I won't lie to you. You won't feel better for a long time. Maybe not ever. All you can do is try to piece together little bits of goodness to keep patching up the hole. You need to make right whatever you can."

"That's why we're here," Evie said. "Let me ask one question. Does it ever heal?"

Rachel hesitated, then said, "No. Not really."

"Well, that's just peachy." Evie eyed the leaf pile forlornly, clearly wishing she hadn't tossed the smoke. "So. I know why we're here. You know why we're here."

"I do," Rachel said. "So how do you want to handle this? Good cop, bad cop?"

"After the day I've had, I'm more in the mood for bad cop, bad cop."

"I can do that."

They approached the ranch-style home. It was faded beige with white trim, with a slate-gray gabled roof, aluminum siding, and an attached garage. A rusty John Deere sat surrounded by overgrown grass on the unkempt lawn. The house would have felt dated twenty years ago.

Evie rang the doorbell. They heard a shuffling sound from inside. A minute later, the front door opened, revealing a man of about sixty wearing a light-blue terry cloth bathrobe, an undershirt stained yellow. His craggy, unshaven face was covered in white stubble. He had an irritated grimace like Evie was there to ask him to undergo a colonoscopy.

"Electricity bill is paid up," he said. He looked the women up and down, a crooked smile spreading on his thin, chapped lips. "You two're better looking than the fella they usually send to harass me."

"Unfortunately for you, we're also a whole lot meaner," Evie said. "Timothy Ruddock?"

"Yes?" the man said, with an obvious distrust for anyone who knew his full name.

"Mr. Ruddock, we're here to talk to your son."

The smile on his face disappeared. "What do you want with Benny?"

Rachel said, "That's between us and him."

"Boy goes off on weekends. Think he goes looking for strange, like most kids his age," the elder Ruddock said, eyeing his slippers. "You'll have to come back another time."

"I'm sorry . . . he goes looking for what? Strange?" Rachel asked.

"Strange," Timothy Ruddock said. "You know—strange pussy."

"Charming," Rachel said. "Your family knows how to raise gentlemen."

"Know what? I don't think you're with Central Electric," Ruddock said, folding his arms across his chest.

Evie clapped sardonically. "Give the man a prize."

Ruddock's eyes bounced between the two women. "So then who the hell are you? And what do you want with Benny?"

"My name is Rachel Marin, and this is my associate, Evelyn Boggs. We want to talk to your son about Bennett Brice. You may have heard that a man named Bennett Brice was shot and killed last night. Your son has had some dealings with him. We think he can help us find who did it."

Ruddock spat a glob of yellowed phlegm into a hedge off the porch.

"Good distance," Rachel said.

"If only there was an Olympic sport," Evie replied.

"I got nothing to do with that Brice fella, and any *dealings* my son might have had with him are his business and his business alone."

"Your son is a high schooler and has made thousands of dollars working for a man who was just murdered," Rachel said. "And you look about as bothered by your son's possible criminal activities as you do about global warming."

"What are you, Mother of the Year?"

Rachel said, "Compared to you I'm June fucking Cleaver."

Evie said, "Listen, Mr. Ruddock. We just want to talk to your son. Then we'll be on our way."

Ruddock eyed them both, debating whether to trust them. His breath smelled like he ate too much meat and smoked too many unfiltered cigarettes.

"Are you cops?" Ruddock asked. "Like, undercover? I don't see no badges on you."

"We're not cops," Rachel said. "But I assure you that we could have the cops here before you can brew a pot of coffee."

"But we don't want that," Evie said. "We just want to talk to Benjamin. We think he has information that can help save someone's life. We don't want to get anyone in trouble, and that's the truth. He can do the right thing here. He's made mistakes. Now's his chance to make up for them."

"My boy . . . ," Ruddock said, absently scratching the inside of his nose, his eyes with a faraway look. "He's a good boy. Never gotten into any trouble."

"I think you might be a little off there, Dad of the Year," Rachel said.

"I might know where he is," Ruddock said. "But I need you to swear there won't be no cops coming around here once you're done."

"Funny," Evie said. "I would have expected you to ask us to swear not to hurt your son."

Ruddock let out a small dismissive laugh. "What, you ladies? One thing about Ruddocks—we grow 'em *strong*."

Lightning quick, Evie reached out and grabbed Timothy Ruddock's crotch. He let out a yelp so high pitched that Rachel wondered if he'd ever considered a career in opera.

"Tell me where he is," Evie said, "or I twist off your manhood like cherry stems."

"Stop! OK!" Ruddock squealed. "He's . . ."

They heard a shuffling noise from inside the house. Ruddock senior's eyes flickered. He knew they'd heard it.

"Back door," Evie said.

"On it," Rachel replied.

Before Rachel could move, they heard a banging noise and the sound of footsteps on grass.

"Back door! Ben is running!" Rachel shouted. "You go that way. We can flank him."

Both women sprinted away from the front door, Rachel around the right side of the house and Evie around the left. On Rachel's side, a six-foot-high wooden fence separated the front of the house from the back, latched with a padlock.

Just my luck, Rachel thought.

She stopped, stepped back, and measured. There were no footholds. The top of the fence was formed into wooden spikes. She took a breath, put her hands in between the spikes, and pushed herself up. She managed to swing one leg over the fence, but as she was bringing the second leg over, she felt someone grab her pant leg and pull her backward.

The top of one of the spikes raked a gash deep into her inner thigh. She felt a searing pain, immediately followed by wetness as blood began to flow. She looked down to see Timothy Ruddock, bathrobe flailing as he tried to pull her down. She gave him a solid kick to the Adam's apple. He went down, eyes bulging, hand at his throat. Rachel threw herself over the fence before he could recover.

She landed hard, and the world swam. Her head pounded. Her leg throbbed. It took her a moment to regain her equilibrium.

The backyard ran parallel to Mulligan Avenue. Rachel sprinted ahead, ignoring the fire in her leg and snare drums pounding in her head.

"Come on!" Evie shouted. She was a good twenty feet ahead. Rachel could see Benjamin Ruddock sprinting away from them. Pedestrians stopped to watch. Rachel figured it wasn't too often they saw a teenage boy fleeing from two women. He was young. Fast. In good shape. Rachel was no slouch, but she didn't think they could get him on foot.

At least not if they played fair.

"That asshole stole my phone!" Rachel shouted. "Someone stop him!"

Ruddock kept running, but Rachel saw a woman reach out and try to grab his arm. Ruddock shrugged her off, but it slowed him down. A man stepped into Ruddock's path, but Ruddock managed to dodge his grasp. But again, it slowed him down. Evie was maybe ten feet behind Ruddock. Rachel twice that. But they were gaining.

Suddenly a grizzly bear of a man stepped into Ruddock's path. He was about three hundred pounds, with a thick black beard and wearing an unzipped leather jacket with only a tight white T-shirt underneath. When Ruddock tried to evade him, the man, displaying a shocking amount of agility given his size, mirrored Ruddock's step, grabbed hold of his shirt, and tossed him to the ground like an unpaid bill.

Ruddock tried to get up, but the man literally took a seat on the boy's back, pinning him to the ground.

"You're not goin' anywhere until these ladies get a word with you."

"They're lying!" Ruddock shouted, prone on his stomach like a trapped butterfly.

"Oh, yeah? Then why you running?"

Evie and Rachel jogged up to the pair. Rachel caught her breath, her leg and head pumping blood. She laughed, thinking about the doctor telling her to take it easy given her head wound. Ruddock slapped pitifully at the large man's legs.

"Oh, so you like to play patty-cake?" the man said, smacking Ruddock's hand hard enough to elicit a yelp.

"Thank you, sir," Rachel said, between breaths. "The four-hundred-yard dash was never my strongest event."

"Don't mention it," he said. "Tyler Rodenhouse. At your service. Squirmy little bastard, ain't he?"

"You don't know the half of it," Evie said. "I'm Evie. This is Rachel. We owe you."

"You owe me nuthin', lady. Want me to call the cops?"

"No thanks," Rachel said. "He's not worth the trouble. We just want to get this over with, get back what he stole, and get home to our kids."

Evie said, "I think we have it under control from here. You can let him go. Just wish I hadn't smoked for the first time in years before this kid pulled a Dr. Richard Kimble on us."

Rodenhouse stood up, and Ruddock immediately leaped to his feet. He threw a punch at Evie, but Rachel was able to grab his wrist before it connected. She brought her foot down into the back of Ruddock's knee, driving him to the ground. He went to backhand Rachel, but Evie grabbed his wrist, twisted it behind his back, and shoved his face into the dirt.

Rodenhouse looked at the two women, eyes wide. "Uh, yeah. I'd definitely say you have it under control. Just remind *me* never to get on your bad side."

"I don't think that'll be a problem," Rachel said.

"Your leg's bleeding," Tyler said, pointing at Rachel's thigh. "You should get that looked at."

"I will," Rachel replied. "And . . . Tyler?"

"Yeah?"

"Thanks. You're one of the good ones."

He smiled. "Gonna tell my wife you said that."

Tyler walked away, leaving Benjamin Ruddock on the ground, Rachel and Evie standing over him.

"The hell do you want?" Ruddock said, blowing dirt as he spoke. "I didn't do anything."

"You nearly got me killed," Rachel said. "And if you don't start talking, you just might get a kid killed too."

"I didn't have anything to do with what happened to you," Ruddock said. He picked up a small pile of dirt with his free hand and flung it weakly into Evie's shin.

"You're telling me when I was following you and my son, you didn't call Bennett Brice?"

Ruddock tried to roll over, but Evie forced him back down.

"Sure. I called Brice," Ruddock said. "But I never spoke to Peter. I just told Brice you were there and he needed to handle it. I didn't know what would happen next."

"You mean with the Spivaks," Evie said.

"Look. However Brice decided to handle it, that's on him."

"That's crap," Rachel said. "A boy—a *boy*—put a gun to my head. You knew exactly what would happen. And now that boy's father is dead. You have one chance, *one chance*, you bulbous undergrowth, to do maybe the only good thing you've done in your life and tell us where to find Peter Lincecum. I know you don't want his blood on your hands."

Ruddock seemed to deflate. He stopped fighting. And then, he began to sob.

"I never wanted anyone to get hurt," he said, his voice cracking.

"I find that *very* hard to believe," Rachel said.

"Well, it's *true*!" Ruddock sat up. He looked up at the two women. The fear and shame in his eyes let Rachel know he was done. "Brice came to me three years ago. My dad had just lost his job. He couldn't pay our mortgage. Our electricity got turned off. We were going to get evicted. He didn't care. He just kept drinking."

"You want us to feel sorry for you?" Evie said.

"I don't care *what* you feel," Ruddock said. "It's the truth. Brice told me I had two choices: work with him and see money. *Real* money. Or say no and end up like my dad. He called him 'useless.' You know what it's like to hear someone call your dad that and know it's true? Brice tells me the world is screwing me over. That people like me are getting left behind. That I'm owed my share. And he's going to help me get it."

"Go on," Rachel said.

"Brice tells me I'm smart. That I have good grades. I do, you know. That with his help I can pay my dad's mortgage, pay for *anything* I want. I tell him he's full of it. But then, he shows me." Ruddock looked at Rachel. "In two years, I've made two hundred and forty thousand dollars. That's more money than my dad has made in ten years."

Rachel paused, then said, "You stole the rat from the biology lab."

"Huh?" Ruddock said, but his hesitation gave it away.

"What was its name? Midge. You stole Midge from Ashby High. The one that was used to torture Matthew Linklater."

"I didn't know what it was going to be used for, I swear. I thought they were just going to scare him."

"They?" Rachel said. "I know that two people together killed Matthew Linklater. One of them did the dirty work. That was Randall Spivak. But the other had to get him to open the door. That was you. *You* helped kill him."

"No way. I swear on my life I wasn't there. Brice found out that Mr. Linklater knew about YourLife."

"How did he know?" Evie asked.

"I don't know. I really don't. Brice always relied on the Spivaks for the really bad stuff. OK, I stole the rat. I figured it was going to be a prank. But I wasn't anywhere near Mr. Linklater's home the night he died."

"Killed," Rachel said. "The night he was killed."

"Where is Peter Lincecum?" Evie said, the patience in her voice wearing thin.

"I don't know," Ruddock said. Evie twisted Ruddock's arm behind his back, and the boy squealed.

"Talk," Evie said, "or you'll spend the rest of your life with your ulna and radius bones held together by a twist tie."

Spittle dangled from Ruddock's lips. "You can break my arm," he said, "but you both know what Randall Spivak is capable of. I'm not scared of you."

Evie twisted Ruddock's arm harder, and the boy screamed again. Rachel placed her hand on Evie's wrist and gave her a look that said, *That's enough.*

"Tell me where Peter is," Evie said. "Maybe you're not afraid of a broken arm. But I have contacts inside Pinckneyville who would just love to know about a good-looking guy about to serve time. A guy who hurt young kids."

Ruddock looked at Evie, true fear now spreading across his face. "You wouldn't."

"If you think I wouldn't," Evie said, "then you don't know me."

"OK. But I don't know where Peter is. That's the honest truth," Ruddock said, snot bubbling from his nose. "But I know who does."

CHAPTER 45

Rachel was about to press the buzzer when she saw them standing across the street, waiting for the light. Gabrielle and Tony Vargas were each carrying three large grocery bags, stuffed to the brim.

Rachel's eyes locked with Gabrielle's. She gave a slight nod that said, *We've been waiting for you.* Gabrielle acknowledged Rachel but seemed far from happy to see her.

When the light changed, Gabrielle and Tony crossed the street. Tony spun around in the crosswalk, heavy bags outstretched, as though trying to impress his mother with his strength.

Tony was five eleven, with sharp cheekbones, close-cropped black hair, and a wisp of a mustache. He wore a plain black T-shirt, just tight enough that Rachel could see where it strained slightly against his shoulders and biceps. His chin had just the slightest bit of pudge, but it would melt away soon enough. Rachel could see the faded red scar on his neck, like an errant mark from a watercolor, more translucent than red. Her heart hurt for the boy. She could only imagine what the wound had done to him, inside and out.

Tony was growing into a tall, handsome young man. He had a full life ahead of him. Gabrielle Vargas looked like she hadn't slept in weeks. Her eyes were bloodshot, the circles underneath them dark enough to hide coal. Her hair was tangled and stringy, and her white blouse was wrinkled and worn. But whatever was weighing on her, it hadn't affected her son.

"Ms. Marin," Gabrielle said as they stepped onto the sidewalk. Her voice was pleasant but suspicious. "I'm sorry, did we have a meeting?"

"No, Ms. Vargas, I apologize for showing up like this."

"That's all right," she said, artificially perking up. "And you are?"

"Evie. Evie Boggs." Gabrielle shook Evie's hand, gently.

"She's a friend," Rachel said. "From back in the day."

Gabrielle smiled lightly. "This is my son, Antonio."

"Tony," the boy said. He held out his hand. Rachel shook it, as did Evie.

"Firm grip," Rachel said.

"Coach Gleeson said I have the inside track to be starting outside linebacker next year," Tony said. He flexed his bicep. "Benched two twenty-five for six reps this week."

Rachel whistled but couldn't stop staring at the scar on the boy's neck. He noticed her looking, and his confident demeanor evaporated. He seemed to withdraw and moved closer to his mother.

"Is that . . . blood?" Gabrielle pointed at the torn fabric on Rachel's pants, where her leg had been gouged on the fence by Timothy Ruddock.

"It's been a day," Rachel said, wearily.

"So, ladies, why are you here?" Gabrielle said.

"Actually, Gabrielle, we were hoping we could talk to Tony."

Tony's eyes narrowed. Gabrielle's widened.

"Me?" he said.

"Him?" his mother said. "What do you want with my son?"

"I'm hoping you can help us find someone. His name is Peter Lincecum. I think you know him," Rachel said. Her voice was sympathetic but firm.

Tony's face became a shield. His eyes narrowed. His cheeks sank as he muttered "Don't know him" with such utter conviction that only a fool wouldn't know he was lying.

Rachel stepped forward. Tony automatically retreated. Gabrielle stepped between them.

Rachel said, her voice calm, "We know Tony knows Peter. Peter's life is in danger. His father was killed by someone looking to do him harm. And that person is *still* looking for him. I have a feeling Tony knows all this. All we want to do is find Peter before he's hurt. Or worse."

Evie tried to push between Gabrielle and Tony. "Listen, kid, we—"

Rachel put her hand on Evie's shoulder and pulled her back. For a moment Evie resisted, then relented.

Rachel said, "I'm willing to bet that scar on your neck was given to you by one of the Spivak brothers."

"You need to leave," Gabrielle said. "My son has nothing to say to—"

"It was Raymond Spivak," Tony said. Gabrielle turned around. Tony's face was ashen. Eyes wet. "They need to know the truth. For Peter's sake."

"Antonio, I . . ."

"Raymond was nice at first," he continued. "Came around a lot when he and my mom were seeing each other. My dad had just been sent away, and I was angry. So angry. I don't think I saw it because I didn't want to see it. But, Mom, he was a *monster*."

"Baby, I—"

"Sometimes I wouldn't load the dishwasher right. Or I'd have music playing too loud in my room. Or I'd be playing Xbox when his show was coming on. And you could see it in his eyes. That he wanted to hurt me."

"Raymond never touched you," Gabrielle said softly.

"No, but Randall did," Tony said. He looked at the women. "I was in my room, reading. Raymond didn't know I was there. You were at the store. I heard Raymond talking to Bennett Brice on the phone. They were talking about hurting people. Taking their money. I knew I wasn't supposed to hear what they were saying. I was afraid to come out of my room. When you came back and opened my door, Raymond knew I'd heard it all. He left without saying a word. You thought he was mad at you. Remember? You cried all night because he didn't come back. He never came back. And you thought it was your fault. I was too scared to tell you the truth. I'm done being too scared to tell the truth, because people keep getting hurt by it."

"Antonio," Gabrielle said, her eyes welling up. "I'm so sorry."

"I was walking home a few days later from a pickup basketball game at the Murray courts," Tony said, his voice catching in his throat. "Randall appeared out of nowhere and shoved me to the ground. He put a steak knife to my neck. He told me if I ever told anyone what I heard, he would tie me to a chair, cut my mom's head off, and serve it to me on a dinner plate so I could see your dead eyes. And then he did this." Tony drew his finger along the scar on his neck, gently, as though recalling a memory on his skin. "Just to let me know he was serious."

Gabrielle put her hand on Tony's cheek.

"That's why there are no photos of him in your album from that time," Rachel said. Gabrielle nodded. She turned to Tony. "And I bet that's when you stopped writing too."

"Felt kind of silly writing about superheroes," he said. "That day taught me one thing. Nobody's coming to save you. You're on your own. Superheroes don't exist. It's just me and my mom. She's the only hero in my life."

"And he's mine," Gabrielle said, placing her hand on his arm. "I didn't want my son to be reminded of what happened. Maybe I didn't want to be reminded either."

"We can't shield our children from pain forever or pretend the pain didn't happen," Rachel said. "We can only help them try to move on from it."

"Maybe I didn't allow that," Gabrielle said. "I did what I thought was right."

"Now you have a chance to do what's right," Rachel said to them. "Tony, help me find your friend. Tell me about Peter Lincecum."

"I've known Pete since we were, like, five," Antonio said. "He lived in Ashby for a while. Played some little league. He was a pretty good shortstop. Couldn't hit worth a damn, but he could field a hot grounder like his glove was coated in superglue. But Pete hated it here. He wanted to live in a big city, like New York or LA. At some point his dad moved them to Carltondale. Pete never knew why. He got a job delivering pizzas on his bike, but his dad took all his tips and bet on long shots. One-eyed horses at, like, fifty to one, things like that. Pete wanted to save up to be able to leave his dad behind without having to ask for a dime. Without ever saying goodbye. Said when you've been left behind so many times, people don't deserve a goodbye."

Rachel saw Evie's lower lip trembling. She knew what Evie was thinking. Hearing how these children got kicked around and abandoned made her understand why they'd found Bennett Brice's offer so attractive. Even if it came with a cost, freedom itself was priceless.

"That's how Bennett Brice found him," Rachel said.

Tony nodded. "Brice knew about Pete's family situation. And that if he really wanted a better life, and if he had the work ethic to make it happen, Brice could give him an opportunity. Brice told him he would take care of him. And Pete bought it."

"My brother had a good heart," Evie said. "He *wanted* to help these kids. He wasn't strong enough to stand up to the Spivaks once things got violent."

"Bennett Brice was your *brother*?" Gabrielle said. Her voice became hostile. "How *dare* you come here and tell me he's a good man. He destroyed lives."

"We're here for Peter. That's it. We can deal with everything else later," Rachel said.

"I still don't know what you want from us," Gabrielle said. "My son told you everything he knows."

"I'm not so sure about that," Rachel said. "I think Tony knows where Peter is."

"Even if I did, why would I tell you?" Tony said. "She admitted she's Brice's sister. Brice and the Spivaks were, like, best buds. I should trust her when she says she wants to help Pete? For all I know she's going to lead Randall Spivak right to Pete."

"I was arrested for trying to kill Raymond Spivak," Evie said. Tony's head snapped to face her. "That's the truth. There's an arrest report. Rachel has seen it."

Tony looked to Rachel. "Is that true?"

Rachel nodded. "It's true."

Evie added, "I have as much affection for the Spivak boys as I do for the bubonic plague."

"Why did you try to kill him?" Tony asked.

Evie sighed. "It's a long story. I'll tell you when this is over."

"Why can't we just call the police?" Gabrielle said. "I spoke with Detectives Serrano and Tally before. I have their numbers. Wouldn't we want their help?"

"The Ashby PD doesn't have jurisdiction on this," Rachel said. "They'd have to kick it over to the Carltondale PD. Intercity police politics is like high school, only more petulant. Do you really want to play a game of telephone with someone's life? And I promise you this: Randall Spivak is not waiting around. He doesn't care about bureaucratic red tape. And if he finds Peter, nobody will ever see him again."

"Why do you two care so much about Pete?" Tony said. "He's been screwed over his whole life by everyone. His birth mom abandoned him. His dad was a loser. His stepmom was a junkie. Bennett Brice used him. And now you want to save him?"

"With every ounce of blood in my body," Evie said, with a gritty conviction that startled Rachel.

Tony looked at his mother. Gabrielle's eyes pleaded with her son, but Rachel could tell she was unsure what exactly she wanted him to do.

"Antonio," Gabrielle said, "you can just go upstairs. You don't need to get involved. You know what this man is capable of."

"That's why I have to help them," Tony said. He looked at Rachel and Evie. "I'll bring you to him."

"No way," Rachel said. "Just tell us where he is, and we'll handle it."

"Pete is *my* friend. If anything goes wrong, I'm the only one I trust a hundred percent."

"No," Gabrielle said. "Antonio. *Please.*"

"I'll be back for dinner," he said. He kissed his mother's cheek, and she closed her eyes, gripping his hand.

"Promise."

"I promise."

Tony walked off and gestured for the women to follow. Rachel said to Gabrielle, "I promise you we won't let anything happen to your son."

"Good, because if anything does happen to him, I will make your life hell every single day for the rest of your life."

"I believe you," Rachel said.

"So go find that boy. And keep mine safe. Act like these boys are your own. Do whatever you need to do to make sure no harm comes to them."

"From one mother to another," Rachel said, "I will."

CHAPTER 46

John Serrano and Leslie Tally sat in a conference room at the Ashby central precinct rifling through a mountain of papers. Bank statements, phone records, email printouts, and employee records blanketed a three-by-six-foot table. Bennett Brice's life boiled down to a miasma of busywork.

What lay in front of them was a tangled mess of millions of dollars that had threaded its way into dozens of crevices around the world, like a fiduciary Snakes and Ladders. They had learned, with the help of a forensic accountant the department had brought in (who was definitely deserving of a nice Christmas bonus), that Bennett Brice had personal bank accounts in the Cayman Islands holding somewhere in the vicinity of $7 million.

They found another $2.4 million stored in a legitimate trust account. No recipient was named, so they couldn't tell who Brice had earmarked the money for. That was the money Chester Barnes was referring to. It was money Brice had paid taxes on and wanted to be able to legally declare. The rest, though, was shadier than an umbrella on a Miami beach in August.

Rachel had been right. Brice had been using mules to deposit money into Cayman accounts for at least ten years. Serrano wondered what the legality of exhuming someone was just to put them on trial for fraud.

Serrano stifled a yawn, ran his fingers through his hair, pinched his sinuses, and tossed back the dregs of his fourth cup of coffee that day.

"So let's unpack all this. YourLife itself seems to be a legitimate business. At least on the surface. But because of the sporadic nature of the incoming revenue, Brice is able to use the company as a filter-slash-laundering service for the Spivaks. He also squirrels a chunk of it away in the Caymans to keep it from the IRS."

"And uses front men to deposit it for him," Tally said, "but pays taxes on enough of it so he doesn't arouse suspicion."

"Ruddock was giving couriers account and deposit information— those manila envelopes Rachel saw him carrying," Serrano said. "Now, you have to figure there's a Benjamin Ruddock, a 'captain,' in at least a few towns adjacent to Ashby, including Carltondale, where Peter Lincecum lives, and Brice has himself a nice little mini-Mafia thing going on."

"And if you look at this," Tally said, handing Serrano a folder, "other than the mortgage on his home and the lease on the YourLife office, Bennett Brice is actually fairly frugal. He even owned a Civic and flew economy."

"Didn't want to arouse too much suspicion," Serrano said. "But he had enough bling—the watch, the home—to impress the impression-able youth of America."

"Brice set up more than fifty different bank accounts for YourLife employees himself. Most were trusts that couldn't be accessed until the recipient turned eighteen."

"He sets up accounts for the kids so he can go around their par-ents," Serrano said. "There are deposits totaling hundreds of thousands if not millions of dollars. Again, it all looks legitimate. Taxes paid."

Tally flipped through the pages and said, "I recognize a lot of the names these accounts are registered to. They're Penny's classmates. I see Benjamin Ruddock. I see LeRoy Burns. I see Martin Glickman." She looked at Serrano. "And he already set one up for Eric Marin. There's ten thousand dollars in it."

"Nice little signing bonus," Serrano said.

"So here's what's been eating at me," Serrano said. "We know why Brice and Ruddock approached Eric Marin. They wanted to keep him close after Linklater's email to Rachel and use him as leverage to distract Rachel but also intimidate her. It was a bargaining chip. If she ever came after Brice, it would seem like a vendetta."

"And Rachel didn't do herself any favors showing up at Brice's office to threaten him," Tally said. "But if they thought they could intimidate Rachel, they didn't think this whole thing through."

Serrano said, "But how could Brice know *exactly* which kids to target? He would need financial records, social security information, to know which kids were most vulnerable."

"He'd have to have a source," Tally said. "Someone with access to all that information."

Serrano began sifting through the piles of paper. Dozens of pages fell to the floor.

"What are you doing?" Tally asked.

"Brice's phone records," Serrano said, holding up a batch of pages.

He laid out the pages. The technicians had underlined all numbers Brice had communicated with frequently, both calls and text messages.

"Look at this," Serrano said. "There's only one phone number that Brice routinely called *and* texted over the last two years."

He brought the pages over to Tally.

"Ninety percent of calls and texts tend to take place between the hours of nine a.m. and nine p.m. That percentage goes up if you remove people between the ages of fourteen and thirty. Kids, people who are single, and people who work odd hours. But look at this number. There are calls and texts from Brice at all hours of the day. Early morning. During the day. Many of the messages coming in groups in the middle of the night. But what's strange is that the phone is *also* registered to Brice."

"He wasn't calling himself," Tally replied. "He must have bought the phone for someone else to use."

"Exactly what I'm thinking."

Tally said, "The icon next to the texts means there were media attachments with those texts."

Serrano nodded. "Look here. May eighth. Two pieces of media sent at one thirteen a.m. Followed by a video at one eighteen a.m."

"How do you know that one is a video?" Tally said.

"Look at the data usage. One hundred and thirty-six megabytes. That's over two minutes long."

"You thinking what I'm thinking?"

"Bennett Brice was getting some sexy-time videos sent to him in the middle of the night." Serrano pulled out another piece of paper. "According to the phone company, the social security number used to register this phone is also registered with another cell phone. Different company, different service provider."

Tally said, "Someone wanted to keep their extracurricular activities separate from their work activities. Whoever this phone number is registered to was seeing Bennett Brice on the sly and using a phone Brice provided them to keep it quiet."

Serrano handed her another page. He underlined a phone number at the top with his finger. "This is the other line. Very little media, ninety-nine percent of texts and calls between the hours of seven a.m. and nine p.m."

Tally took the page. When she saw the number, she gasped.

"What is it?" Serrano said. "You know that number?"

"It's Tamara Alvi," Tally said. "She's the principal at Ashby High."

CHAPTER 47

Tony walked fast, his long teenage legs practically galloping along as he led Rachel and Evie toward some nebulous destination. Every block or two, Evie would ask Tony, "Are we there yet?" Tony ignored her. Rachel could see Evie's hands clenching into fists. She seemed impatient. Rachel wanted to find Peter Lincecum as well, but this seemed personal for Evie, like she was trying to prevent Lincecum from being hurt on account of her brother's criminal ties.

Normally the young man's brisk pace wouldn't have been an issue, but between the aching wound in her leg and the aftereffects of the concussion, Rachel felt like she'd been squeezed into a blender and tossed around on "pulse." She wanted to find Lincecum, get him safely to the authorities, and then nap until the next lunar eclipse.

The sun was setting. A cool breeze came from the northeast. Ashby during springtime was a glorious place to be. Rachel loved the smell of freshly mowed lawns. Smiled at the way young couples intertwined their fingers, a simple smile saying more than words ever could.

She remembered a day from a lifetime ago when she walked a sunny street with the man who would become her husband. They'd met in winter, at a dive bar on karaoke night. They spent the evening making fun of the singers who took it a *little* too seriously, kissed chastely at the end of the evening, then had dinner the next night. Rachel knew right off the bat that Bradley Powell was the one.

They spent December through February cozying on his couch, in her bed, sipping hot chocolate in the morning and red wine at night, making love like their bodies needed air and only intimacy could provide it. He cooked for her on his electric stove. She helped decorate his small, sparse apartment.

Then, when summer came, she bought a closet's worth of sundresses, all floral patterns and bright colors. The first time she saw him wearing a T-shirt and shorts, his pale appendages poking out like bones, she practically leaped into his arms. Rachel never thought of herself as a "girly girl." She didn't buy into fairy tales, considered red roses to be red flags, and assumed men who acted like Prince Charming probably kept a pile of severed heads in their closet. She did not believe in being swept off her feet . . . until she found herself floating.

Rachel knew Brad loved her before he ever said it. One afternoon he led her into a park, refusing to tell her where they were going or why. She dutifully followed, lost in the aphrodisiac of mystery and romance. Finally, she found herself underneath a massive oak, its base wide enough for two people to sit against. Waiting for them was a picnic lunch in a brown wicker basket. Her heart swelled. She told him he was lucky it hadn't been stolen.

He removed two sandwiches: soppressata, mozzarella, roasted red peppers, arugula, and garlic aioli on ciabatta for him. Honey-maple turkey with swiss, alfalfa, tomato, and brown mustard on whole wheat for her. He even had a bottle of chardonnay, which he'd kept cool with plastic bags full of ice. Dessert was homemade chocolate chip cookies, whipped cream, and fresh berries.

When they finished the meal, they leaned back against the tree, stomachs and hearts full. At that moment, if he'd asked, she knew she would've said yes. To marriage. Family. A life.

But as was the tendency with men, he waited another three months before asking.

On the day of their wedding, as she kissed him at the altar, the limitless possibilities of life stretched before them like a highway. She believed their wedding day was merely the beginning of a journey together. Rachel never really thought about the last part. *Till death.* It was not even a consideration.

Knowing what came after the wedding, knowing what happened to Brad, knowing the horrors he endured, that his death would shatter their family and tear apart any hope she had for a normal life, she had asked herself if she still would have gone through with it. But every time she looked at Eric and Megan, Rachel knew, even if she felt guilty admitting it, that it was worth all the hell for the heaven of their children.

"We're here," Tony said.

Rachel snapped to attention.

They were standing in front of a four-foot-high metal fence. A rusted nameplate on the gate read **SALLY DUBOIS PARK**. The fence was flaked with rust. The gate was shut with a padlock that looked like it would snap open if sneezed on.

"It's a playground," Evie said.

"*Was* a playground," Tony said. "It's been abandoned for years. My mom told me never to go near it. She said the only people who hang out here now are addicts and dealers. And if I touched anything inside, I would need a tetanus shot."

"She's probably right on all counts," Rachel said. Through the gate Rachel could see a moldy wooden seesaw, its green paint yellowed, broken in half so that both ends rested pitifully on the ground. Next to it was a swing set with only one seat, four empty chains dangling down from metal bars like boneless limbs. There was an empty sandbox, the wooden floor cracked and soiled, and a slide whose plastic had warped so sharply that if you took a fast ride down it was liable to cut you in half.

"This place looks like Disneyland got sucked into the seventh circle of hell," Rachel said.

"Sally Dubois was nine years old when she died of non-Hodgkin's lymphoma," Tony said. "That was ten years ago. She was diagnosed when she was four and spent the last five years of her life raising money and awareness. When she died, they named this park after her. A few years after that, the city slashed its parks budget. And then she was forgotten about. And this park was forgotten about. It used to be beautiful."

Rachel said, "I bet it still could be beautiful."

Tony said, "I was four when Sally died. And I think about her more than the people who promised they'd never forget her. Adults like to act all virtuous, but kids are the ones who get left behind. We get used, and then they forget about us."

With that, Tony vaulted over the fence. Evie followed suit. Rachel did the same, feeling pain in her leg and an ache in her head when she landed.

Tony led them through the jungle of twisted metal, cracked plastic, and swollen wood. Rachel wondered how many small feet had once climbed up the jungle gym. How many little hands had gripped the chains with wide smiles as parents pushed them on the swings. And how many people had had to turn a blind eye to allow such a joyous place to decay.

"Where is Peter?" Evie said. She grabbed Tony's shoulder and spun him around. The boy stumbled backward, his heel catching on the rusted bottom of a spring rider in the shape of a seahorse, its once-yellow paint spoiled to a dark orange. Rachel managed to grab the boy before he fell.

"Take it easy," Rachel said to Evie, helping Tony back up.

"Sorry," Evie said. "Just . . . we need to make sure he's safe."

Tony glared at Evie, then said, "Come on."

At the far end of the playground was a wooden shack, about eight by twelve feet and surrounded by patchy grass. It was chained with a padlock. But unlike the padlock at the front gate, the thick padlock on the shack's door looked like it could withstand a shotgun blast.

Tony approached the door and rapped on it twice with his fist, waited three seconds, rapped twice more, waited again, then rapped four more times.

Then he took a key chain from his pocket, selected one, and unlocked the padlock.

As soon as he opened the door, the smell of mildew, rust, and feces wafted out of the structure. Piles of equipment were stacked haphazardly, most of it looking well beyond repair. Lawnmowers, shovels, bags of peat moss, spades, a dulled pitchfork, several rakes, and a dozen pairs of heavy-duty gloves. A shelf housed all sorts of paper goods and chemicals: towels, toilet paper, half-used cleaning solvents, and dirty rags. Rachel guessed they could get half a dozen different diseases or infections if they weren't careful.

"Pete?" Tony whispered.

Rachel looked down. Evie was gripping her wrist. *Hard.* Rachel looked up at her. Evie's face was etched with worry. Then they heard a sound behind the shelving.

Rachel saw a lock of sandy-blond hair peek through the maze of boxes, followed by a pair of scared blue eyes. She heard Tony exhale in relief.

"Dude," Tony said. "For a second I thought you might have booked it."

From behind the mass of debris, Peter Lincecum stood up. Rachel could see a mess of fast-food bags, empty soda bottles, and candy-bar wrappers at his feet, as well as a soiled pillow and thin blanket. Peter limped around the boxes, heavily favoring his left leg. His clothes were dirty and damp. Rachel could see a makeshift bandage on his injured right knee, an athletic brace wrapped with surgical tape, the white strips caked with dirt.

Rachel felt Evie's fingernails dig into her skin.

"Ow," Rachel said. "What the hell?"

Then Peter saw Rachel. His eyes went wide.

"What the hell is she doing here?" the boy said. He stumbled backward, knocking against the far wall of the shack. Sharp tools and implements rattled around him.

"It's all right," Rachel said, hands outstretched. "I'm here to help."

Peter didn't look sold. Then he saw Evie, and his jaw dropped.

"What is *she* doing here?"

Evie let go of Rachel's arm and pushed her way through the maze of detritus. She approached Peter, tentatively, a look of absolute shock on the boy's face. Rachel looked at Tony. He appeared to be as confused as she was.

Then, to Rachel's surprise, Evie gathered Peter into her arms and held him, sobbing into his soiled shirt. The boy did not move, but then, slowly, he brought his arms up and wrapped them around Evie.

Tony looked at Rachel and mouthed, "What the hell?"

"I don't know," she replied.

Evie took Peter's head in her hands and gently kissed his filthy forehead. A smudge of dirt remained on her lips when she let go.

"Mom?" Peter said. "What are you *doing* here?"

"Mom?" Rachel and Tony said simultaneously.

Evie said, "I'm so sorry, Peter. I'm so—"

Then a gunshot shattered the air. Evie fell, eyes wide as her blood splashed across her son's horrified face.

CHAPTER 48

Rachel did not hesitate. She just reacted. First, she slammed the door closed and then, without thinking about the various dangerous objects scattered about the room, dived forward and yanked Peter Lincecum down just as a shot exploded through the door, splintering wood and passing through the air where the boy had stood a millisecond ago.

Randall Spivak.

Rachel looked around, her heart pounding. The door was closed. Whoever was out there could not see inside the shack—but all he had to do was wait. Rachel heard a faint *clink-clink* from outside. The sound of a gun being reloaded. She cursed under her breath. She couldn't rely on Spivak running out of ammo. Too many shots and nowhere to go.

Rachel crawled over to Evie. She was on her back, breathing heavily. Blood was soaking through her shirt, her face already turning pale.

"Mom?" Peter said. *"Mom?"*

He touched her shirt. His hands came away covered in Evie's blood.

"Shh," Rachel said to Peter. "He can't see us. Don't let him know where you are."

Peter nodded, his face white beneath the specks of red.

"Give me your shirt," Rachel whispered to Tony. The boy did not move. He was on the ground, knees tucked against his chin. He was shaking. Terrified. *"Antonio. Shirt. Now."*

The boy snapped to, took his shirt off, and gave it to Rachel. Rachel looked into Evie's eyes.

"This is going to hurt," she said. Evie nodded, biting her lip. Rachel probed the wound. The bullet had entered Evie's left upper back, near her shoulder. She could feel the entrance wound, slick with blood. Evie gasped as Rachel's fingers explored.

"There's no exit wound," Rachel whispered. Evie needed medical attention, immediately. The bullet had more than likely shattered Evie's collarbone and possibly cracked her shoulder blade. But the larger issue was the damage to blood vessels in the area. Given the amount of blood, the bullet had probably clipped her subclavian artery. If there were any floating bone fragments, they could shred blood vessels with every breath she took.

"Randall," Evie said softly.

Rachel nodded.

Rachel placed Tony's shirt on the wound and pressed. *Hard.* Evie let out a cry, and a moment later another gunshot rang out, this one embedding itself in a crate a foot from Evie's face.

"Hold it there," Rachel whispered, placing Peter's hand over the cloth.

Rachel sent a text to 911 and cc'd it to John Serrano and Leslie Tally.

Gunfire @ Sally Dubois park. Gunman psbly Randall Spivak armed/dangerous. Evie Boggs wounded. Send police/EMTs NOW.

Then she surveyed the shack. There were a hundred things inside that she could use as a weapon—but none of them were faster than a bullet. It was possible someone had heard the gunshots and called the police, but even then it would take several minutes for them to arrive. Spivak could empty a clip indiscriminately and likely find flesh. They couldn't take that chance.

Rachel tapped Peter on the shoulder. He was trembling. She put her hand on his cheek. He looked at her, looked at Evie, and said, "Mom?"

She held a finger to her lips. Mouthed the words "Can't let them hear us."

Peter nodded.

"Where's the way out?"

Peter looked surprised. Rachel knew the moment Tony'd unlocked the shack that there had to be a separate exit other than the front door. There was no way Tony was locking an injured boy inside without an alternate exit.

Peter crawled to the left side of the shack, grimacing as he pushed off his bad leg. He gently moved a pair of large, damp cardboard boxes, revealing a narrow tunnel dug into a hole between the floorboards. Rachel turned on her cell phone flashlight and peered into the tunnel.

"Where does it go?" she mouthed.

"Outside. Under a mailbox."

"How far?"

"Not far."

"Can you make it?"

Peter nodded.

The tunnel was wide enough for boys their size. Rachel was reasonably sure she could wriggle her way through. But then she looked back at Evie, her shirt soaked with blood, blood draining from her body. There was no way Evie could shimmy through a narrow dirt tunnel given her condition. Even if she managed to get inside, there was a very real chance she could pass out from blood loss. In which case they might all be trapped. Unarmed. They would be target practice.

The tunnel must have been dug some time ago. She guessed that given the park's derelict state and the faint odor of smoke and pot inside the shack, kids and junkies used it to light up. Shoot up. A minor miracle the whole structure hadn't gone up in flames yet.

Rachel grabbed Peter and Tony by their shirts. She mouthed, "You two. Go."

Peter's eyes filled with worry. "My mom," he said.

Rachel gripped Peter's shoulders and looked into his eyes.

"If you don't go, we all die. We help her by surviving."

"My leg. It hurts. I can't."

"I promise you, a bullet will hurt more."

Peter nodded, grimly. Tony took a deep breath and slid into the tunnel. Peter crawled over to Evie and kissed her forehead.

"I love you."

Just then a shot rang out, and another hole was blasted through the door.

Evie managed to push herself off the ground. She brought Peter's face toward hers, his face sparkling red with her blood.

"Go," Evie said. "I love you too."

Peter climbed gingerly into the mouth of the tunnel.

"I love you," he said again. Then he slid into the darkness.

Evie's face was ashen. Blood had soaked through Tony's shirt.

Rachel crawled to Evie. Her breathing was ragged, but her eyes raged with fire.

Evie pointed toward the tunnel. "Go."

Rachel could hear Randall Spivak's footsteps on the grass outside. "Go."

Rachel nodded. She leaned down and whispered in Evie's ear.

"Nobody is dying today. Not you. Not your son."

Then she dropped into the tunnel.

Whoever had dug the narrow passageway hadn't cleared all the roots and rocks. Rachel pushed her way through, feeling all sorts of detritus tearing at her clothes, her skin. She could hear the two boys ahead of her scrabbling through the dirt. Every time Peter Lincecum pushed off his injured leg, he cried out in pain. But he kept going.

Every second mattered. Spivak couldn't see inside the shack, but given that nobody had returned fire, he could assume they were all unarmed. Still, there were four of them. Evie and Rachel could handle themselves in a fight, and Spivak couldn't know how badly Evie was wounded. But the cops *would* be coming. Spivak didn't have all day to wait. He would have to smoke them out. Either with gunfire, or . . .

Oh, no. Evie.

"Hurry," Rachel whisper-yelled to the boys. They picked up their pace. Rachel ignored the wetness on her arms and legs where rocks and roots had raked her skin.

Then, up ahead, the boys stopped. They must have reached the end. She heard the sound of metal and Tony Vargas grunting. A moment later, both boys had disappeared. Rachel pulled herself forward and saw sunlight.

At the end of the tunnel, she saw an exit hole and the blue metal bottom of a mailbox. A metal grate had been moved to the side. A pair of hands reached down into the darkness, and Rachel took them. Tony and Peter helped Rachel shimmy out on her back so as not to slam her head against the underside of the mailbox.

The boys were panting and covered in dirt. Antonio looked around, terrified. Peter held his knee, his face racked with pain. They were outside the park, shielded by a row of hedges surrounding the metal fence. Rachel could still see the tops of the dilapidated swing sets. She visualized the park's layout. They were about thirty feet from the shack, with the fence between them. The trajectory of the bullet that had hit Evie suggested Spivak was slightly northwest, but he could have moved.

She had to go back for Evie.

Peter limped toward the hedges. Rachel grabbed the boy and held him back.

"Both of you, get out of here," she said. "Find a store or a building with a doorman. Somewhere public. The cops are on their way. Just stay safe and stay together."

"But my mom . . . ," Peter said.

"I've got her," Rachel said. "Now *go*."

Tony took Peter's arm and put it around his neck for support, and they went off as fast as Peter's injured leg could move.

Rachel turned back to the park. Between the hedges she saw an opening through which the park grounds were visible. The door to the shack was slightly open. Somewhere inside, Evie was bleeding. She could see bullet holes in the door.

Randall Spivak stood just a few feet from the door. He held a gun in his hand. He was being tentative, smart. He knew not to barge into the shack, gun blazing. He didn't know what waited for him inside. But he also knew the cops were en route. His time was limited. Which is why Rachel froze with terror when she saw the lighter and a small bottle of clear liquid in his other hand. Lighter fluid. He was going to burn Evie alive.

If there had been any doubt in Rachel's mind that Randall Spivak had killed Matthew Linklater, it was now gone.

Rachel crouched down, pushing through the hedge. Spivak's back was to her. He was kneeling at the front of the shack. Rachel heard the *pfft* of a lighter. Within seconds, she saw black smoke wafting into the air. The shack was on fire, with Evie inside.

Rachel hurdled the fence, landing on a spot of dry earth. Staying low, she went as quickly and quietly as she could to the nearby merry-go-round, placing her hand on a corroded metal bar. There were maybe twenty feet between her and Spivak.

"I just want the boy," Spivak said, his back still to Rachel. "If he comes out, I'll let the rest of you go. If he doesn't, by the time the ambulance gets here, you'll look like overcooked bacon."

Spivak's voice was even, unhindered. As though killing four people was merely a hitch in his day.

"You have five seconds," he said. "And then I'll just let you all burn."

Rachel darted out from around the side of the merry-go-round. Spivak counted down. As he got to two, Rachel increased her speed, lowered her shoulder, and drove it into the soft section of Spivak's side between his rib cage and pelvis. Rachel felt thunder crackling in her head as she lifted him off his feet.

Spivak landed with a grunt, Rachel to his side. She quickly stood up and stomped on his wrist, hearing an audible crack as several of his carpal bones shattered. Spivak cried out and dropped the gun. Rachel kicked it away. Spivak tried to get to his feet, but Rachel drove her fist into his stomach, doubling him over and taking the breath from his body. But she was slow. Tired. The exhaustion had finally caught up to her, sapping her strength and stamina. Before she had time to react, Spivak backhanded her across the temple, and Rachel crumpled to the ground.

Her head felt like it had been trampled by a rampaging bull. Her vision swam. Her eyes couldn't focus. She managed to get to her knees, but Spivak kicked her in the ribs, sending her flying into a heap.

She curled up. Couldn't breathe. Couldn't see. Her vision was cloudy, as if she were viewing the world through gauze. Spivak brought his foot down into the center of Rachel's back, driving her to the ground, mashing her face into the dirt and grass.

She rolled to her side. Her ribs felt like they'd been pressed against a grill. From the prone position, Rachel could see Spivak pick up his gun.

"No," she said weakly. He cradled his maimed arm and looked at her with a mixture of curiosity and pity.

"You got out," Spivak said. "Maybe the boys did too. But someone is still in there. Otherwise you wouldn't have come back. I'm guessing it's our friend Ms. Boggs. I've despised that cunt for years. And given what a pain in the ass you've been, Ms. Marin, I'm glad you get to smell her cook. And then I'm going to find those boys, and I'm going to tear them apart."

Rachel pressed her fist into the ground to steady herself. She took a lurching step toward Spivak and fell to a knee. She dry-heaved. Spivak watched, a thin smile spreading across his lips, like he was watching an infant trying to take its first trembling steps.

"You don't give up," he said. "I could say I admire your fortitude, but I'd be lying. If you were less stubborn, you might have lived to see your family again."

Rachel got back to her feet. Took another step. Stumbled.

"This is sad to watch," Spivak said.

The fire was rising, spreading across the walls of the shack. Rachel could not hear or see Evie and prayed the woman hadn't already passed out.

Spivak walked over to Rachel. He knelt down, his face level with hers.

"Misery loves company. Why don't you join your friend?"

Spivak took Rachel's wrist and began to drag her toward the shack. Rachel resisted, weakly. Spivak turned back to her and laughed. As he did, his grip relaxed ever so slightly.

Now!

Rachel stood up, placed her free hand atop Spivak's head, and in one simultaneous movement, pushed down on his cranium as she brought her knee up swiftly, viciously, to connect with the front of his face. The crunch told her she'd shattered his nose and perhaps an orbital bone.

Spivak lurched backward, blood spurting from his broken face. The gun fell from his hand, and Rachel kicked it across the park. It settled underneath a set of monkey bars that had gone green with neglect. Flames had begun to lick at the roof of the shack, smoke pouring through the cracks and crevices. She could feel the heat coming off the wood in waves.

Evie.

Rachel barreled forward. She threw the doors open. A burst of flame shot out at her like a tongue, and Rachel fell backward. She turned just in time to see Randall Spivak come at her, swinging a tree branch. She managed to deflect the blow with her forearm, but it knocked her off balance. Spivak swung the branch back at Rachel, flecks of blood flying off his face. But Spivak had slowed, and Rachel was able to duck, then bring her leg up and hammer Spivak between the legs.

Spivak let loose a moan that resembled air being slowly released from a balloon and sank to the ground. Blood dripped onto the dirt. Rachel turned back to the fire. She couldn't see anything through the thick smoke.

"Evie!" she shouted, moving forward. She held her shirt up to her mouth. "Evie, where are you?"

She heard nothing except the crackle of fire splitting wood. Rachel was dizzy, her vision blurred, her senses off. She did not hear Spivak swing the branch again, only felt something heavy crack against the back of her head. And then she hit the ground.

Rachel rolled onto her back. Smoke billowed out above her, and Randall Spivak stood over her, his face covered in blood, flames licking the air behind him like they were announcing the arrival of the devil himself.

Spivak lifted the branch over Rachel's face.

She closed her eyes and mouthed two words.

"Eric. Megan."

But Spivak did not bring the branch down. Rachel lay there, breath coming in ragged gasps. Spivak hovered over her, unmoving, as if someone had pressed "Pause."

Why am I not dead?

Then she opened her eyes and saw the blood.

It did not come from Randall Spivak's face, where she had struck him, but from a hole right above his Adam's apple. Then Rachel saw what had caused the wound. A pitchfork had been thrust into Randall

Spivak, its three rusted, barely sharp prongs sticking out of his neck, chest, and abdomen.

Spivak brought his hand up and touched the tip of the uppermost prong as though testing its sharpness. Blood poured from him in rivulets, soaking his shirt red in seconds. And then Randall Spivak fell forward, the pitchfork protruding from his back like a gruesome handle.

Behind him stood Evie Boggs, her body a mess of red, her face ghastly pale.

"That was . . . gross," Evie said, and then she collapsed onto the ground next to Randall Spivak.

CHAPTER 49

Rachel walked into the lobby at Mackenzie North Hospital, thinking she'd had more than her fill of hospitals and blood. Two people she cared about had just gotten out of surgery. The first, Peter Lincecum, had had his ruptured patella tendon repaired. The injury caused by Rachel had been exacerbated by the lack of medical attention. Thankfully, the doctor said, he'd seen worse knee injuries sustained by football players, and if *they* could return to the field, Peter would be up and at 'em in six to eight months.

Tony Vargas had gone with Peter to the hospital, their hands intertwined, the day's trauma and violence forming a bond that could never be broken. Rachel was heartened to hear about Peter's prognosis but knew she would carry around the guilt of his injury far longer than his recovery time.

As for Evie, the situation had been decidedly more grim. The bullet from Randall Spivak's gun had shattered her collarbone like a drinking glass dropped on the floor. A shard from the bone had cleaved her subclavian artery nearly in two. By the time the EMTs got to her, she had lost nearly a third of the blood in her body.

Rachel prayed that Evie would survive, if only to answer her many questions. She knew now that when Evie had referred to needing to protect her son, she'd been referring to Peter Lincecum.

Rachel could barely stand herself. Her head rang like an abused xylophone, and her body ached like it had been beaten with sticks. Still, after a sleepless night, Rachel found herself dragging her bedraggled self up to the hospital receptionist, who looked at her disheveled appearance with disapproval.

"Laundry day," Rachel said with a shrug.

"Miss . . . do you need help?"

"Yes. A lot of it. But not medical. I'm good there," Rachel said. "Evelyn Boggs's room, please."

The woman smiled nervously and punched the name into her computer. The smile quickly turned into an apologetic frown.

"I'm sorry, Miss . . ."

"Marin."

"Ms. Marin, Ms. Boggs is under police guard. I'm afraid I can't . . ."

Rachel took her ID from her purse and showed it to the woman. It was temporary and did not grant her the full amenities of a sworn-in officer, but she hoped it would be enough to sate a hospital receptionist. She looked at the ID and said, "Room 237. Take the elevators past the cafeteria, then make a left when you get off."

Rachel thanked her. When she got to the second floor, Rachel saw Officers Lowe and Chen seated in the hallway. Lowe was reading a paperback book. Chen appeared to be texting. As Rachel got closer, they both looked up and then stood to greet her.

"Ms. Marin," Chen said. "We heard about everything. Glad you're on your feet."

"We can't let you in to see her," Lowe added. "She's in critical condition. No visitors."

"I know. I just wanted to . . . I'm not sure." Rachel leaned to her side, just far enough that she could see a white curtain covering the length of the bed, shielding Evelyn Boggs from onlookers. Then Rachel was overcome by dizziness. Lowe held her arm, allowing her to steady herself. "Thanks, Officer Lowe. How is she?"

Lowe looked at Chen, as if debating whether to answer. Lowe said, "Hanging in there. Docs say it's touch and go."

"If she wakes up, tell her I came by."

Chen smiled and his eyes softened. "We will, Ms. Marin."

"Thank you, Officers."

Rachel took the elevator to the fourth floor and went to room 410. There were no cops outside the door. Everybody who had wanted harm to come to the patient inside was either in prison or dead.

"Hey, Peter," Rachel said, stepping inside. "How's the wheel?"

Peter Lincecum was propped up in bed, his surgically repaired leg hanging from a sling in an air cast.

"Can't really feel it right now, which I guess is a good thing." The boy's voice was slow, slurred due to the medication. "How's Evie?"

"So you call her Evie?"

"Never really known her as 'Mom.' All these years she kept saying she'd come back to Ashby. That we could try to be a family. But she never came. Said her brother could take better care of me than she could. I guess she had more important things to do than watch her son grow up."

Rachel took a seat next to the bed.

"I'm sorry about this," she said. "I'm sorry for what I did."

Peter made an exaggerated, drugged wave. "I deserved it," he said. "I was the one with the gun. I swear I wasn't going to use it. We were just trying to scare you. I don't think Bennett wanted you hurt. I mean really hurt. I'm so, so sorry, Ms. Marin."

"It wasn't your fault," she said. "I'm just glad you'll be OK. And that you weren't quicker on the draw."

"Is Evie going to live?" he asked.

"I hope so. Your mom is tough as hell."

"Did she really kill Randall Spivak with a pitchfork?"

Rachel laughed. "She did."

Peter smiled proudly.

"Listen, Peter. Evie made mistakes. The kind you can't just apologize for. I think even she'd admit that. But she's going to live. And I have a feeling she'll do whatever she can to make it up to you."

Peter nodded, his eyes drowsy.

As Peter began to drift away, Rachel heard footsteps. Two pairs. She immediately straightened up, knowing there was no security outside the room. She was gripping the steel leg of her chair—in case she needed a weapon—but relaxed when Gabrielle and Tony Vargas appeared at the doorway. Tony wore an Avengers T-shirt. Between the bright splashes of color on his shirt and the boyish smile when he saw his friend, he looked like a new person.

Peter's eyes slid open, and he managed a lazy smile.

"Hey, man," he said to Tony. "How do I look?"

"Like you picked a fight with the Hulk. Maybe we can just sit you on a skateboard and push you around the school caf," Tony said. "Hey, look on the bright side. Sympathy works. I bet Esther Lowenstein will finally realize you're alive."

"Esther does too know I'm alive," Peter said, defiantly. "Besides, this is partly your fault anyway."

Tony chuckled uncomfortably and said, "Don't make Ms. Marin break your other leg."

Rachel could see a smile spread across Gabrielle's face as the boys bickered. Tony went to Peter's bedside. Peter was fighting to stay awake but looked happy to have the company.

With the boys preoccupied, Rachel spoke to Gabrielle.

"How are you?" Rachel said, softly.

"I'm not sure, honestly. I'm just glad the boys are OK." Gabrielle turned to Rachel. "Can I ask you something?"

"Of course."

"Is it . . . all right to be glad that someone's dead? Bennett Brice and now Randall Spivak. I always taught Antonio not to hate. Hate only drags you down. But I can't help but think how much I hated those men and how glad I am that they're dead."

"I'm not in any place to judge. I've wanted people hurt before. As long as you raise your boy right, nobody can judge you. Sometimes I think that's all parenting really is—not letting your kids pay for your mistakes."

"What mistakes have you made?" Gabrielle asked.

Rachel smiled and said, "That's for another time. Over a few bottles of wine."

"It's a date."

Rachel watched the boys and smiled. They seemed so joyful and lighthearted in the face of such evil.

Then Rachel thought about what Peter had said just moments ago, and she had to stifle a gasp.

This is partly your fault, anyway.

Peter had said that to Tony in his painkiller-fueled stupor. *Your fault.*

The other assailant the day she'd followed Eric and Benjamin Ruddock. The one who nearly knocked her brain out of her skull while she was tending to the wounded Peter Lincecum.

It was Tony Vargas.

For all he knew, the woman who'd just snapped his friend's patella tendon was about to finish the job. So Tony brained Rachel, helped Peter get the hell out of there. He then hid him in Dubois Park, knowing that with the job having been botched, the Spivaks would come for Peter.

Rachel stared at the scar on Tony's neck, wondering if it ever still itched.

She decided to allow Tony to move on with his life unhindered. That was the least she could do for the boy. The Spivaks had already nearly cut his throat. He'd only attacked Rachel because he was terrified for his friend's life and his own.

As Peter's eyes began to close, Tony turned back to look at his mother. Gabrielle blew him a kiss. He returned the kind of *ew, gross* look perfected by teenage boys around the world. Then Tony's eyes caught Rachel's. They held for just a moment. *I know*, and *I know you know.*

"I'm sorry," Tony mouthed.

Rachel simply smiled, put her finger to her lips, and said, "Shh."

Tony nodded and turned back to his friend.

Rachel recognized the sound of boots and knew Serrano and Tally had arrived. John wore heavy-duty tactical sport boots when he was on duty. They were heat resistant, waterproof, and oil resistant, with a side zipper (for those dexterously challenged who didn't have time to tie laces before heading out to duty). They were black and bulky and ugly as hell, and if he were not a cop, they would have already had a conversation about Serrano's style—or lack thereof. But at the same time, hearing the sound of the rubber soles clomping against the linoleum of the hospital floor made Rachel's heart sing.

She missed him. Needed him. She longed to spend a night—maybe several—curled up with Serrano on the sofa underneath a soft blanket, a bottle of shiraz warming them from the inside. Then, once the bottle was empty, she wanted their clothes in a pile on the floor, nothing between them for the rest of the night but a thin layer of sweat.

She smiled at Serrano and Tally.

"Detectives," she said.

Neither of them returned the pleasantry. Serrano did not even look at her.

"Ms. Vargas," Serrano said. His voice was stern and unsympathetic. "Could we have a word with you?"

No. Rachel knew what was about to happen. *Please. Leave her be.*

"Everything all right, Detectives?" Gabrielle said. Her voice was questioning, confused, but her eyes were scared.

Then it all came together, puzzle pieces snapping into place.

"Step outside, please," Tally said. Rachel knew exactly what was going to happen in the next five minutes.

Gabrielle tentatively stepped forward.

"John," Rachel said, putting her hand on Serrano's arm. "Please. Don't."

"Stay out of this, Rachel," Tally said. The boys had stopped talking. They turned to see what was going on.

"John," she said, "she has a son. This family has been through hell. Don't drag them back down. You of all people should understand the importance of being able to move on."

"This isn't about me or you or Eric or Evan," Serrano said, his voice low but tinged with anger and emotion. "This is my job, Rachel."

"Screw your job," Rachel said. "What would you give to have one more day?"

"Enough," Tally said. "Rachel, you're out of line."

"Gabrielle," Rachel said, "call a lawyer. Do it *now*."

"Why—"

"Please step outside, Ms. Vargas," Serrano said, though he was staring daggers at Rachel as he spoke.

Tony said, "What's going on?" He stepped between his mother and Detective Serrano.

"Please," Tally said to Gabrielle. "Let's do this outside."

"Do what?" Tony said, defiantly. "Anything you say to her, you can say to me."

"Antonio," Rachel said, taking his arm, using the boy's formal name for the first time. "Let's let them talk . . ."

"*No*," he said, pulling away. "I have a right to know what the cops want to say to my mom."

"Antonio, stay in here with Peter for a minute," Gabrielle said. "*Please.*"

Tony stepped back. Gabrielle went into the hall with the detectives. Tony eyed the corridor like a sheep wary of wolves outside the paddock. Rachel followed them into the hall. Gabrielle's hands were shaking. They all knew what was coming.

When they were out of earshot of the hospital room, John Serrano said, "This isn't easy for me to say. But we need you to come with us."

"Why?" Gabrielle replied, her words more of a plea than a question.

"I believe you know why," Tally said. Gabrielle said nothing. "Ms. Vargas, I'm asking you to come with us of your own volition. Don't make us force you. Not in front of your son."

"I don't understand," Gabrielle said.

Tally said, "We need you to come down to the precinct. Once there, we are going to formally question you about your roles in the murders of Matthew Linklater and Bennett Brice."

Gabrielle shook her head. Her voice was manic, disbelieving. "No, no. I can't. I need to stay here with Antonio. He's been through so much."

"Ms. Vargas," Serrano said. His voice was sympathetic, trembling. "Just come with us."

"No," she said. "I can't."

Serrano pinched the bridge of his nose and closed his eyes. Rachel could tell he was struggling. She wondered if he was thinking about his son, Evan. Serrano's family had been torn apart, and now he was pulling another parent away from her child. Serrano was doing his job. But Serrano also knew the cold, cruel ramifications of what doing his job meant.

"Please don't make this harder than it needs to be," Serrano said.

"John . . . ," Rachel said, her voice trailing off. "John, please. They're a family."

"They can come back from this," Serrano said. "I never had that chance. They do."

"John . . ."

"Rachel, *stay out of this*," Tally said. "Ms. Vargas, you can go back in and tell your son that you're coming with us. Do you have any family in Ashby? Someone Tony can stay with?"

Then Gabrielle Vargas began to cry.

"Please," she said. "I didn't have a choice."

"We know you didn't," Tally said. "But you still have to answer for their deaths."

"Go talk to your son," Serrano said. "I promise you will see him again. We'll wait for you right here."

"Don't make us come get you," Tally added.

"*Detective Serrano*," Rachel said, her voice taking on both an urgency and anger that made both Serrano and Tally turn to attention. "She is a mother. A mother who was protecting her son. What would you have done to protect your son? Please, don't do this."

Serrano took Rachel by the arm, gently. She thought about pushing his hand away but didn't want to cause more of a scene. Serrano led her aside.

"This is not about me or my son, and don't you dare use Evan's memory like this. Gabrielle is coming with us whether you like it or not. Don't get involved. And keep my boy's name out of your mouth."

Rachel softened. "I'm sorry, John. But you're a father. I'm a mother. I *know* what I'd do for my children, and it isn't pretty. Just tell me. What did you find?"

Serrano looked at Tally. Gabrielle had gone back into the hospital room to talk to her son. Tally nodded at Serrano in a way that seemed to say, *Deal with her*.

"We subpoenaed Bennett Brice's phone records. We found a number of exchanges between Brice and Tamara Alvi."

Rachel took a step back. Her head began to swim.

"The principal at Ashby High," she said.

Serrano nodded. "We believe Brice and Alvi were in a sexual relationship. We talked with Alvi earlier. She confirmed that she had been in a consensual relationship with Brice on and off for some time and that he had access to her files and computer. When we searched her computer, we found a keylogger program that Brice had installed. When we compared that to the cached history in Brice's computer, we found that Brice had used the program to gain access to Alvi's files. Including all student applications."

"Which would give him access to families' financial records," Rachel said.

"That's right," Serrano said. "We believe that's how Brice was able to target kids like Tony Vargas and Peter Lincecum. He found applications that noted financial difficulties and other weak points and leveraged them against the families."

"Did Alvi know?" Rachel said.

"At this moment, we don't believe so. But her career is over."

"So Principal Alvi is ruined because a man took advantage of her love and loyalty," Rachel said. "That makes me sick. And I still don't see what this has to do with Gabrielle Vargas."

"On the morning of June fifth," Serrano said, "there was a text message chain between Brice and Alvi. Brice asked Alvi about one of the teachers at her school."

Rachel said, "Matthew Linklater."

"Yes. In the course of their conversation, Alvi told Brice that Mr. Linklater was dating the parent of a student."

"Gabrielle Vargas," Rachel said.

Serrano nodded. "When we questioned her previously, Alvi claimed not to be aware of any relationship. We believe Bennett Brice told Gabrielle that harm would come to Tony if she didn't help Randall Spivak gain access to Matthew Linklater's home."

"No. No way."

"We obtained a search warrant for the Vargas home," Serrano said. "In Gabrielle's closet, we found handgun cartridges. Ballistics confirms they match the ammunition used to kill Bennett Brice." He paused to let the information sink in. "Gabrielle Vargas was the one who knocked on Matthew Linklater's door the day he died. She did it to protect her son. But she still did it. And here's the thing, Rachel—I think you knew *all* of this. But you wanted to protect Gabrielle. Like you said yourself: what a mother would do for her son isn't pretty."

And there it was. The truth.

"Randall Spivak maimed Tony," Rachel said. "If she hadn't gone along with it, they would have killed him."

"I know that," Serrano said. "And I'm sure the judge or jury will take that under consideration."

Gabrielle Vargas came out of the hospital room, her eyes swollen and red. Tony was behind her, his eyes blazing.

"They made us do it!" Tony shouted. At this point, the entire hospital floor began to notice the commotion. An elderly man walking slowly with an IV stopped to watch. A nurse picked up the phone and asked for security. People peeked out of hospital rooms.

"Antonio, that's enough," Gabrielle said.

"No, it's not!" He drew a line across the scar on his neck. "Randall Spivak did that to me! He told me if I didn't do what he and Mr. Brice said, they'd cut my throat and kill my mom. Why do you think I hit Ms. Marin?"

Serrano looked at Rachel. "Did he . . . ?"

Rachel nodded. "He was the one who clocked me after I disarmed Peter Lincecum. And I formally decline to press charges."

Tony ran up to Rachel and grabbed her wrists. It was not aggressive, but pleading, remorseful. "I swear to God I never would have done it in a million years. But after what happened to Mr. Linklater, I thought if I didn't do what they said, they'd hurt my mom. I swear I didn't mean it, Ms. Marin. I *swear* it."

Rachel took Tony's hands and squeezed them. Tears spilled down his cheeks, his eyes a mix of fire and fear.

"This is all my fault," he said, voice trembling. "Mom, I'm so sorry."

"John," Rachel said, turning to the detectives. "Leslie. Detectives. Do something about this. Gabrielle Vargas doesn't belong in a cell. They did what they did because they were protecting their family from monsters."

"I know they were," Serrano said. "But nobody is above the law. Not me. Not them. Not you."

"Come on," Tally said, ignoring Rachel. She placed her hand on the small of Gabrielle Vargas's back and gently pushed her down the hall.

"Go home, baby," Gabrielle said, looking over her shoulder. Tony stood there, catatonic. "I promise this will all get figured out. We're a family, and we always will be."

"How do you know that?" Tony said. "How?"

Gabrielle did not answer.

"Detective Tally," Rachel said. She ran to Tally and grabbed her arm. The detective spun away.

"Ms. Marin, step *back*."

At first Rachel did not move. But when Tally's hand slid down toward her handcuffs, Rachel relented.

"I don't want to fight you, Detective," Rachel said.

"Well, then, that makes two of us. Let me do my job."

"You *know* Gabrielle doesn't deserve this."

"That's not my job to decide. And it's *definitely* not yours. There's a system in place for this, Rachel."

"The system doesn't work," Rachel said. "The system let the man who tore my family apart back on the street. It let Randall Spivak and Bennett Brice poison children. I shouldn't have trusted the *system* then, and I sure as hell don't trust it now."

"Go home, Rachel," Tally said. "Or I'll be booking two people today. One of these days, you'll do that *before* I have to threaten you."

Tally led Gabrielle Vargas away. Tony stood there, shaking, as if the anger and confusion and sadness inside him were all fighting for supremacy.

The elevator door opened. Serrano, Tally, and Gabrielle Vargas stepped inside. Tally's face was placid, emotionless. Serrano's eyes looked haunted. Gabrielle opened her mouth to say something. The doors closed before she could speak, and then they were gone. Tony Vargas sank to his knees. Rachel put her hand on his shoulder but said nothing. There were no words that could comfort him.

CHAPTER 50

One Week Later

"Look at this," the boy said. He gently placed his crutches on the chair. He then tentatively lifted his right knee in the air, balancing on his heavily bandaged left knee. The leg wobbled, and he had to stretch his arms out for balance, like a tightrope walker high above the ground. "Not bad, huh?"

"Peter Lincecum, stop that right now," Evie said. "If you pop your stitches, I'm going to sew your leg back up myself with piano wire and superglue."

Peter put his good leg back on the ground and picked the crutches up, inserting them under his armpits. "These things give me rashes."

"Stop complaining. I have a butt rash from these sheets. I'd kill to have an armpit rash instead."

"That's gross, Evie."

"Mom," she said. "You can call me Mom."

Peter nodded but didn't say the word.

"I know," Evie said. "It'll take some getting used to. For both of us."

There was a knock at the door, and they turned to see Rachel Marin standing there. She had dark circles under her eyes but an easy smile on her face.

"They haven't kicked you out of here yet?" Rachel said. The color was returning to Evie's face, which held a shade of pink just paler than cotton candy. Her arm was in a sling, her shoulder wrapped in bandages. She wore a generic hospital gown with a drab floral pattern.

She'd lost a considerable amount of weight, her muscle tone softening, her reddish-brown hair thin and untamed. But she was awake. And she would survive.

"Funny thing," Evie said. "When you lose almost half the blood in your body, they don't let you run off so fast."

"Good thing they're in charge here and not you. How's the leg?" Rachel said to Peter.

"Hurts like hell."

"That's because you're doing too much," Evie said, sternly. "You're supposed to stay off it, not perform circus tricks like some teenage seal."

"Circus tricks? I was just showing you I could balance—"

"OK, children, that's enough," Rachel said. "Peter, can your mom and I talk for a bit?"

Peter's eyes went to Evie.

"It's OK," Evie said. "Go get a snack. There's money in my purse."

"Remember, Mom, I have my own money," Peter said. "Oh. Right. Guess it's too soon to talk about that. Back in a few, ladies."

The boy went off, crutches thumping on the floor. They watched him until he turned the corner and was out of sight.

"*Ladies*," Evie said, with a laugh. "He sounds so proper. Like we should be sipping mimosas and talking about our French writers."

"Lucky for you I've picked *Les Misérables* as the first official selection of my 'nearly set on fire by a psychopath and lived to tell about it' book club. We meet every other Thursday at Applebee's."

"I'm in," Evie said.

Rachel sat on the side of the bed and took Evie's hand. Her grip was weak.

"How are you?" Rachel said.

"Physically, like I got run over by a tractor. Like I got run over by a tractor and then doused with battery acid. Plus I have eight pins and a steel plate holding my collarbone together, and I'll never be able to do a full jumping jack again. Otherwise, I'm doing peachy."

Rachel looked down, then said, "Why didn't you tell me about Peter?"

Evie shifted in her bed, grimacing in pain.

"I've only trusted one person in my life," Evie said. "My brother, Bennett. When Peter was born, I was a mess. I drank, smoked, injected, and inhaled anything and everything I could get my hands on. I had no money. I was already taking care of one son, and not very well at that. I was ready for a second kid like I was ready for a cannonball to the face. I suppose I could have done something about that before I told my ex not to bother with protection. But hindsight is twenty-twenty, right?"

"So you gave Peter up for adoption?"

"It was the best thing for him. I couldn't afford a sandwich. You know who saved us? Bennett. He visited my crappy shoebox of a home. I was drunk off my ass, using my TV as a babysitter for my preschooler, with an infant crying in the other room like he was being tortured. I was too out of it to even comfort my own son. When Bennett saw what was going on, he told me the baby needed a new home. I told him to go to hell. He said I didn't have a choice. He said he would make sure the baby would be taken care of."

"So he arranged for Peter to be adopted by Lloyd and Stefanie Lincecum."

"When you have enough money, it becomes a whole lot easier to dictate the terms for adoption," Evie said. "But the Lincecums were crap parents too. When I sobered up, I told Bennett I wanted Peter back. But by that time, the Spivaks had brought Peter into YourLife. And Bennett had put enough money aside for Peter so that he'd never have to want for anything ever again. So I pretended that the universe knew better than I did when it came to my son's well-being. Funny thing about the universe: it doesn't know squat either."

"I have to ask . . . Why did you try to kill Raymond Spivak?"

Evie laughed, then coughed into her hand. "I wasn't *actually* going to kill him. Well, maybe. Bennett was in deep with the Spivaks. I didn't like them. I'm a good judge of character; can't you tell?"

Rachel smiled but said nothing.

"Anyway, I told Bennett to cut ties with the Spivaks. They knew I was trying to pry Bennett away, so Raymond told me he was going to gut my son like a fish if I didn't mind my own business. I just went to Raymond's place to let him know that if anyone's entrails were going to wind up on the floor, they would be his. And then I end up killing his brother with a pitchfork. Go figure."

"So what now?" Rachel asked.

"Weirdly enough, nearly dying can bring people closer together. Kind of like you and me, Blondie, right?"

"Yeah. We're peas in a messed-up pod."

"So I'm going to give it a go. Try to be a mom again. My oldest doesn't need me—he's got life figured out. Unlike his mom. But Peter does need me. So I guess it's time to see how Ashby fits this old broad."

They sat in silence for a while. Finally Evie spoke.

"What you did or didn't do to Stanford Royce," Evie said, "will never pass these lips."

Rachel nodded. "You'll understand if I don't believe you."

"I understand. But you saved my boy. You came back for me. I might be an asshole, but I'm a loyal asshole."

"That would make a heck of an epitaph."

"Thankfully, I'm not going to need one anytime soon." Evie paused. "So what's happening with the Gabrielle Vargas case?"

"Gabrielle got a pretty good lawyer. They're going to push self-defense. Given all the terrible things the Spivaks did to her family, she can legitimately say she believed their lives were in danger if they didn't comply. I talked to Serrano. He thinks the DA will offer a plea. She might even avoid jail time."

"She killed my brother," Evie said.

"And your brother nearly got her and her son killed," Rachel replied. "You loved Bennett. But you know what he did."

"You're saying my brother had it coming. That he deserved to die."

335

"I'm saying you can only push someone so far before they push back."

"Is that how you live your life, too, Blondie?" Evie said.

"I don't know," Rachel said. "Ask Stanford Royce."

Rachel closed the front door, kicked off her shoes, and sank into the living room couch like it was a warm bath. She could feel the exhaustion in her bones.

She could hear beeps and blips coming from upstairs; Eric was slaughtering a thousand pixelated space blobs. She knocked gently on his door.

"Come in," he said, without hesitation.

When she entered, Eric paused his game and swiveled around. That alone made her heart full. She couldn't remember the last time he'd actually paused a game for her.

"What's new?" she said. He shrugged.

"All anyone can talk about are Tony Vargas and Benjamin Ruddock," he said. "Rumor is Ben is getting expelled. Like weeks before graduation. I heard he's going to take a plea and testify all about Bennett Brice and his business with those Spivak creeps. Probably stay out of jail. People are saying he's got a ton of cash squirreled away and as soon as this is over, he'll leave Ashby and never come back."

"Probably best for everyone," Rachel said. "What about Tony?"

"Tony's actually a pretty good dude. We've been talking a bit."

"He is. Never hurts to have friends. Especially ones with moms who are a little . . . different."

"You're different in a good way," Eric said. "But I know Ms. Vargas is too."

"Do you think they'll fire Principal Alvi?"

"I honestly don't know," Rachel said. "She lied to the cops. But I don't think she really knew how dangerous Bennett Brice was. She couldn't have known what he would do."

"Even if she didn't, a lot of people think she did."

"Sometimes what people think is very different from the actual truth. Learning to spot the difference is a valuable life skill."

Rachel sat on his bed. She smoothed out the covers as if by habit.

"I was thinking," she said, "that it'd be a good idea for you to talk to someone. Professionally. About your dad. About anything you want. You can always talk to me, but even though I think I'm kind of smart about some things, I can be very dumb about others. And I'm smart enough to know that there are other people who are trained to help in ways I can't. I'll always be here for you. But I know I can't be the *only* person you rely on. What do you say?"

"All right."

"Wow. Really? That quick?"

"Yeah," he said. His voice grew soft. "I don't want to feel this way forever. And I know you've been messed up, too, right?"

"I have been," Rachel said. "Maybe more than I've let on. And I should do a better job of talking to you and your sister about how I feel. I love you more than the earth and stars, and I don't want to ever seem as distant as they are."

"Me either."

"You know, maybe I should talk to someone too," Rachel said.

"I think that's a really good idea."

"And if you want to talk to me about what you talk about in there, you can."

Eric said, "Is it OK if I don't?"

Rachel smiled and said, "Of course it's OK."

"Thanks, Mom."

"Hey, are you free this weekend?"

"I think so, why?"

"I planned a little family trip. Keep your schedule clear."

"OK. Should I be worried?"

"Only if you like fun," she said with a smile.

She went to hug Eric, and to her surprise he opened his arms and let her in. Tears came to her eyes.

"Look at me," she said, embarrassed. "You're not supposed to cry in your son's arms."

"You can cry wherever you want," Eric said. "Sometimes crying is good for you."

Eric's cell phone vibrated with an incoming text. The ID read *Penny Wallace*. Eric looked up at her, blushing.

"What are you waiting for?" she asked. "Text her back."

Eric smiled and picked up the phone. Rachel left and closed the door behind her.

The door to Megan's room was open a crack. Inside, she could see her daughter hovering over reams of paper, no doubt a forthcoming Sadie Scout adventure. Rachel knocked.

"Hi, Mom," she said, without looking up. "I'm kind of busy. Sadie is getting ready to swing over a moat filled with really hungry crocodiles in a bad mood, and we *really* need to concentrate."

"We?" Rachel said. She stepped into the room and looked at the page. "I hope Sadie plans on changing her shoes. I imagine it would be awfully hard to swing over a crocodile-infested lake in heels."

"Not for Sadie Scout," Megan scoffed. "She rescued the Prince of Cheetonia from the evil Dr. Blurg while she was wearing heels."

"Well, if she can rescue the Prince of Cheetonia . . . ," Rachel said. "Hey, this weekend. You, me, and Eric are going to take a little trip. That all right?"

"Sure!" Megan said, looking up with an expectant smile. "Where are we going?"

"It's a secret," Rachel replied, "but it's something we should have done a long time ago. And when we get back, I'm going to help you get your stories together so we can maybe look to get your Sadie Scout books published."

"Wait, are you serious?" Megan said.

"I'd never joke about something involving Sadie Scout."

"You're the *best*." Megan leaped up and hugged Rachel.

"Now, get back to your story," Rachel said. "I need to know if Sadie makes it across that moat."

Megan gave her a thumbs-up and turned back to her pages. Rachel went to ease the door shut but instead left it open a crack.

Downstairs, she took a beer from the fridge. She was in the mood for wine but didn't think she could finish a whole bottle herself. A month ago, she would have called John Serrano to come share it with her. Tonight, the thought didn't cross her mind before she'd taken her first sip.

It was when she took her second that her cell phone rang. The ID registered *John Serrano*. Rachel picked it up.

"Hey, John," she said.

"Rach. How are you?"

"Having a beer. Why don't I drink more beer?"

"I've wondered that about you," he said. She could practically hear him smiling on the other end. "Any chance you have an unopened cold one in the fridge?"

"Sorry," she said, "only had the one."

The lie came shockingly easy.

"Too bad. I'm thirsty."

"Drink some water. Any updates on Gabrielle Vargas?"

"Pleaded not guilty."

"What do you think?"

"Between us? She's got a case. Given everything that's come out about Brice and the Spivak brothers, sympathy is on her side. Especially when Tony testifies about how he got that scar. DA says it'd be hard to find a jury member who couldn't see themselves doing the same thing, given the circumstances."

Rachel let out a breath. "That makes me happy. We both know that family doesn't deserve to suffer any more."

There was a pause on the other end. "Listen, Rach. I know things between us have gotten tangled lately. Maybe neither of us realized how tough it would be to mix, you know, business and pleasure. But I care about you. A lot. More than I've cared about anyone in a long time. And I don't want this—us—to end."

Rachel slipped a fingernail underneath the label on the beer bottle and slowly pried it away. It left adhesive residue on the bottle, which she ran over with her thumb.

"I care about you too," she said. "A lot. And I don't want us to end either."

"I'm glad we feel the same way," Serrano said. "If now's not a good time, what are you up to this weekend? Want to have dinner? With or without Megan and Eric."

"Actually, I planned to take a little trip with the kids this weekend."

"Oh yeah? Any room for a stowaway? I'm great at carpool karaoke."

"Any other weekend, I'd welcome your terrible singing voice in a heartbeat. But this is a trip that we need to do as a family. It's something I should have done a while ago, and it needs to be the Marin family. And just the Marin family."

Serrano paused for a moment, then said, "I understand. Have a great time. Call or text me when you get back."

"I will," she said, and she meant it.

"Tell the kids I miss them. Tell Megan I want to read the next Sadie Scout book. And tell Eric we're overdue for a *Lord of the Rings* marathon."

"I will. They'd like that. Talk to you soon, John."

Rachel hung up. She wished she had invited him over for that beer.

CHAPTER 51

Megan and Eric were thrilled when Rachel told them they were taking the car as opposed to flying. Rachel wasn't quite sure why—the flight itself would have been barely an hour and a half, whereas the drive would need to be split up over two days. But Rachel wanted the kids to see the outside world, different cities and towns, to remind them there was more out there than just Ashby.

"Road trip! Road trip!" they chanted as they loaded up the car. Megan had her pens and markers and a ream of fresh paper. Eric had an iPad, e-reader, four print books, and a pair of Bluetooth headphones. He had enough entertainment to keep him busy for at least a week, maybe two.

They spent the night at a Marriott outside Pittsburgh. The skies were gray and rainy, and the three of them curled up in bed and watched a superhero movie. Rachel didn't care for it much, but at the end the dazzling and daring female superhero kicked the snot out of an army of computer-generated space creatures, which seemed to make both Megan and Eric happy, so for those reasons she enjoyed it immensely. The next morning, after nearly emptying out the breakfast buffet, the Marin family hit the road.

As the hours passed and they got closer to their destination, Rachel felt a palpable sense of fear and anxiety. She had tried to forget about this place, to push it from memory, because all it had brought her was sadness. But she had finally realized that she'd been making a decision for her children without their consent, keeping them from their past.

Pretending a wound was nonexistent was not the same as letting it heal.

"Mom?" Eric said, a whisper of fear in his voice. "Are we going . . . home?"

"In a way," Rachel said.

"Where's home?" Megan chimed in.

"Darien," she replied. Megan had been just a baby when Rachel had uprooted the family, and for better or worse she did not remember their lives, did not have the same memories her brother did. But Megan deserved to know more about that life. About who her family once was.

"We're not going to our old house," Rachel said, assuaging Eric's fears. That would be too much, too triggering.

"So where *are* we going?"

Rachel did not answer. Ten minutes later, she pulled the car into the lot of a self-storage company called UR-STUFF.

"Uh, you drove us halfway across the country to see a storage unit?" Eric said as they got out of the car, stretching their arms and legs.

"Just come with me," Rachel said.

Rachel led them inside the facility. A young man behind the desk did not look up from his cell phone when he said, "Help you?"

"We're good," Rachel said, "but thanks."

They took an elevator to the third floor. Storage units with orange garage doors, most of them padlocked, lined the corridors. Rachel led them down the hallway. They stopped at unit 314B.

She took a key chain from her purse, selected a key, and opened the large padlock. Then, taking a deep breath, she rolled the door up and flicked a light switch on the side of the interior wall. The light flickered for a moment—it had not been used in several years—then illuminated what was inside.

"It's not a storage unit," Rachel said. "It's a treasure chest."

Eric's eyes grew wide. Megan's mouth opened.

"Oooh," she said. "Can I . . ."

"Yes. All of this is yours."

The storage unit was filled with duffel bags and trunks, pictures, heirlooms, jewelry, clothing, books, toys, and random bric-a-brac. Everything from their old lives that Rachel had stored because she couldn't bear to look at it. Dresses she'd worn on dates with her husband. A blue "power" tie he wore the day he got a promotion. Onesies once worn by the children who were now looking at them with the awe of reawakened memory.

It felt like Rachel had opened the door to a world she had pushed aside and her children never had a chance to experience.

I need to remember. They deserve to know.

She remembered packing all these bags and boxes in the weeks after Bradley was murdered, tears dripping onto torn strips of duct tape as she sealed off her life. Ghosts of love and loss, but also mementos of joy.

Rachel felt a tug at her heart. A pain, but not an unwelcome one, like the feeling of a strenuous workout after a long sedentary period, where your muscles ache but it feels good to know they still work.

"Hey, Mom?" Eric said. "What's this?"

"That," Rachel said, sliding her way over to where her son was standing, "is a record player."

"A what, now?"

"Record player. Back in the Stone Age, when me and your dad were younger, he used to play actual records. They were old fashioned even then, but he *insisted* that vinyl sounded better than CDs."

"What's a CD?"

"God, I'm old," Rachel said. "Come. Look at this."

Rachel pulled off a plastic covering to reveal about two dozen records, all sheathed in their jackets. She took one out.

"The Rolling Stones. *Exile on Main Street.* You have no idea what this album sounded like on this record player. It was like . . . *life.* Eric, you probably don't remember this, but your dad could dance."

"Dad could *dance*?" Megan said, no less shocked than if Rachel had told her that her dad had been born with four heads.

"He most certainly could."

"That must have been really hard for him," Eric said, smirking. "I mean, I've seen *you* dance."

Rachel gave him a playful punch in the shoulder.

"Megan, come here. There's something I want you to see. This is part of the reason we came here."

Rachel maneuvered between bags and boxes until she stopped, knelt down, and picked up a red shoebox. She blew a layer of dust off it and opened the lid.

Immediately Rachel felt her heart clench. Tears welled up and trickled down her cheeks. Her children peered inside.

It was still in good condition. A little frayed. A little worn. It had some of its original texture, but the original gray was now more of a light silver, the rich brown faded to the color of sand. But when something was worth loving, it didn't matter if it looked loved. And until she'd met her husband, Rachel had never loved anything the way she'd loved what she now held in her hands.

Rachel took the stuffed rabbit from the box and gently handed it to Megan. Her daughter accepted the bunny with an *"Oh!"* that was so full of love and wonder that Rachel could have floated away. Megan cradled the bunny in her arms and rocked it like a baby, gently stroking its ears.

"It's beautiful," Megan whispered, as though not wanting to wake the stuffed bunny. The sight of her daughter holding the rabbit made Rachel's heart swell in a way that reminded her of the first time she held each of her children, how it expanded to a size she never thought possible.

"That was mine," Rachel said, holding back tears. "I got it when I was a little girl just a little younger than you are now. I used to hold it the same way you're holding it."

"It's so soft," Megan said, petting it gently. "Can I . . . have it?"

"Yes. That's why I brought you here. I wanted you to have it," Rachel said. "That little rabbit is worth more than everything else in this place combined. Times a hundred. Times a *thousand*."

"No way," Megan said, eyes wide. "Did it belong to a princess?"

"It does now," Rachel said.

Rachel knelt next to her daughter and stroked the bunny's ears. Its button eyes were frayed, the threads coming loose, but it was nothing a sewing kit couldn't remedy. The seams were still tight. If it was taken care of, which Rachel knew it would be in Megan's hands, the rabbit had many, many years of love ahead of it.

"This little bunny holds so many memories," Rachel said. "It was there for me when I needed love the most."

"Don't you still need love, Mommy?" Megan asked.

"I do. Everyone needs love. And I'm lucky to have you and your brother."

Megan looked up at her mother, wide eyed, tears beginning to form at the corner of her small, perfect eyes even if she didn't fully understand why.

"Mom?"

"Yes, sweetie?"

"What's the rabbit's name?"

Rachel smiled and said, "Marin. Its name is Marin."

Megan smiled. "Like us."

Rachel leaned in and pressed her forehead against her daughter's.

"Yes. Like us. I got Marin at the time when I was happiest in my life. I named it Marin, because that's where I was when I got it. So I always associated its name with joy. That's why when we needed to leave our sadness behind, I thought of how much happiness Marin had brought me. And I hoped that name would rub off on us. Give us happiness like it had given me."

"If you got Marin when you were little," Megan said, "why did you put it in here? Why didn't you show it to me before?"

"Oh, baby, I should have. But I thought leaving all this behind meant I could leave all my sadness behind too. I was wrong. Sometimes even the sad memories are worth remembering. I want you to take the very best care of Marin."

"I will," Megan said. Her eyes twinkled. "Mom, I just had the best idea ever."

"What's that?"

"In my next book, Sadie Scout is going to get a new rabbit friend."

"I think that's the best idea ever too."

"I have a question, though. If Marin is the rabbit's first name, and Marin is also our last name, then wouldn't the rabbit's name be Marin Marin?"

Rachel laughed and said, "I guess you're right. Welcome home, Marin Marin. Welcome home."

ACKNOWLEDGMENTS

The second book in a series might be the most difficult one to write. With the first book, you have the element of surprise. Readers are meeting these characters for the first time and, if you're fortunate, will want to invite them back into their lives again. I'm indebted to many people who helped mold and shape this book, allowing me to deepen and enrich the characters and expand the world of Ashby.

My editor at Thomas & Mercer, Jessica Tribble, has been an ongoing champion for me and these books, and for that I am eternally grateful. I once sent Jessica a gift of Writers' Tears whiskey (yes, there is such a thing, and I wholeheartedly recommend you try it). But in reality, working with Jessica has been an absolute joy. Maybe one or two tears of joy, but I swear that's all.

Kevin Smith, my brilliant developmental editor, has worked his magic yet again. He pushed me to make this book even better. If you enjoyed what you've just read, Jessica and Kevin deserve a large amount of credit and many bottles of whiskey.

A big thanks goes to Megan Beatie, who has worked tirelessly to get the word out about my books. Writing is done in solitude, but you don't want the books to remain in the dark, and Megan has made sure that mine have not.

Working with Thomas & Mercer has been a dream, and I'm proud to call it Rachel Marin's home. My sincere thanks goes out to Grace Doyle, Sarah Shaw, Ashley Vanicek, Lindsey Bragg, Laura Barrett, and the rest of the T&M squad for welcoming Rachel and me into your family. I'd been a fan of the Thomas & Mercer list from afar, and it's an honor to now be a part of it.

At the Jane Rotrosen Agency, Amy Tannenbaum has been a phenomenal agent, sounding board, consigliere, friend, and guide. While I was writing this book, Jessica Errera also joined the team and gave me even more outstanding notes to help sharpen the story and characters.

The mystery and thriller community has been the backbone of my professional—and often personal—life for going on two decades. It is here that I have found endless inspiration, support, joy, and, OK, maybe a drinking buddy or two. Here's to many more years spent talking shop at hotel bars.

These books would not exist without the three most important people in my life: my daughters, Ava and Lyla, and my wife, Dana. I could not have written these books before I became a father to the two most amazing girls, and I would not be the father I am without being fortunate enough to have a wife who is endlessly caring, patient, and loving. My heart grows every day I'm with them, and even though there is darkness in these books, I also believe there exists a great deal of hope, and it is because of my family that this hope burns brightly.

A final thank-you to readers like you who have embraced Rachel Marin and these characters and have brought them into your homes and on your travels. I hope these stories stay with you the same way they have stayed with me.

ABOUT THE AUTHOR

Photo © 2017 by Jason Rhee

Jason Pinter is the bestselling author of seven novels for adults—*Hide Away* (the first Rachel Marin thriller), the acclaimed Henry Parker series (*The Mark, The Guilty, The Stolen, The Fury,* and *The Darkness*), and the stand-alone thriller *The Castle*—as well as the middle-grade adventure novel *Zeke Bartholomew: Superspy!* and the children's book *Miracle.* His books have over one million copies in print worldwide. He has been nominated for numerous awards, including the Thriller Award, the *Strand* Critics Award, the Barry Award, and the Shamus Award, and *The Mark* was optioned to be a feature film.

Pinter is the founder of Polis Books, an independent press, and was honored by *Publishers Weekly's* Star Watch, which "recognizes young publishing professionals who have distinguished themselves as future leaders of the industry." He has written for the *New Republic*, *Entrepreneur*, the *Daily Beast*, *Esquire*, and more. He lives in New Jersey with his wife and their two daughters. Visit him at www.JasonPinter.com, and follow him on Twitter and Instagram @JasonPinter.